UNKNOWN RIDER

JACK STEWART

SEVERN RIVER
PUBLISHING

Severn River Publishing
SevernRiverBooks.com

This is a work of fiction. Names, characters, businesses, places, events and incidents are either the products of the author's imagination or used in a fictitious manner. Any resemblance to actual persons, living or dead, or actual events is purely coincidental.

ISBN: 978-1-64875-483-8 (Paperback)
ISBN: 978-1-64875-575-0 (Hardcover)

ALSO BY JACK STEWART

The Battle Born Series
Unknown Rider
Outlaw
Bogey Spades
Declared Hostile

To find out more about Jack Stewart and his books, visit
severnriverbooks.com

For my dad,
Who taught me I could fly.

1

USS *Mobile Bay* (CG-53)
Off the coast of Southern California

Damn the torpedoes.

The immortal phrase inscribed on the warship's superstructure was nearly impossible to read through the inky darkness as it rose with a cresting wave. The *Ticonderoga*-class guided-missile cruiser shuddered as her bow plunged into a trough, showering her five-inch gun and forward vertical launching system with frigid seawater. Had the ship's bell not been secured, even its clanging would have fallen silent under the tempest of the sea.

In her stateroom, Captain Bethany Lewis smoothed her hair back, then perched the dark blue baseball cap on her head and pulled its brim low to shield her tired eyes. She stared at her reflection in the mirror, unable to keep her gaze from wandering to the gold embroidered scrambled eggs on the bill of her hat. This wasn't her first command, but not moving up from executive officer brought its own unique challenges.

Taking command of a warship on its final voyage even more so.

She took a deep breath and scanned down the length of the mirror, inspecting her uniform before leaving her sea cabin. With twenty-two years in the Navy, most spent waging an uphill fight in the traditionally male-dominated battle space, she knew appearances mattered. It was why she worked out daily, watched what she ate, and paid particular attention to her uniform standards.

Unlike the service dress uniform she wore while in port, Beth had donned her normal "at sea" attire of a blue one-piece coverall. The khaki-colored nylon belt cinched tight around her trim waist identified her as an officer or chief petty officer, though as one of only two dozen women aboard the warship, there was no confusing her with anybody else.

"*You* are the captain," she said, as much a pep talk as a reminder of the burden she carried.

The newly pinned and matching silver eagles, whose heads pointed forward, adorned her collars and stood vigil on either side of the lump in her throat. After two decades in the Naval Service, Beth had finally made it to the pinnacle of her surface warfare career.

There was a knock on her door, and she cleared away the lump before speaking.

"Enter!"

The door opened, and Master Chief Ben Ivy stuck his head through the crack, blocking out the dim red glow from the passageway beyond. "Ready, ma'am?"

Beth reached up and flipped the switch to extinguish the fluorescent light over the mirror. She turned for the door, and her momentary hesitation vanished. "Let's go."

Master Chief Ivy was a large man with ebony skin who glided through the passageway like a phantom, his size-thirteen steel-toed boots placed quietly and deftly on the polymeric resin–coated deck as he listed with the gentle rolling of the ship. His quiet demeanor had earned him a solid reputation among the ship's sailors, but his unyielding loyalty to their new captain had earned him her respect. She had always believed that Chiefs ran the Navy and saw no reason to change tack now.

Master Chief led the way, simultaneously ducking while stepping over knee-knockers. Beth stood tall, following in his wake while only lifting her feet. He towered over her by more than a foot, and the few sailors they encountered in the passageway stepped aside to watch their diminutive new captain walking with self-assuredness. A few murmured shy greetings as she passed, but most only offered polite nods in recognition.

"Captain's in Combat," Ben said as he led them into the Combat Information Center's cramped quarters. Only the Tactical Action Officer, Lieutenant Martin Schaeffer, acknowledged her presence by turning to welcome her to the darkened space.

"*Abe* just entered flight quarters and will begin the launch at the top of the hour," Martin said, motioning to the large red numbers on the digital clock mounted on the bulkhead.

"Very well," she replied, taking her place in the captain's chair at the center of the room.

Martin sat in the seat next to her, ignoring the hulking Master Chief's presence as he strolled behind the operators at their consoles. The upcoming evolution was their capstone exercise and would set the tone for her command. She had to be better than perfect. "Latest intel shows enemy forces marshaling north of San Clemente. They will attempt to circumvent our air defenses to make a run at the carrier."

Beth grinned, remembering her time as TAO aboard the USS *Stockdale*. She recalled with fondness the war games she had participated in during the pre-deployment workup cycle and knew they were always more exciting than real-world operations. Martin was young and enthusiastic, and she envied his ability to look upon the looming exercise with wonder.

"I would expect so," she replied. "How many air contacts do we have?"

Martin gestured to the large screen across the cramped space, showing an expanded view of the airspace around the *Mobile Bay*. His Operations Specialists manning the radar consoles catalogued each of the air contacts in their operating area, defining them as either hostile, friendly, or unknown. "Nine contacts holding north of the Desired Commit Line and an additional three unidentified within Whiskey Two Ninety-One."

He referred to the Warning Area above them that was set aside for military air training. Most of the carrier strike group sailed in what was known as SCORE, or Southern California Offshore Range, while completing a series of tests that evaluated their ability to deploy. Of all the ships in the strike group, none was more important than the aircraft carrier. But her little cruiser came close.

"Keep an eye on them. They've disguised hostiles as white air before," she replied, knowing exercise planners sometimes hid adversaries within the flight profiles of commercial aircraft.

"Yes, ma'am, that was our thought too," Martin said.

She nodded. Her predecessor had trained his crew well, and she had inherited a combat-ready team more than prepared for the upcoming test.

A commotion near one of the radar consoles caught her attention, and she craned her neck to observe two young sailors chattering and gesturing at the screen. One of them turned to Martin with a panicked look. "Lieutenant!"

Before Beth could inquire about the problem, the portable radio she carried everywhere squawked to life with, "Captain to the bridge! Captain to the bridge!"

Master Chief Ivy also heard the radio call and intercepted her at the door. She knew her way around the ship, but the protective Master Chief wasn't about to let his new skipper face whatever problem awaited without his wise counsel at the ready. Only this time, he was the one trying to keep up, listening to Beth's size-six boots pounding on the steel deck.

Once on the bridge, she didn't announce her presence and walked straight to her executive officer, a Navy commander who had been her Plebe at the Naval Academy. "Talk to me, XO," she said.

"I don't..."

He trailed off, and Beth followed his gaze through the open hatch on the starboard side of the ship. Instead of the pitch black she had expected, a half dozen bright lights glowed through the thick fog just above the horizon, swirling and dancing as they multiplied and circled the warship. Her mouth fell open.

"What the hell?"

"Ma'am?"

Beth had spent years of her life sailing the world's oceans and had seen strange and unusual things, but nothing could have prepared her for the unexplained phenomenon at a pivotal moment in her career. As she stepped out onto the bridge wing, she craned her neck upward and watched the glowing orbs swirling in the late evening mist like massive fireflies.

You are the captain, she reminded herself.

"Ma'am?" her XO prompted again.

"Radio the *Abe* and have them suspend the launch," she ordered. "And call away the SNOOPIE team. I want to know what *the fuck* those things are."

USS *Abraham Lincoln* (CVN-72)

Fifteen miles south of the *Mobile Bay*, Navy Lieutenant Colt "Mother" Bancroft sat in the darkened cockpit of a brand-new Marine Corps F-35C Lightning II Joint Strike Fighter. As a guest pilot, he was respectful of the trust the squadron's commanding officer had placed in him. But as one of the most experienced JSF pilots in the Navy, the eighty-million-dollar jet was in good hands.

The sights and sounds beyond the canopy were familiar to him, but he felt a little out of place and took his time to prevent making careless mistakes. The Black Knights were only the second squadron operating the JSF from an aircraft carrier, and the first for the Marine Corps. To say there was pressure on them to succeed was an understatement. His job was to make sure they had the tools needed to integrate the fifth-generation fighter into the strike group.

They had already completed a check-in with the airborne E-2D Hawkeye Air Intercept Controller and received their seven-line Defensive Counter Air brief. He fought for control over his nerves as he waited for the Tophatter department head to initiate their event's check-in.

"Taproom, Bolt check Aux, Taproom Three One."

"Taproom Three Two."

"Taproom Three Three."

"Taproom Three Four."

The first four jets in their event were FA-18E Super Hornets, highly capable platforms in their own right.

"Bolt Four One," Colt said, craning his neck to look over at Smitty, a junior captain and the only other pilot flying the new fighter in the event.

"Bolt Four Two."

The air wing leveraged the lethal integration of fourth- and fifth-generation fighters, and an additional four Super Hornets and two JSFs would launch near the end of their vulnerability window to relieve them on station. But Colt and his flight were first up, and he hoped to get a crack at the adversary aircraft orbiting north of them. A yellow-shirted plane director walked up to his plane and held his hands up above his head before patting himself on the chest, signaling that he was taking control of Colt's jet.

Here we go, Colt thought.

The Marines around his jet responded to the plane director's signal to break him down by removing the chocks and chains and freeing him from the flight deck as he prepared to taxi. Colt clicked his oxygen mask into place and armed his seat, prepared to follow the yellow shirt's lighted wands from his parking spot forward of the island to the number four catapult on the port side of the ship.

His heart pounded in his chest when the yellow shirt crossed and uncrossed his wands, signaling for him to release his brakes and begin moving. He advanced the throttle and felt the turbofan engine spool up as he released the pressure on his brake pedals and inched forward, following the lighted wands and tuning out the rest of the flight deck's activity.

"Looks like you're first up," Smitty said over their tactical frequency.

Colt double-clicked the microphone switch, acknowledging the transmission but too focused on taxiing to come up with something witty in reply. The yellow shirt passed him off to another in the landing area who steered him behind the outermost waist catapult before crossing his wands to stop him, then directing him to spread his wings. He selected the command on the touchscreen PCD, or Panoramic Cockpit Display, in front of him and confirmed it by clicking on the cyan box.

The butterflies bouncing around in his stomach settled, and he focused on the mission ahead. They all knew the scripted exercise would turn into a notional shooting war at some point during the night when their adversaries tripped the stringent Rules of Engagement. Then the gloves would come off, and they would bring to bear the might of the entire *Abraham*

Lincoln strike group against the make-believe enemy. That was when Colt would get to witness what he'd come for.

As the first event to man Combat Air Patrols against the adversaries, Colt thought they would get to see action before being relieved on station and forced to return to the ship for their recovery. He was combat experienced, well trained, and was flying the most advanced fighter the Navy and Marine Corps had to offer. He was ready.

The yellow wands uncrossed and began moving in short arcs, and Colt replied by taxiing forward across the jet blast deflector. After lining up behind the catapult shuttle, the yellow shirt again stopped him and ordered him to lower his launch bar. Again, he chose the command on the touchscreen and clicked on the cyan confirm box, longing for the simpler analog days of the Hornet. He felt the launch bar drop into place with a satisfying *thunk.*

Colt looked over and saw Smitty lined up behind the catapult next to him. The orchestrated chaos of an aircraft carrier never failed to amaze him, especially at night, when only the tower's dim sodium lights illuminated the precise ballet of planes and people dancing on the flight deck. Shadows stretched across the non-skid surface and enveloped everything in darkness.

"OAKINE," Smitty said.

Once A Knight Is Never Enough...

The yellow shirt uncrossed his wands again and taxied him forward until he felt the holdback fitting tug on his jet and hold him in place. Then the yellow shirt rotated his torso and shot a wand outward, giving the signal to take tension. Colt released the brakes and felt the nose strut squat as the yellow shirt handed him off to the Shooter. He advanced the throttle, manipulated his side stick to exercise the control surfaces, and stepped on the rudder pedals in both directions. At last, he flipped the switch to turn on his exterior lights as the signal he was ready to go.

The Shooter saluted him, then tapped the flight deck with his wand in a fencer's lunge before raising it to point at the blackness beyond the flight deck edge lighting. Colt placed his helmet back against the headrest and waited for the catapult to fire and fling his Joint Strike Fighter off the pointy end of the ship.

When it did, he broke into a smile behind his oxygen mask. Nothing would ever dull the thrill of a catapult launch, not even the terrifying few seconds before he assured himself he was flying.

Good airspeed, he thought, watching the numbers in his Helmet Mounted Display tick upward into three digits, relieving him of the fear of a soft catapult shot. His body jerked forward with the sudden loss of acceleration at the end of the stroke.

"Three oh seven, airborne."

Colt raised the landing gear and climbed away from the water, activating his combat systems in preparation to rendezvous with the tanker overhead the carrier to top off his fuel tanks.

"Three oh seven, tower, switch rep."

Colt scanned his engine instruments, wondering why the Air Boss in the tower wanted him to talk to the squadron's representative in the Carrier Air Traffic Control Center.

"Three oh seven," he replied.

He dialed up the assigned frequency and caught the last of the broken transmission. "...oh seven, you up?"

"I'm up. What's going on?"

"Hey, Colt, they're suspending the launch. Alpha Whiskey reported unknown air contacts in the area."

He chuckled. "Isn't that the whole point of an ADEX?" he asked, referring to his Defensive Counter Air mission in the Area Defense Exercise.

"Yeah, but these are interlopers. Real-world bogies."

His smile vanished. Just his luck, he was flying in the strike group's most capable fighter but had no weapons loaded. There wasn't much he could do other than gain a visual on the unidentified aircraft and bring back video from his EOTS, or Electro-Optical Targeting System, for the intelligence types to pore over.

"Copy. How many made it airborne?"

"Just you."

"What do you want me to do?"

The rep keyed the microphone to speak, but then released it. The E-2D Hawkeye was still airborne, and they were probably trying to decide whether it was worth pushing him to their control or just recover him early.

He began a climbing turn to the left to set up an orbit over the carrier while awaiting their decision.

"Three oh seven, push Banger."

"Three oh seven," he replied in an even tone with a silent fist pump, thankful they had pushed him to the Hawkeye controller for tasking instead of leaving him sidelined.

2

"Right full rudder," Beth said. "Steady on course zero nine zero."

"Steady on course zero nine zero, aye, ma'am," the helmsman said, spinning the wheel to the right while watching the gyro compass. Every few seconds, his eyes shot up to look through the forward windows at the glowing lights swirling above their ship.

"*Abe* suspended the launch, but not before a JSF got airborne," her XO said.

Shit!

She kept her face passive, trying to shield her sailors from her concern. If she remained calm and collected, they would follow suit and be the professionals she knew them to be. But dammit if it didn't bother her—they had unknown air contacts swirling around the strike group while one of the air wing's most valuable assets flew around defenseless.

"Let's put some distance between us," she said, hoping to use her ship as a decoy and draw the swirling lights away from the carrier. As the strike group Air Warfare Commander, known as Alpha Whiskey, it was her responsibility to protect the carrier from air threats. And until they had more information, the swirling lights were definitely threats.

"Ma'am, steady on course zero nine zero," the helmsman said, centering the needle on his compass to point due east.

"All ahead flank three," Beth said.

"All ahead flank three, aye," the lee helmsman replied, smoothly advancing the throttles to full power, opening up the gas turbine engines to propel the five-hundred-and-sixty-seven-foot guided-missile cruiser through the dark waters.

"Ma'am," Master Chief Ivy said over her shoulder. "Do you want to call the crew to general quarters?"

This can't be happening, she thought. They were off the coast of California for a pre-deployment exercise, not in hostile waters. She shouldn't have to rouse her crew to prepare for combat. She turned and looked into Ben's stoic face, then nodded reluctantly.

The Master Chief picked up the handset for the 1MC public address system and flipped the brass switch to sound the klaxon before speaking into the microphone. "General quarters, general quarters. All hands, man your battle stations. The route of travel is forward and up to starboard, down and aft to port. Set material condition Zebra throughout the ship. Reason for general quarters is imminent unidentified aircraft. This is not a drill."

Beth leaned forward and rested her knuckles against the porthole as she stared through the fog at the glowing lights. They no longer appeared to swirl around her ship but matched pace with the cruiser as it raced east for the California coast.

She glanced up at the digital display above the centerline pelorus.

Thirty knots.

What the hell are these things?

She ignored the flurry of activity around her as the rest of her four-hundred-sailor crew moved to their battle stations. Her eyes drifted from one glowing orb to the next, trying to discern a pattern in their positioning but seeing only randomness.

Her confusion only multiplied when a speaker set to Net 15 squawked with a report from Combat: "Aside from the strike group's other ships, the surface picture is clear."

"Well, these *things* had to come from somewhere," she said to herself, knowing full well she was losing her battle to keep emotion from her voice. She turned to the Gunnery Liaison Officer standing near the Mk 20 Electro-Optical Sensor System. "Get me an ID on these targets, Chief."

"Aye, ma'am," he replied.

Though designed to provide accurate targeting information for the ship's five-inch gun, the EOSS was a capable system that might allow them to gain a visual on the unidentified flying objects through the fog and track them to their place of origin. Her first thought had been that they were commercial drones operated from a civilian ship in the area, but the speeds they could maintain and the absence of unidentified surface vessels in the area ruled that suspicion out. Maybe the EOSS would offer another clue.

"Range to *Abe*?" Beth asked.

"Eighteen miles," the radarman replied.

Not enough, she thought. She needed to put more distance between them and the carrier and draw the orbs away, maybe close enough to shore where other Navy ships could aid in identifying them.

"Ma'am!" the Officer of the Deck shouted, pointing through the window.

The lump in her throat returned.

Bolt 41
Marine F-35C

Colt saw the glowing orbs right away. Once Banger control had vectored him in the right direction, he spotted them circling the dark Navy ship without the aid of his advanced sensors, but he directed his targeting system onto the ship anyway. Without weapons of any kind, the only thing he could do was be a high-speed cheerleader and record the event for posterity.

Between the EOTS's Infrared Search and Track capability and his visor-projected night vision, he only had to look through the canopy into the night sky to see nearly a dozen tiny squares surrounding the lights. As he neared the *Mobile Bay*'s location, the sight of the swarming orbs left him speechless.

"Bolt Four One, Banger, status?"

"I...uh..."

He couldn't find the words. His jet's core processor had designated the targets, but he couldn't make heads or tails of what he was witnessing. They looked like bright orbs of light encircling the ship and keeping pace as it raced through the water.

"Bolt Four One, Banger, take angels twenty and reset."

He shook his head, his eyes bouncing from one square to the next. For whatever reason, the Hawkeye controller wanted him to climb to twenty thousand feet and return to his CAP location twenty miles to the west.

Well, that's not gonna happen.

"Negative, Banger. I've got a visual on multiple bogies," he said.

From his vantage point, he could see a green-hued guided-missile cruiser steaming at maximum speed to the east, her massive props churning the water to create a bioluminescent wake visible through the dense fog. Instead of climbing to twenty thousand feet, Colt banked the Joint Strike Fighter and entered into an orbit over the ship.

"Bolt Four One, Banger, Shogun actual directs reset," the controller said in a firm tone.

He knew what that meant. The Commander of the Air Wing, CAG himself, had directed him to depart station and return to CAP.

"Stand by, Banger," he replied.

He might as well have said "Fuck off, Banger," since that's what he really meant. He didn't become a fighter pilot to tuck his tail and run, but he was a guest pilot and didn't want to rock the boat either. If he pissed off CAG, his commanding officer back at the US Navy Fighter Weapons School in Fallon would get an earful. And that meant *he* would get an earful. That combination usually didn't bode well for future career aspirations.

Dammit.

He keyed the microphone to acknowledge the order but stopped himself when the eight-by-twenty-inch PCD flickered in front of him. It lasted less than half a second before returning to normal, but he felt his face flush. He had more hours in the F-35C than almost any other pilot in the Navy, and nothing that unnerving had ever happened to him before. His skin prickling with anxiety, he wondered if it was the first indication of an impending electrical failure—the absolute last thing he wanted to deal with at night over the water.

"Banger," the controller replied.

Colt again keyed the microphone to let the controller know he intended to comply when the portal on the right side of the PCD shuffled through multiple pages on its own. He reached up to navigate back to the air-to-surface radar page just as the adjacent sub-portal maximized and replaced his flight controls display with an air-to-surface weapons page.

"What the hell is going on?"

He glanced over his left shoulder as he passed abeam the cruiser and cut across its bow, still bewildered by the mysterious lights circling it. He wanted to stay and provide whatever support he could to the tin can sailors, but the electrical anomalies were starting to worry him.

Again, he tried replying to the Hawkeye controller, but his words caught in his throat when the jet suddenly overbanked, almost as if rolling in to begin a bombing run. He tried countering the roll by slamming against the sidestick, but it continued until he was inverted and hanging in his straps.

Fuck fuck fuck fuck fuck...

As his nose fell through the horizon, he abandoned his attempt to reverse the roll and added left pressure instead. *If you can't beat 'em, join 'em.* But his wings remained level with the greasy side up and shiny side down.

Ten degrees, he thought, watching his nose track lower into a dive.

Colt stared through his visor at the ship racing up at him, hardly noticing the glowing halos around the orbs shrinking.

Twenty degrees.

He yanked his throttle to idle, trying everything he could think of to slow his closure with the water. But the engine refused to respond, and his airspeed ticked upward rapidly. The gnawing fear he felt just under the surface threatened to erupt into full-blown panic, and he stabbed at buttons and switches, seemingly at random, hoping to stumble upon a solution. Nothing in his training had prepared him for this, and his efforts seemed futile.

Thirty degrees.

Suddenly, the jet rolled upright but continued diving directly at the *Mobile Bay*. The *whoop-whoop* of his radar altimeter warned him that he was racing through five thousand feet and only seconds from impacting the ship, or, if he was lucky, the black abyss of the Pacific Ocean. He pulled harder on the sidestick, wishing the JSF had a physical connection to the flight controls he could muscle into submission.

Four thousand feet.

"Come on!"

Colt dug his forearm into the armrest and tried to increase his leverage on the immobile stick. Sweat poured from underneath his helmet and down the front of his face and stung his eyes. He blinked it away and ignored the aching in his forearm as he stared in horror at the increasing airspeed and decreasing altitude.

Three thousand feet.

He took his hand off the throttle and positioned it between his legs, wondering at what point he would decide to abandon his attempt to save the jet in favor of saving himself. Over his thousands of hours at the controls of a Navy fighter, he had never considered pulling the ejection handle. Not once.

Two thousand feet.

The fingers of his left hand wrapped around the knurled black-and-yellow ejection handle, but his right wasn't willing to give in and continued pulling back on the sidestick to try to level off before it was too late.

"PULL UP...PULL UP..."

The Ground Collision Avoidance System aural warning and flashing red X's across his displays shook him free from his paralysis. He took his hand off the stick and mated it with the one already on the ejection handle, prepared to do what he never thought he would. He pressed his helmet back against the headrest and braced himself for the ejection, only partially aware that his PCD had flickered again.

This can't be happening...

As Colt tensed his shoulders and prepared to pull the handle, the engine wound down to flight idle, and he felt the G-forces increase as his nose began slowly tracking up to the invisible horizon. He hesitated, knowing the envelope for ejection was shrinking. He needed to either commit to making a last-ditch effort to save the jet or get out. Indecision was a killer, and it was time to shit or get off the pot.

One thousand feet.

He took his hands off the ejection handle and snatched at the sidestick, overriding the G-limiter to increase the pull and stop his descent before it was too late. His vision narrowed to the size of a soda straw that was filled almost entirely with the guided-missile cruiser.

"PULL UP...PULL UP..."

He wanted to scream at the jet but grunted instead as his narrow tunnel of vision disappeared. The last thing he saw was the ship's superstructure and main mast reaching up to knock him from the sky.

3

USS *Mobile Bay* (CG-53)

Beth fought against her instinct to dive away from the kamikaze jet, but in the end, the overpowering sense of self-preservation prevailed. In a flurry of panic, she flung herself to the deck and collided with several of her sailors, cursing under her breath at the audacity of the pilot to imperil her crew. Her heart raced as she waited for the collision, but as the seconds ticked by and the sound of the jet faded into the distance, she jumped to her feet full of piss and vinegar.

"Who *the fuck* does that guy think he is?" she roared.

Master Chief Ivy rose next to her and gripped her arm gently. "Ma'am, are you okay?"

"I want his wings!" She ripped her arm free, livid at the jet jockey. "Get me their CAG! I'll have his ass for this stunt!"

"Ma'am!" the Officer of the Deck shouted again.

Still fuming, she spun toward the window and looked up in time to see one of the glowing orbs disappear. Her racing heart slowed, and she leaned forward into the glass to look at another, just as it too disappeared in the fog. One by one, the lights extinguished until darkness again ensconced the ship.

"All stop!"

"All stop, aye, ma'am," the lee helmsman replied, standing up the throttles to silence the cruiser's motors.

Beth spun away from the window and darted through the door onto the open-air bridge wing. She looked up into the sky, barely able to make out a few of the brighter stars through the thick fog, but the orbs that had harassed them for the last half hour were notably absent.

She unclipped the radio from her belt and brought it to her mouth. "TAO, Captain. What's the air picture?"

Martin's response was immediate. "They're gone! They just disappeared."

"Closest contact?"

"Bolt Four One is overhead our position."

Her anger at the jet jockey returned, and she looked up, knowing full well she wouldn't be able to spot the single F-35C Joint Strike Fighter flying over her ship. She would take him to task for his circus stunt, but she couldn't afford to let it blind her from her responsibilities.

You are the captain.

"Surface contacts?"

"New contact. Unknown merchant vessel bearing zero two zero for two zero miles," Martin replied. He added, "It was in San Clemente's shadow."

"What about AIS?" Beth asked. The Automatic Identification System used transceivers on board ships to supplement surface search radars in identifying contacts. She had seen Iranian vessels attempt to cloak their movements by turning off their AIS transponders, but for a vessel to do so in international waters so close to America's coast was unheard of.

"Off," he said.

She stormed back onto the bridge and walked to the radar console, looking at the blip of the unknown surface contact just beyond the dark outline of San Clemente Island. She still thought it unlikely the objects harassing her ship had originated from a ship so far away, but she didn't believe in coincidences.

"All ahead full," she said. "Left full rudder, steady on course zero two zero."

Damn the torpedoes, she thought. *Let's find out who you are.*

Bolt 41
Marine F-35C

Colt's vision slowly returned after he relaxed his white-knuckled grip on the stick, and he exhaled into his mask with relief. He scanned his airspeed and altitude and felt his tension evaporate after assuring himself he was in a climb and had averted a disastrous collision with the warship. But his hands shook with the aftereffects of a boatload of adrenaline.

"Thank you, Jesus."

He leveled off at five hundred feet over the water, four miles to the ship's stern, and banked left to regain sight of the *Mobile Bay*. Gasping for breath, he barely noticed when one of the orbs disappeared. The digitally created square around it remained for a second and a half before it too disappeared.

What the hell?

He flew across the glowing wake as a second orb disappeared, followed quickly by a third. The targeting processor scrambled to keep up, but the artificial squares also disappeared after a short lag. Momentarily forgetting that CAG had ordered him to break contact and return to the ship, he rolled out on a heading to parallel the ship's course and quickly designated the *Mobile Bay* as a target and allowed the EOTS to slave to the ship.

By the time he flew abeam the cruiser, the last remaining ball of light had vanished. *Poof.* Into thin air.

He raced by the ship at three hundred knots before banking the jet in a climbing left turn, thankful it seemed to be responding to his control inputs again. Crossing the bow, he craned his neck to look at the ship over his shoulder, only subconsciously aware it had come to a dead stop. Continuing to circle, he surveyed the infrared image of the ship on his display, searching for any sign of the orbs. But they were gone.

What the hell is going on?

"Bolt Four One, Banger, status?"

"Banger, the bogies appear to have...uh...vanished," he said, still unable to believe it, and unable to put into words what he had just experienced.

They were over twenty miles from the nearest piece of land without another ship in sight, but still he directed his radar into a surface search mode, looking for any plausible explanation for the orbs' disappearance.

"Banger copies. The bar is open. Shogun directs buster."

Shit.

The message was clear enough. An open bar meant the flight deck was clear and ready to recover him aboard the carrier. CAG directing him to buster meant he was to proceed directly to the ship. Do not pass Go. Do not collect two hundred dollars. For once, he agreed. He needed to explain to CAG what had happened with his jet so he could ground the fleet before whatever cancer had infected the software caused any real harm.

He circled the *Mobile Bay* again, watching as she turned to point her bow north before once more kicking up a bioluminescent wake. He couldn't help himself and looked along her projected course, spotting a ship floating just north of San Clemente Island. With a few quick hand gestures, he designated the ship on his surface search radar as a target and slewed the EOTS to the new target.

"How copy, Bolt Four One?"

With one more glance at the ship centered under the crosshairs on his display, he sighed and keyed the microphone. "Bolt Four One copies."

He turned and pointed his nose at the *Lincoln*.

USS *Mobile Bay* (CG-53)

"Where's he going?" Beth asked.

She was standing next to the chief supervising the Mk-20 EOSS operation, her eyes glued to the nineteen-inch display and the vessel centered in the crosshairs. The seaman manipulated the joystick control, firing a laser at the merchant ship to update their range to the target.

"Eighteen point five nautical miles and holding, ma'am," he said, not answering her question but still giving her a crucial piece of information.

"Is he running?" Beth asked, turning to look at her XO, who was hovering over the radar display.

"His course would put him in the heart of commercial traffic in and out of Long Beach," he replied.

"All ahead flank three," she commanded.

"All ahead flank three, aye, ma'am," the lee helmsman replied.

They lurched as the massive engines again increased to full power, pushing the mighty warship to its maximum speed. She still didn't know if the vessel they had spotted hanging in the shadow of San Clemente Island had played a role in the orbs circling her ship, but it had disabled its transponder and was trying to get lost in the clutter of America's second busiest port. That made him guilty in her mind.

"Range to target?" she asked.

There was a pause as the sailor fired the laser again. "Eighteen point four nautical miles and closing slowly, ma'am."

"How far is she from the anchorage?"

Her navigator leaned over the chart and measured the distance from the commercial vessel to the southern end of the field where ships sat at anchor waiting their turn to enter the port and offload their cargo.

"Forty-eight point six nautical miles," he replied.

She didn't need a slide rule to know there wouldn't be enough time to intercept the vessel before it could lose itself among the other ships. She resisted the urge to slam her fist down onto the nearest console and instead deliberately folded her arms across her chest.

"Ma'am, a word?" Ben said, standing apart from the other sailors.

She saw his contemplative expression and could tell from his posture he was preparing to give her sage counsel, whether she wanted to hear it or not. She nodded and stepped closer, allowing him to speak without fear of being overheard by the crew.

"What is it, Master Chief?"

"Once we cross north of San Clemente, we will be out of position to provide sanitization for tomorrow's missile test. I recommend we hand off this contact to the Coast Guard and return to our assigned station."

She had a feeling that was what he was going to say, and she admitted it was the right thing to do. But she had never backed down from a fight in her life. She was a scrapper and had fought to get where she was. It stuck in her craw not to see this through.

"But you are the captain," Ben added as a gentle admonishment.

"Thank you," she whispered, then stepped around his hulking frame to address the bridge. "XO, break off the intercept and return us to our station. Radio Coast Guard Los Angeles-Long Beach and hand off the unidentified merchant vessel, then secure from general quarters."

The commander stepped forward. "Aye, ma'am."

She turned and placed a hand on Ben's shoulder, giving it a gentle squeeze in quiet thanks for his reminder. The ship's crew were in excellent hands with Ben Ivy as their Master Chief.

He nodded at her, and she slipped off the bridge for her cabin to complete her report of the evening's events. She still wasn't sure what to tell the admiral about the orbs, but she sure as shit knew what she was going to say to the CAG; there was a certain pilot who would soon learn what happened to those who crossed her.

4

Lance Corporal Adam Garett shuffled along the passageway, blinking away his fatigue as he made his way forward to Ready Room Four. He still hadn't found his sea legs and cursed when a gentle swell toppled him into the white bulkhead and scuffed his green coveralls.

"Dammit," he muttered. *Gunny's gonna get on me for that.*

He wasn't the poster Marine by any stretch, but he still made an effort to keep up appearances. If for no other reason than it allowed him to stay under the radar of the senior staff noncommissioned officer's withering stare. He would do anything to breathe in fresh air on the roof with the chain monkeys, but instead his recruiter had doomed him to a life stuck indoors.

Battle to belong. My ass!

"Hey, Garett, Gunny's looking for you."

He looked up and saw his sergeant walking toward him. Unlike Adam, Sergeant Narvaez, a short and stocky Puerto Rican from the Mott Haven neighborhood of the Bronx, was the perfect Marine. His green coveralls were starched with sleeves rolled tight around his defined biceps and legs bloused neatly above his tan combat boots. Under other circumstances, he could have been the perfect role model.

"Yeah, yeah," he replied. "I'm on my way."

Narvaez brushed by him, and Adam turned the corner with trepidation. It wasn't that he was afraid of working for the hard-nosed gunnery sergeant; it was that he woke every day dreading a life stuck with this job. *Aviation Logistics Information Management Systems Specialist.* It had sounded important when the recruiter pointed it out to him.

"Garett! Where da fuck have you been?"

He took a deep breath and ignored the gravelly voice as he walked through the door and took his seat at the computer that had become his rifle. Instead of storming the beaches of Iwo Jima or wading through the jungles of Guadalcanal, he was given charge of a broad spectrum of network infrastructure and information systems. You never saw that job on any of the recruiting posters.

"Sorry, Gunny," he muttered.

"Sorry don't cut it in *my* Marine Corps." He always said it like that, as if he had been a wet-eared private at Tun Tavern. But he shifted the plug of chewing tobacco to the opposite cheek, swatted at the air, and moved on. "Day check fucked up some MAFs, and I've got the MO on my ass."

Fortunately, he moved on to something Adam knew he could do. He might not have been a model Marine, but he knew a thing or two about computers and had become the "go to" in the Black Knights for navigating the brand-new Operational Data Integrated Network, known as ODIN.

"What tail?" Adam asked.

"*Tails,*" Gunny corrected.

Adam groaned, knowing it would take him longer to discover where the errant Maintenance Action Forms had disappeared to. He didn't mind having the task to occupy his time while confined to the prison-like office space, but he knew the Maintenance Officer wanted an answer sooner than he could probably get it to him. And that meant Gunny would ride him like a swaybacked mule until he delivered. Shit really did roll downhill in the Marine Corps.

"Maintenance, flight deck," the handheld radio perched on Gunny's desk squawked.

Gunny saw Adam hesitate. "Get started, Garett."

"Aye, Gunny." He spun back to his terminal and logged in while keeping an ear turned to the radio.

"Go ahead," he growled.

"They scrubbed the launch and are shutting everyone down."

This time, it was Gunny who groaned. Without planes in the air, the focus would be on his department to get them ready for the next day. "Roger. Put 'em to bed, then come down off the roof."

"We still got one airborne," the staff sergeant on the other end of the radio said.

Gunny muttered a string of colorful curse words under his breath while Adam held his. "Which one?"

"Three oh seven."

Adam couldn't help himself. He glanced over at the flight schedule and saw they had assigned 307 to the visiting TOPGUN pilot. He exhaled, thankful it wasn't one of the Marine pilots in his squadron. It wasn't that he felt any particular allegiance to them; he just didn't want the added distraction of knowing the guy at the controls.

Chen hadn't given him all the details of what was supposed to happen, only that a jet wasn't going to make it back to the ship. In truth, he didn't want to know the details. He would have felt better if she hadn't told him it was supposed to happen at all.

Now, as he sat in front of the computer, pretending to sift through thousands of ODIN files in search of the missing MAFs, his heart raced with anxiety. He knew somewhere out there, one of his squadron's jets was going to crash. And some lieutenant he had never met before was going to die.

"Maintenance, CATCC," the radio on Gunny's desk squawked.

This is it, Adam thought. Any moment, Gunny was going to learn aircraft 307 went into the drink—the newest and most expensive fighter in the fleet vanished into the murky depths of the Pacific Ocean. Then he would direct Adam to lock down the files to prepare for the mishap investigation.

And Adam would act like any other lance corporal in the Marine Corps and follow his orders.

Gunny spit a long stream of tobacco juice before answering. "Go ahead."

"Three oh seven checked in bravo."

Bravo?

Adam spun in his seat and looked over at Gunny, who was hanging his head in despair. The Maintenance Officer was already on the staff noncommissioned officer for open maintenance actions that weren't even downing discrepancies. They were "up gripes," which meant the jets could still fly and were Partially Mission Capable, or PMC. But a jet coming back "bravo" meant that it was Non-Mission Capable, or NMC, and would require maintenance before it flew again.

Down, but not gone. Like she had told him it would be.

"Roger," he replied. "What for?"

"He didn't elaborate."

Adam couldn't help but wonder if whatever he was down for was somehow related to what Chen had told him would happen. It was obvious things hadn't gone the way she had expected. He pushed back from the computer and stood. He didn't have a good excuse, but he needed to get word to her that the F-35C was coming back.

Gunny spit the plug of tobacco into a Gatorade bottle wrapped in athletic tape. "Where you goin', Garett?"

"Gotta use the head, Gunny."

The maintenance control chief nodded his bald head and went back to pecking on the computer. Adam hesitated for a second before turning for the door, figuring he had time to send his message before the JSF made it back. He had just stepped out into the hall when he heard Gunny's voice boom after him.

"And change that fucking uniform! You've got paint all over it."

―――――――

A few minutes later, Adam rotated the long-armed handle on the watertight door and pushed it open, exposing only pitch black. He stepped out onto the catwalk, then closed and dogged the door behind him, standing with his back to the steel hull as he let his eyes adjust to the darkness and listened to the water rushing by sixty feet below him. The edge of the flight deck was just above his head, and a short climb up the ladder to his right would take him to what he really wished he was doing instead of being stuck indoors as a glorified paper pusher.

While most of his fellow Marines with an aviation Military Occupational Specialty, or MOS, had gone to Pensacola for advanced training, Uncle Sam had sent him to Newport, Rhode Island. For a foster kid from California who went to boot camp in sunny San Diego, that one winter in the Northeast was enough to convince him he belonged on the West Coast. The jury was still out whether he belonged in the Marine Corps.

Adam rarely spent time on the flight deck, and never during flight operations, but he was convinced that was where he wanted to be. Every time he sat down at his computer and waited for the system to log him in, he daydreamed about the warm sun washing over him as he ducked under exhausts and dodged spinning propellers. Compared to the purgatory of maintenance control, the flight deck was a wondrous splendor and the proverbial greener pasture.

But even though that was what he wanted, it still terrified him. He would have preferred waiting until daylight when he could see more than six inches in front of his face and spot the dangers lurking around him, but he couldn't wait that long to send his message. So, he ignored his pounding heart and pushed through the fear to make his way along the bulkhead to the railing aft of the Sea Sparrow launcher.

He was at the stern of the ship, just to the port side of the landing area, and knew he wasn't supposed to be there. But he didn't have a choice.

How did I end up in this mess?

But he knew how, and it wasn't overly complicated. A beautiful woman had been the downfall of many men through history, but he had never thought he would fall victim to something as banal as sex. Until, of course, Chen approached him at the Shore Club in Pacific Beach. Within five minutes, he knew he would do anything she wanted.

And he hated himself for it.

Committing treason had seemed so simple in the abstract. But now, as he skirted along the haze-gray painted steel to the platform just above the R2-D2-looking Phalanx Close-in Weapon System, he couldn't help but question every choice he had ever made. Part of him was relieved that whatever fate had been planned for the F-35C failed to materialize and that the Navy pilot would return safely to the carrier.

"I'm so stupid." His words sounded hollow against the wind whipping through the missile launcher behind him. It was an empty chastisement but made him feel marginally better.

Adam gripped the railing and stared into the distance, barely able to make out the carrier's wake in the starlight. He caught sight of a pair of slow-blinking wingtip strobe lights flying closer to the ship and recognized them as belonging to the once doomed fighter. There was no question the chicken had come home to roost.

With sudden understanding, he turned and looked past the Sea Sparrow launcher, noticing for the first time the gaggle of men in white float coats standing on a platform next to the landing area. The Landing Signal Officers, known colloquially as Paddles, were there to guide the JSF back aboard the carrier. And he had given himself a front-row seat.

"So fucking stupid."

The last place he wanted to be as the fighter landed on the carrier was only feet from the flight deck, so he removed the modified Nintendo Switch from his back pocket and hurried to turn it on. As it booted up, he performed the now familiar sequence of control inputs required to access the handheld video game system's partitioned hard drive.

Up, up, down, down, left, right, left, right, B, A, plus.

He knew it was a play on the original Konami code, adapted for the new console, and he covered the screen to prevent its glow from giving him away. In the night's blackness, even the faintest light pollution would be a beacon to his unwelcome presence, and he couldn't afford to be caught with the device out in the open.

"Come on, come on, come on," he said, urging it to finish booting up so he could transmit his message and return to the safety inside the ship.

When Chen had first given him the device while they lounged in bed one Sunday morning, he had thought it was a joke and started it up to play Mario Kart. But then she told him to turn it off and restart it while entering the faux-Konami string of inputs during the boot-up sequence. Now, just as he had seen then, a black reverse video screen replaced the familiar red screen, identifying the Covert Communication Partition.

He took his hand off the screen and saw only two icons labeled "Send" and "Receive."

He tapped on "Receive" and held the device at arm's length, screen facing skyward, and waited for the progress bar to fill. Once complete, he pulled it close and looked at the words displayed on the screen.

NO NEW MESSAGES.

He hadn't expected any, but still felt dismayed she hadn't shown the least bit of concern he was hanging himself out in the wind for her. With a groan, he opened the access panel and inserted the microSDXC card he kept hidden in his uniform, then tapped on the icon labeled "Send."

He followed the commands on the screen, selecting the memory card and the message he had rushed to compose, then hit "OK." As before, he held the device out with the screen facing the sky and waited for the progress bar to show his message had been transmitted to the orbiting satellites overhead. Once filled, he read the message on the screen.

DONE.

Adam thought it anticlimactic but didn't really care how the technology worked. He removed the microSDXC card and slid it back into the hidden pouch in the waistline of his coveralls, then powered down the device. The next time he turned it on, it would boot up like any other Switch without even a hint that it was more than it appeared to be.

He tucked it back into his pocket and ducked around the Sea Sparrow launcher just as the JSF crossed the ramp and slammed down onto the flight deck above his head with a deafening roar. It should have startled him, but he was already fearing the response to his message. He knew he was just a minor cog in the wheel of global espionage, but part of him still hoped his actions might mean something, that he was important to somebody.

The JSF pilot pulled the throttle back, and silence once more filled the night. Adam took a deep breath and opened the watertight hatch to return to the belly of the beast.

5

Colt stepped off the bottom peg of his boarding ladder, thankful to be back on a naval aviator's version of solid ground. He was amazed by the silence of the normally chaotic flight deck and heard only the wind howling through the chains securing the stock-still aircraft to the ship.

A staff sergeant stepped around the stubby nose of the stealth fighter jet and walked up to him. "Good jet, sir?"

Colt turned and looked up at the hulking staff noncommissioned officer, trying to read his stoic expression. As usual, he gave nothing away as he stared down the pilot who had dared to risk damaging his jet by taking it flying.

Colt shook his head. "I don't..." The fear tightened around his chest. "I don't know what's wrong with her."

The staff sergeant gave him an odd look and waited for an explanation, but when Colt failed to deliver, he turned back to continue supervising his Marines and forgot about the lieutenant who walked on shaking legs aft to the tower, already lost in thought. Colt took the ladder outboard from the carrier's superstructure and descended to the catwalk suspended above the water. From there, he opened a watertight hatch and stepped into a darkened anteroom before dogging it behind him and opening an inner door to the passageway lit up in red.

He passed the Air Transfer Office that coordinated transportation on and off the carrier, then turned left in the main passageway, heading for Flight Equipment, where he could remove his helmet and secure it inside the case designed to protect the state-of-the-art workspace. The custom-fitted helmet, made of Kevlar-reinforced carbon fiber, had a visor that acted as both night vision goggles and a display for the Distributed Aperture System, giving him access to real-time imagery from six infrared cameras located around his aircraft. It cost $400,000, and Colt would be damned if he let something happen to it.

He took two steps before running into Smitty.

"What the fuck happened, bro?"

He had thought of nothing else since he almost blacked out and crashed into the *Mobile Bay*. But the bitch of it was, he couldn't explain it. For a person who was supposed to be an expert in the F-35C, that troubled him the most. "I don't know…"

"You can tell me later," Smitty said with a dismissive wave. "You need to give me your helmet and go straight to CVIC."

Colt shook his head in disbelief. "What? Why?"

"CAG and the skipper are waiting to talk to you."

Oh, shit.

He doffed the helmet and handed it to his wingman, who stowed it inside the case, then he turned around and reluctantly headed forward to the Carrier's Intelligence Center. If he hadn't been distracted thinking about the ass-chewing he was about to receive, he might have seen the Marine in time to avoid the collision. But, as it was, both men weren't paying attention, and Colt ran right into the enlisted man and almost knocked the poor kid backward onto his butt. A handheld video game device clattered to the tile and skittered across the floor.

"Dammit!" the Marine exclaimed.

Colt froze in stunned disbelief and watched him scramble for the video game before getting to his feet and dusting himself off. He wore green coveralls with a VMFA-314 patch on his right chest opposite a black leather name tag adorned with a gold embossed Eagle, Globe, and Anchor.

"I'm sorry, Lance Corporal…" Colt read the name tag on his left breast. "…Garett. Are you okay?"

Garett nodded, clutching the handheld device protectively against his chest, and stepped back against the bulkhead to give the pilot room. "It was my fault, sir."

"You sure?"

He nodded again, and Colt looked him over once more, then brushed past and continued across the blue tile bound for whatever fate awaited him in CVIC.

He didn't have to wait long. After entering the code that unlocked the door with an audible *click*, he saw CAG had cleared the space of everybody except his deputy and the Black Knights' commanding officer. Even the air wing's intelligence officers were notably absent, and they practically lived there.

He glanced at the Marine skipper, who shook his head ever so slightly, warning him to keep his mouth shut, then back to CAG, Captain Patrick "Footloose" Meyers, a double anchor who had commanded a Super Hornet squadron in Colt's first air wing. Though a natural rivalry existed between pilots and weapon systems officers, CAG had never given him a reason to think he was anything other than a fair and reasonable leader. A few shots of whiskey at the Silver State Club in Fallon after a particularly brutal debrief had solidified Colt's opinion that CAG flew hard and fought hard, but he drank and played harder.

"What the *fuck* don't you understand about a direct order, Lieutenant?"

Guess he's not playing, Colt thought.

"Sir, there's something wrong with—"

"I asked you a question!"

His eyes snapped back in front of him, and he came to attention like he was a Plebe on I-Day, forgetting his rehearsed platitudes under CAG's withering stare. "Sir, I..."

Footloose jumped to his feet and crossed the tile floor to stand nose-to-nose in front of him. He felt CAG's anger radiating like heat in the still room and suddenly wished he were back in the darkened cockpit of his possessed Joint Strike Fighter, struggling for control while chasing bogies in the pitch black over the Pacific Ocean.

CAG clenched his jaw as he seethed, inches from Colt's face. At last, he spoke through gritted teeth in an ominous tone. "I just got off the phone with a pissed-off *Mobile Bay* skipper, and she's out for blood. You have *one* chance to explain yourself, and if I don't like what you have to say, I'm taking you to mast under Article 90 of the Uniform Code of Military Justice. Do you know what that is?"

Colt thought he might, but he kept his mouth shut. "No, sir."

"DCAG?"

CAG's deputy stepped forward and spoke in a calm and emotionless voice. "Disobeying a superior commissioned officer."

"And am I a 'superior commissioned officer'?"

"You are," DCAG replied.

"What are the penalties if found guilty?"

"Up to ten years' confinement and dishonorable discharge," his deputy replied.

Colt swallowed.

"Further, based on your reckless flying, I am going to recommend that your skipper convene a *fee-nab* when you get back to Fallon to determine your suitability to continue flying as a Naval Aviator."

Worse than the potential for prison time and a boot from the Navy, a FNAEB, or Field Naval Aviator Evaluation Board, was a death knell. One of the potential outcomes from the board was being stripped of his wings and losing his entire identity as a pilot. Everything he had worked so hard to achieve could be taken from him with a simple up-down vote from three senior aviators.

"Lieutenant Bancroft, do you understand the gravity of the situation?"

Colt studied CAG for a sign he was anything but one hundred percent serious. Seeing only fierce determination in the face before him, he nodded. "Yes, sir. I do."

"Very well," CAG replied. "Then, what do you have to say for yourself?"

Colt took a deep breath to calm his fraying nerves. He still didn't know how to describe what had happened to him over the *Mobile Bay*, but he needed to convey the severity of the situation. "Sir, I almost died tonight."

CAG's face softened slightly as he heard the tremor in Colt's voice. "What do you mean, son?"

Colt shook his head. "I don't know how to explain it, but there's something wrong with the jet's software." He paused, again remembering the impotence he felt when his connection to the jet was severed. "Just as I arrived on station, my PCD flickered, and I lost control of the jet."

CAG rolled his eyes. "You lost control? Like, you departed?"

Again, he shook his head. "No, sir, I'm saying the jet wouldn't respond to my commands. It rolled in on the ship on its own, and I couldn't pull out of the dive. I couldn't stop the roll. I couldn't stop the dive. *Nothing* I did worked."

"So, how'd you recover?"

Colt glanced over at the Black Knights' skipper and saw a worried crease on his brow. He was certain the lieutenant colonel was questioning the safety of his fleet, but he wasn't willing to stand up to Footloose and recommend grounding the Joint Strike Fighter. He looked back into CAG's face and saw the concern that had been etched there slowly fading away. He was losing his sympathetic ear.

"I don't know what I did," Colt replied honestly. "I wish I could say it was my knowledge or skill that saved me, but I'm afraid it was just dumb luck. All I know is that the jet rolled in on the ship on a kamikaze attack, and I was helpless. We almost lost a guided-missile cruiser tonight."

Saying the words out loud shaded the events in a completely different light. The possibility of crashing and being lost at sea was an inherent risk of his chosen profession. But taking out a strategic asset and critical component of the carrier strike group made it seem targeted. It was almost as if nothing that happened had been random or could be explained away as a simple glitch.

He saw CAG's jaw harden, and he knew his time was up.

"You disobeyed a direct order. You put our greatest asset at risk, and now you want me to cover up your reckless flat-hatting by grounding my entire fleet of F-35s? Well, I'm not buying it."

Colt held his breath.

"Go directly to maintenance control and complete your paperwork, then straight to your stateroom. I'm grounding you and confining you there pending a review of the maintenance data."

Colt exhaled through pursed lips, though he knew he wasn't out of the woods yet. His entire fate rested on a report generated by a jet that had already betrayed him. Without concrete evidence validating his claims,

CAG would likely take him to mast. Or, worse, he would recommend a FNAEB to have him stripped of his wings.

CAG turned to the Black Knights' commanding officer. "Skipper, you will accompany me to maintenance control so we can get to the bottom of this."

"Aye aye, sir."

CAG gave Colt one more appraising glare. "You're dismissed, Lieutenant."

Colt's stomach dropped, but he performed a parade-worthy about-face and marched out of CVIC on unsteady feet.

6

Long Beach, California

NCIS Special Agent Emmy King sat at a waterfront brewery and stared over the railing at the empty slip in the yacht club where *TANDY*'s boat should be moored. She ran a finger along the side of her glass, rubbing away the condensation that had collected there while trying to ignore the man sitting across from her. It wasn't that she didn't like him. After all, her father's best friend had been part of her life for as long as she could remember. Rather, she didn't like how he reminded her of things she'd just as soon forget.

"Can I get you anything else?" the waitress asked.

Emmy took her eyes from the yacht club and glanced up, shaking her head. "I'm fine. Thank you."

The young woman, who was probably a junior or senior at Cal State Long Beach, started to walk away to check on her other tables, but Rick Cole stopped her. "Actually, we'll have another round."

The waitress smiled at Rick and said, "Certainly."

Emmy raised her half-empty glass in silent toast to the studious waitress, then took a sip of the West Coast–style IPA, savoring the undercurrent of zesty orange and piney hops. They had been sitting at the table against the terrace's railing well before the sun had set, watching boats transiting the inlet in and out of Alamitos Bay without seeing what Rick had promised would be there.

"I really need to get going back to San Diego," she said.

"What's the hurry, Punky?"

She gave him an impish smile, and he chuckled. Few people knew Rick better than she did, not even his fellow special agents at the FBI, and she knew he was only trying to get under her skin. He had bestowed on her the nickname when she was just a little girl with dark hair in pigtails and rosy cheeks, but she never gave him the satisfaction of knowing she secretly liked it.

She tipped back her glass and drained the rest of the beer. "I have a two-hour drive," she said. "One beer is enough."

She wasn't dressed for a night on the town and wore dark gray jeans, ripped at the knees, with a plain white T-shirt that was loose and anything but flattering. A pair of red Vans and a red zip-up hoodie completed her casual ensemble and clashed with Rick's obnoxiously bright Hawaiian shirt that made him look like a Black Magnum, P.I., minus the mustache.

He drained his glass when he noticed the waitress returning with two fresh ones, then nodded across the water. "Why go back? It's still early, and my boat's just over there."

"Don't you mean the Bureau's boat?"

Rick shrugged and flashed her a toothy smile as the waitress set the beers on the table between them and absconded with the empty glasses. "That's what I meant."

For as long as she could remember, Rick loved to tease her. But sooner or later, he was going to have to come to terms with the fact that she had grown up; she wasn't his best friend's daughter, but his colleague.

"You can let me know what happens," she said. As close as they were, she hadn't come all this way just to have a drink with him on a random Thursday. She had kept him at arm's length for a reason, but it would have been worth it if his intel had paid off and *TANDY* had shown. But without a fucking boat in the fucking slip, they had nothing.

"Stubborn like your daddy," he muttered.

Damn him.

"I didn't get to where I am by being docile." She pushed back from the table and jumped to her feet. "Enjoy your beers, Uncle Rick."

"Oh, come on," he said, holding his hands up in mock surrender. "I was only messing with you."

She appraised him silently for a moment. "No, you weren't."

If she was being honest, she *was* stubborn like her daddy. It was probably one of the few traits she'd inherited from him that had helped her in life. But she considered herself patriotic and duty bound, beholden to the ideals of the Founding Fathers. She had a job to do, and she didn't think digging up the past and sharing stories aboard a fifty-foot Hatteras fishing boat would help their cause.

Though she admitted the ten-minute drive to the marina would be better than the two hours it was going to take her to get back to San Diego, she'd rather walk the hundred miles than tread through a minefield of shared history that was better left buried.

"It's a boat. You're in the Navy now."

"I'm *not* in the Navy," she reminded him.

"Close enough."

They stared at each other in silent defiance for a moment before she felt her phone vibrate in her hand. His phone must have also vibrated, because he ended the staring contest and fished it from his pocket. She took the opportunity to check the notification on the screen and saw that there was a message waiting for her in the secure portal. After a cursory glance over her shoulder, she unlocked her phone with a six-digit passcode and biometric scan, then opened the secure messaging application and entered another unique passcode to connect to the encrypted network.

Her momentary desire to leave gone, she sat back down while her phone completed the download process. Feeling the first bit of hope she'd had all night, she leaned forward in her chair and opened the inbox, ignoring Rick, who was probably doing the exact same thing. She entered the onetime code to decrypt the message, eager to see the latest message from the National Security Agency.

The NSA had been monitoring routine communications between *KMART*, a sailor aboard the aircraft carrier *Abraham Lincoln*, and *TANDY*, an unknown person located somewhere in Southern California. Based on the sophistication of the encrypted messages, they suspected *TANDY* worked for a hostile foreign intelligence organization, necessitating a joint operation with the Federal Bureau of Investigation. Her Uncle Rick had been assigned to track down the operative while she focused on unmasking the traitorous sailor. For the last three months, it had been her priority.

More like obsession, but whatever.

She couldn't bear the thought of some low-life pond scum sullying the good name of her father's Navy by giving secrets to the enemy. Worse, she couldn't stomach the nameless piece of shit putting lives at risk for a paltry sum or piece of pussy. Workaholic or not, she lost sleep over the sailor she knew only as *KMART*.

She opened the message and read through it twice, each time with increasing dread.

TEXT FROM INTERCEPTED TRANSMISSION FOLLOWS.

FROM: KMART

TO: TANDY

1. TARGET AIRCRAFT SURVIVED. OPERATION FAILED.

2. SEND INSTRUCTIONS.

Target aircraft survived? What the fuck?

She looked across the table and saw Rick's normally stoic face creased with a worried frown. He glanced up at her, and they made eye contact. His voice lowered to a hush, barely audible over the surrounding clamor of the microbrewery's patio. "What operation?"

"Not here," she said.

He nodded and pulled out three twenty-dollar bills, tossing them onto the table next to the untouched beers. Together, they rose and headed for the exit, weaving their way through the crowded patio. After leaving the bar, they descended to the parking lot for a modicum of privacy and walked to the far side where she had backed her car into a spot.

"None of their previous communications mentioned an operation," she said, leaning against the driver's door while scanning their surroundings. "What do you make of it?"

Rick looked away and stared at the breakwater that defined the channel into Alamitos Bay. "It doesn't sound good," he said. "It sounds like our boy *KMART* is doing more than just giving up secrets."

She had to admit she read it the same way. "If there was some type of sabotage on the carrier, the entire fleet will be buzzing with rumors. I need to get back down to San Diego and see if anything shakes loose."

"Punky, it's late. Let's just nab *TANDY* when he shows."

She shook her head. "We can't risk losing his connection to *KMART*. We need to stop him, Uncle Rick."

Without waiting for his concurrence, she swung open the door and dropped into the tan driver's seat. Rick closed the door and leaned in over her. "You sure you can handle this?"

The question could have been taken any number of ways, but she knew what he meant. The men in her life had been making the same assumptions for as long as she could remember. She was too feminine to play water polo, too pretty to go into law enforcement, and too timid to drive her dad's restored 1974 Corvette Stingray. Each time, she answered by letting her actions speak for themselves.

I can handle anything.

She turned the key, and the car shuddered as the starter cranked over the 7.4 V8 and caught with a throaty growl. She put her foot on the gas pedal and goosed the throttle, answering his question with a smile.

"I'm gonna catch the bastard," she said, then smoked the tires as she peeled out of her parking space.

Rick watched the Corvette that had belonged to his best friend tear out of the parking lot and remembered when Terry had brought it home. It was almost as vivid as the memory of when he had brought Punky home too. Even as a baby, the girl had spunk. But the version she had grown into was one Terry would have been proud of.

You should see her, bro.

She was prettier than she knew; tall and athletic, with piercing blue eyes over an olive complexion that hinted at her mother's Israeli heritage. But it was her smarts and toughness that came from Terry—qualities that had made him one hell of a SEAL, and her one hell of a counterintelligence officer.

With a shake of his head, he watched the Corvette disappear, then climbed into the silver BMW M5 sport sedan that had come with the boat. If he was going to act the part of a rich pleasure boater, it wouldn't do to have him spotted coming and going in an overly pedestrian vehicle, like a Ford Focus. But unless *TANDY* showed, it really didn't matter what kind of car he was in.

It was a short drive from the bar to the yacht club where the boat was docked, and he spent the time wondering where he had gone wrong. Between the NSA's intercepted communications and correlated hits on an airborne *Stingray*, the intel had been solid enough to grant him dedicated air support for surveillance. But still nothing. He pulled into the marina's lot and parked next to a blue Jeep Wrangler, then descended onto the dock and sauntered to his slip.

Rick stepped from the dock onto the fifty-foot fishing boat's stern and glanced across the water at the brewery's bright lights before unlocking the cabin and stepping into the spacious saloon. The boat was connected to shore power, so he flipped a switch to turn on the lights and descended to the small galley to splash lukewarm water on his face. After drying it with a dish rag, he slipped an earpiece into his ear and glanced at the chronometer on the wall to estimate when he would hear from the pilot.

"Delta One, Air One," the voice said in his earpiece.

Speak of the devil, Rick thought. "Go ahead."

"On station. Currently tracking multiple small craft, but no bites."

He groaned and paced across the saloon, stepping out onto the aft deck to look up into the air. Somewhere up there was a Cessna Turbo Stationair from the Surveillance and Aviation Section fitted with an electro-optical and infrared sensor mounted on the fuselage. But it was the *Stingray* on board that would be their secret weapon.

"Copy. Keep me updated."

"Air One, out."

Rick turned and climbed up to the fly bridge, plopping himself into one of the vinyl chairs overlooking the sleek bow. The boat was far nicer than the ones he had spent time on in his previous life, but he had a sense of familiarity being alone on the water in the darkness. Now, the bastard just needed to show up.

In the sky above Long Beach, the FBI pilot turned his Cessna west and went feet wet over the coastline headed out to sea. He had to admit the prospect of the assignment was better than what he normally worked on. When they had sent him to Long Beach, he had assumed he would be tasked with tracking subjects suspected of money laundering, or, at best, collecting intelligence on one of the many drug cartels that had moved into the area. But this? *This is some real Jack Ryan shit!*

"Cessna Four Oh Two Charlie Whiskey, switch to So Cal on twenty-five, thirty-five," the Air Traffic Controller said.

"Twenty-five, thirty-five," he parroted. "See ya."

He changed the frequency, then looked down at the surveillance equipment's control panel.

Nada.

The FBI's fleet of single-engine turboprop Cessnas all carried the same basic gear, but a few were modified based on the needs of the operation. An external sensor pod hung on the left side of the fuselage and transmitted video to a monitor inside the cockpit. But so far, the boats sailing up and down the coast hadn't triggered his suspicion. At least not to the threshold of espionage.

"So Cal, Cessna Four Oh Two Charlie Whiskey, VFR at two thousand feet, squawking two two five one," he said, letting the controller know his transponder code so the turboprop could be identified on radar.

"Cessna Two Charlie Whiskey, So Cal, radar contact. Maintain VFR."

He steered the Cessna 206 Turbo Stationair toward Catalina Island under Visual Flight Rules and pressed his face against the window, looking down on the dim lights of container ships anchored and waiting to offload their cargo in the ports of Los Angeles and Long Beach. Delta One believed a spy was somewhere down there, but so far, the *Stingray* had been silent. He double-checked his equipment just to be sure.

"Zilch," he muttered.

Even more than the electro-optical and infrared sensor pod, the *Stingray* would make or break this surveillance. Designed to simulate a cell tower, it tricked targeted phones into connecting to it, then collected their

GPS location, call history, and text messages. Assuming Delta One was correct and the spy was on one of those boats beneath him, all *TANDY* needed to do was turn his cell phone on, and it would automatically connect to the *Stingray* and provide all the information they needed to take him out. Game over.

"Come to papa," he said.

7

USS *Abraham Lincoln* (CVN-72)

Adam sat at his desk in the corner of maintenance control near Ready Room Four, doing his best to ignore Sergeant Narvaez explaining to Gunny why his "hunt and peck" method of typing would stunt his career growth. Time at sea wasn't measured by weeks or days or even hours, but by the sheer volume of meaningless and asinine conversations one engaged in to pass the time. But this was Adam's first real experience with being underway, and he found the discussions between the two staff noncommissioned officers to be both dull and unworthy of his attention. As such, he wasn't paying attention when a third voice interrupted their discussion.

"Gunny, what did you find with three oh seven?"

He might not have been listening, but Adam's heart rate spiked when he heard the tail number of the jet that was supposed to have crashed. He stopped scanning the batch of files he'd been reviewing and looked over his shoulder to see the skipper standing at the counter next to a stern-faced CAG. They made eye contact, and Adam swallowed.

"Nothing, sir," Gunny replied. "Ran it through every test we have in our pubs, and it passed with flying colors."

"That's disappointing," the skipper replied. "We need some answers."

"Did you want to see the write-up?"

"I want to see it," CAG said, stepping around the skipper to belly up to the counter. "And I want you to make a copy of it and the raw data while you run it through the computer again."

Gunny looked from CAG to the skipper, then back to the senior officer. "Aye aye, sir."

Adam choked with fear and tried to cover it up by coughing.

Gunny barked, "Got something to add over there, Garett?"

"No, Gunny." With one more glance at the two officers, Adam turned back to his terminal. But instead of returning to the batch of files he'd been sifting through, he searched for the file containing the data they had downloaded from the crippled jet. He had a feeling somebody would come looking for it sooner or later, but he had hoped for a bit more time. Now he needed a little luck and some sleight of hand to keep them from finding anything that could point to foul play. Or worse, to him.

"Gunnery Sergeant, how long is this going to take?" CAG asked, obviously annoyed with being made to wait for something he thought should take as long as it took him to snap his fingers.

"I'll make a copy of the MAF right now for you, sir. It will be just a minute to run the data through the computer again to look for any anomalies."

"I asked how long," CAG snapped.

The skipper—one of the few officers Garett actually respected—stepped in to run interference for his Marines. "Sir, you don't need to stick around for this. Why don't you go back to your office, and I'll bring it straight to you."

"Fine. Straight to my office," he said, the sound of his retreating footsteps echoing in the passageway.

When the footsteps had faded, Gunny addressed the lieutenant colonel. "What's got him wound so tight, sir?"

"Don't make me answer that, Gunny. Just make those copies and run the data again so I can tell him if something is wrong with these jets."

Adam's face flushed, but his fingers kept flying across the keyboard to find the file. He needed to replace it with another one before it was too late.

"Garett, make the skipper a copy of three oh seven's history."

He didn't reply. He didn't trust his voice not to crack under the strain as he frantically clicked his mouse to open folder after folder, drilling deep into the system's archives to find the file that might implicate him in treason and attempted murder. He didn't hear the skipper walk through the door, but he felt his presence hovering over him.

There!

He spotted the file and, clicking on it, he quickly pressed Alt + *V*, followed by the *H* and *S* keys. The file vanished.

"Find it?" the skipper asked.

Adam forced himself to exhale slowly before answering. When he did, he kept his eyes fixed on the computer and exited the folder he had been in, then opened it again. "I don't get it," he said, his voice quavering and little more than a whisper. "This is the right folder, Skipper, but the file isn't here."

The skipper exhaled loudly in exasperation, and Adam took the momentary distraction to copy aircraft 305's maintenance data and move it into the folder for 307. Then he exited the folder and leaned away from the computer while trying to act confused.

"What do you mean it ain't there?" Sergeant Narvaez asked, pushing back from his desk to join the younger Marine at his terminal.

"See, Sarge? Should be right here in this folder."

Adam opened the folder and groaned when he saw the copied file. "Oh," he said.

The stocky Marine leaned over Adam's shoulder and saw what he thought was the correct file, right where it was supposed to be. "Garett, you're some kind of special."

"Sorry, Sarge."

"Do you have it or not?" the skipper asked.

"We've got it, sir. I'll make you a copy right now." Narvaez inserted a USB flash drive into the side of the Toughbook laptop and copied the file from the ODIN servers.

The wrong file, Adam thought.

Colt sat on the edge of his rack in his stateroom and stared at the opposite bulkhead, numb with worry. He replayed the incident over in his mind, racking his brain to come up with a plausible explanation for why his jet had betrayed him. That had never happened to him before, and he couldn't recall ever hearing of something like that happening to any other pilot either.

Frustrated, he stood and paced the cramped space. He ran through the entire event in his mind, from startup to shutdown, trying to pinpoint where it had gone wrong. The start and launch had been normal, and aside from being the only fighter to get airborne during the event, nothing stood out to him as unusual that could have given credence to the way his jet refused to respond to his control inputs. It was a dreadfully normal flight.

Except for the orbs...

The knock at his door halted his thoughts before he could closer examine the strange lights swirling the cruiser. He turned and opened the door, not surprised to see the skipper standing there.

"Colt," the skipper said.

"Skipper."

"Mind if I come in?"

Colt opened the door wider for the lieutenant colonel and stepped back to permit him entrance. The skipper pulled a chair away from the desk built into the bulkhead and turned it toward Colt.

"What did you find, sir?"

"Have a seat, Colt."

His stomach dropped, and fear gripped him as he waited for the skipper to speak. But he pulled up a second chair and nervously sat. The skipper took the seat opposite him and leaned forward.

"Give it to me straight, sir."

The lieutenant colonel sighed. "We didn't find anything."

The pit in his stomach shot to his throat, and Colt leaned back in his chair as if he had been slapped. "What?"

"We ran the data through the computers again and couldn't find any irregularities to account for an uncontrolled roll or dive."

"But..."

"Colt, I'm sorry."

"Did maintenance run it through any tests?"

The skipper nodded. "Could not duplicate on deck."

Colt shook his head. "This doesn't make any sense. There *has* to be a logical explanation!"

"Colt..."

"Can you ground the planes until we get a tech rep from Lockheed out here?"

"Colt, CAG made up his mind."

He stood and looked down at the skipper, not wanting to believe it had come to this. "About what?"

"He's not going to ground the planes."

"But..."

The skipper jumped to his feet. "Get ahold of yourself, Lieutenant!"

Colt snapped his mouth shut and stared straight ahead, focusing his eyes beyond the skipper's stern face. It had been close to a decade since he graduated from the Naval Academy, but he still knew how to compose himself despite the torrent of emotions threatening to sweep him away.

"I fought for you," the skipper said. "But CAG made up his mind. He doesn't believe your story and doesn't think there is anything wrong with the Joint Strike Fighter. He's putting you on the first COD off the boat in the morning."

Colt swallowed hard and reined in his anger before speaking. "Roger that, sir."

"I'm sorry, Colt. But he's going to recommend your commanding officer convene a FNAEB when you get back to Fallon."

His eyes fell to the floor, and he felt his sails collapse in the stillness. Even his anger faded away to a simmer, and Colt was left with nothing but a feeling of hopelessness. His entire identity as a fighter pilot was on the brink of being ripped from him, and there was nothing he could do to stop it.

"I'd be happy to speak to the board on your behalf," the Marine offered. "You're a good officer and a skilled pilot, Colt. I don't know what happened up there, but I don't believe you did anything wrong."

"Thank you, sir," he said, his voice barely a whisper.

The skipper put a hand on Colt's shoulder and squeezed it. "I'm sorry, Colt."

At least I'm not going to mast, he thought.

8

After the skipper left his stateroom, Colt went forward to sit alone in the "dirty shirt" wardroom at the front of the ship, wishing for something stronger than the fountain drink in his plastic cup. He hadn't been entirely surprised CAG had ordered him off the ship, but he naively believed the older aviator might have at least listened to him with an open mind. He knew there was something wrong with the F-35C, and it was going to kill somebody or succeed in taking out a ship if he didn't find the problem and fix it. Soon.

"Mind if I join you?"

He didn't bother looking up and motioned for the other pilot to join him.

There were two wardrooms on the aircraft carrier where officers gathered to eat their meals. Most of the ship's company ate in the XO's wardroom, located deeper in the bowels of the carrier, but the air wing officers and those who spent their time on the roof ate in the one located just below the flight deck. Known as the dirty shirt, it had once been the only wardroom to allow flight suits and flight deck jerseys, but even after the rules changed, it was still where the air wing's pilots went to congregate.

"What the hell happened?"

Colt looked up and saw Smitty take the seat opposite him. "Thanks for taking my helmet," he said without answering.

The Marine dismissed the comment with a wave of his hand. "Want to talk about it?"

He took another sip of his root beer, still trying to calm himself from the whole ordeal. After leaving CVIC, he had gone to Flight Equipment to strip out of his flight gear and maintenance control to complete his paperwork, but his mind was still in the darkness out over the ocean. He saw the displays flickering and the pages cycling, and his heart raced as he relived the horror of almost blacking out and colliding with the guided-missile cruiser.

Smitty leaned forward and ducked his head lower to make eye contact. "Bro?"

But Colt's vacant stare was fixed on the nightmare ordeal.

He couldn't help thinking that the jet had spent decades in development and had been run through the wringer by test pilots at every phase. But, to his knowledge, nothing like this had ever happened before. If an experienced pilot like him had struggled to regain control, what would happen to a brand-new nugget pilot?

"What did you see out there? There's some strange rumors," Smitty said.

Colt cocked his head to the side. "What rumors?"

Was the entire air wing already talking about the TOPGUN pilot who CAG had kicked off the ship and recommended to a FNAEB? Was his reputation already so damaged that even if he managed to keep his wings and come back to the fleet, he'd be nothing more than a punch line? Reputation was everything in this business.

Smitty looked over both shoulders, but they were alone in the forward part of the wardroom. Their table was next to a large stainless steel contraption aviators lovingly referred to as the "dog machine," and it hummed a low harmonic that drowned out the surrounding noise. Satisfied he wouldn't be overheard, Smitty leaned even closer. "What did you *see* out there?"

Colt leaned back in his chair as it dawned on him. Smitty wasn't talking about Colt's insubordination, alleged flat-hatting, and subsequent exile from the carrier. He wasn't talking about almost crashing into a warship and dying. He was talking about those glowing orbs that had been harassing the *Mobile Bay*.

"I don't know," he replied honestly.

"Some of the Hawkeye guys said there were drones or something?"

Colt had to hand it to him. He was trying every angle he could think of to get the tight-lipped pilot to spill his guts. But as much as he wanted to validate or disprove whatever theory Smitty had concocted in his head, he didn't have much to go on.

"I just saw lights, man."

"Lights?"

"Yeah. Just lights. Like ten or so swirling around the ship." Colt let go of his plastic cup and circled his hands around it like it was a tin can full of sailors instead of a chalice for his root beer. "I don't know what they were, but then they..."

The memory of the terrifying moments flooded back to the forefront of his thoughts and froze him.

"They what?"

Did the orbs disappear after he'd regained control of his jet? Was it just a coincidence? Though his body still vibrated from the raw fear that had gripped him in those moments, he couldn't be certain his memory was accurate. Maybe he had the timing wrong. Maybe it didn't even matter.

He looked up at Smitty. "They just disappeared."

The Marine pilot furrowed his brow, clearly not satisfied with the eyewitness testimony. "What did they look like?"

Colt picked up his root beer and took another sip. Though he thought it likely his jet's strange behavior was linked to the orbs in some way, he knew he needed somebody to listen to his concerns. And not how CAG had listened with open skepticism, but with earnestness. "Listen, forget the lights."

"Were they UFOs?"

Colt shook his head. "Forget the lights. There's something more important you need to know."

"What?" Smitty's dubious look disappeared, and he leaned in again, waiting for Colt to drop a bombshell on him.

"I think there's something wrong with the jet's software. Something happened tonight, and I lost total control."

Smitty's eyes grew wide, but he remained silent.

"The jet rolled in on a perfect thirty-degree dive targeting the cruiser. It wouldn't respond to any of my control inputs, and I almost crashed right into the ship. At the last minute, I regained control and almost blacked out trying to recover. I have no idea what could have caused it, but I need to figure it out before it happens again."

"Does maintenance know?"

Colt nodded. "I wrote it up, and they ran it through a bunch of checks, but the skipper said they didn't find anything. They're going to sign off the MAF and send it up again."

"Could not duplicate on deck," Smitty said.

"Could not duplicate on deck," Colt echoed, parroting the skipper's own words. To aviators, it was a cop-out. It was maintenance control's way of saying they investigated the pilot's concern but found nothing to corroborate the gripe. It would be their way of dismissing his experience and signing it off safe-for-flight, believing as CAG did that the guest pilot had lost his mind.

"Why not get the raw data?" Smitty asked.

Colt opened his mouth to answer but snapped it shut. If he had the raw maintenance data, he could get it to somebody at Lockheed who understood the engineering of how the jet worked, somebody far smarter than a political science major from West Texas.

"Colt?"

But he would need more than just his jet's data so they could compare his with one that hadn't been possessed. Without another word, Colt got up from the table.

Adam sat in maintenance control and did his best to avoid looking like he was paying too much attention to Gunny and Sarge bickering over yet another meaningless fact of life aboard an aircraft carrier. It was too early to congratulate himself for deceiving the skipper and CAG with maintenance data for the wrong jet, because sooner or later, somebody would recognize the mistake and come looking for the right data.

"You mean to tell me you do your *own* laundry?" Narvaez asked incredulously.

"Gunnery sergeants don't let strangers wash their unmentionables," Gunny replied, deadpan.

Adam shook his head but decided he needed to permanently delete aircraft 307's history. While the two staff noncommissioned officers bickered, they weren't paying attention to what he was doing, and he drilled deeper into the ODIN servers, navigating to the folder where he had hidden the file.

"Hey, Gunny, was wondering if you could do me a favor," a new voice said.

Adam turned and saw the Navy pilot standing at the counter. As expected, the lieutenant didn't even acknowledge his presence. Aside from the skipper and a handful of other officers, most didn't think a lance corporal warranted their time or attention.

"Well, that depends, sir. What can I do for you?"

"The skipper said you guys ran some tests on three oh seven?"

"Ran it through every one in our pubs," Gunny replied.

"And you didn't find anything?"

"No, sir," Gunny said, then spit a string of tobacco juice into his taped-up Gatorade bottle. "Did you want to add more to your write-up?"

It wasn't unusual for pilots to remember some small tidbit of information and return later to add it to the MAF. Every tiny detail mattered because the maintainers relied on them to diagnose the malady. Just as doctors used every symptom to help narrow down a patient's illness, aircraft mechanics used a pilot's experiences to trace the problem to a root cause. But Adam started worrying the pilot had remembered something that might uncover what *really* happened.

That wouldn't be good.

"Nothing else to add," the lieutenant said.

Adam exhaled and turned back to his terminal. He had a feeling he knew what the lieutenant was about to ask, and he wanted to delete the file before Gunny or Sarge turned their focus on him and the deception he was trying to accomplish.

"Anything else I can do for you, sir?"

"Well, I'm headed back to Fallon tomorrow, and CAG wants me to bring flight data back for the Lockheed engineers to go over. Can you make copies for me?"

Adam groaned to himself, but it wasn't unexpected. He opened aircraft 307's folder and again glanced over his shoulder to see if anybody would see him making the file appear out of thin air so he could scrub it completely from the servers.

"Sure thing, sir. Come on back," Gunny said. Then, "Garett, make the lieutenant here a copy of three oh seven's history."

"I'm sorry," the lieutenant said. "Not just three oh seven's history."

"Not just three oh seven? Which ones?"

"All of them."

Adam turned around in his seat and stared at Gunny, hoping the bald staff noncommissioned officer would tell the Navy pilot that was unwarranted and excessive. A simple sleight of hand wouldn't be enough to disguise the data, because it would be obvious one was missing.

"All of them, sir?"

"That's what CAG said."

Sergeant Narvaez stood and walked over to Adam's desk. "I got this, Garett. Why don't you take a break and let me handle it."

He stared at the stocky Marine but didn't move. If he got up and walked away, Narvaez would quickly realize that one of the files was missing, and he was too good with a computer to not conclude that the data they had copied for the skipper was the wrong one. "That's okay, Sarge. I can do this."

Narvaez cocked his head in surprise, then gestured for Adam to continue. He probably thought Garett had finally decided to show some initiative and take his job seriously. "Be my guest," he said.

Adam inserted a USB flash drive into the Toughbook laptop and created folders for each of the squadron's jets. Then, one by one, he dragged the files over from the server, intentionally skipping aircraft 307 and creating a duplicate file from aircraft 305. A warning of the error popped up on the screen, but he quickly dismissed it, hoping it went unnoticed.

"I think you made a duplicate," Narvaez said.

Dammit. Adam's face flushed, but he tried to act nonchalant. "Did I?"

"I think you copied three oh five's history twice."

Adam had one more card to play, and he opened 307's folder to show Narvaez that it was empty. "See, Sarge? The file's already been moved over."

"Did you try looking for hidden files?" Gunny asked.

Gunny had called his bluff, and his heart rate spiked. How the *hell* did that hunt-and-pecking Neanderthal know to look for hidden files?

"How do you do that?" Garett asked.

"Alt and *V*, then *H* twice."

Adam already knew how but had hoped the senior NCO didn't. Dismayed, he tapped on the requisite keys, and the file appeared right where it had been all along. Reluctantly, he finished copying the remaining files to the USB flash drive.

"Don't worry, Garett," Gunny said. "Lance corporals don't become gunnery sergeants overnight."

Once the last file had been copied over, Adam removed the flash drive and handed it over to the lieutenant. "Here's the data, sir."

"Thanks, Lance Corporal."

Adam felt his stomach twist into knots when the Navy pilot spun for the door. Narvaez went back to dogging Gunny for the way he typed, and Gunny went back to the endless paperwork the Marine Corps ran on. Adam stared at the incriminating file on his computer and wondered what Chen would do when she found out the aviator had whatever information it contained.

I have to tell her.

9

MV *Yonggan De*
Anchored off Long Beach, California

North of the Southern California Offshore Range, a ship sat at rest for the first time in twenty-two days, eight hours, and thirty-seven minutes. That was how long it had taken the Merchant Vessel *Yonggan De* to transit from Qingdao Port in China's Shandong Province to the coast of California. Smaller compared to many of the larger New Panamax vessels sitting at anchor on either side of her, the *Yonggan De* still carried close to five thousand twenty-foot equivalent units' worth of cargo bound for the American consumer.

As the largest exporter of consumer goods to the United States, China accounted for almost twenty percent, totaling over $430 billion. The *Yonggan De* had crossed the Pacific carrying electrical machinery, oilseeds and oleaginous fruits, mineral fuels, and medical instruments. But it was the cargo not listed on the manifest, the cargo stevedores wouldn't offload, that was the real reason for her long passage across the ocean.

Twenty-two days, eight hours, and thirty-seven minutes, Xi Jian thought.

He zipped up the canvas duffel that sat at the foot of his bed, then turned to the stark metal desk built into the small stateroom's bulkhead.

The Toughbook laptop computer he had removed from the container sat open with a progress bar showing how much more data needed to be copied over to the memory card before he could throw the computer overboard. Then he could get off this godforsaken ship and back onto dry land where he belonged.

...99...100.

Without so much as a smile, Xi Jian removed the memory card and tucked it into the front pocket of his black jeans, knowing Mantis would want the information it contained. The jeans were slim fitting but had a stretch that made them ideal for navigating the crowded cargo deck. He wore a dark gray turtleneck underneath a hip-length black overcoat to help curb the damp ocean air. Scooping up the plain, black wool watch cap, he pulled it down over his head before closing the Toughbook and turning back to his bag.

He slung it over his shoulder and, with laptop in hand, left the stateroom that had felt like a prison cell. *Twenty-two days, eight hours, and...*

"The dinghy is almost here," the voice said, startling him from his thoughts.

Xi Jian looked up into Wu Tian's blank face. The slender chief mate was one of only three people on the *Yonggan De* who knew of his mission.

"Very well," he replied. "And we are on schedule?"

Wu Tian nodded but still gestured to the ladder in a not-so-subtle hint he would feel better once Xi Jian had left the larger Panamax merchant vessel for the inflatable dinghy on its way to retrieve him.

"And the transponder?"

"Back on," he replied. "Once the Navy ship turned back, we activated it to blend in with the rest of the commercial traffic."

Xi Jian nodded. The mission had looked to be a success at first, but then it all went to shit. The jet hadn't crashed into the guided-missile cruiser like it was supposed to, but thankfully, the memory card in his pocket contained the data Mantis would need to refine the waveforms. He had failed but knew it was the cost of doing business with an untested weapon.

At least I don't have to make the transit back, he thought as he turned for the ladder leading up to the main deck. He heard the chief mate's heavy boots on the treads behind him, but his thoughts were already on deep-sixing the Toughbook and making his way aft to the boarding ladder they had set up to prepare for his debarkation.

At the top of the stairs, he rotated a lever to open the watertight door, then stepped out onto the weather deck. He walked across the narrow walkway on the starboard side of the ship to the cream-colored and rusted steel railing and looked out over the edge into the darkness below. He could barely see the murky water, but he hoped it would be deep enough to do the job.

"It'll do," Wu Tian said, reading his thoughts.

Xi Jian looked to his left toward the bow of the ship and the lights twinkling on the coast. "How deep?"

The chief mate shrugged. "Ninety feet or so. We're in one of the deeper anchorages about five miles south of the port."

Xi Jian looked up and down the vacant deck of the ship, then flung the Toughbook computer over the side and watched it tumble through the air before crashing into the water with a quiet *splash*. He watched it disappear, then turned right and started walking aft to the rope ladder and his parole.

Wu Tian followed on his heels, keeping a watchful eye on him until he could verify he was off the ship and they had removed all evidence of contraband. Xi Jian heard his heavy footfalls behind him but was too busy thinking about a hot shower and soft pillow-top bed to pay him any mind. But when he heard the radio squawking at the man's waist, he stopped dead in his tracks.

Did he say Coast Guard?

Wu Tian's wide-eyed expression amplified his command. "Go!"

Xi Jian looked into the darkness beyond the railing for the approaching dinghy. He had hoped that reactivating their transponder after the Navy ship turned away would eliminate them from suspicion. But the radio call from the bridge dashed that hope to pieces.

"Go," he said again.

"The container..."

Wu Tian waved away the comment. "I'll take care of it." Then, bringing the radio to his mouth, he said, "I'm on my way. Respond that we are ready to receive them."

Xi Jian hesitated.

"*Go!*"

He watched the chief mate turn for the bridge, then sprinted aft for the boarding ladder. He needed to be off the boat before Coast Guard Cutter *Forrest Rednour* pulled alongside to board them.

Or before Wu Tian sanitized the container.

A few minutes later, he descended from the rope ladder's bottom rung onto the bobbing bow of the Rigid-Hull Inflatable Boat. He had barely steadied himself when the driver put the transmission in reverse and lurched away from the merchant vessel, bringing him to his knees.

"Sit *down!*" the voice hissed.

He scrambled off the front step plate and scurried around the center console to the aft seat, collapsing against the backrest as the one-hundred-horsepower Honda outboard propelled the small boat forward.

They were running without navigation lights, and the driver steered them clear of the dim halo of illumination surrounding the merchant vessel. If they could remain invisible from the Coast Guard, they might make it to shore none the worse for wear. But if somebody spotted them without their navigation lights...

"Was it a success?" she asked, craning her neck to look over her shoulder at him.

The faint red glow from the instrument cluster lit up half her face, and Xi Jian could tell she was beautiful. The Ministry had increased its use of women in the field over the half century following Katrina Leung's infiltration of the American Federal Bureau of Investigation. But at least he didn't have to spread his legs to complete his tasks.

His eyes wandered from her face, down to the body she had tried hiding underneath a wool peacoat. But even its bulk wasn't enough to disguise her shapely figure, and his eyes traced further down to her ass. His face cracked into a smile.

She stood the throttle up, and the motor behind him fell silent. "I asked you a question!"

He shot his eyes back to her face, saw it contorted with anger, and shook away his thoughts. "N-n-no," he stammered.

"No?"

"The hack failed," he said.

"Was it the drones?"

He glared at her through the darkness. "The drones did exactly what we wanted them to do. They lured the target aircraft into range."

"So, what happened?"

He shook his head. "I don't know. The hack...it just stopped."

If he had expected some sort of absolution for his failure, she didn't give it to him. "Do you have it?"

"What?"

"The mission data!"

He nodded his head.

"Give it to me."

He shoved his hand into his front pocket and pulled out the memory card. He felt its miniature form between his thumb and forefinger and held it out across the fiberglass hull, still unnerved by the dichotomy of the woman's appearance and her demeanor. He had never been spoken to with such disdain, let alone by a woman.

Like a viper, she snatched it from his grasp and slipped it into her pocket. Then, without another word, she turned back and advanced the throttles to bring the twenty-foot craft up on plane to escape the approaching cutter. Xi Jian huddled behind the woman, who stood tall at the console, peering into the darkness beyond the bow. He tucked himself close, her slender body blocking most of the wind while jostling against the eddies that swirled on either side of them.

"Where are we going?" he shouted over the din of the wind and water and four-stroke motor.

"Escaping before your blunder costs us," she shouted.

He felt his temper flare. "*My* blunder?"

She glared over her shoulder at him but remained silent. How could she think he had any control over the effectiveness of the weapon someone else had developed? He had been taught how to use it before leaving port, but whether it performed as advertised was well beyond his dominion.

The RHIB hit a trough, and it shuddered underneath them, the salty water spraying over the bow and soaking them both. He removed his watch cap and wiped his face. She didn't move an inch.

"What does a woman know?"

He should have kept his mouth shut but couldn't help himself. He thought of her as little more than a *xiagongpeng*, the lowest form of prostitute in mainland China. Who was *she* to question his actions when her service to the state was best done on her back?

Or on her knees, he thought.

He traced the curves of her body again, and he felt himself flush at the depraved thoughts. She would take him to shore, then he would take what he wanted and reward himself for the month-long passage with a roll in the sack. When he was done with her, she would drive him to the consulate and arrange transportation for him to return to Shanghai.

"Just drive the boat," he said. "Let the experts fix the weapon."

She glanced back at him and caught him again staring at her ass. When his eyes met hers, he saw her features harden. He smiled at her, but when she turned away, it vanished, and he felt anger flush his face.

Maybe I'll bend her over instead...

She again stood the throttle up and coasted to a stop, only this time she turned the key to kill the motor. Leaning against the steering wheel, her body rocked with the gentle rolling of the boat as she scanned the horizon in every direction. Over two miles behind them, the Coast Guard Cutter *Forrest Rednour* had pulled alongside the *Yonggan De* to conduct its search. Other Panamax and super-Panamax vessels sat at anchor in the mooring field to await their turn in the saturated Port of Long Beach, but otherwise they were alone on the water.

He watched her expression change as if she had donned a purple Peking Opera mask portraying serenity and a sense of justice. "I'll forgive your lack of manners," she said. "And won't put it in my report to Mantis."

Mantis?

His thoughts of taking the woman as his prize evaporated in an instant. If she truly reported to Mantis, then he had underestimated her. And he had unwittingly put himself in grave danger. "Th-th-thank you," he stammered.

"You've been at sea a long time, yes?"

He nodded.

"I can forgive your behavior and chalk it up to..." She opened the front of her peacoat, unveiling a dark, long-sleeved shirt that clung to her breasts. "A lack of *social interaction*. Is that about right?"

Again, he nodded.

"It's understandable you want to spend the night with me," she said. It was a statement, not a question. "But I'll need you to do something in return."

He licked his lips as he watched her move like a snow leopard, elegant and graceful, emoting barely constrained violence. He stared into her face as she circled the helm and slid her legs in between his knees, spreading them as she descended onto him. She hovered over him, and he swallowed back his nervousness.

"What?" he asked, managing not to stutter or fumble with his words.

With both her legs between his, she reached down and caressed the bulge in his pants. He hadn't been touched by a woman in so long.

Twenty-two days, eight hours, and...

His eyes closed as he succumbed to the pleasure he felt owed to him. He had earned it. He deserved this reward for being a faithful servant of the State, for imprisoning himself for a month at sea to steal their enemy's secrets and use them to strike...

"To die," she replied.

Her velvety words elicited such desire and passion that he missed the sensation of cold steel against his neck. When the icy tendrils across his trachea erupted in burning agony, his eyes shot open and stared into the black void of the woman leaning over him. He brought both hands to his neck to stanch the blood, distantly aware that she held a fillet knife in one hand and continued stroking his erection with the other.

Then she whispered in his ear, "This is my gift to you."

He felt himself climax as his eyelids drooped closed and he gave in to the warm embrace of death.

10

The smile on Chen Liling's face vanished the moment his life ended. It hadn't been part of her plan to kill him, but his failure to crash the American fighter into the warship jeopardized her greater mission, and she couldn't afford to overlook such an error. Mantis might complain she had exceeded her authority, but that didn't bother her. Leverage had its uses, and she wouldn't hesitate to use hers if the punishment doled out was more than a slap on the wrist.

She watched the man's chin slump to his bloody chest, then wiped the fillet knife on his overcoat before sliding it back into the sheath at her waist. She stood and admired her masterpiece of duality, the *yin* of taking his life while pleasing him with the *yang*.

With a shove, she toppled Xi Jian's body into the cold, dark waters of the Pacific Ocean and watched it bob like a cork next to the blacked-out RHIB. She drew the knife again, then bent over the side tube and plunged it into his chest to pierce his inflated lungs. There was no hatred or malice in the blows, just the calloused efficiency of a professional. Each time, the slender blade slid between his ribs and withdrew with a gurgling hiss.

Three, four, five times she stabbed him; each time, his body sagged lower in the water. At last, it slipped beneath the surface and disappeared from view. She stood and looked up at the cargo ships anchored around her. She was still a ghost on the water, a fantasy and myth, and nobody had witnessed her rescuing the Chinese spy from certain capture by the US Coast Guard. Or sentencing him to death.

A deafening explosion echoed across the inky water, and she spun back to see fire erupt from a container on the *Yonggan De*'s deck.

"Fucking idiot!"

She lunged for the console and turned the key to crank the Honda motor. The engine caught with a quiet cough, and she advanced the throttle, steering away from the inferno's flickering glow for the jetty east of the breakwater. Wu Tian was supposed to have waited until well after she was gone to destroy the container, but now his recklessness had put her at risk. First, Xi Jian. Now, Wu Tian. Even her asset had disappointed her by not warning her of the operation's failure.

She knew other vessels would respond to the fire, and she turned up her peacoat's collar to guard against the stinging spray as she sped for the shore. A mile from the breakwater, she flipped a switch to turn on her navigation lights, guiding the RHIB between the boats racing in the opposite direction, bound for the burning merchant vessel.

Rounding the breakwater, she reached inside the waterproof glove box and removed her cell phone. Powering it on, she waited for it to connect to the nearest cellular tower, then opened the application disguised as a calculator. A notification banner indicated she had a waiting message, and she entered *9413*, followed by the minus sign and *4059*, then concluded the passkey by tapping on the equals sign. Instead of returning an answer, the calculator opened a partition that allowed her to send and receive encrypted messages over a satellite network.

Much like the modified Nintendo Switch she had given the hapless, lovesick Marine, the application offered her two options. She tapped on "Receive" and waited for her phone to query the orbiting satellites. After several seconds, the progress bar had reached one hundred percent, and she looked down at the screen.

1 NEW MESSAGE.

Without fear or hesitation, she tapped on the icon and waited for the message to download, dividing her focus between the phone on the console and the dark waters in front of her. When another window opened on the screen, she glanced down and read the message.

1. TARGET AIRCRAFT SURVIVED. OPERATION FAILED.

2. SEND INSTRUCTIONS.

She glowered at the screen, at first relieved the Marine had taken risks to inform her of the mission's failure but annoyed by his presumption. He had proven useful in providing her with detailed maintenance logs for his squadron's fleet of F-35C Joint Strike Fighters but hadn't quite grasped the nature of their relationship. He thought he was her partner, at least a bishop or knight on the board instead of the pawn she played him for. She needed to consider how to rectify the situation before responding.

She closed the application and navigated to her phone's native internet browser. The information she had just recovered was time sensitive, and she couldn't afford to rely on her normal method of delivery via the consulate's diplomatic channels. Mantis would want it delivered in person. She navigated to the website hosting a vacation rental forum and searched for the post she had made when first arriving in the United States a year earlier.

Hawaii, Maui, Sands of Kahana, 1BR.

Selecting it, she scrolled past half a dozen comments from legitimate users asking for more information, which she had provided to keep the post active while giving credence to her cover. When she reached the bottom, she saw that the last comment was hers.

Available for rent.

She had posted it before leaving the marina earlier that evening, signaling to Mantis that she was commencing the operation's first phase. She clicked on the icon below to post a reply and tapped out a simple message, indicating the mission had been a failure.

Off the market temporarily for renovations.

Almost immediately, her phone vibrated with a notification she had received a message in Signal, a secure messaging application Mantis only used for time-critical communications. She knew Mantis was displeased, and she opened the application to read the cryptic message.

192.0.2.1

At first glance, it looked like a computer's IP address. But Chen knew better. Mantis had presented her with the simple code to guide her to dead drop locations along the California coast. The first three-digit number was meaningless, a mere placeholder to disguise the code, but the other three numbers told her everything she needed to know.

"Shit," she said, pushing on the throttle to keep the twenty-foot Brig Navigator at top speed until the last possible moment.

The first of the three remaining numbers was the priority. The lower the number, the more immediate the need to make the handoff. A "1" meant she had twenty-four hours to reach the location. A "2" gave her twice that. But a "0" meant she needed to drop everything she was doing and proceed there posthaste.

The next two numbers corresponded with a four-by-four grid she had long ago memorized. Beginning at one of the four corners, she counted spaces to land on the designated location. The starting corner changed daily, adding another layer of security to the already unbreakable code. Today's assigned corner was the top right, so she moved down two spaces and in one.

Dexter Lawn.

While most of the locations were in and around the Bay Area, some were further south and easier to reach. Teeming with college students most of the year, Dexter Lawn would be nearly deserted this early in the summer. But that wasn't the reason the spymaster had chosen that location for the drop.

She passed the 72nd Place Lifeguard Station on her left and slowed the RHIB to an agonizing crawl as she entered the inlet. An incessant ticking clock counted down in her head, reminding her of the urgency with which she needed to make the drive north. It took incredible willpower to keep her right arm from pushing forward on the throttle and ignoring the "No Wake" signs on her way to the slip.

"Zero," she said.

Mantis had never used a zero.

The Marine could wait.

11

3,000 feet over Seal Beach, California

The FBI plane crossed the shoreline and went feet dry when its *Stingray* issued an audible alert, signaling the targeted cell phone had finally connected to it. The pilot looked down at the display in disbelief, recognizing the phone number Rick had given him, and quickly pulled up a chart overlay on the screen. The computer-generated icon of the cell phone's location entered the channel into Alamitos Bay just north of his position.

"Well, I'll be damned," he said, banking the Stationair north so he could aim its sensor pod at the target boat and gain a visual. He had almost given up on the target showing.

He selected the encrypted radio and keyed the push-to-talk rocker switch on the control yoke. "Delta One, Air One."

"Go ahead, Air One."

"Got a hit on your target cell phone entering the channel now. Should be in visual range shortly," he said.

"Nice work, Air One," the deep voice replied. "Remain on station."

He glanced at his fuel, figuring he had another hour of loiter time before he needed to return to the Long Beach airport and gas up. He could stretch it maybe another fifteen minutes, but he didn't want to go much beyond that without a really good reason. He had done his job and verified the target. Now it was up to Rick to do the rest of the work.

"Delta One, I've got about an hour of play time left."

The FBI special agent double-clicked his microphone switch in reply.

Slewing the sensor pod's crosshairs onto the channel, he zoomed in on a smaller boat where a lone figure stood tall at the center console. Using the driver's height as a reference measurement, he estimated the boat was twenty to twenty-four feet in length; probably a Rigid-Hull Inflatable Boat with a single outboard. It was far smaller than the other boats at the yacht club and probably only useful for short jaunts to and from a larger ship at anchor.

"Delta One, Air One, looks like you're looking for a RHIB."

"Roger."

Alamitos Bay Yacht Club
Long Beach, California

Rick had come to the same conclusion as the Stationair pilot and guessed that the RHIB was returning from a ship at anchor. Either *TANDY* had dropped something off or picked something up, but he figured it didn't matter much one way or the other. He leaned forward in his seat and strained through the darkness to make out the navigation lights of the smaller boat idling from the channel toward the mouth of the basin.

He felt a bubbling nervousness now that their months of tedious and fruitless investigative legwork was about to pay off. He was about to put eyes on *TANDY* for the first time. The boat entered the basin and motored for an empty slip two down from his. He remained still and squinted at the figure in a dark wool coat.

Something's not right.

"Delta One has a visual," he said.

"Air One."

"Going dark."

When the RHIB disappeared behind the neighboring boats, Rick removed the earpiece from his ear and descended from the fly bridge to the main deck. Halfway down the ladder, he felt his phone vibrate, and when he reached the bottom, he pulled it out and saw another message waiting in the secure portal. He glanced in the target's direction then back to his phone, deciding he had time to check the message before regaining a visual. There was only one way off the dock, and it led right past his position from the deck of *Morning Wood*.

Rick unlocked his cell phone with a six-digit passcode and biometric scan, then opened the secure portal. Entering another unique passcode, he connected to the server and downloaded the waiting message. Over the last several months of monitoring communications between *KMART* and *TANDY*, their pattern had been consistent. The sailor sent one message at night, and his handler replied in the morning. It was predictable.

This was out of the norm, and it worried Rick that *KMART* had sent another message so soon.

After downloading the message from the secure server, he read it through quickly and felt his face flush. He read it again, then glanced in the direction of the RHIB and cursed.

"Well, shit."

He exited the secure portal and dialed Punky.

Punky had cleared the bulk of Los Angeles area traffic and had the convertible Mille Miglia Red Corvette purring like a kitten. But she couldn't keep her mind from racing with worry.

What aircraft had been targeted?

What was supposed to have happened?

Why did it fail?

Her hair thrashed in the wind as she pushed the classic muscle car south to San Diego. The speedometer needle cracked ninety miles per hour, and she instinctively veered into the left lane to pass slower-moving traffic. Patience might have been a virtue, but it wasn't one she had been blessed with. At least not when it came to rooting out traitors and putting them behind bars, where they belonged.

A modern sports sedan veered out in front of her, and she swerved back to the right and stomped on the gas, avoiding the temptation to flash her badge—or middle finger—at the offending driver. As much as she refused to admit it, she wasn't any closer to uncovering *KMART*'s identity, and she doubted a midnight detour into her office at the Naval Criminal Investigative Service Southwest Field Office would help. But what choice did she have?

Her phone rang as the traffic in front of her opened up. She slipped in her AirPods as all two hundred and seventy ponies shoved her back into her seat. "What's going on, Uncle Rick?"

"We got another one," he said.

"Another...?"

"Message."

"So soon?"

"This doesn't sound good," he said.

"The *last one* didn't sound good. What makes this one worse?"

Aside from the fact there had been a predictable cadence in communications between *KMART* and his handler, and that an increase in tempo hinted at something major in the works, she had a suspicion she wasn't going to like the content. Her foot pressed harder on the pedal.

"Where are you?"

"An hour from the base. Are you going to tell me what it said? Or am I supposed to guess?"

Rick sighed on the other end, and she knew he was struggling with the idea of discussing classified material over an unsecured line. Rick was a good agent, but sometimes the cumbersome rules put in place to protect their country from its enemies hindered those who were trying to stop them.

"Spit it out."

"The message said, and I quote, 'Navy pilot downloaded aircraft data. Potential compromise.' End quote."

She felt her first glimmer of hope. Instead of floundering about in reports she had already read at least a dozen times, hoping to find a needle in a haystack and a new morsel of information that might lead her to the traitor, all she needed to do was find the pilot. If *KMART* thought the pilot had information that could compromise him, then she needed to find the pilot.

"What's bad about this? This is good news," she said.

"Punky. What do you think *TANDY* will do if *KMART* is worried about the pilot having this information?"

Her foot came off the gas pedal a smidge. She hadn't considered the danger to the pilot just because of whatever knowledge he possessed, and she tried convincing herself her motives for finding him had changed. "I'll find him," she said.

"Punky..."

"Uncle Rick, you said it. If there's a target on his back, I have to warn him before..." She almost said, *Before we lose our only link to* KMART. "Before something happens to him."

"He's on an aircraft carrier," Rick reminded her. There were hardly more secure places than an American aircraft carrier at sea, but she knew that wasn't good enough. She knew she wouldn't be able to rest until she found the pilot and learned what he knew.

"And?"

"And how are you going to get there?"

"I'll figure it out."

She heard a commotion on the other end of the line before Rick's voice came back in a rushed whisper. "I've got to go. Don't do anything without me."

"I've done everything without you." The words came out harsher than she intended, but thankfully he had already hung up.

Punky took her AirPods out of her ears before reaching across the center console to remove her holstered .40 S&W SIG Sauer P229 from the glove box. While balancing the steering wheel between her knees, she clipped the handgun to her belt above her right hip, slipped a magazine pouch with two spares onto her left side, and pulled her hoodie low to conceal them. Then she pressed hard on the gas pedal once more and launched the Corvette back above ninety miles per hour.

It's time to go home.

12

Alamitos Bay Yacht Club
Long Beach, California

Chen docked the RHIB in the same slip she had departed from hours earlier, then jumped the narrow gap to the dock and secured her lines to the weathered cleats. She was hardly a skilled seaman but had plenty of experience working with ropes, and she was confident the boat would still be there when she returned. She had paid for the slip through the end of the month, but only needed it for one more day.

The dinghy looked miniature compared to the fishing boats and motor yachts occupying the neighboring slips, but with names like *Wet Dream* and *Morning Wood*, she reasoned their owners still thought size mattered and could use the ego boost. Without so much as a glance over her shoulder, she strode up the dock toward her four-door Ocean Blue Metallic Jeep Wrangler in the parking lot.

"Ahoy there," a slurred voice called from the deck of *Morning Wood*.

Chen gave the Black captain in a Hawaiian shirt a furtive glance but gritted her teeth and kept walking. As much as she would have loved to embarrass him by exposing his inadequacies, Mantis had made it clear time was of the essence. And she still hadn't figured out what to do about the Marine and his ineptitude.

When she reached her Jeep, Chen opened the door and climbed inside. She opened the calculator app on her phone and again entered the passkey that gave her access to the partitioned communications portal she used to send and receive messages with her asset. She had a long drive ahead of her and wanted to send him something simple, like *DO NOTHING*, to keep him from striking out on his own and taking action that might jeopardize the entire operation.

She clicked on "Receive" and waited for the progress bar to fill, hoping he hadn't made the fatal mistake of sending a second message in the same night. She knew the American National Security Agency monitored all manner of electronic communications, but those coming from a strategic asset like an aircraft carrier likely received additional scrutiny.

1 NEW MESSAGE.

She tapped on the icon and waited for the message to download while growing increasingly frustrated with the man. She had recruited him for one very simple reason, and it wasn't to break from protocol and inundate her with meaningless information at a critical phase of the operation. No matter how useful he might have been in getting them to that point, she couldn't abide carelessness that risked exposing them and jeopardized her opportunity for advancement.

The message downloaded, and she read it with some surprise.

Maybe he has some use after all, she thought.

She exited the application without replying. She still had several hours before a reply was even necessary, and it might teach the impatient Marine a lesson in sticking with protocol. Send one message a night, at most, and check for incoming messages in the morning. How hard could that be?

Without programming her destination into her phone, she scrolled along her planned route, looking for traffic that might delay her arrival in San Luis Obispo. Chen was familiar with the area and knew her route would take her across Naples before turning to parallel the San Gabriel River north to Interstate 405. She would pass through Torrance, Hawthorne, and Inglewood, bypassing both the Long Beach airport and larger Los Angeles International before traffic slowed her. Southwest of

Burbank, she would merge onto the 101 and pick up speed as she traveled west on the north side of the Santa Monica Mountains. From there, she would hug the coast through Ventura and Santa Barbara, before finally reaching the sleepy college town on the central coast.

She switched back to the calculator app and read the message again.

1. NAVY PILOT DOWNLOADED AIRCRAFT DATA. POTENTIAL COMPROMISE.

Though she doubted the data could lead engineers to conclude the jet's software had been manipulated via remote hack, she thought it possible they could use it to discover the fissure that allowed it to happen in the first place. That would change everything and put months of planning at risk of being wasted. She would have to respond to this, but first she needed to get moving. Mantis didn't like to be kept waiting.

Chen put her phone in the cradle mounted on the dash, backed out of her spot, and began her drive. Normally, she'd spend at least an hour completing a surveillance detection route before proceeding to her destination, but time was short, and she elected to bypass it. Spotting a tail before San Luis Obispo would be child's play.

Rick watched the spy climb from the RHIB onto the dock while he mentally catalogued her appearance for his later reports. *Asian, most likely Chinese. Early thirties. Five foot two or five foot three. One hundred and ten to one hundred and twenty pounds. Shoulder-length black hair. Narrow face with almond-shaped eyes.*

She sauntered past the neighboring yachts, and by the time she'd pulled even with his, he had recovered enough to act inebriated and call out to her. "Ahoy there."

She flashed him a halting smile but continued moving up the dock with effortless grace, confident that she was a woman to be desired, the mistress of her domain. He made note of that characteristic as well, then pulled the earpiece out from under his collar and slipped it into his ear.

"Air One, Delta One."

"Go for Air One," the pilot said.

"Subject is moving toward the parking lot. Female, Asian. Early thirties."

"Air One has a visual."

Rick waited until she had disappeared into the parking lot, then slipped into the saloon, where he turned out the lights. He returned to the aft deck to contemplate his options. "Maintain your visual, and let me know when she's on the move."

"Subject is in a four-door Jeep Wrangler," the pilot said.

Rick heaved himself over the transom and stepped on a stern line to draw the fishing boat closer before leaping to the dock. He willed himself not to run, but in the distance, he saw the Jeep back out of the space next to his loaner BMW and leave the parking lot.

"Delta One is in pursuit, maintain your visual."

"Air One copies."

When the Jeep had gone a hundred yards and disappeared, Rick leaned forward and sprinted up the dock to reach the BMW. Driving a flashy car had seemed like a good idea at the time, but as he climbed into the driver's seat, he regretted his decision not to go with a boring government sedan.

He backed out of his spot and put the German car into gear, tearing out of the parking lot onto Ocean Boulevard to eat up some of the lost ground. "Status?"

"Subject is turning north on Claremont," the pilot replied.

Rick zoomed in on the BMW's navigation display to see the street names and purposely drove past the street she had turned down. He suspected *TANDY* was only cutting across to Second Street and the quickest route to the freeway, but the residential street was a good place to begin a surveillance detection route. "Copy, I will pursue on..." He squinted at the street names on the moving map. "Pomona."

"Air One will be bingo fuel in one five mikes."

He cranked the steering wheel over to turn down Pomona Avenue, paralleling *TANDY*'s route as he tried to close and regain the visual before his air support had to return to the Long Beach airport to refuel. He bit off an acerbic reply and simply said, "Copy."

Rick pressed hard on the gas pedal, ignoring the beach cottages and parked cars whirring by as he sped through the Belmont Shore neighborhood. He scrambled to come up with a backup plan before he lost his dedicated air support.

"Subject at Claremont and Second Street," the pilot said.

Rick glanced down at the map and saw that he had narrowed the gap to five hundred yards, albeit on different streets. "Air One, can you get a license plate?"

"Negative."

"If I can get eyes on, can you run the plates?"

There was a pause. "Affirm. Subject turning east on Second Street."

Rick felt a surge of excitement. If he could get eyes on and have Air One run the plates, there was a chance he could use the Vehicle Identification Number to access Mopar's Electronic Vehicle Tracking System and receive real-time position updates. Barring that, he would have to maintain surveillance the old-school way, because once the Cessna returned to Long Beach, he would be on his own.

At the end of the block, Rick slammed on the brakes and brought the M5 to a complete stop before inching his nose out into the intersection. The Jeep Wrangler pulled out onto the main drag as he craned his neck in its direction. With a quick glance to his left to look for oncoming traffic, he made the right turn and quickly sped up to narrow the gap between them. Closing the distance to a subject under surveillance was counter to everything they had ever taught him, but there was no way around the mess he was in.

He passed Roe Seafood doing almost seventy miles an hour and cursed when the light in front of him turned yellow. But he pressed harder on the gas pedal and darted his head in both directions as he launched through the intersection and onto the bridge.

Up ahead, the light turned red, and he breathed a sigh of relief when he saw the Wrangler's brake lights illuminate. He took his foot off the gas, maneuvered into the right lane, and coasted to a stop as he squinted through the darkness and read off the license plate number to the pilot overhead. "California plates. Seven. Tango. Yankee. Papa. Two. Niner. Zero. How copy?"

"Good copy. Wait one."

When the nose of his BMW was even with the spare tire on the back of the Jeep, the light turned green. He eased his foot off the brake and watched the Wrangler drive away with increasing anxiety as he waited for a response. After what seemed like an inordinate amount of time, he prodded the pilot. "Talk to me, Air One. I'm about to lose her."

Silence followed for several more seconds before the pilot's voice returned. "Okay, we've run the plates, but it's not good."

He felt his skin flush. "What?"

"They belong to a 1997 Chevrolet Camaro."

He groaned, though it shouldn't have been all that surprising TANDY had swapped plates. "Copy. I'll just have to go old school."

Chen took her time driving through the residential neighborhood of Belmont Shore, watching the yacht club retreat in the rearview mirror. She wouldn't run a full surveillance detection route, but she still planned to follow protocol and use every opportunity to look for a tail. Nobody followed, and when she pulled out onto Second Street, she saw only the normal flow of traffic she had grown accustomed to at that late hour.

Crossing the bridge onto Naples, she spotted a European sedan behind her running a red light. Her skin prickled with nerves, and when the light in front of her turned red, she braked the Wrangler, thankful for the opportunity to draw the car closer for a better look. But as it slowed in the lane next to her, she couldn't make out the driver's face in the darkened interior.

When the light turned green, she lifted her foot off the brake and continued through the intersection. But the sedan appeared less eager than it had moments earlier, and as the distance between them grew, she dismissed it. The citizens of greater Los Angeles moved about like those in Shanghai or Beijing, but with less purpose. The sedan's driver was just another example of one seeming only to exist for the sake of existence.

Chen scanned her mirrors every few minutes, noting the unique pairs of headlights behind her. Some were round or square, and others were narrow, but she never saw the pair belonging to the sedan again. She saw dim halogen bulbs and bright LEDs in various patterns, and she tracked them in her mind, noticing when they sped past or fell further behind. She spotted new ones joining the thickening flow of traffic and noticed when others exited.

But none were following her, of that she was certain.

She was clean.

Passing Los Angeles International, she bent over to look up through the windshield at the lights in the sky, making their approach to the parallel runways. Thousands of people were on board, oblivious to the conflict raging in the world around them. But that would soon change.

A war was coming—one America wasn't prepared for.

13

San Diego, California

Driving across the bridge to Coronado still felt like coming home. It was after midnight when Punky crested the sweeping overpass and saw the sleepy beach town spread out before her, anchored by the vast open space of North Island Naval Air Station to her right and the tombolo known as the Silver Strand on her left. Though she had inherited and still owned the modest cottage she had grown up in, she rarely made the drive across the bay to see it. Once full of hope and laughter, the house was now just a constant reminder of what she'd lost.

She steered the Corvette to follow the bridge's arcing descent onto Fourth Street, watching the tip of Point Loma in the distance disappear behind the red spired roofs of the Hotel del Coronado. Gritting her teeth, she focused her attention through the windshield and the problem ahead of her. By the time she passed under the concrete remains of the plaza that last collected tolls in 2002, she had decided on a course of action.

Less than a quarter mile after the defunct tollbooth, the two-way traffic on Fourth Street split, and Punky angled right on Pomona for the short jog to Third Street, continuing past quaint palm-lined neighborhoods to the interior of the island. As much as the houses on either side of her reminded her of happier times, she kept her focus on the looming Stockdale Gate and what it meant to her and the thousands of men and women who embodied the ideals of the Navy.

The gate's namesake, Admiral James Stockdale, had represented everything *KMART* debased. After he was shot down over North Vietnam in 1965, Stockdale created and enforced a code of conduct that governed the behavior of his fellow prisoners. When his captors informed him they intended to parade him in public, he cut a gash in his scalp to avoid being used as propaganda. And when they covered the wound with a hat, he bashed a stool into his face until it was disfigured and swollen beyond recognition. For eight years, Stockdale continued fighting his own war against the enemy despite being a prisoner.

It made her sick that *KMART* wore the same uniform.

The gate was necked down to one open lane at that late hour, and Punky flashed her NCIS credentials to the Navy Region Southwest civilian police officer, who waved her onto the compound. She had been to North Island countless times over her life, visiting as a dependent long before she became a special agent with the Naval Criminal Investigative Service. But she still felt like an outsider. Even after growing up in Coronado, attending Coronado High School, and leading the Islanders to a CIF state water polo championship her senior year, she always felt like an outsider on base.

She continued driving along Stockdale Boulevard, passing a massive parking lot on her right that was filled with cars belonging to sailors embarked aboard ships at sea. She knew many of them belonged to sailors aboard the *Lincoln*, and one in particular to the traitor she had made it her personal mission to unmask.

As the airfield came into view, she turned left on Quentin Roosevelt Boulevard and drove through a round-about alongside a painted cinder block wall that blocked her view of the flight line. A ghost-like formation of disparate aircraft on display passed along her left side as she continued driving west to her destination. She recognized the Sikorsky H-60 Seahawk, though she wasn't sure which of the three models based at North Island was on display. She also recognized the Lockheed S-3 Viking, a carrier-based anti-submarine jet that had made North Island its home during her childhood. But it was the third plane on display that had brought her there.

Punky turned into the parking lot on her right, across the street from the manicured grounds of shaded Spanish-style cottages with red terra-cotta tile roofs and white stucco walls. The sign at the entrance announced it as the home to the Providers of Fleet Logistics Support Squadron 30, the only squadron flying the Grumman C-2 Greyhound in the Pacific fleet. Known as a COD, for Carrier Onboard Delivery, the C-2 delivered high-priority cargo, mail, and passengers to aircraft carriers at sea.

And Punky wanted a ride.

She parked the Corvette in the parking spot reserved for "CO's Guest" and walked across the blue-and-yellow-striped walkway to the entrance under a blue awning. She opened the door and entered an anteroom, known as the quarterdeck. Aboard Navy ships and in buildings on naval bases, it was the designated reception area for guests visiting the command. Punky approached the sailor dressed in the Navy Service Uniform and waited for him to look up from his phone before speaking.

He looked startled when he noticed the dark-haired woman standing at the counter, and he jumped to his feet and approached. "Can I help you?"

She eyed his uniform, consisting of black trousers and khaki shirt adorned with gold aircrew wings and a short stack of ribbons above his left breast. She noted the eagle with two downward-facing chevrons on his lapel and black name tag before speaking. "Yes, Petty Officer Williams. I'm Special Agent King with NCIS." She flashed her credentials to the watch stander. "I need to be added to the manifest for your flight to the *Abraham Lincoln* in the morning."

To his credit, the sailor examined her credentials more thoroughly than most before turning to the clipboard behind him. He lifted it off the hook screwed into the wall and studied the top sheet for a moment before answering. "First flight isn't until zero seven hundred, but we manifest passengers at the terminal in the morning. Do you know where that is?"

She nodded her head but wasn't ready to relent. "This is a matter of national security. Is there somebody you can speak to? The officer of the watch, perhaps?"

He studied her for a minute, then nodded. Picking up the phone from his desk, he dialed a number and held the handset to his ear while he waited for the phone to connect. When it did, he turned his back to her and spoke in hushed tones with whoever he had called to plead her case. She put her hands on her hips and waited for him to finish his conversation, trying her hardest not to let her impatience show.

The second-class petty officer hung up the phone and walked around the desk to approach her. "I'm sorry, ma'am, but you'll need to speak with the aircraft commander when he gets in."

"When will that be?"

He held her gaze before answering. "His brief is at zero five hundred. I would expect him to arrive just before that."

Punky looked over the sailor's shoulder at the clock mounted on the wall. It was too late to drive all the way back to her apartment at the north end of Balboa Park, but she had avoided the cottage on F Avenue for a reason. Seeing Uncle Rick had reminded her that she still wasn't ready to face her past.

USS *Mobile Bay* (CG-53)

Beth sat behind the desk in her office and read through the report she intended to send to the admiral. She had a trove of photographs and video taken from the ship's nautical or otherwise photographic intelligence exploitation, or SNOOPIE, team, but none of it seemed relevant. It was hard to imagine a swarm of unidentified lights circling the cruiser could be insignificant, but because of the actions of a single fighter pilot, she had bigger fish to fry.

There was a knock on her door, and Beth looked up from the report before answering, "Enter."

Master Chief Ben Ivy opened the door and stuck his head in. "Is this a bad time, ma'am?"

She leaned back in her chair. "Come on in, Master Chief."

He walked in and took a seat across from her desk, appraising her silently as she gently massaged her temples to coax her headache into hibernation. It had already been a long night and would probably be even longer, but she knew she needed to get some sleep before their next tasking.

"Are you sure you're okay, ma'am?"

She gave him a slight, crooked smile. "Fine. Just a little headache."

He reached into his pocket and pulled out a travel-size container of Excedrin, popping the top off to fish out two caplets for her. "These should help."

"Is there anything you don't do?"

Ben chuckled and handed her the caplets. She tossed them into her mouth and threw her head back as she swallowed them without water, then she leaned back into her chair and closed her eyes. These brief moments of peace were fleeting for a ship's commanding officer.

"Do you want to get some sleep before we talk about tomorrow?"

Though her head throbbed, and the memory of the kamikaze attack still haunted her, Beth felt her body sink deeper into the chair. If she had allowed it, she could have been asleep within seconds. But the nagging reminder of the burden she carried repeated itself in her mind, refusing to allow her a moment's rest without first considering the mission or her crew.

You are the captain.

She opened her eyes and leaned forward. "No. Let's go over the details now."

"Ma'am..."

"I'm fine, Master Chief," she said. "Really. Let's go over the plan of the day."

He nodded, then cleared his throat and began. "As of zero two hundred local time, CSG-3 authorized us to depart station and steam for the Point Mugu Sea Range. We have officially been chopped to NAWCWD for the duration of the test."

She nodded and understood that she had relinquished her responsibility as air and missile defense commander for the USS *Abraham Lincoln*. The Naval Air Warfare Center, Weapons Division, would be the ones calling the shots until the test was complete. And that worried her.

Though he had only known her for a short while, Ben had an uncanny ability to read her mind. "Do you think it's a good idea to continue with the test?"

She pursed her lips as she contemplated the same question she had asked herself several times over the last hour. "The CAG assured me it was an isolated incident caused by a rogue pilot."

Again, he discerned her thoughts with ease. "But you don't believe it."

She shook her head. "It doesn't make any sense to me."

"Do you think it's somehow tied to the lights?"

She glanced down at the report on her desk where she had openly expressed that same concern to the admiral. It was a little too coincidental in her mind that a fifth-generation fighter had tried ramming her ship only moments after a swarm of lights appeared out of nowhere. "I really don't know. The evidence the SNOOPIE team collected was pretty inconclusive."

Ben nodded. He had already seen the photographs and video, but unlike most of the crew who thought the orbs were piloted by little green men, he thought it more likely the culprit was closer to home. "And the way they just disappeared..."

"The timing is suspect, for sure," Beth agreed. "Why did they disappear right after the jet broke off and climbed away?"

"I'm not a pilot, but isn't there a black box or something that records the whole flight?"

Beth bit her bottom lip and recalled asking the CAG the same question. "They reviewed the data and saw nothing out of the ordinary."

Ben shook his head. "Well, like I said, I'm just a simple ship driver, but I'd say trying to ram a multimillion dollar jet into a warship is pretty out of the ordinary."

You can say that again, she thought.

"Either way, the test is going as scheduled. So, let's go over this plan so we can catch a few winks before it begins."

"Aye, ma'am."

14

San Luis Obispo, California

Early the next morning, Chen exited Highway 101 onto California Boulevard in San Luis Obispo and drove between towering palm trees onto the campus of California Polytechnic State University. It wasn't her first time visiting the campus, but it was her first time doing it under such urgent circumstances. Normally, she would have had more time to conduct a thorough surveillance of the area before making the drop. But that just wasn't in the cards.

She reached a three-way stop bordered by green crosswalks and the words "CAL POLY" painted in white, and she steered the Jeep to the right onto Campus Way. The sun was still hidden behind the nearby Santa Lucia range, and the early morning fog had yet to burn off. Between the weather and most of the student body being gone, the college campus was eerily quiet at that hour, making her task all the more difficult.

Cresting the hill on Campus Way, Chen saw the University House shrouded by trees in the distance and turned left to park in a spot reserved for staff at the bottom of the hill. Before exiting her Jeep, she opened the calculator app on her smart phone and again entered the passkey. She tapped on "Receive" and waited for the device to connect with the satellite network overhead. When she read the resulting message, she sighed with relief.

NO NEW MESSAGES.

Maybe he had gotten the hint. She returned to the main menu and tapped out the reply she had been formulating all night. It would put the Marine at risk, but if what he had said was true, she would rather risk compromising her asset than allow the Americans to learn their newest fighter aircraft had been exploited. When she finished composing the message, she reviewed it and tapped on "Send," waiting for the progress bar to fill before slipping the phone in her pocket.

Climbing down from the Jeep's driver's seat, Chen took a moment to stretch her road-weary frame, then crossed Perimeter Road to pass between the natatorium and an abandoned structure in Mission Revival style known as the Powerhouse. With her head held high, she scanned the road and continued past Crandall Gymnasium and the Engineering West building to reach the southwestern corner of Dexter Lawn.

Chen paused and examined the green space for hidden observers, ensuring she was alone before she exposed herself. Seeing nothing out of place, she stepped out and strolled onto a wide, red brick walkway on the near side of the lawn. She moved with deliberate nonchalance, but her eyes never stopped scanning. Trash can. Bench. Tree. She glanced briefly at each location, searching for the signal.

There.

When she saw it, she forced herself to continue walking at the same pace. Six inches into the grass on the left side of the path was a plastic fork stuck into the ground with its tines facing upward. Had the prongs been buried into the dirt, she would have known the primary dead drop location had been compromised and would have made a lap around the campus looking for an alternate signal site. Had it been any utensil other than a fork, she would have turned around, returned to her Jeep, and abandoned the drop.

But the signal was what she had expected.

Dead drop location clear.

She continued strolling along the walkway until she had pulled even with the seventy-five-foot coast redwood in the middle of the lawn. There, she turned and crossed the manicured grass, headed directly for a concrete bench on the opposite side. It felt good being free from the confines of the Jeep, and she enjoyed the brief reprieve as she breathed in the fresh air and scanned the surrounding buildings for interlopers. Just before reaching the bench, she knelt to tie her shoe and surreptitiously surveyed the length of the lawn and the path behind her.

A flash of movement near a sycamore caught her attention. She untied and retied her shoe, focusing on the spot at the west edge of the lawn until satisfying herself that it had been nothing more than the wind. She was alone. She turned and sat on the bench, then slipped the memory card from her pocket and reached under the front edge to insert it inside a hollowed-out nook. With the drop complete, she leaned back and took a deep breath of the fragrant air with satisfaction before standing to resume her leisurely circuitous route around Dexter Lawn.

She had been on campus less than twenty minutes, but already the coastal overcast was beginning its slow retreat back to the sea. It was shaping up to be a beautiful day and was a small consolation prize for having to spend the next several hours behind the wheel. She was exhausted but couldn't rest until she had returned to Long Beach and notified Mantis she was in position for the evening's operation.

Only this time, I'll do it myself, she thought.

She glanced up at the redwood as she circled around to the south side of the lawn, then resumed looking for anybody who might have witnessed her completing the dead drop. But she had been careful. She hadn't spotted a tail during her drive north from Long Beach, and she hadn't seen a soul on campus. She had only one more task to complete before she could leave.

Nearing the signal, she bent over and scooped up the fork, carrying it to the nearby trash can at the end of the walkway as her countersignal that the drop had been loaded. Though she hadn't seen anybody who might have witnessed the act, she reasoned that if they had, they would have just assumed she was your typical California co-ed, removing litter from the green space.

But she was alone. She felt it.

She deposited it into the receptacle, then turned at the Engineering West building and continued at a relaxed pace for her Jeep.

Despite the comfort of the BMW sedan, Rick was exhausted from maintaining his tail throughout the night. After Air One had departed station to return to the Long Beach airport, he closed the distance to within five car lengths. Maintaining his visual on the Jeep took priority, and it was a nerve-racking drive north on Interstate 405 through Los Angeles. But by the time his quarry merged onto Highway 101 north of the Santa Monica Mountains, he had perfected his technique.

He thought of it like casting and drifting, setting the bait and letting the current carry him toward his target. He weaved in and out between cars and blended in with the surrounding traffic, at one point even passing the Jeep Wrangler and exiting the freeway before rejoining several car lengths behind. His only goal had been to keep his movement as random as possible to avoid her detecting a pattern and making him. The technique worked until the traffic thinned out, leaving his BMW as one of only a handful of cars remaining on the road.

In spite of the challenging conditions, he had managed to maintain his visual on the Jeep until she turned onto California Boulevard in San Luis Obispo. After driving only a few blocks, she quickly turned down a side street and came to a stop alongside the curb. It was a classic countersurveillance technique and only the first since leaving Long Beach. To Rick, that meant she was nearing her destination.

He kept his speed constant and drove past the side street, only looking at the Jeep from the corner of his eye. Her brake lights were still illuminated, which meant she hadn't turned off the ignition and intended to continue driving. He drove another four blocks before turning into an apartment complex parking lot where he doused his lights and waited to see if the Jeep returned to the main road. After several minutes, his patience was rewarded, and he spotted the blue Jeep continuing toward the campus. He breathed a sigh of relief.

Keeping his lights off, he pulled out onto the road two hundred yards in trail of the Jeep, feeling a giddy nervousness with each passing minute. By the time his target had reached the Cal Poly campus, he was reasonably certain she hadn't spotted him. But he didn't want to take chances, and he drifted further behind and watched from a discreet distance as she turned right on Campus Way.

As the Jeep's taillights retreated up the hill, he used the trees lining the street as cover and turned to follow. With his heart pounding in his chest, he glanced at the navigation display to try to predict where she was headed. He saw the Jeep pull into a parking space at the bottom of the hill, and he quickly turned right and pulled into a parking lot in front of a white stucco building and coasted to a stop. He kept his foot off the brake pedal to avoid illuminating his taillights, then shifted into park and turned off the engine.

What is she doing?

He adjusted his rearview mirror to observe the area around where *TANDY* had parked the SUV. She could have been executing another countersurveillance technique, waiting to see if any other cars pursued her down the hill before driving away. But, after several minutes, she surprised him by emerging on foot and walking away from him and deeper into campus.

He quickly climbed out of the car and crossed the street to the sidewalk alongside Cuesta Avenue. In the distance, he saw the back of *TANDY*'s head, her dark hair bobbing rhythmically as she crossed another street and disappeared into the shadows between two academic buildings.

"Shit!"

Fearing what might happen if he lost her, he started jogging down the hill while musing over his decision to wear the brightly colored Hawaiian shirt. While it might have helped him blend in at the yacht club, he stood out like a sore thumb on the deserted campus.

When he pulled even with the blue Wrangler, he removed a small magnetic tracking device from his pocket and slipped it inside the Jeep's grill without breaking stride. He ignored the heat radiating from the hood in the cool morning air and removed his phone to check that the tracking device was working. But before he could, his phone vibrated, and he saw a notification banner that the NSA had intercepted another message.

Rick stopped and hurried to access the secure portal, where he downloaded the pending message. He felt time and his target slipping away from him but needed to know what the message said.

TEXT FROM INTERCEPTED TRANSMISSION FOLLOWS.

FROM: TANDY
TO: KMART
1. PROVIDE DETAILED INFORMATION ON NAVY PILOT.
2. BE ALERT FOR OPPORTUNITY TO ELIMINATE.

His heart rate quickened, knowing that the woman who had sent that message to a sailor aboard the *Abraham Lincoln* was less than one hundred yards in front of him. He dialed Punky as he resumed his chase, eager to fill her in on what he had discovered since she left. His call was answered after three rings.

"Uncle Rick." She sounded breathless. "What time is it?"

"Early." He heard rustling in the background and assumed she was still in bed.

"Oh, shit! I'm late!"

"Late for what?"

She didn't answer. "Where are you?"

"I'm following *TANDY*," he said. "She's at Cal Poly in San Luis Obispo."

The rustling continued, and Punky's voice sounded strained. "San Luis...wait. Did you say *she*?"

"Yeah." Rick darted between the buildings where he had last seen *TANDY*, hoping to regain his visual before she disappeared for good. He recited the description he had built the night before as she walked past *Morning Wood*. "Punky, our subject is a woman. Asian, most likely Chinese—"

"Ministry of State Security," she muttered.

Rick ignored the interruption and continued relaying his information as he slowed his jog and neared the corner of the building. "Early thirties. Five foot two or five foot three. One hundred and ten to one hundred and twenty pounds. Shoulder-length black hair. Narrow face with almond-shaped eyes."

"Are you on foot?"

Rick heard the unmistakable angry growl of a cold Corvette Stingray starting, and he ignored her question. "What are you late for? Where are you going?"

"Don't get burned. We can't lose her."

He knew he had been on the phone too long already, distracted from the task at hand, but he couldn't help but worry that she was rushing into danger. In the background, he heard the Corvette's engine rev. "I placed a tracker on her car," he said. "She won't get away."

"Hang back," Punky warned. "If she sees you, it's over."

Rick stepped out from behind the corner of the building and saw her.

She was walking across a wide lawn with her back turned to him, and he edged away from the walkway toward a sycamore tree and shrubs at the west end of the open space. Suddenly, she stopped and knelt to tie her shoe, and he froze. He knew she was checking for a tail, which meant something was about to happen.

"I've gotta go," he whispered. "Don't do anything without me."

"I'm not a kid anymore, Uncle Rick."

When she hung up, he clenched his jaw in frustration, as much with himself as with her obstinance. But when he watched *TANDY* quickly stand and walk to a concrete bench, he forgot he had called to warn his stubborn adopted niece that the Navy pilot was in even more danger than before.

15

Professor David Wang watched the whole thing while sitting nestled in the trees at the east end of Dexter Lawn. He was in his early forties but often mistaken for someone ten years younger, a happy accident he attributed to not owning a car and either riding his bicycle or walking everywhere he needed to go. San Luis Obispo was a coastal town located halfway between the Bay Area and Greater Los Angeles but enjoyed a cool Mediterranean climate. It was the perfect place for an active and modest lifestyle, and it suited him well.

Like most professors at the university, David wore slacks and a collared shirt to lecture, but was often distinguishable on campus by his bright green Outdoor Research GORE-TEX rain jacket. Even when rain wasn't in the forecast and the early summer temperatures ranged from the mid-fifties to the mid-seventies, the damp ocean air chilled him to the core, and he wore the jacket more often than not.

But this morning, he had left it at home, favoring more subtle attire that allowed him to blend in with his surroundings. He fancied himself one of the more popular members of the faculty, at least in the College of Engineering, and rarely was able to walk across campus without being noticed. Most of his students, undergraduate and graduate alike, recognized him and hailed him with friendly waves or shouts of, "Hey, Professor Wang!" He smiled at the thought, already missing most of his students who had moved off campus for the summer break but glad for their absence at the moment.

The campus had been planted in the middle of a roadless barley field, but Cal Poly sprouted into an institution with rich arboreal roots. From the orchards maintained by students in the 1900s to the Canary Island date palms lining the entrance to campus, David found peace in the abundance of greenery. Over the years, he had identified several carefully selected spots, known only to him, where he could escape the chaos of the classroom and breathe in the fresh air to rediscover his calm and practice the art of being still.

He sat in one of those spots now, absorbing the sound of the wind whispering to him through the California redwood, deodar cedar, and London plane trees, while admiring the woman Mantis had sent. She appeared confident and demonstrated competent tradecraft as she made her way to the designated dead drop in remarkable time, but it wasn't entirely surprising she hadn't seen him hidden in the trees.

The girl was beautiful, he thought. Mantis had spoken often of her, lauding her ability to recruit assets, so it came as no big surprise when the spymaster had assigned her to the operation. Even if she had missed him observing her, he didn't really blame her. Even the mongoose sometimes misses the viper in the wild.

But it was that *other* thing she had missed that bothered him.

She hadn't seen the Black man in a colorful shirt follow her onto the lawn and duck behind a sycamore tree before she'd made the drop. At first, David had been worried the man would move to recover what she had left behind. But when the stranger followed her from Dexter Lawn, David was both relieved and concerned. Relieved that he could collect what she had brought him but concerned that her carelessness put him at risk.

David remained still until both Shanghai's darling and her shadow disappeared. He waited another twenty minutes and observed his surroundings before standing with a heavy sigh and slipping out into the open. He crossed quickly to the bench, stooped to reach underneath and retrieve the memory card, then pocketed it and returned to his perch hidden in the trees.

He spent several more minutes watching the campus come alive around him as he organized his thoughts. He knew he needed to return to his office in the Computer Science building adjacent to the lawn to begin his task, but he had another appointment to keep first. More important than the damage it might do to his career aspirations if he missed it, he knew his absence might draw unwanted attention to the job that would occupy most of his day.

At last, he stood and walked along the red brick path bound for the five-thousand-square-foot 1928 Mission-style home. He would share his morning tea with the University president, like he did every morning. He would engage in small talk and hint at his desire for tenure, also like he did every morning, then he would lock himself away in his office to see what she had brought him.

But there was one more thing he needed to do first.

David crossed Perimeter Road and saw the University House sitting atop a squat hill, its ornate wooden door still cloaked in the early morning shadow. He paused at the bottom and pulled out his phone to place a call he was loath to make. It was answered after one ring.

"Hello?"

"I'm sorry," he said. "I was trying to reach Donna."

There was a pause on the other end. "I think you have the wrong number."

"I'm sorry. This isn't six four two one?"

"Six four two two," the woman replied.

"My mistake."

He ended the call, satisfied he had notified Mantis of the danger to her operative. Whether she chose to warn the girl or simply cut her off was none of his concern. His only concern was to analyze the information contained on the memory card and fix whatever errors had caused his waveform to fail.

But first, it's time for tea.

He tucked the phone in his pocket and started up the hill to begin his day.

16

USS *Abraham Lincoln* (CVN-72)

Colt barely slept a wink that night. It wasn't because they had stuck him in a crowded stateroom and forced him to sleep in a three-high bunk with only eighteen inches of clearance, because they hadn't. As a guest pilot, they had assigned him to one of the two-person staterooms on the port side of the ship close to the dirty shirt wardroom. He had the entire room to himself and hadn't been forced to suffer the intolerable snoring or bodily gas expulsions that had defined each of his previous experiences aboard an aircraft carrier. But still, he barely slept.

He rolled out of his rack just before six in the morning and let his bare feet cool on the worn linoleum floor while he held his head in his hands. As fresh as the memory was, the fear was already receding. He was embarrassed at being forced to leave the ship early but consoled himself by remembering he had a copy of the squadron's maintenance data, and that if he got it into the right hands, he might avert a disaster.

With a groan, Colt stood up from the rack and crossed the short distance to where his towel hung on the open locker door. Other than the large parachute bag containing his flight equipment, he had only brought a small duffel with the essentials, including a week's worth of fresh underwear and socks, clean T-shirts, and workout gear. He threw on one of his powder-blue TOPGUN T-shirts, slipped on his shower shoes, and grabbed his toiletries before tossing the towel over his shoulder and opening the door.

The hallway was still darkened, bathed in a faint red glow from the previous night, but before he had taken two steps, that changed. Bright white lights flickered on to replace the soothing red, and Colt squinted against the offense.

The 1MC confirmed what he had already suspected. *"Now reveille, reveille, all hands heave out and trice up. Give the ship a clean sweep down fore and aft. The smoking lamp is lit in all authorized spaces."*

With eyes barely more than slits, he shuffled along the passageway to the officer head located a short distance from his stateroom. There were only two shower stalls in the smaller head, but for most air wing officers, reveille was often a clue that it was time to put the Xbox controller down and go to sleep, not get up and prepare to leave the ship in disgrace. He felt confident he wouldn't have to wait for an empty stall.

Colt turned the corner with his gaze lowered and saw a pair of black leather boots just in time to avoid a collision. Startled, he looked up and saw his wingman from the night before.

"Hey, Colt," Smitty said.

"You're up early."

"You know, early bird and all that bullshit."

Colt nodded and waited for the Marine pilot to move aside, but Smitty just stood there with a concerned look on his face. He felt his waning anxiety return and wondered if he would ever regain his confidence.

"So, Colt..."

Here it comes.

Smitty's voice lowered into a conspiratorial tone. "Did you get it?"

He felt his face flush with sudden fear that his theft was about to be unveiled. It took a second for Colt to brush aside the cobwebs and remember that it had been Smitty's idea to steal the maintenance data in the first place. But still he struggled with the idea of letting the Marine in on the secret. If he was discovered, the last thing he wanted to do was drag someone else down with him.

When Colt didn't answer, he stepped closer. "Did you?"

Colt shook his head. "You don't want to know."

Smitty recoiled as if slapped. To a Marine, the motto *Semper Fidelis* was an eternal and collective commitment to the steadfast loyalty to those they served alongside. Colt knew he had probably offended Smitty by intimating that he didn't trust him to have his back, but he couldn't bear the thought of making Smitty complicit in his crime.

"*Yeah*. I do. Besides, I think I have an idea that might help."

It was such a simple comment, but one that gave him hope and made him believe he wasn't alone. Despite CAG's open disbelief and Colt's subsequent ostracism from the community he considered a family, before him stood a lone Marine who risked his own career to stand beside him. Still, his optimism was somewhat guarded. "What?"

"I think you should talk to my college roommate."

Colt felt himself deflate. As much as he appreciated Smitty's attempt to help, he needed something more concrete than an old college roommate to escape this mess unscathed. "Thanks, but—"

Smitty cut him off. "No, I'm serious. Do you know Bill McFarland?"

"Jug?"

Smitty nodded. "He's a test pilot stationed in China Lake with VX-31."

"Yeah, we were partners during Air Combat Maneuvering in Kingsville," Colt said. After getting winged, the Navy had ordered the pair to separate coasts. Their friendship went the way of most of those forged in the military, and they lost touch. Then it dawned on him. "Jug is your college roommate?"

Smitty nodded. "If you can get the maintenance data to him..."

"*If* I had it." Colt wanted to give Smitty every chance to preserve his deniability.

But the Marine was having none of it. "Yeah, whatever. As I was saying, if you can get it to him, I'll let him know you're coming and that he needs to help you."

"What makes you think he'll listen to you?"

Smitty grinned. "Spring break, senior year, Negril, Jamaica."

Despite feeling about as hopeless as he'd ever felt in his entire life, the comment made Colt smile. He considered the offer for a moment, letting it hang in the air between them, knowing that Smitty was risking not only his reputation but his friendship to help him out. He could have simply turned his back on him, and Colt wouldn't have thought any less of him for it.

At last, he looked Smitty in the eyes and asked, "Are you sure?"

"Oh yeah," he replied with a grin. "These photos are *very* compromising."

He laughed and slapped the Marine on the shoulder, then nodded. "Okay. Let him know I'm coming and that I'm not crazy."

"Can't vouch for the crazy part."

Colt chuckled. "That's valid."

Smitty nodded and his smile vanished, resuming the stoic Marine facade under his high-and-tight haircut. "Good luck, brother."

Colt waited until Smitty had turned the corner before continuing to the head, eager to shower and catch the COD to shore. There was a dim flicker of hope on the horizon, and he had locked in on it like a heat-seeking missile.

"*Sweepers, sweepers, man your brooms. Give the ship a clean sweep down fore and aft...*"

San Diego, California

Punky launched her dad's restored Corvette Stingray through the intersection at Alameda before stomping on the brakes to avoid blowing through the guard post at Naval Air Station North Island's main gate. She held up her NCIS credentials and waited impatiently for the Security Forces sailor to wave her aboard, then floored the gas pedal and raced west on Stockdale toward the flight line.

She knew it had been a bad idea sleeping in her childhood home but hadn't wanted to risk missing the flight out to the carrier. Ironically, sleeping there had most likely caused her to do just that. She had suppressed her initial hesitation and arrived at the cottage in the middle of the night, sneaking inside like she had done countless times as a teenager. She moved through the tiny house as if on autopilot, ignored its ghosts, and crashed onto the bed she had grown up in without setting an alarm.

When Uncle Rick had called, it had taken her a moment to remember where she was. But that moment was all she needed to recall she was supposed to already be on base, begging the aircraft commander for a ride out to the *Abraham Lincoln*.

Reaching the flight line, Punky turned left and spurred the Corvette down the straightaway until she reached the VRC-30 hangar across the street from the iconic I-Bar at the Bachelor Officer Quarters. Her rear tires let loose as she careened around the corner, and her stomach lurched when she saw a C-2 Greyhound on the ramp beyond the hangar with its propellers already spinning.

"No," she said in disbelief. She drove straight at the chain link fence before again slamming on the brakes and screeching to a halt. She jumped from the idling muscle car and stared in open-mouthed horror at the cargo plane preparing to taxi away.

"*No!*" she shouted.

In reply, the sound of the churning propellers rose in pitch as the COD began rolling forward. When it turned away from her, she looked beyond the lowered ramp into the gaping darkness of the interior and saw several pallets of cargo and rows of empty seats.

One of which she should have been strapped into.

She wanted to cry but knew it would do no good. What she needed to do was figure out how to get in touch with the pilot who had downloaded the aircraft data and get it to somebody who could analyze it for clues leading her to *KMART*. But without a ride out to the ship, she was back at square one.

What would Uncle Rick do?

She shook away the thought, reminding herself that she had gotten to where she was on her own and didn't need anybody else's help. But the thought of her father's best friend reminded her of the early morning phone call, and she replayed the conversation in her mind.

She removed her cell phone to check for missed texts or phone calls and noticed a notification of a waiting message. She unlocked the phone, opened the secure message portal, then entered her passcode to download the pending message. After decrypting it, she felt the blood drain from her face.

TEXT FROM INTERCEPTED TRANSMISSION FOLLOWS.

FROM: TANDY

TO: KMART

1. PROVIDE DETAILED INFORMATION ON NAVY PILOT.

2. BE ALERT FOR OPPORTUNITY TO ELIMINATE.

"Holy shit," Punky said.

She backed away from the chain link fence and looked up into the sky in time to see the Greyhound climbing slowly into the air toward Point Loma before banking and turning out to sea. If she thought the pilot had been at risk before, this message made it crystal clear *TANDY* wanted him out of the picture. Espionage, sabotage...murder. The *Abraham Lincoln* was getting way more than she bargained for during her workups.

She might have missed the first COD out to the Lincoln, but there was still a chance she could pull some strings and find herself on the next one. She slipped her phone back into her pocket, then smoothed back her hair and pulled it into a ponytail before turning for the hangar and the door leading to the VRC-30 quarterdeck.

17

San Luis Obispo, California

Rick climbed back into his BMW after watching *TANDY* deposit something at a dead drop location on campus. He had been torn between following her or recovering whatever it was she had placed under the bench, but in the end decided he couldn't afford to lose her. He had placed the tracking device on the Jeep, but there was no guarantee she wouldn't ditch it for new wheels, and he needed to be prepared for that eventuality.

Still, his walk back to the M5 was more relaxed. The pulsing blue dot on his phone's map showed the Jeep leaving campus and returning to Highway 101, and he felt confident he could home in on the beacon and close the distance gradually. He backed out of his space and drove down the hill, passing a man walking in the opposite direction toward a Mission-style house set back in the trees. He turned left on Perimeter Road and drove toward the stadium, before making another left to exit the campus.

Within minutes, Rick was back up to speed on the highway, contemplating the significance of *KMART*'s handler driving through the night to Cal Poly to complete a drop. Was somebody at the university involved in the conspiracy? He reached across the center console for the pen and notepad sitting on the passenger seat and hastily scrawled three words.

CAL POLY FACULTY?

Chen sat behind the wheel of the Jeep, focused on returning to Long Beach to prepare for the night's operation. Though the brief walk through campus to the dead drop had shaken off some of her fatigue, the prospect of sitting behind the wheel for several more hours was daunting. She cracked the windows to allow the cool sea breeze to waft over and invigorate her, but it wasn't until she received a message in Signal that her fatigue evaporated.

YOU ARE BEING FOLLOWED.

Of course, her first instinct was to glance into her rearview mirror to look for a car she might have seen more than once. But she resisted, not wanting to look suspicious and spook whoever was following her. She had been careless during the night, but it wasn't too late to turn the tables. Mantis wouldn't have sent her the message if she wasn't certain, which meant that the professor had been watching her make the drop and spotted the tail.

How could I have missed it?

Without changing speed or giving any outward sign that she had become more aware, she scanned the road ahead and saw an exit coming up. She changed lanes with furtive glances in her mirrors to see if anybody moved to follow and took the single lane off-ramp up a small hill to a four-way stop. When nobody exited behind her, she turned left onto an overpass and glanced down at the steady flow of traffic on the highway below.

Where are you?

As eager as she was to return to the freeway and continue to her destination, she knew Mantis had given her an opportunity to remedy her mistake. The spymaster could have easily cut her off from all support and thrown her to the wolves, but she hadn't. She still might at some point, which meant Chen needed to rectify the situation and get into position before it was too late.

The road continued east away from the highway and crossed a narrow bridge over the San Luis Obispo Creek into the rural countryside. She turned right at the end of the road and passed alongside a small grape vine-yard, but she still hadn't seen anybody leave the highway to follow.

Could Mantis be wrong?

She shook away the thought. It was possible, but unlikely, that the woman responsible for the Ministry's West Coast network had made such a gross error. No, Chen was certain somebody was following her. Now it was her job to turn the hunter into the hunted.

Rick slowed when he saw the flashing blue beacon exit the highway and cross over into the foothills on the east side. He was tempted to follow, but with the tracking device providing him real-time position updates, it didn't make sense to risk exposing himself. A quick survey of the map showed that the road *TANDY* was on led back to the highway just before Shell Beach.

He pressed his foot down on the gas pedal and felt the sport sedan surge forward, pushing him back into the bolstered leather seats. If he could get to the exit before she rejoined the highway, he might be able to set up surveillance from in front of her and resume his "cast and drift" technique while blending in with the traffic.

Rising into the hills, Rick saw the coastal overcast blanketing the sky in front of him, but he was focused on finding the right exit. When he reached it, he steered the M5 down the off-ramp and coasted to a stop at the bottom. To the right, the road led to Avila Beach. The road ahead led to Shell Beach. And, to the left, he expected to see a blue Jeep Wrangler approaching at any minute from underneath the highway overpass.

He looked at the flashing beacon on his phone and saw it nearing his location from the other side of the highway. Gambling that *TANDY* intended to return to the freeway after completing a brief SDR, he floored the gas pedal and made a sharp left and immediate right, guiding the BMW back onto the freeway.

"Please don't be wrong," he muttered.

18

San Diego, California

Punky slammed the door open on her way back out into the parking lot. Still seething at missing her flight out to the ship, her anger only intensified when she learned that the only other scheduled COD flight that day had no available seats. No amount of begging, pleading, or cajoling could convince the squadron commanding officer to make room for her on the flight out to the carrier. She stood under the blue awning, her eyes pinched shut and head tilted skyward as she tried to rein in her emotions.

In the distance, she heard an unfamiliar, violent thrumming that reminded her of a high-tempo base drum. Similar to the sound of large propellers spinning on the ramp, she knew it wasn't another C-2 Greyhound, but whatever it was, it sounded big. With nothing left to do but accept her situation and come up with an alternative plan of action, she turned right and walked back to the chain link fence where she had made her unfortunate discovery earlier that morning.

There, on the ramp, in front of the newer adjacent hangar, was an off-white plane she normally saw painted in olive drab or even flat gray. Calling it a plane was a bit of a stretch, because both massive proprotors were turned skyward and resembled a helicopter more than anything else.

She knew the Navy had decided to retire the C-2 Greyhound and replace it with a version of the V-22 Osprey tilt-rotor aircraft designed for aerial assault and special operations missions, but this was her first time seeing it.

Propelled by her curiosity as much as by her hope, she walked to the adjacent hangar, where she saw the mural of a kneeling man holding the world on his shoulders. The hangar was home to the newly commissioned Fleet Logistics Multi-Mission Squadron 30, and her last chance for catching a ride out to the carrier.

Punky walked onto the quarterdeck and was greeted by a sailor similarly dressed as the one next door. "Can I help you, ma'am?"

Again, she displayed her NCIS credentials. "I'm Special Agent King with the Naval Criminal Investigative Service. I have an urgent need to get out to the USS *Abraham Lincoln*."

Unlike the sailor's response from the night before, however, the petty officer on duty nodded his head eagerly. "Let me call my chief," he said.

She knew better than to get her hopes up, but she couldn't help feeling a twinge of excitement that the cards might finally start falling her way. After months of dead ends in her search for the *Lincoln* sailor, he might have finally made a gaffe that would usher in his demise. She listened to the one-sided conversation while tempering her expectations. Even if they were willing to help her, there were still so many variables at play that there was a very real chance she could leave feeling as dejected as she'd felt when she walked out of the hangar next door.

The sailor hung up the phone and cracked a smile. "My chief is on his way downstairs. Do you mind waiting?"

Well, it's not a no...

She took a deep breath and nodded, stepping to the side while tapping against her thigh in a metronomic tic as she waited for the noncommissioned officer to come speak with her. When the stairwell door opened a minute later, she turned and saw a tall Black man wearing a one-piece olive drab flight suit worn by aviators with a pair of gold aircrew wings embroidered on his name tag. He walked up to her and held out his hand.

"Ma'am, I'm Chief Cooper. I understand you're in need of a ride?"

She shook his hand and felt her anxiety evaporate in his warm smile. "I am. Is there any way you can get me out to the *Lincoln*?"

His smile grew wider, displaying a mouth full of brilliant white teeth. "You're in luck. We actually have a parts run leaving in a few minutes."

"And you have room for me?"

"Let's go see the skipper. He's the aircraft commander for the mission and the one who will make the call."

Chief Cooper turned and held the door to the stairwell open, gesturing for her to lead the way. She gave him a warm smile in thanks, then started climbing the stairs. With each step, she felt her hope rise.

A short while later, Punky sat with her back to the fuselage on the port side, ignoring what she suspected was a view of San Diego retreating in the distance through the circular porthole over her left shoulder. Flying out to sea in the Osprey was unlike anything she had ever experienced before, and she swallowed hard to combat the nausea gripping her stomach.

As if feeling sick to her stomach wasn't bad enough, she felt claustrophobic with an olive drab horse collar flotation device zipped up tight around her neck and held down by thin nylon webbing of the shoulder harnesses keeping her pinned to the seat. She wore foam hearing protection under a hard-sided cranial and a pair of bulky goggles pulled down to cover her eyes. In a way, she envied the aircrew who looked far more comfortable wearing flight helmets that allowed them to speak to one another over the intercom system.

Despite her discomfort, she kept an eye always trained on them. The aircrew would know long before her if they were about to ditch or make a crash landing, and she continually read their body language for signs that her fears were warranted. Chief Cooper saw her looking at him and gave her a thumbs-up, but even that didn't seem to settle her nerves, and her leg bounced as if trying to keep pace with the massive proprotors.

After what seemed like an eternity, she noticed the aircrew talking to one another and gesturing animatedly at various items around the cabin. The taste of sour spit filled her mouth, and she leaned forward in her seat to focus on the men who had become her security blanket.

Chief Cooper walked up and spoke.

Punky scrunched up her face, unable to hear over the din of the engine noise and her double hearing protection.

He leaned close and put his mouth to her ear. "Ten minutes!"

She gave him a thumbs-up in reply, then tugged on the bitter ends of her harness to make sure she was cinched down good and tight.

Aside from the museum on the USS *Midway*, she had never been aboard an aircraft carrier. Punky had spent her entire life, minus the four years she'd spent at USC, living in one of the largest Navy towns in the world, and she'd still never set foot on one. Only the sober nature of her mission to stop a traitor blunted her excitement at being less than ten minutes from a ship that carried an air force more powerful than seventy percent of the countries in the world.

"Five minutes!"

Her stomach knotted. She still couldn't hear him but had learned to read his lips.

USS *Abraham Lincoln* (CVN-72)

Adam watched the CMV-22B Osprey make its approach with mild fascination. The Marine Corps had been flying the Osprey from amphibious assault ships for some time, but this was a new undertaking for the Navy, and he was curious to see how it would fare. The off-white-colored paint scheme made it appear decidedly inferior to the Marine version, in his mind.

He had come to the viewing area on the island known as Vulture's Row to watch them launch the COD carrying the Navy pilot who had absconded with the maintenance data. On the one hand, he was happy the lieutenant was leaving the ship for the beach. But on the other, he worried what might happen when he got there.

Sure, Adam had finally managed to erase the data after being forced to make the pilot a copy, but it was only a matter of time before CAG or the skipper noticed the deception and came along looking for answers. And he hadn't the foggiest what he might say.

Unlike the fixed-wing jets and planes that flew aboard the aircraft carrier, the Osprey approached from astern with its proprotors tilted skyward, looking more like a helicopter than a plane. He watched the enlisted landing signalman guide the tilt-rotor aircraft to the flight deck behind the number one wire, then taxi it forward in the landing area before handing off control to a yellow-shirted plane director.

The fear Adam felt when he was on the flight deck was absent high on Vulture's Row, where he had a God's eye view of the orchestrated chaos. But he still bristled with nervous energy and looked around to make sure he was alone before pulling out the Nintendo Switch and powering it on.

He knew he had broken protocol by sending her a second message in the same night, but he didn't want to even contemplate the ramifications if the maintenance data the pilot carried off the boat showed clear evidence of foul play. It would be bad enough if they found out the jet's malady wasn't an error in the software, but it would be catastrophic if they figured out he was the one who had supplied the Chinese with the information needed to develop the weapon. Aside from taking matters into his own hands and tossing the lieutenant overboard in the middle of the night, his only solution was to tell Chen and hope she could remedy the problem. She usually did.

After entering the faux-Konami code, Adam waited for the covert communication partition to boot up and provide access to any instructions she might have sent him overnight. He glanced over his shoulder again before tapping on the icon labeled "Receive" and watched in agony as the progress bar slowly filled. His gaze fell on the Osprey while he waited, but then he saw a window open on the reverse video screen.

1 NEW MESSAGE.

He knew there was a good chance she would be angry with him for breaking protocol, but it was too late to worry about that now. He tapped on the icon to download the message and held his breath while he waited for it to appear.

"Beautiful day, isn't it, Marine?"

The voice startled him, and Adam fumbled the Nintendo Switch, almost losing it over the side of the railing onto the flight deck below.

"Good lord, my boy!"

Adam turned to face the older, silver-haired man and came to attention. Even without the silver stars on the collar of the man's khaki uniform shirt, he would have recognized the commander of the carrier strike group. He was a popular figure among most of the sailors and Marines embarked aboard the *Abraham Lincoln*, and with good reason.

"Admiral!"

"At ease, Lance Corporal."

But he couldn't relax. Even the bemused expression on the admiral's face wasn't enough to calm his surprise at the most powerful man on the ship sidling up next to him. He wondered if the admiral made it a habit of poking his head into random spaces aboard the ship, just to see how his troops responded. After all, he had his very own version of Vulture's Row from which he could observe the comings and goings on the flight deck, why would he climb another level above the flag bridge to—

"Oh," Adam said with sudden realization. "I'm in the wrong place."

"Nonsense!" The admiral turned away from Adam and looked down on the CMV-22B Osprey being chocked and chained in the landing area just forward of the island. "Nobody ever comes up here to watch airplanes flying with me. I'm happy to share it with you."

Adam glanced down at the video game console in his hand and read the message before clearing it and powering down the device. He didn't think the admiral would pay much attention to it, but he still felt uncomfortable standing next to him. Especially after the message Chen had sent.

1. PROVIDE DETAILED INFORMATION ON NAVY PILOT.

2. BE ALERT FOR OPPORTUNITY TO ELIMINATE.

He swallowed hard and tucked the device into his pocket.

Eliminate?

Adam knew what he had gotten himself into, but he rationalized it by telling himself the Marine Corps had brought it upon themselves. They had lied to him and used him as just another warm body, subjecting him to a life of mediocrity with a fancy title. Worse, they misused his talents and took an enthusiastic teenager and turned him into a jaded idealist.

The Marine Corps had turned its back on Adam, while Chen had welcomed him with open arms. And legs.

He turned to face the admiral. "By your leave, Admiral?"

The old man sighed and nodded at the Osprey. "Very well. Guess I should stop ogling the pretty girls and get back to running my strike group."

Adam followed his gaze and watched a slender woman in jeans and a red hoodie with jet-black hair tucked under an ill-fitting cranial follow a tall Black man in a flight suit from the back of the Osprey toward the island. She wasn't dressed like a sailor, or any other member of the military for that matter, and he watched her until she disappeared from view.

The two men turned and looked at each other for a moment before the admiral broke away with a curt nod and turned for the flag bridge. Adam turned the opposite direction for the door leading to the down ladder while his mind swam with conflicting thoughts.

USS *Mobile Bay* (CG-53)

A short distance north from the *Lincoln*, Beth sat in her chair on the bridge, brooding over the day's coming events. She had managed four hours of sleep after Master Chief finished briefing her on the plan of the day and the timeline for the upcoming missile test, but she knew she would need more than a cup or two of Trident coffee to make it that far.

She lifted the gold-rimmed ceramic coffee mug and took a sip of the steaming elixir, savoring one of the few guilty pleasures she allowed herself in her otherwise Spartan lifestyle. Staring through the forward windows, she took in the vastness of the Pacific Ocean beyond the bow, but her mind continued replaying the events of the night before.

"Ma'am?"

Beth turned and saw the Officer of the Deck standing over her shoulder. "Yes, Lieutenant?"

"We just crossed into the Point Mugu Sea Range."

Beth stepped down from her chair and followed the young lieutenant junior grade to one of the ECDIS, or Electronic Chart Display and Information System, stations to review their position in relation to the sea space overlay. The thirty-six-thousand-square-mile sea test range was ideally suited for coordinated exercises with submarines, surface ships, and aircraft to engage targets both in the air and on the water.

"Very well," she said. "Go ahead and begin area sanitization."

"Aye aye, ma'am." The OOD spun away and picked up the Net 15 handset to inform the Surface Warfare Coordinator they were in place and ready to begin.

Beth watched the confident young officer work and again marveled at the skill and professionalism of her crew. It felt like only yesterday when she had been in his shoes, just over two years in the Navy and a graduate of the six-month Division Officer course at SWOS, the Surface Warfare Officer School, in Newport, Rhode Island. The future had seemed so exciting and the possibilities endless, but she had no idea what to expect.

She certainly never would have expected what happened the night before.

"Lieutenant, what's the air picture?"

He glanced at her to acknowledge the query, then spoke again into the handset. Within seconds, she heard the speaker squawk: "Air picture clear."

She nodded. No matter what the CAG had told her, she still felt uneasy about having an F-35C Joint Strike Fighter flying in the airspace above, armed with an advanced anti-shipping missile no less. But one thing was for certain. She wouldn't be caught with her pants down and would prepare her crew for the unexpected.

"Captain, Combat," came the voice over the Net 15 speaker.

Beth turned and picked up the handset. "This is the captain."

"The target is within range."

"Very well. I'm on my way there."

Beth turned and strode for the door, confident she was leaving the bridge in good hands.

19

USS *Abraham Lincoln* (CVN-72)

Adam was still recovering from his brief encounter with the admiral as he made his way aft in the hangar bay toward the fantail to reply to Chen's message. It worried him that their frequency in communication had increased, but not as much as the idea of being caught because the Navy pilot found something incriminating in the maintenance data. With his message sent, he left the cavernous hangar bay and tried putting it from his mind. He didn't need to report to maintenance control for at least another hour, but he also knew he couldn't stay away from his workspace if he wanted to avoid suspicion.

For most sailors aboard the carrier, as well as the Marines in Adam's squadron, learning how to get around the ship had been relatively simple. He only needed to know how to get from his assigned berthing and work-space, both on the 03 level, to the mess deck four levels beneath him, where he ate his meals, usually alone.

After reaching the top of the ladder, he turned inboard for one of two main passageways running the length of the ship. Maintenance control was located off a short hallway on the port side, and with some hesitation, he turned for it and walked through the door. Both Sarge and Gunny were in their usual places, preparing the logbooks for the upcoming first event. "Morning, Gunny," he muttered.

"Garett," Gunny replied, before spitting a thick stream of tobacco juice into his bottle.

"Skipper came by this morning," Sergeant Narvaez said, turning to look at him. "We couldn't find the data from last night's event. Did you move it somewhere?"

Adam felt his heart bolt like a startled doe, but he breathed through his nose to tamp his fear before replying. "Not since we made a copy for the lieutenant."

Acting like it wasn't a big deal, he crossed to his workstation and sat down in the chair and put his back to the other men. He could already feel beads of sweat forming on his brow, and he wanted to avoid drawing even more attention to himself. But if the others thought the missing data was a big deal, they didn't show it and went back to the normal busywork that defined their jobs on the boat.

Adam logged in to the computer while continuing to breathe through his fear. He needed to lose himself in his work and forget the message he had sent to Chen. He should have felt relief the pilot would soon be off the carrier, but he was starting to wonder how deep down the rabbit hole of treachery he was willing to go. She might not have ordered him to pull the trigger, but he had pointed the gun for her.

There's no turning back now.

———

As Punky followed Chief Cooper from the back of the Osprey and across the flight deck, she couldn't help but stare in open-mouthed amazement at the bedlam surrounding her. Everywhere she looked, she saw sailors in different colored jerseys scurrying about in an unorganized fashion performing various tasks she assumed were somewhat important to the daily goings-on aboard an aircraft carrier.

"This way, ma'am," Chief Cooper yelled, turning to ensure she was still following in his wake.

She remained on his heels, not daring to step away from the invisible path he was treading. To their left, she saw a man in camouflage trousers with a long-sleeved green turtleneck and green vest standing at the nose of an F-35C Joint Strike Fighter. His green cranial swiveled from side to side as he supervised others in green, brown, and white jerseys crawling underneath the jet. He turned in her direction, said something into the microphone attached to his cranial, then turned back to the others and started barking orders.

To her right, an E-2D Hawkeye started its engines, and the propellers began spinning violently in the humid marine air, dangerously close to where she and Chief Cooper were walking. But the seasoned crew chief didn't seem fazed by it, and he walked with confidence toward the starboard side of the ship, just forward of the island. She breathed a sigh of relief when he led her from the flight deck down a short set of stairs onto a catwalk, then into the ship through a watertight door.

It took a moment for her eyes to adjust to the darkness, but when he led her through the next hatch, the smell of fresh paint intermixed with grease and oil permeated the dry conditioned air and hit her square in the face. The chief stopped in front of a door marked "ATO" and removed his helmet. She followed suit and removed the cranial and horse collar flotation device the squadron had loaned her, handing them back to the chief.

"Do you know where you're going from here?"

She just stared at him, perplexed. She figured people who flew out to the aircraft carrier usually had somebody expecting them or at least had an idea of the ship's layout. She had neither.

Chief Cooper sensed her hesitation and put a comforting hand on her shoulder. "If you want my advice, find a pilot in a flight suit and ask one of them to help you. Most of them are underworked and bored out of their mind."

She grinned. "Know where I could find one of those?"

"Each squadron has a ready room where they usually hang out. All the ready rooms are on this level, so if you walk up and down this passageway," he pointed to the corridor at the end of the small hallway they were standing in, "I'm sure you'll find who you're looking for."

"Thanks, Chief."

Colt pulled his stateroom door closed before slinging his duffel bag over his shoulder. He had thirty minutes before they expected him to show at the ATO to manifest for his ride back to North Island, which was more than enough time to collect his gear from Flight Equipment.

His mind was in a fog as he walked aft through the main passageway, then cut across to the starboard side of the ship. He stepped around sailors who were busy touching up paint or polishing brass, but his focus was on collecting his flight gear, getting on the COD, and flying back to North Island. He could worry about hitching a ride to Montgomery Field once he got there.

When he arrived in the small space where the Black Knights stored their flight equipment, Smitty and another Marine pilot were already there getting dressed for the first event of the day. He had never felt embarrassed or ashamed to be in the presence of other fighter pilots, but the dark cloud of his damaged reputation hung over his head and was impossible to ignore. He just wanted to get his gear and leave.

"I can come back," he said, starting to back out.

Smitty turned. "Forget that, dude. We're almost done."

The other pilot gave Colt a nervous smile, then turned to Smitty. "I'll meet you on the roof."

Smitty nodded, then watched his wingman skirt around Colt to leave the cramped room and waited until he was gone. "Grab your shit and I'll walk with you to the ATO."

The Marines who took care of their flight gear had already packed his away in an olive drab parachute bag. After finding the right bag, he stuffed his duffel inside, zipped it closed, then hefted it off the floor and slung it across his back. Smitty led him out into the main passageway, then turned toward the ATO. Every few steps, he looked over his shoulder to see if Colt was following, then stopped in a vacant stretch.

Colt spoke first. "I really appreciate your offer to help, Smitty."

"Dude, don't worry about it. That's what we do, right? We look out for each other."

He looked up and down the passageway, but aside from a woman in jeans and a red hoodie several frames forward walking in their direction, they were alone. He lowered his voice anyway. "Did you talk to Jug?"

Smitty nodded. "Called him on the POTS line just before my brief."

The POTS line, or Plain Old Telephone Service, was a phone that could be used like any other landline. Normally only squadron commanding officers and other higher-ranking officers had access to the service, but enterprising aircrew often found ways to work around the restrictions so they could call home. Colt felt his heart beat a little faster. "And?"

Smitty removed a scrap of paper from his flight suit pocket and handed it to him. "He's expecting your call."

Colt saw a number scrawled on the sheet of paper and slipped it into his pocket, overwhelmed by a sense of gratitude for the Marine pilot. He had only known Smitty for a few weeks, but already he felt as if they had known each other much longer. "Thank you, brother."

Punky walked hesitantly through the main passageway, stepping through knee-knockers as she looked for somebody who could help. Up ahead, she spotted two pilots talking to each other, but unlike Chief Cooper's prediction, they didn't appear bored or overly eager to help. One wore a high-and-tight haircut and was outfitted in cumbersome flight gear, but the other only carried a bulky gear bag on his back. She stopped when the two men embraced.

The acoustics weren't great on the ship, and a deep humming sound radiated through the steel bulkheads around her. But it was quiet enough that she could just barely make out their hushed voices.

"Keep me posted," high-and-tight said.

The blond nodded. "I'm going to figure out what happened."

"I know you will."

Punky cocked her head to the side, wondering if she was reading too much into what she had overheard. The blond's comment could have meant anything, but she latched onto it and figured she had nothing to lose by playing her hand early. She stepped through another knee-knocker and approached them.

"Excuse me," she said, flashing them her credentials. "I'm with NCIS and looking for a pilot who might have been the target of sabotage last night."

The men looked at each other, then back to her. "What's the pilot's name?" high-and-tight asked.

"I don't know. I was hoping you could help me find him."

The blond looked at his watch, then moved to step around her. "I'm sorry, I'm going to be late for my flight."

"You're leaving?"

"I'm on the next COD, and if I miss it..." He trailed off before adding, "Excuse me."

She watched him walking toward the ATO, where Chief Cooper had just deposited her, then turned her attention to high-and-tight. "What about you? Got somewhere to be?"

"I'm actually heading to the flight deck for the first event." He paused. "But if you walk with me, I can take you to our ready room on my way. Somebody there ought to be able to help."

"Thank you. I'd appreciate that."

With a resigned sigh, high-and-tight glanced at the other pilot once more, then started walking aft. Punky was tall and had long legs, but she found that she needed to quicken her pace to keep up with the pilot. Either he was late or deliberately trying to make it difficult for her to follow, but she didn't have a choice. She needed to find the pilot before it was too late.

"So, you said something about sabotage?" high-and-tight asked over his shoulder. "What happened?"

"I don't really know," she replied. "Just that a jet was supposed to have crashed, and now a pilot is in danger because of some information he downloaded. I don't know anything about—"

She almost crashed into high-and-tight, who had stopped dead in his tracks. He spun to face her. "Did you say the pilot is in danger?"

20

Pismo Beach, California

Chen had completed her brief SDR and returned to the highway without spotting anything amiss. All around her, she saw only the normal flow of traffic for an early Friday morning, but she wasn't willing to ignore the warning Mantis had sent her and resolved to be more observant. Twice more, she exited the highway and completed an abbreviated SDR before returning to the freeway and continuing south.

The clouds had retreated entirely back out to sea, and the sky overhead was a deep, smog-free blue. Every few minutes, she craned her neck forward to look up through the windshield, trying to spot an airplane that might be orbiting overhead. Each time, she leaned back in her seat, frustrated that she still hadn't seen the signs she was being followed.

When a notification appeared on her phone, she unlocked it and opened the calculator app. She entered her passkey, then clicked on "Receive" and waited to see if the Marine had come through for her. She moved into the left lane, giving a wide berth around a car parked on the shoulder, when her phone chirped.

1 NEW MESSAGE.

She felt a nervous excitement and tapped on the icon to download it, then glanced up to complete a scan of her mirrors and surrounding traffic. When nothing triggered her acutely honed sense of awareness, she moved back into the right lane and forced herself to continue driving just below the speed limit.

1. *NAVY LT COLT BANCROFT. TOPGUN INSTRUCTOR.*

2. *ABOARD COD FOR NORTH ISLAND.*

She still needed to shake her tail and get out from under whoever was surveilling her, but now she had a name. She had a target she could prosecute. If the pilot wasn't already on the ground in San Diego, he would be soon. And she needed to make sure that's as far as he got. She abandoned caution and switched from the encrypted messaging application to Signal, found the number for her man in San Diego, and placed a voice call.

When he answered, she said, "We have a problem."

"I'm listening."

She took a deep breath and considered her break from protocol. The urgency of the situation necessitated that she forgo her normal coded communication methods in favor of an expedient solution. "Colt Bancroft," she said at last. "He is a Navy lieutenant with information that could jeopardize our operation. I need you to kill him."

"Where and when?"

Chen tapped up on the cruise control to increase her speed. "He is flying to North Island from the carrier. I don't know when."

"I'll take care of it," he said, then ended the call.

She should have felt relief that the Marine had come through for her and given her what she had asked for, but she couldn't shake the nagging sensation that events were spiraling out of her control. Chen was meticulous in how she ran her operations, and she was unaccustomed to playing back on her heels. She tapped up to increase her speed further, succumbing to her subconscious need to play offense.

With her men taking care of this *Colt Bancroft*, she could focus on what troubled her most.

Rick sat on the side of the road while trying Punky's phone again. When it went to voicemail for the third consecutive time, he cursed and switched back to the tracker application to check on *TANDY's* location.

"Oh, shit!"

The flashing blue beacon was less than half a mile behind him, and he quickly glanced into his side-view mirror as he put the BMW in drive and prepared to pull out behind her. Within seconds, he spotted the Jeep Wrangler he had been following all night and watched it move into the left lane to pass him. He turned and watched the SUV move back into the right lane and continue south on the highway.

Dammit.

He knew it had been a bad idea to pull off on the side of the road, but after noticing the beacon exit the highway twice more since leaving Avila Beach, he began to wonder if the increase in SDRs meant she had somehow detected him. Without air support, he needed to ensure she didn't ditch the vehicle, and the only way of doing that was by getting eyes on. Still, he knew she had seen his car now and would become suspicious if she spotted it a second time.

Rick waited until the Jeep had gone half a mile, then pulled out into traffic and quickly accelerated to match her speed. He tried reaching Punky again but was met with the same frustrating result, so he put the phone down and focused on maintaining his surveillance. Now that he was in view of the subject, he couldn't afford to become complacent and make careless errors.

He saw the Jeep's turn signal flash, and he eased his foot off the gas. *Here we go again.*

As she took the off-ramp for Price Street, he allowed the M5 to coast and preserve the separation he had established. He knew she was likely completing another surveillance detection route and would be looking to see who followed her off the highway, but he couldn't simply drive past and wait for her to catch up again now that she had already seen him on the side of the road.

By the time he reached the exit, the Jeep was at the stop sign at the end of the off-ramp. He continued slowing as she made a right turn, back-tracking up the coast on the Business 101, forcing him to choose between two equally unappealing options. If he turned left, he would lose sight and she could pull into any of the hotels or restaurants lining the beach to swap out the Jeep for a clean vehicle. But if he chose to follow her, she could double back unexpectedly and spot him.

"Dammit, Punky..."

Following a subject with two vehicles was infinitely easier and would have precluded him from having to make this decision. And even though it wasn't her fault that she wasn't there to help, he couldn't help but allow his frustration at her ignoring his warnings to bubble over into his own predicament. At last, he rolled the dice and turned right, hoping TANDY intended to backtrack to the previous on-ramp and return to the highway.

As Chen made the right turn at the bottom of the off-ramp, she glanced into her rearview mirror and saw a silver car also exiting. Something about the car seemed familiar to her, but she couldn't place it and fought the temptation to simply dismiss it as paranoia. She had good reason to be paranoid, and until she satisfied herself it was nothing, she treated it like everything.

Okay, let's find out who you are.

She kept her speed low as she watched the silver car near the stop sign behind her, then she turned left and descended into the Shore Cliff Hotel parking lot. She was certain that if the sedan was following her, its driver would have seen her make the turn. She coasted down the hill and parked in a spot reserved for electric vehicles, angling her rearview mirror so she could see the road, and waited to see if the car continued driving north.

When she saw a flash of silver, she quickly backed out of the spot and raced back up the hill to the street. She looked left and watched the silver sedan continuing north on Price Street as if nothing was amiss. But still, something bothered her about the car, and she racked her brain to try to figure out what it was.

Two hundred yards up the road, the silver car turned right and drove under the freeway. She pulled out onto the road and followed, knowing full well that if the driver had been following her, he would have seen her leave the hotel parking lot. He would know he had been burned and would attempt to disengage, but Chen wasn't about to let that happen. She reached alongside her seat and felt for the Glock 19 peeking out above the center console.

This ends now, she thought.

She turned right to follow the sedan underneath the overpass and spotted it on the other side, driving up a hill to an access road on the other side of the highway. If its driver had been following her, he gave no outward sign that he had been burned and drove like any other Southern California driver.

But she was tired of pretending. She pressed on the gas and sped up, narrowing the distance between them. She wanted the driver to see her closing on him and wanted to startle him into making a mistake she could exploit. When she got within one hundred yards, the sedan turned right and drove up a hill. A quick glance at her map showed that it was the only way in or out of the parking lot for Pismo Preserve.

Gotcha.

21

California Polytechnic State University
San Luis Obispo, California

Professor David Wang closed the ornate wooden door behind him and stepped out into the brisk morning air. For the first time in months, since he had begun taking morning tea with the University President, he felt hopeful and content. It had been a long journey from his poor upbringing in Heilongjiang province to receiving tenure at long last, but that wasn't why he walked with a bounce in his step.

At the end of the sidewalk, David turned right and strolled down the well-manicured hillside on the southern edge of campus. Trees of various shapes and sizes—there were over five hundred diverse and distinct species on campus—towered around him, obscuring the surrounding hillsides that disappeared in the low-hanging clouds. But, unlike most mornings, he allowed his mind to wander away from the beauty of nature and settle on his work.

He admitted the first iteration of the waveform had used brute force to attack the fifth-generation fighter's network encryption, much like the 2017 collision attack by CWI Amsterdam and Google against SHA-1. When Centrum Wiskunde & Informatica, the Dutch national research center for mathematics and computer science, discredited Secure Hash Algorithm 1, the world of cryptography changed.

Unlike then, his goal now was to break the encryption without letting the Americans know. Because if they knew, they would change their encryption method completely and he would lose the advantage. If he wanted his weapon to work, he needed to be careful how he approached it.

David entered the building and walked quietly to his dank office, a room that had an almost closet-like feeling to it compared to some of the more roomier office spaces of more senior professors. He didn't mind it, though, as most of his students and fellow faculty knew he was more likely to be found outside enjoying the California weather than stuck inside. That made it one of the more secure places for him to undertake such work, since it was unlikely somebody would come looking for him there and disturb him while he focused on the task at hand.

He sat down at his desk and powered on his computer. He knew it didn't come close to possessing the power required to alter the waveform from its current state to one that would withstand the Joint Strike Fighter's advanced defenses—the defenses that had successfully repelled their most recent attack. Fortunately, his position in the university gave him access to the Amazon Elastic Compute Cloud, also known as EC2, a secure and scalable cloud-computing service that he could leverage to run his program.

Powered by NVIDIA A100 Tensor Core GPUs, Amazon EC2 P4d instances were deployed in hyperscale clusters that allowed him to rent only as much computing power as was required to complete the task. And since his department often used this service, he could charge the cost to the university and further shield his work from the prying eyes of American law enforcement or the National Security Agency. Not that they would even have a clue what to look for, but for added security, he logged in under one of his colleague's accounts.

Each UltraCluster performed like the most powerful supercomputer in the world, and after entering the test results into his program and uploading it to the cloud, David leaned back in his chair and watched it perform the work for him with growing unease. He had scaled the processing power such that he knew the program would deliver results in less than an hour, but he couldn't stand the thought of sitting in his office any longer than he had to.

David turned off the monitor and pushed back from his desk. A leisurely stroll around the campus would suit him well and give him a chance to show his face while he hacked into America's most advanced stealth fighter.

A short while later, David sat on a bench outside the faculty offices on the east side of Centennial Lawn, watching the sun trace a path upward through one of his favorite trees on campus. The lone Queensland kauri stood over forty feet tall and cast an elegant shadow across the grass. It was the perfect place to sit and wait for the Amazon EC2 UltraClusters to finish crunching his program and produce the final waveform.

There had been a time early in his career when he felt conflicted about the work he did for the Ministry. He had always considered himself an academic above anything else, earning his bachelor's at Harbin Institute of Technology and master's at Shanghai University. It wasn't until he had finished his doctorate at Johns Hopkins University that the Ministry approached him about conducting research on their behalf. Of course he said yes. He was Chinese and always would be.

He squinted as a ray of sunlight broke through the branches and caught him in its warm glow. He had traced the movement of the sun through the tree's branches, trying to ignore how much time had elapsed since he started running the program. He was content just sitting outside, breathing in the fresh air, and enjoying the sun's caress on his skin.

His phone vibrated, and he removed it from his pocket and saw a notification that the program was complete.

He didn't smile, didn't pump his fist in celebration, and didn't hasten to leave one of his favorite places. He simply slipped his phone back into his pocket and stood, letting his spine elongate with a deep inhale of satisfaction and long exhale of contentment. Then, he walked west across the grass and placed his hand on the tree's trunk, thanking it for the beauty it provided.

His office in the computer science building was less than a five-minute walk, just on the other side of the Engineering East building. He took his time, walking with his regular gait that was easily spotted by other faculty and students alike.

"Hey, Professor Wang!"

He turned to see one of his former students, a sophomore, he thought, offering him a friendly wave as she walked into the Baker Science building. He returned the gesture with a genuine smile but continued to his destination without another thought. She wouldn't feel slighted by his response. It was just his way.

He turned into his building at the southeast corner of Dexter Lawn and took the stairs down to his basement office. Most of those who had shared the level with him were either away on sabbatical or had moved to more comfortable spaces with windows that looked out on the beautiful campus. But David never saw the need because he spent so little time there.

He unlocked his office door and reached in to flip on the light before stepping inside. He didn't bother locking the door behind him and walked across to his desk, where he sat down in the uncomfortable office chair and turned on his computer monitor. As expected, the results were waiting for him, and he quickly scanned through the program's output, looking for an obvious reason why the first iteration had failed.

"Ahhh...there you are."

He saw it almost right away and chastised himself for missing something so painfully obvious. He had designed the weapon to target the JSF's Autonomic Logistics Information System, known as ALIS, the first-generation cloud-based information exchange that was designed to allow the jet to transmit performance data back to those who maintained it. But after fielding several iterations of the flailing system, the US military had adopted ODIN, the Operational Data Integrated Network.

The results from the previous night's mission showed that the waveforms still targeted much of the older system's architecture and hadn't been adapted for its replacement. Of course, he should have predicted that, but with the pace at which the Navy and Marine Corps upgraded their fleets, he didn't see how he could have known which environment they were operating in. But with this latest waveform, he was certain they would be able to complete their mission.

He packaged the results in an encrypted compressed file and transferred it to a device he kept locked in his drawer. It wasn't one the university had provided, but it also wouldn't draw too much attention since the faculty often worked on experiments in their free time. The Ministry had provided the device to him for the sole purpose of transmitting the software update to a dedicated satellite in geosynchronous Earth orbit where it would broadcast to the weapon's operators.

Once the software package had been uploaded to the device, David shut down his computer and locked up his office. It was a short walk to the Engineering building, where he had access to the Cal Poly CubeSat Lab that had been established over the last several years to develop a complete X-band transceiver to support deep space missions. The device the Ministry had provided him integrated seamlessly into the student project and allowed him to transmit his software updates without even leaving campus.

David ascended from the basement and stepped once more into the fresh air, feeling instantly rejuvenated by the sunlight. Even with his budding excitement, his gait was still relaxed and measured as he walked across the courtyard into the Engineering building. Within ten minutes, his software patch would be uploaded, and his role in the operation would be over. It deserved a celebration, and he decided on a bike ride around campus to commemorate the occasion.

22

USS *Abraham Lincoln* (CVN-72)

Colt sat in the back of the C-2 Greyhound and blinked his eyes against the stinging jet exhaust as it wafted over him. The cargo plane's upgraded eight-bladed propellers spun in violent arcs on either side of the fuselage in preparation for the flight deck crew to break them down for taxi to the catapult after the event's fighters launched. Through the open hatch at the rear, Colt saw the air wing's Super Hornets and Joint Strike Fighters moving under the guidance of plane directors, and he felt a pang of disappointment.

Fighter pilots belonged strapped into ejection seats, not forced to sit facing backward in a cargo plane. He gave a little shake of his head to clear away the negative thoughts, then froze when he saw a sailor in a white float coat leading another passenger onto the COD. She looked odd wearing jeans and a red hoodie with an olive drab horse collar flotation device around her neck and ill-fitting cranial and goggles over her long, black hair.

The NCIS agent.

His heart raced with fear as he wondered if she had come to arrest him for taking the maintenance data without permission. It wasn't exactly classified but was sensitive enough that he knew he would be treated the same as if it had been. But other than Smitty and the Marines in maintenance control, nobody knew he had it; certainly, nobody who could have tipped off the NCIS with enough time to send an agent out to the boat.

Colt took several calming breaths to try to rein in his pounding heart as he watched one of the Greyhound's aircrew help the lady agent up onto the cargo ramp and forward to an empty seat next to him. He couldn't help but notice how out of place she seemed in the back of the cargo plane, and he nodded to her in greeting as she sat down next to him.

With trembling fingers, she strapped herself into the seat, affixing the last buckle when the cargo ramp closed shut, sealing them inside the jostling airplane. Colt recognized the subtle shifts in movement and the sounds reverberating through the fuselage and knew they had been broken down and were being led to one of the catapults. He turned to look at her and saw her eyes pinched shut and lips moving as if she was reciting a frantic prayer.

"You'll be okay," he shouted, loud enough to be heard through her hearing protection and over the roaring turbine engines.

Her lips stopped moving, and she turned to look at him with pleading eyes. They made eye contact, and he felt his heart stagger as her pale blue eyes drilled into him. "How do you ever get used to this?"

He grinned. "You don't."

Her eyes grew wide in surprise, then narrowed as if he had said something utterly terrifying. At last, she looked away, staring straight ahead at the back of the plane as they neared the catapult. He couldn't help having a little fun at her expense but admitted there was nothing more uncomfortable than being stuck inside the back of a Greyhound as they were flung off the front of a ship. He hated it, but he had done it enough times to have picked up a few tips to make it at least bearable.

Colt elbowed her, and when she turned to look at him, he gestured down at his feet. He had placed his toes on a ledge at the bottom of the seat in front of him, and he watched her lift her red Vans to mimic him. Then he reached up and grasped the opposite shoulder harnesses with each hand, crossing his arms over his chest. Again, she mirrored him and gave him a questioning look, and he nodded to her in approval.

Finally, he pressed back against the seat's headrest and braced himself for the catapult shot. Unlike when he flew in the cockpit of a Hornet or Joint Strike Fighter, the passenger seats on the Greyhound faced backward, which meant the thin nylon straps of the seat belt and shoulder harnesses were the only things keeping him in his seat. He had learned that putting his toes on the seat in front of him allowed the use of his legs to help brace against the sudden acceleration, but there was little else he could do to make a catapult shot bearable.

He felt the plane squat and heard the turbine engines rev louder, and he shouted across the din to warn the NCIS agent. "Get ready!"

The plane shook from side to side, his seat vibrating against the force of the twin Allison turboprop engines at full power. He kept his eyes focused straight ahead, pressing his head back into the seat as he waited for the holdback to break. He felt a pressure on his thigh and looked down to see the agent's fingers digging into his leg.

Ignoring his initial hesitation about the agent, he reached down and placed a comforting hand on top of hers just as the catapult fired. In an instant, they were flung forward in their straps as the cargo plane went from a dead standstill to flying airspeed in less than three hundred feet. He tensed his legs against the seat in front of him and noticed her doing the exact same thing.

One potato...two potato...

The acceleration ended abruptly and pushed him back into his seat. She turned to him with a look of terror on her face, and he gave her a reassuring smile. "We're flying."

Colt saw her visibly deflate, but she kept her hand on his leg.

He didn't mind.

A short while later, the C-2 Greyhound touched down on the runway and Colt at last felt the agent relax. Despite his assurances, she had been tensed up since leaving the *Lincoln* and had kept her hand on his leg. But when the wheels hit the tarmac, she removed her hand and leaned back into the seat, panting as if exhausted from the twenty-minute flight.

"Don't like flying?"

She turned and gave him a curious look. "Actually, I love it. I just hate being trapped in a tube with no way of knowing if we're going to crash."

He smiled and, with a shake of his head, admitted he wasn't very fond of being a passenger either. He watched the cargo ramp lower as the Greyhound taxied clear of the runway and made its way to the apron in front of the hangar, then pulled out his cell phone and turned it on. He waited for it to establish a connection with the network, gave the NCIS agent a hesitant glance, then dialed the number Smitty had given him.

He pressed send and brought the phone underneath the cranial to his ear, straining to hear the ringing over the engine and hydraulic noises reverberating through the cabin. He probably could have waited to make the call, but he couldn't help but feel as if there was an invisible timer counting down to something horrible happening. Something he needed to stop.

"Hello?"

"Jug!" he shouted. "It's Colt."

"Colt? Where are you? Sounds like you're inside a blender."

He gave the agent another sideways glance, saw her knees bobbing up and down with nervous energy, and reminded himself to choose his words carefully. "Just landed in North Island."

"COD?"

"Yeah," he said. "The blender."

Jug laughed, apparently sharing his view of riding as a passenger instead of piloting the plane himself. "Smitty told me you had something you needed my help with, but he wouldn't say what."

"Yeah, I do. I can fly up to Inyokern and be there in a few hours—"

Jug interrupted him. "Sounds serious."

Again, Colt glanced at the NCIS agent before responding. "It is."

"Well, don't come to China Lake. I'm at Point Mugu for the weekend."

Colt felt himself deflate. "Mugu?"

"I'll explain later. Can you come here?"

He sighed with relief. "Sure. I'll call you later."

He ended the call and slipped the phone back into his pocket, then placed his hands on his knees and looked out at the base through the rear opening to wait for the lumbering cargo plane to stop. When it did, he didn't waste any time in unstrapping from his seat and removing the safety equipment he had been forced to wear. The sooner he found a ride to Montgomery Field, the sooner he could figure out what the hell was going on.

He watched the NCIS agent fumbling with the buckle and hesitated. Part of him wanted to be as far from her as possible, but another part felt obligated to help his fellow prisoner escape.

"You need help, ma'am?"

When she didn't answer, he leaned down and twisted the center of the buckle, releasing the shoulder straps and freeing her from the seat.

"Thank you," she said.

They locked eyes for a moment before he broke away and made for the rear of the plane as the pilots shut off the engines and the massive propellers slowed to a stop. He lifted the parachute bag containing his flight gear from the deck, slung it across his back, and dropped down from the ramp. The ocean breeze washed across the sprawling naval air station and cooled the perspiration that had accumulated on his skin during the short flight, and he took a moment to get his bearings before setting off for the hangar fifty yards away.

"Lieutenant!"

He heard her call out to him but ignored it. They had forged a bond of solidarity during the flight from the *Lincoln*, but he still felt uncomfortable being so close to her. There was something about what she had said when she approached them on the carrier that bothered him.

I'm with NCIS and looking for a pilot who might have been the target of sabotage last night.

Though he didn't see how it could have been sabotage, he was the only pilot who had flown the night before and had had something extraordinary happen to him. And he couldn't allow anybody to keep him from finding out what.

"Wait, Lieutenant!" she shouted again. "You're in danger!"

He froze in his tracks.

23

Punky watched the pilot stop and slowly turn to look at her. He had been kind to her on the flight from the ship, but he seemed overly eager to get away from her, an all-too-often unfortunate byproduct of her being a law enforcement officer. Of course, normally only the guilty ran.

"What do you mean I'm in danger?"

If the story the Marine pilot had told her was true, she was almost certain Lieutenant Bancroft was the pilot she had flown out to the carrier to find, but she wasn't quite ready to answer his question. She walked quickly to close the gap between them so she wouldn't have to yell across the ramp. "What happened to you last night?"

She saw his eyes glass over as he recalled a memory she could tell he'd just as soon forget, then he shook his head. "Nothing."

"Nothing?"

He opened his mouth but quickly closed it.

"Who's Jug?"

His eyes narrowed, then he turned and continued walking back to the hangar. She took a deep breath and looked up into the clear, blue sky, second-guessing her decision to press him for information. She was certain she was on the right track, but she knew she couldn't bully her way into getting the answers she needed. If she wanted to find *KMART* and stop him before he succeeded in killing somebody, she needed to get Colt to trust her.

"Wait," she said. "Colt!"

Again, he stopped and turned back, dropping his parachute bag on the tarmac.

She held up her hands in a calming gesture. "The Marine pilot you were talking to on the ship? Smitty? He told me you might be the one I'm looking for."

Colt's eyes closed, and his head drooped in resignation.

She pressed her advantage. "Look, we're on the same team here. I'll tell you everything I know, but I can't help if I don't understand what happened."

His eyes snapped open, and she could tell she hadn't quite gotten through to him. "What happened," he said, "is that something took control of my jet, and I almost crashed into the water. And when I tried warning CAG that something was wrong with the jet, he kicked me off the ship and promised to take my wings away."

Punky had never served in the military, but she had been around the Navy her entire life. She knew what those wings of gold meant to Navy pilots and why Colt was so upset. "What if that *something* was a hostile act?"

"Like sabotage," Colt said, echoing the word she'd used earlier.

She nodded. "But there's more you need to know."

"Go on." He folded his arms across his chest, waiting for her to convince him to trust her.

She didn't know what information he had that put him in danger, but she couldn't just let him leave and lose her only link to *KMART*. She looked around and saw that they were alone on the empty tarmac, but it still wasn't exactly the privacy she wanted before having this conversation.

"Outside?" She gestured to the parking lot. "Maybe I can give you a ride somewhere?"

He hesitated, then scooped up his parachute bag and nodded.

She led them through the hangar and out the same door she had exited in disgust earlier that morning. Next to the blue-and-gold starburst logo adorned with Pegasus, she saw her car still parked in the "CO's Guest" spot and walked to the rear to open the trunk for him.

"A Corvette?" Colt asked, his tone one of both shock and amusement.

Like most fighter pilots, he probably had an affinity for things that were flashy and went fast, but she didn't want to tell him it wouldn't have mattered if it were a Mercury Bobcat. She didn't drive it for the cool points, and her reason for having it was really none of his business, anyway. She opened the trunk and gestured for him to put his gear inside.

She climbed into the driver's seat and waited until he had stowed his gear and climbed in next to her before turning the key and firing up the V8. Without another word, she backed out of the space and left the parking lot on Quentin Roosevelt Boulevard, driving north toward the traffic circle where she had seen the aircraft on static display. She took the first exit from the roundabout and drove east for the main gate on McCain Boulevard.

"So where am I taking you?"

"Montgomery Field," he said as he ran his hands along the smooth dash, appreciating the car in a way she never would. She knew her dad had admired the Corvette's lines in the same way. He leaned back into the seat and turned to her. "Know where that is?"

"Yes," she said. "I know where that is."

She steered the Corvette through the main gate, crossed Alameda Boulevard, and stomped on the gas, pressing them both back in their seats. The muscle car's engine roared, echoing off the beach cottages on either side of the street, but her eyes never stopped scanning the familiar island scenery.

"So, what do I need to know?" Colt asked, shouting to be heard over the wind noise.

Punky raced around slower-moving cars, weaving the nimble sports car in and out of traffic as she made for the bridge. She checked her mirrors but saw nothing that set off alarm bells, and she turned to look at the pilot, who appeared at ease in the passenger seat.

It was a beautiful morning in the San Diego area, and Li Hu didn't mind the break from the monotony. He and several others had been assigned to the Southern California city as a sort of Quick Reaction Force for the Ministry's agents if they found themselves in need of firepower. But since their job was to remain within the shadows and avoid drawing undue attention to their activities, Li Hu thought of his posting as a brief respite following his decades in special operations.

"Ping it again," he said.

The man in the passenger seat tapped an icon on the tablet computer resting in his lap. "It's moving."

Li Hu nodded, feeling a slight fluttering of excitement welling from within. After all, he was unaccustomed to a life of peace or of sitting on his hands, waiting for a chance to put his skills to use. So, when Chen had called and told him she needed him to kill a Navy pilot, he felt a tiny sliver of hope that his boredom was nearing an end.

"Where is it?"

"On McCain Boulevard, headed this way."

Li Hu put his foot on the brake and shifted the large SUV into drive. He glanced in the rearview mirror and saw two more of his men sitting in silence as they scanned their sectors through the side windows. He picked up his phone and dialed Chen, listening to the call connect through the earpiece in his ear.

"Yes?"

"We are in position," he said.

"Any sign of him?"

Almost as if the man in the passenger seat had heard the question, he pinged the target's cell phone again. "Nearing the gate," he whispered to Li Hu. "Ten seconds."

"Ten seconds," he told Chen.

He heard the men in the back seat slide the bolts back on their Heckler & Koch MP7 submachine guns, verifying their condition, before rotating the fire control levers off safe. The man next to him tapped the tablet computer again, then looked up through the windshield as a red Corvette launched through the intersection.

"Is that him?" Li Hu asked.

The man tapped the screen again, then set the tablet down and turned to him. "That's him."

He took his foot off the brake and pivoted it to the gas, smoothly and quickly pulling away from the curb. He turned right on Fourth Avenue, several cars behind the classic muscle car, looking at the back of a feminine head sitting behind the steering wheel. "We're in pursuit," he told Chen through his earpiece. "He's with a woman."

"Who is she?" Chen asked.

Li Hu turned and looked to the man sitting next to him. "Find out who the woman is."

He picked up the tablet computer in response and opened a separate app. Li Hu kept his eyes glued to the matching pair of twin round tail-lights on the back of the Corvette, marveling at the way the woman veered the car in and out of traffic. He spoke into his earpiece. "What are my orders?"

Chen didn't hesitate. "Kill them both."

Pismo Beach, California

Chen ended the call and watched the silver sedan disappear into the Pismo Preserve parking lot. She was tempted to follow but instead made a hasty U-turn and returned underneath the highway overpass.

She wanted to finish this and get out from under the sedan's surveillance, but she would do it on her own terms. She had turned the tables and harried her pursuer into a corner, making him question his resolve in continuing the chase. He would continue, of course, but she had bought herself some breathing room.

She dialed another number and waited for the person on the other end to pick up.

"Hello?"

"It's me," she said. "I can't make it to the primary pickup location."

"Do you have an alternate?"

She turned left on Price Street and accelerated past the Shore Cliff Hotel again, continuing south into Pismo Beach. "Santa Maria," she said.

"They just left there."

Undeterred, she asked, "Well, how soon can they be back?"

There was a pause on the other end as he calculated the change in route. "An hour fifteen. Hour thirty, tops."

"Good. Tell them I'm on my way. I need to take care of something first."

He paused again, as if considering what that something might be. "Are you clean?"

She gritted her teeth, loath to admit that she wasn't, but knew there was no point in keeping it a secret. Mantis already knew. "No, but I will be."

"You know the code."

He ended the call, and she took her foot off the gas, allowing the Jeep to slow as she neared the congested beach town's center. As with most such towns, tourists wandered the sidewalks and clogged the streets with their aimless meandering, unaware of the pursuit that was taking place under their noses. Chen didn't want to set her trap in the heart of Pismo Beach, so she continued south along the divided main thoroughfare, scanning the cross streets for a southbound on-ramp.

There were signs advertising veterinary services and decorative garden art, and even a few quirky ones that proclaimed *all happiness depends on a leisurely breakfast* and that *wine is sunlight held together by water*, but she hadn't seen any showing her where to go. So, she pressed on, stopping at stop signs and yielding to pedestrians, but otherwise driving with the singular focus of escaping Pismo Beach and putting some distance between her and the silver sedan.

By the time the road crossed Pismo Creek, the downtown area had drifted into the distance behind her, and the traffic had become sparse, allowing her to plant her foot on the gas pedal and inch the speedometer needle upward. She didn't know how long her pursuer would remain at Pismo Preserve, but she knew his car was faster and could gain ground quickly. Her only hope was to find a suitable spot. And find it soon. She merged back onto the freeway and raced south while checking her mirrors.

Still no silver sedan.

Where are you, my friend?

In Arroyo Grande, she exited the 101 and headed south on Halcyon Road. In terms of mileage, it wasn't any longer than staying on the highway, but it was forecasted to take another ten minutes to reach Santa Maria—ten minutes that would be well spent if her plan worked. After cresting a slight rise above the expansive agricultural fields, Halcyon Road merged with Highway 1, and Chen removed the pistol tucked next to her seat and slipped it into her waistband at the small of her back.

Ten minutes later, she reached the small town of Guadalupe and found what she was looking for. On the right side of the two-lane road was a dealership with an eclectic assortment of used cars parked in a dirt lot underneath black and yellow streamers lining the property. On the left was a facility she suspected was used to store and distribute fertilizer or some other agricultural commodity. But it wasn't the product that interested her. It was the large warehouse bordering the street.

She pulled the Jeep into the dirt lot and parked it in a space facing the road, then she jumped out, locked it, and quickly crossed the street to duck inside the warehouse. She started a timer on her watch, knowing that at the earliest she needed to be at the Santa Maria airport in forty-five minutes. If the sedan didn't show in twenty, she would send the signal to her ride and proceed to the pickup.

But as it turned out, she didn't have to wait even half that. From the shadows just inside the open garage door, Chen saw the silver sedan that had been following her slow as it neared the used car dealership, confirming her suspicion that her pursuer had somehow tagged her vehicle with a tracking device. As the BMW M5 sport sedan came to a stop, the memory of a car running a red light in Long Beach flashed in her mind.

Could it be?

It was hardly the only silver BMW in Southern California, but it was too much of a coincidence to ignore. She leaned forward, straining to see the driver through the dark tint, but flinched when the driver's door flew open. This time, she needed no help in remembering where she had seen this person. It wasn't often you saw a muscular Black man in a brightly colored Hawaiian shirt.

"Son of a bitch," she said. Then she stepped out into the light.

24

Rick stared with dismay at the Jeep through the windshield. He suspected *TANDY* had made him in Pismo Beach, and ditching the Jeep for a clean set of wheels all but confirmed it. He glanced down at his phone and saw the blue beacon of the GPS tracker pulsing from the used car dealership on his right.

"Well, shit," he said, shifting the BMW into park.

He opened the door and stepped out into the warm California sun, looking across the roof of his car at the metallic blue Jeep resting in a space bordering the street. He walked around the front of his car and approached the lot, stepping over the rusted chain draped between two poles in front of the Wrangler.

The SUV was still warm. Heat radiated from it as he reached his hand into the grill and felt for the tracking device. It was right where he had left it. He pulled it out and slipped it into his pocket just as the front door to the small brick building opened and a thin man with short-cropped dark hair and tanned skin walked out.

"Help you?"

Rick smiled at him, though he didn't feel much like smiling. "Just looking," he said.

The man furrowed his brow when he saw the Jeep, obviously questioning whether it belonged in his inventory. "Those four-door Wranglers are pretty nice," the salesman said, deciding to just go with it.

Anything for a sale, right?

Rick scanned the lot, looking for a clue that another car had been taken. "Sell many?"

"Not really," the man said as he neared the Jeep. "Haven't had one on the lot for some time."

"How long have you had this one?"

He gave Rick a confused look. "To be honest, I'm not even sure this one's in our inventory. But I'm sure I can help you..."

An honest used car salesman after all, Rick thought.

"No, that's all right," he said. "You didn't happen to see who parked it here, did you?"

The salesman's confused look turned into one of suspicion. "Can't say that I did."

Rick gave him a placating smile and nodded. "Well, thanks for your time."

"What did you say your name was?"

He noticed the salesman had remained on the other side of the Jeep and was appraising him with a healthy dose of skepticism. Not that Rick blamed him, but it was interesting to see how quickly he had gone from expecting an easy sale to wondering if Rick was involved in something shady.

"I didn't," Rick said. "Thanks again."

He turned back to his car and stepped over the rusted chain, scanning up and down the street for any sign of his prey. He supposed she could have ditched the Jeep and taken a car from the parking lot next door, but with so many to choose from at the dealership, why would she go to the trouble?

Rick opened the door and slipped into the Napa leather seat. He gave the salesman an uneasy wave through the windshield, then put the car into drive and pulled away from the curb. Consulting his map, he figured he could cut across the Santa Maria Valley and rejoin the 101. He glanced down at the passenger seat to the note he had scrawled.

CAL POLY FACULTY?

There was something there, and he needed to pursue it more.

Rick turned left on West Main Street and waited until he had passed the residential neighborhoods on both sides of him before picking up his phone. He was tempted to call Punky again but figured it would just go straight to voicemail, and he wasn't sure he could handle the frustration. He had decided on calling his supervisor to update him on the surveillance, but he stopped when he saw a message waiting for him in the secure portal.

"What now?" he groaned.

He logged in and waited for the message to download, glancing up at the straight stretch of road in front of him. He saw nothing but commercial fertilizer tenders and other large trucks on both sides of the road cutting between fields of broccoli, cauliflower, and lettuce. A glance in his rearview mirror revealed the distant grill of a Kenworth semitruck, distorted by the heat shimmering from the pavement.

"Yeah, the M5 was a good choice," he said, chastising himself for borrowing the low-slung BMW sport sedan.

He lifted the phone to his face and cursed when he read the message he should have caught earlier.

1. NAVY LT COLT BANCROFT. TOPGUN INSTRUCTOR.

2. ABOARD COD FOR NORTH ISLAND.

Rick exited the portal and dialed Punky's number. "Come on, kid. Pick up!"

To his surprise, she answered his call after one ring, and he heard the Corvette's exhaust rumbling beneath the wind noise. "Uncle Rick!"

"Have you seen the latest?"

She ignored his question like she usually did. "Is everything okay? Did she make you?"

He didn't want to tell her that she *had* made him and that she had ditched the marked vehicle and was in the wind, so he took a page out of her playbook and ignored her questions. "Listen, she knows the pilot's name. He's on his way back from the ship."

She paused, then said, "He's with me."

"With you?"

"Yeah, I'm taking him someplace safe."

"Punky…"

A flash of movement distracted him from completing his thought, and he glanced up into the rearview mirror in time to see the red-and-white Kenworth logo filling his rear window. Instinctively, he stomped his foot on the gas to feed fuel to the twin-turbo V8, but the subtle lag was just enough to delay accessing all six hundred horses, and the semitruck had already reached ramming speed.

In the instant it took his turbochargers to spool up, the Kenworth veered to the left as if to pass, then pulled even with his rear wheels. He recognized the signs of an impending classic PIT, or Pursuit Intervention Technique, but not early enough to stop the truck from darting back into his lane and clipping his tail.

He felt the rear end give out and tried turning into the skid, but it was too late. He lost control.

San Diego, California

Punky held the phone against her ear in horror as she listened to what sounded like a car accident unfolding on the other end. She heard screeching metal, the faint tinkling of glass, and the pained grunts of her partner and father's best friend.

"Uncle Rick!" she screamed.

The call ended, and she quickly hit redial.

"What's going on?" Colt asked from the passenger seat.

She ignored him as she waited for her partner to answer his phone. "Come on, come on…"

"Hey," Colt said again. "Talk to me."

Punky threw the phone down in frustration and downshifted, shoving them both back into their seats as she veered the Corvette onto the off-ramp at Kearney Villa Road. She continued accelerating up the hill, barely tapping the brakes as she slid around the corner, regained traction, and raced toward the Interstate 805 overpass.

"Something bad happened," she said, more to herself than to the Navy pilot sitting next to her.

"What? What happened?"

She followed the road around a bend, but her foot had eased off the gas pedal as she fought to rein in her emotions. She knew Rick had been following *TANDY* on his own, and there was a good chance he had been made. But did that mean he had been targeted by a countersurveillance team and taken out? She came to a complete stop at the intersection with Aero Drive, then turned right.

"You okay?" Colt asked.

She turned to look at him, surprised to see he appeared calm and unfazed by her erratic driving. "That was my uncle...my partner. He called to warn me that they know your name."

This *did* seem to faze him. "*They*? Who are *they*?"

She gave a little shake of her head. "We think it's the Chinese. The Ministry of State Security."

Colt held his hands out in front of him as if trying to stop the Corvette through telepathy. "Whoa, hold on a second. Why do the Chinese know my name? Why do they even care about me?"

Tall palm trees lined the road on their left, and Punky continued driving the muscle car as if she didn't have a care in the world. The truth was, she was using the opportunity to open the aperture on her situational awareness and look for things that didn't belong: idling cars at the curb or down side streets, pedestrians on the phone who gave the red Stingray more than the usual amount of attention, or dark SUVs with tinted windows. Like the one she saw in her rearview mirror following her onto Aero Drive.

"I've been investigating a sailor aboard the *Abraham Lincoln*, code-named *KMART*, who's been in regular communication with who we believe is a foreign intelligence operative."

"*KMART*?" Colt chuckled. "You're joking, right?"

She took her eyes off the rearview mirror and gave him a deadpan look. "I wish I was."

His lilting smile vanished. "Okay. But why *KMART*?"

"In 1985, John Anthony Walker, a former sailor, was arrested for selling secrets to the Soviets. When asked later how he had managed to get his hands on so many classified documents, he replied that 'Kmart has better security than the Navy.' So, now this bastard is *KMART*."

The entrance to Montgomery-Gibbs Executive Airport appeared on their left at the next intersection, but Punky turned right on Sandrock Road, keeping her speed low while staring in her rearview mirror.

"Uh, you turned the wrong way."

"No," she said. "I didn't."

The black Chevrolet Tahoe made the right turn behind her, and alarm bells started going off in her head. Two consecutive turns was hardly concrete proof they were being followed, but given what Rick had just told her, it seemed an unlikely coincidence.

Colt noticed her gaze fixed to the rearview mirror and started to turn, but she stopped him. "Don't. Keep your head forward."

"What's going on?"

She made another right turn onto Glenhaven, slowly increasing her speed through the residential neighborhood. If the Tahoe followed, she would have no choice but to take evasive action and prepare for contact. "Open the glove box. My backup gun should be in there."

"Gun?" He seemed shocked but didn't hesitate and opened the glove box to remove the holstered SIG Sauer P365XL she normally carried when off duty. "You're starting to freak me out here."

She glanced over and saw him remove the pistol from the holster and conduct a press check to verify it was loaded. He appeared competent with firearms, but it still made her nervous having an unproven shooter with an unholstered weapon sitting next to her. "You've fired a gun before, I take it?"

He gave her a look that said, *Are you kidding me?* "I have the exact same gun, though mine has the ROMEOZero Red Dot."

The Tahoe turned the corner behind them. "Shit. Hold on."

This time, she didn't stop Colt from looking over his shoulder. She stomped her foot down on the gas pedal, and the Corvette's engine roared a battle cry as it surged down the residential street, passing parked cars, white picket fences, and delinquent trash cans with shocking speed. Her eyes darted in front of her, looking for threats, and she took her hand off the shifter and tugged on her red hoodie, giving her a clear path to draw her pistol if it came to that.

"Is that the Chinese?" Colt yelled, twisting in his seat to keep sight of the Tahoe while pointing his muzzle at the floorboard.

"I don't know. But I don't want to find out."

That was when the first shot rang out.

25

Colt had been in combat before, but from thirty thousand feet above the battlefield. Hearing bullets snapping through the air around his head and plinking into the Corvette's rear end was a far cry from the type of combat he had experienced. To her credit, the NCIS agent comported herself well and ignored the gunfire as she focused on reaching the next cross street.

"Shit! It's a school," she yelled.

Colt turned and looked through the windshield at a tall chain link fence bordering a tan building with a blue roof. He racked his brain, trying to remember when school let out, but gave up when he saw mobs of children running on the playground. He wasn't sure whether it was normal play or in response to the sounds of gunfire echoing up the street.

"Turn right!"

Without looking for crossing traffic, she cranked the steering wheel and skidded around the corner. Colt twisted his body and brought the pistol up, aiming it at the intersection as he waited for a shot. The Tahoe came into view just as the Stingray regained its traction and surged north on Afton, knocking his aim off. He took his finger off the trigger.

"No shot," he yelled, then reached behind him and unbuckled his seat belt so he could plant his right knee in the seat and brace himself with his outstretched left foot on the floorboard. "Keep it steady!"

"I'm trying to get us outta here!"

The Tahoe wasn't as nimble or as quick as the Corvette, but the driver was doing a remarkable job keeping pace with them. He didn't see how she was going to build enough separation so they could bug out and make it to his plane. Colt craned his neck over his shoulder and saw the looming traffic light glowing yellow.

"Go straight," he said.

"It's turning red!"

"Run it!" He felt her press harder on the gas pedal and listened to the engine straining as they closed to within one hundred yards of the intersection. The light turned red, and he shifted his body to sit in the seat, scrambling to buckle in as he urged her on. "Faster! Faster!"

Less than fifty yards from the stoplight, traffic began moving on the cross street, and he leaned into his seat belt as he looked for a gap they could dart through. If they made it to the other side, the Tahoe might be stuck behind a wall of traffic, giving them the opportunity they needed. He looked for a side-view mirror to see if their boldness was paying off, but the Corvette didn't have one on his side.

"They're falling back!" she yelled in triumph, as if reading his mind. He felt her ease off the gas.

"Don't slow down!"

Twenty yards from the intersection, he felt another surge of acceleration as her foot dropped to the floor. His head whipped left and right, using his experience in judging closure to assess the crossing traffic.

"It's going to be close!" he yelled.

They reached the intersection just as a white pickup truck crossed in front of them from left to right. They cleared its rear bumper by inches, and Colt thought he could almost reach out and touch it as they blazed across the eastbound lanes. When the truck cleared from his field of view, he looked up in time to see two midsize SUVs occupying both westbound lanes barreling down on them.

"Faster!"

There was nothing he could do but brace himself, but she seemed to coax just a little more power from the Corvette, and they reached the other side with less than a foot of clearance from the second SUV. His heart pounded in his chest, but he again craned his neck to look over his shoulder at the Tahoe, relieved to see it only nosing into the intersection.

"Holy shit!" she yelled, relaxing the throttle only a little.

"Right here," Colt said, slinking back into his seat and closing his eyes with relief.

She made the turn, still faster than normal, but he could feel the Stingray slowing back to a comfortable speed. They had bought seconds at most, but they at least had options. They could run. They could hide. Or they could fight.

His eyes snapped open when she slammed on the brakes, horrified to see a car darting out from a parking garage in front of them. The overheated brakes locked up and the radial tires skidded across the ground, but still she tried turning to avoid the collision, and he felt the back end let loose.

Colt barely had time to brace himself before the Corvette slammed sideways into the Japanese import. His shoulder hit the door hard, and his head snapped to the side, connecting with something solid. The sound of squealing tires and roaring engine was replaced with splintering fiberglass and an anguished cry from the woman sitting next to him.

Like he had been trained to do during water survival, he waited until all motion had stopped before trying to move. The earsplitting clatter ended in an instant, and he tried making sense of the sudden silence. He shook his head, feeling woozy, and tried blinking away the stars twinkling at the edge of his vision. He looked to his right and saw a shattered window with deflated air bag curtains, and he had enough presence of mind to recognize they weren't his.

"You okay?" he asked.

Silence.

He looked left and saw the NCIS agent hunched over with the right side of her face pressed against the steering wheel. Ignoring his own aches and pains, he reached out and shook her. "Hey! Wake up!"

Colt's skull throbbed and his ears rang, but his only thought was on the unconscious woman sitting next to him.

At least until he saw the Tahoe turn the corner.

Colt shook her hard, ignoring the prevailing wisdom not to move a car crash victim. There was a good chance she had suffered at least a concussion—hell, he was pretty sure he had one himself—but if she didn't come to soon, the car full of angry Chinese barreling down on them would be the bigger worry.

"You need to wake up!" he yelled.

He felt her stir but couldn't take his eyes off the Tahoe. It had stopped in the road, twenty yards short of the mangled Corvette, as its occupants assessed the situation. He remained hunched over, his face hidden behind her long, dark hair, trying his best to appear as motionless as possible. Though he didn't think they would simply drive off if he played dead, he needed the time to think.

"Unh..." The NCIS agent started to move, and he kept his hand pressed against her back to keep her still.

"Shhh. Don't move."

"Wha...happen?" Her words were slurred, her voice weak, but Colt knew it wouldn't last long.

The Tahoe's rear doors opened, and two men stepped out onto the street, looking around to check for witnesses. Colt felt an ice-cold fear grip his insides when he saw that the men each cradled a submachine gun. They were too far away for him to make out what kind, but it didn't really matter.

Rubbing his hand lightly on her back, he kept repeating the hushed plea of "Shhh...don't move," while searching frantically around his lap for the pistol he had been holding before they wrecked. Out of the corner of his eye, he saw the man to his left—the one who had exited from the Tahoe's passenger side—spin toward what used to be the Corvette's trunk and raise his gun.

Colt pinched his eyes shut, fearing that the time had finally come.

Then he heard a woman's weak voice call out from behind him. "Please, help me..."

"You sit down," the man said. "Help is on the way."

"Ma...gun," the agent muttered.

He hushed her again, but then thought he understood. He slowly brought his right hand around his waist and reached across the center console to feel for the service pistol she had holstered on her right hip. His fingers probed the Kydex holster, looking for some form of retention, a lever or button that needed to be actuated, but it appeared to be held in place by friction.

"Help me," the woman said, her voice having drifted further to Colt's left and closer to the man pointing a gun at her.

Colt wrapped his fingers around the pistol grip and braced himself, looking through squinted eyes at the two gunmen as they chattered back and forth in what he assumed was Mandarin. The words sounded harsh and clipped, but the tone was universal. The man on the right was losing patience with the woman and wanted his partner to end it.

"Now," the agent whispered.

Colt didn't hesitate. He drew the pistol and brought it up over the top of the agent's back, leaning away from her as he brought the muzzle to bear on his first target. His hand trembled and his vision wavered, but he focused on the front sight post and pulled the trigger the instant it settled on the man's torso.

Crack!

The man staggered, and Colt squeezed the trigger a second time before shifting his aim to the other gunman, who was already raising his submachine gun.

Crack! Crack!

Colt rushed both shots, only clipping the man in the upper arm and spinning him enough to throw off his aim. The return gunfire also went wide, shattering the Corvette's windshield and plinking into the wrecked import sedan. Colt shook his head to clear his vision, readjusted his aim, and fired again.

Crack! Crack! Crack!

The man dropped hard to the pavement, the air behind him a cloud of pink mist, but Colt had been taught to keep shooting until the threat had been eliminated. He glanced over to the first man, saw him writhing in agony, and made the split-second decision to engage the Tahoe.

He couldn't see its occupants but knew both gunmen had exited the rear seats. There was one, maybe two more men inside, and he still had over half a magazine left. He approximated head height on the driver's side and settled his front sight post there before squeezing the trigger.

Crack! Crack!

The Tahoe's windshield spiderwebbed and its rear tires squealed as the driver frantically reversed to escape the gunfire. Colt immediately recognized it as a tactical mistake and shifted aim to the passenger side and continued firing at the fleeing SUV.

Crack! Crack! CLICK.

The Tahoe careened around the corner in reverse, but Colt had heard the loudest sound in a gunfight, and his blood ran cold. Acting on instinct, he thumbed the magazine release and felt the empty magazine fall away and clatter to the Corvette's floorboards. He reached around the agent's waist and probed along her left hip, relieved to find two spare magazines. He removed one and quickly indexed it to the magazine well while keeping his eyes on the street. When it snapped into place, he sent the slide forward and chambered another round.

Back in the fight, he thought.

The agent pushed against his hand. "We need to move," she said.

———

Li Hu clutched at the bullet wound high on his left shoulder, releasing it only long enough to crank the steering wheel over and reverse the SUV out of the kill zone. It had been a mistake to assume the target was unconscious after coming upon the accident, but his price would only be a nasty scar. His men would never know the price they'd paid.

"Find me a way out!" he yelled, looking over his shoulder as he angled the Tahoe to the curb so he could put it in drive and escape before the police showed up. "Huang Bo! Find me a route!"

When the technician refused to answer, he spun to see half of his technician's face caved in, the casualty of a lucky shot. He shook away his anger and put the Tahoe in drive, wincing with pain as he pulled out into traffic and fled the scene. Li Hu could barely see through the windshield and would need to ditch the vehicle, but his priority was getting as far away as possible.

"Dammit!" he yelled, slamming his fist against the steering wheel. How had a Navy pilot and a woman in a vintage sports car taken out three of his men? Three of his highly trained commandos? He replayed the scene in his mind, watching the pilot wield the pistol with calm precision, prioritizing his targets and shifting between them with ease. What was Chen not telling him?

He released his grip on the bullet wound and felt the blood oozing down his chest. He was light-headed and ran his tongue along the inside of his dry mouth, but he couldn't allow himself to be captured. He reached for his phone with trembling blood-soaked fingers and placed an encrypted call to the duty officer at the safe house they used for an operations center.

"Authenticate," the voice intoned.

"Mandate of Heaven," Li Hu replied through gritted teeth.

"Go ahead."

"I've got three dead, two on the scene, and I'm wounded."

"Are they clean?"

His nostrils flared in exasperation. He was on the verge of passing out and trying to let his people know that two of their compatriots had paid the ultimate price and he needed medical attention, and all they wanted to know was whether or not they were clean?

"*Of course!*" Li Hu snapped. "I need help."

"Torch the vehicle and find alternate means of transportation. Proceed to Site Bravo."

The call ended, and he moaned as a fresh wave of pain crested over him. His vision swam and closed in on the hazy street in front of him, but he strained against it and forced himself to stay awake long enough to do what needed to be done. He scrolled to another phone number and tapped on it, wanting to let Chen know that her faulty intelligence had cost him three good men.

But he never got the chance. The last thing he saw before losing his fight to stay awake was a telephone pole rushing toward him.

26

Santa Maria Valley, California

The PIT maneuver had worked better than even Chen expected. The BMW's rear tires had lost all traction and spun the sports sedan into oncoming traffic, where another commercial fertilizer tender slammed into its passenger side, despite the driver locking up his brakes to try and stop. The silver M5 flipped up into the air and crashed down on its roof, skidding across the road in a shower of sparks.

Chen pulled off to the side of the road and dropped down from the cab.

"Call 9-1-1!" the other trucker yelled to her, as he too jumped from his cab and ran to the mangled car.

Chen ignored him and continued running. "Is he okay?"

The truck driver dropped to his knees and leaned his head in through the shattered driver's window, reaching in to check for a pulse or unbuckle the seat belt. She glanced over both shoulders, then reached around to the small of her back and removed the pistol she had hidden there. Holding it out at arm's length, she walked up behind the Good Samaritan, who probably thought he had been to blame for the accident.

"Is he okay?" she asked again.

The man pulled his head from the wreckage and turned to look at her.
Crack!

She squeezed the trigger and shot him in the face. He collapsed like a
marionette with its strings cut, falling to the side in a grotesque lounging
position, but she ignored him and shifted her aim to the man in the car. His
head was tilted to the side, pressed against the caved-in roof, but he was
alert and staring at her in wide-eyed fear.

"Who...are you?" he asked.

Chen grinned, then used the toe of her shoe to shove the dead trucker
out of the way and kneel so she could see the man in the car more clearly.
She glanced at her watch and saw that she still had plenty of time to make
it to the Santa Maria airport before her ride showed up. Normally, she
would have just shot the man and moved on, but he had embarrassed her
in a way nobody ever had. She would still kill him, but not before having a
little fun first.

"I am a ghost," she said. "You will never know my name, but the world
will know what I've done."

He coughed, and blood sprayed across the sedan's wrecked interior.
"What...will you...do?"

Chen could tell the man was in pain. He probably wanted her to put
him out of his misery. She would, but she didn't mind satisfying his curiosity. At least a little while longer. So, she nodded and said, "You answer my
questions first, then I'll answer yours. Who do you work for?"

He coughed again, and his body sagged under its own weight. "FBI."

She had suspected as much, though it bothered her that the FBI even
knew she existed. "How'd you find me?"

He groaned. "My turn."

Chen had to admire the man's grit. He was in pain and had no way out
of his predicament, but he still wanted to make her work for her information. That he would never get the chance to do anything with what she told
him hadn't even factored into her decision to give him this one small
concession. Warrior to warrior, she would honor the terms of their bargain.
She nodded for him to continue.

"What...will you...do?"

"Sink your aircraft carrier."

"Why?"

She waggled the gun in front of his face, reminding him of their arrangement. "Who else knows about me?"

His mouth clamped shut, and she saw a spark in his eye that told her he had no intention of answering the question.

"If you won't answer," she said, pausing to look over both shoulders, "I'm afraid my time is up. Which means your time is up."

"Punky," he said through gritted teeth.

"Who's Punky?"

This time, the FBI agent didn't try reminding her of their quid pro quo. "The person who's...going to stop you."

Chen rocked back on her heels and shot the pistol out like a viper, striking him in the face with it. He grunted but made no move to try to stop her. She wanted to keep hitting him in the face until she had smashed every bone, then keep hitting until his face caved in. But she had tired of playing with him, and this *Punky* was going to learn the hard way.

Crack!

The bullet entered his right eye, and his body fell still. "Goodbye, Mr. FBI agent man."

Chen stood in the vacant road and looked in both directions, then she scanned the fields of broccoli on either side. She couldn't even hear the faint sound of sirens but knew it was time to leave. She slipped the pistol back into her waistband and jogged back to the Kenworth truck she had borrowed. It was a short drive back to Guadalupe to return it and reclaim her Jeep, then a quick sprint to the Santa Maria airport.

And there wasn't a damn thing Punky could do to stop her.

San Diego, California

Colt had wiped away some of the blood from her forehead, then helped her out of the Corvette and set her on the ground, leaning against the front wheel. Seeing that she was alert, he went to check on the woman who had been driving the Japanese import and returned a few minutes later, asking to borrow Punky's phone to call for help. She was already starting to feel more alert but knew the worst of her aches and pains wouldn't set in for another day or two. She removed her phone from her pocket and started to hand it to him when it vibrated with an incoming call.

"Who's Uncle Rick?" Colt asked, seeing the name appear on the caller ID.

She ignored the question, answered the call, and brought the phone to her ear. "Uncle Rick? Are you okay?" She heard noises on the other end like something was rubbing against the phone's microphone, but she couldn't make out anything recognizable. "Uncle Rick?"

Colt knelt in front of her. "Put it on speaker," he said.

She did, and they heard the unmistakable sound of a gunshot. "*Uncle Rick!*"

Then she heard his voice, though weak and woozy, come through clearly. "Who...are you?"

She leaned in closer to the phone, straining to hear the other voice speaking with an elegant feminine crispness. Colt leaned closer as well, understanding that they were eavesdropping on a conversation her Uncle Rick wanted her to hear. She saw him react when they heard the words *aircraft carrier*, but otherwise, he remained silent.

"Punky," Rick's strained voice said, and her heart skipped a beat.

"Who's Punky?" the woman asked.

"The person who's...going to stop you."

She let out a sob and felt Colt wrap his arm around her head, pulling her close to his chest. It was almost as if he knew what she would hear next, but even muffled, the sound of the gunshot made her flinch. He took the phone from her hand and held her there, but all she could think of was finding the woman who had killed the last person she cared about.

Guadalupe, California

Chen walked out of the brick building and closed the door behind her. After delivering the borrowed and slightly damaged fertilizer tender back to the warehouse across the street, she returned to the used car dealership to reclaim her Jeep. The salesman had been more than happy to speak with her in his air-conditioned office, but his eagerness quickly faded.

She watched the security footage before erasing it, confirming that the FBI agent had stopped to recover a tracker he had used to follow her from Long Beach to San Luis Obispo, and ultimately to his demise. With the tracker now on a farm road inside the wrecked BMW, she could continue to the Santa Maria airport without fear of being followed.

She walked across the dirt lot and unlocked her Jeep before climbing inside. The salesman had been another casualty in a growing list of bodies she was leaving scattered across Southern California, but it was another loose end tidied up. All that mattered was completing the mission and proving her worth to Mantis. She started the Jeep and removed her phone to open a dating app she never used for its intended purpose.

She entered a specific set of unlikely search parameters and began swiping through potential suitors, spending more time on each profile's "About Me" section than she suspected most of the app's users spent. She knew the one she was looking for. Without the key phrase embedded innocuously in the profile, she would swipe left and continue her search.

Then she saw it.

"...my other half..."

She swiped right and made a match. It wasn't the phrase itself but the first letters of the three words that mattered. Other Ministry operatives used varied and clever phrases containing the same sequence of letters to spoof the application's algorithms, but always a three-word phrase beginning with M-O-H.

...my own home...

...making our history...

...made over here...

They all referred to one thing: Mandate of Heaven.

The ancient Chinese philosophy justifying an emperor's rule was first used to support the Zhou dynasty and legitimize the overthrow of the Shang dynasty. But the Ministry used the Mandate of Heaven to empower its operatives abroad, and they used it to establish an unorthodox means of seeking assistance without the excessive impediments of going through official channels.

A red bubble appeared over the app's internal messaging platform. She tapped on the icon and read the message.

ARE YOU CLEAN?

She thought about the dead FBI agent in a wrecked BMW, the tracker he had planted now removed from the Jeep, the erased surveillance footage from the dealership, and the salesman who hadn't lived long enough to tell anybody about the Chinese woman interested in a four-door Wrangler.

YES, she replied.

ETA?

She consulted the map on her phone before replying. *20 MINUTES.*

CENTRAL COAST JET CENTER. 30 MINUTES.

Chen backed out of the parking space, then pulled out of the lot and headed south on Highway 1. She could have cut across the valley on West Main Street and approached the airport from the north, but that would have taken her by the scene of the accident. Instead, she followed the highway as it wended along the southern edge of the valley and exited in Santa Maria.

From the highway, it was a five-minute drive north on Blosser Road to the airport. Central Coast Jet Center, the fixed-base operator that provided fuel and basic maintenance services, was located at the south end of the airport between the two intersecting runways. She parked the Jeep in a long-term lot outside the fence line, then walked to a gate located next to RLC, an offshore helicopter transportation company servicing the oil platforms Harvest, Hermosa, Hidalgo, and Irene in the Santa Maria basin off the coast of Point Arguello.

Walking through the gate, the fence line guided her to a side entrance into one of the two buildings. She entered a four-digit access code into the keypad next to the door and waited for the light to turn green before opening the door and walking into the unlit helicopter base.

Standing in the darkness, she listened for a sign that she wasn't alone, then crept through the building for the exit onto the flight line. In the distance, she heard the reverberating echo of a helicopter approaching the airport. She approached the window next to the door and peered through the blinds as a blue and white Sikorsky S-76 lowered its landing gear and approached the landing pad.

Chen smiled as she watched her ride touch down, then opened the door and stepped out into the sunlight.

27

Scorpion Anchorage
Santa Cruz Island, California

Wu Tian paused from his chore to wave at the passing sixty-five-foot catamaran carrying passengers to the pier at Scorpion Ranch. A few waved back, but most were preoccupied looking up at cliffs bearing down on them. He waited until they had moved past, then went back to packing the equipment he had removed from the container into the watertight dry sack. The gentle swell made it more difficult, but as a career sailor, he felt as sturdy atop the Tillotson Pearson forty-four-foot sloop as he did on the *Yonggan De*.

His phone chirped, and he scrambled in bare feet across the sailboat's open cockpit to read the message.

45 MINUTES.

He cursed silently to himself, tucked the phone in his pocket, and resumed packing. Most of his equipment was already aboard the inflatable dinghy, and he could be off the boat and motoring to shore in ten minutes, but he would be cutting it close to reach the ranch in time. And Chen was not one to be kept waiting.

After lowering the last dry sack into the dinghy, he clambered forward to check on his anchor rode, ensuring he had calculated the scope correctly. Even without other boats in the relatively shallow anchorage, it wouldn't do to have his anchor drag. Confident it would hold, even in the unpredictable winds, he moved aft and dropped down into the saloon to tidy everything up before departing.

At last, Wu Tian climbed back outside before closing and locking the hatch. He was about as remote as he could be, even though he was only fifty miles from the second most populous city in the United States with almost four million people, but he didn't want to take any chances. With the boat secure, he climbed over the braided stainless steel safety lines and lowered himself into the dinghy.

Once he had untied the line that kept him connected to the sailboat, he sat down on the inflated side wall and cranked the outboard motor, listening to it cough quietly as he coaxed it awake. He reached up for the shift lever and moved it into the forward position, then twisted the tiller grip to propel the eight-foot tender away from the boat. With one more glance at the sloop, Wu Tian focused on the island and motored for the south end of the beach.

As isolated as it was, Santa Cruz Island was a popular destination for outdoor enthusiasts. Each day, the Island Packers catamaran carried hikers and campers to the island maintained by the National Park Service, but at over sixty thousand acres, it wouldn't be difficult to find the privacy he needed.

Nearing the beach, Wu Tian saw the gentle waves lapping at the rocky shore. There were a few hazards he needed to navigate his way around, but within minutes he felt and heard the sand and water-worn pebbles scraping the underside of his inflatable floor. He quickly pressed the engine cutoff switch and lifted the outboard clear of the water, letting his momentum carry him aground.

Before coming to a complete stop, he swung his legs over the side and dropped down into the ankle-deep water. It was bitter cold but refreshing after sitting under the baking sun all morning. The sand was soft under his bare feet, and he moved confidently toward shore, stepping on the occasional smooth stone while tugging the boat higher up onto the beach. Clear of the water, Wu Tian tied the boat off to a sturdy rock, then made quick work of removing the dry sacks from the boat.

He glanced at his watch.

Ten minutes.

It might have been his ears playing tricks on him, but he thought he could already hear the distant thumping of helicopter rotors approaching the island. Putting that thought aside, he dried his feet and reached into the first dry sack for his socks and Asolo hiking boots, which he quickly laced up. Then he hefted the two dry sacks into a farmer's carry and walked up the beach that would be teeming with recreational kayakers later in the day.

The beach opened up into a valley that stretched between grass and coastal sage scrub-covered hills on both sides. He found the dirt trail leading to Scorpion Ranch and lowered his head against the strain in his shoulders and walked steadily onward, ignoring the laughing and excited chittering from the visitors emptying the catamaran at the pier behind him.

There were few trees on that part of the island, but as he neared the Scorpion Ranch House, an oak woodland with varying species provided a wide canopy of shade from the midday sun. Passing the house made with island rocks held together by a lime-and-cement mortar, the trail opened into a wide gravel path where he heard the unmistakable echoing of an approaching helicopter's rotors off the hills to his left. He grimaced and increased his pace.

At the far end of the settlement, he came to an intersection with trails stretching in each cardinal direction. He meandered off the trail and set the dry sacks down in the shade of a coastal pine. Squatting next to the sacks, he faced north and waited to see the woman he had traveled to the island to meet.

His phone chirped, and he removed it from his back pocket to read the message.

ARRIVED.

He tapped out a reply and hit send. *AT THE RALLY POINT.*

There was still much work to be done before nightfall, but he enjoyed the moment of rest while he waited for Chen to make her way from the helicopter landing site a little over a quarter mile away.

Chen ducked as she stepped from the rear of the Sikorsky S-76 helicopter, carrying only a duffel bag full of supplies. Ten thousand dollars in cash had bought her the chartered helicopter for a ride to the island and was lucrative enough that the Louisiana-based company didn't mind removing it from its regular schedule of ferrying personnel and equipment to Freeport-McMoRan oil rigs.

She passed a bright orange windsock at the edge of the grass helipad, then turned to watch the blue-and-white helicopter lift and turn back to the mainland. It had been a one-way ride, and the text she had just received from Wu Tian confirmed he was in place and that the sailboat was waiting for them to make their escape once the operation was complete.

The helipad sat atop a butte on the northeast corner of the island between Cavern Point and Scorpion Ranch. She slung the duffel over her shoulder and started down the dirt trail, descending the side of the hill toward a modern settlement of tan-colored prefabricated houses. Passing the National Park Service enclave, she continued south on the gravel road and spotted Wu Tian squatting patiently in the shade.

He stood when she approached and slipped a dry sack onto his back, then lifted the other off the ground and handed it to her. "Everything's here," he said.

Chen grasped the shoulder straps and swung the dry sack onto her back, cinching them down to distribute the weight evenly. "Did you have any difficulties transferring the equipment from the container?"

"None."

She looked toward Scorpion Ranch and saw several tourists milling about in brightly colored outdoor recreation clothing. "Think they will give us any trouble?"

Wu Tian followed her gaze, then shook his head. "I take it you brought the supplies we need if they do?"

She patted the duffel bag, feeling the soft cases inside containing the Heckler & Koch MP7 submachine guns and enough ammunition to deter a squad-sized enemy force. "Hopefully we won't need them," she said.

"Agreed," he said, before glancing at his watch. "Let's get moving."

He didn't wait for her assent and turned to begin their trek. She was content letting the former *Jiaolong* commando lead the way, and she settled into a relaxed pace several yards behind him. The trail split when they passed a windmill that appeared functional high up on a wooden tower.

"What do you suppose that's for?" she asked.

He glanced at the windmill and shrugged.

Without consulting a map, Wu Tian took the right fork and followed the trail up the side of the hill. It wasn't a steep climb, but it offered a nice view of Scorpion Ranch to their left. After cresting a small rise, the trail angled south, and the anchorage came into view where she saw the naked mast of a sailboat resting offshore. "Is that her?"

He nodded. "The dinghy is at the south end of the beach."

When they reached the top of the hill, Wu Tian took a trail that cut back to the west. There were no trees offering protection from the sun, and the wind hammered at them as they cut back toward the interior of the island. After walking another half mile, the double-track trail again turned south, and she found herself enjoying the hike despite her almost overpowering exhaustion.

They reached another trail intersection, and he stopped. She would never have admitted it to him, but she was thankful he had decided to take a small break. He lowered his dry sack to the dirt and squatted over it, unrolling the top to remove two Nalgene water bottles. He handed one to her, and she eagerly accepted it, uncapping it and bringing it to her mouth to gulp down the lukewarm water.

"Only a little farther," he said.

She nodded, knowing the comment had been intended for her benefit. Wu Tian was a veteran of the *Jiaolong*, the naval commandos of the People's Liberation Army Navy, whose members were renowned for their toughness. Men like Wu Tian had survived a training pipeline with an eighty-eight percent attrition rate to become "Sea Dragons," the most lethal commandos in the world. A leisurely stroll through the rolling hills of Santa Cruz Island wouldn't even come close to arduous.

He took another sip of water, then capped his bottle and slipped it back inside his dry sack. She handed hers back, and it also disappeared inside. For this mission, they had dressed like every other recreational hiker enjoying the Channel Islands and wore Arc'teryx or Outdoor Research shorts over Asolo hiking boots and brightly colored fleeces and soft-shell jackets that had been removed as the sun bore down on them. She caught Wu Tian casually glancing at her revealing tank top, but otherwise he appeared totally focused.

Their dry sacks weren't filled with the usual equipment and supplies one might expect of backpackers visiting the island. No tents, sleeping bags, or sleeping pads. They carried enough water to last them twenty-four hours, but the other items they carried wouldn't be found on any other hiker.

"Shall we?"

Wu Tian rolled up the top of the dry sack and stood. He shifted the weight of the pack on his shoulders, then turned to take the lead of their two-person column again. He set out at a brisk pace, and she followed, letting her thoughts drift to the upcoming mission. Months of planning had gone into getting them to this moment, and if not for the failed waveform on the previous night's mission, success would have been all but certain.

The trail grew more difficult as Wu Tian led them up a rocky slope through scrub oak, climbing higher up onto Montañon Ridge and traversing toward the southern shore of the island. They hiked for another hour in silence before coming upon a clearing at the summit, eighteen hundred feet above sea level.

She paused and scanned the open space, noting the small concrete utility building and solar panels that ostensibly powered the tall radio antenna stretching into the sky. Then, she looked east beyond Anacapa Island at Naval Air Station Point Mugu, twenty-five miles distant across the dark blue waters of the Pacific Ocean.

Wu Tian stopped and followed her gaze, then turned to her. "We need to set up our hide site."

She nodded but felt a tinge of excitement and let a tight smile crack her stern facade as one thought repeated itself in her mind.

Destiny.

28

Continuing onward, Wu Tian led them down a small finger from the summit that gave them a commanding view of the ocean. Smuggler's Cove was in the distance below and to their left, and Sandstone Point was to their right, but they had no intention of going to either.

There was no trail descending south from Montañon Ridge, but Wu Tian forged his own path down the rugged terrain. Halfway down the steep slope, he found a narrow ledge that was protected on one side by a large boulder jutting up from the ground. Scrub brush dotted the landscape in every direction, but otherwise they had no protection from the elements.

"This will do," he said.

Chen nodded her agreement, then immediately went to work. She dropped her pack to the ground and stripped out of her brightly colored recreational hiking clothing, ignoring Wu Tian's sidelong glances as she crammed the garments into a separate stuff sack before tucking them away in her pack. Then she put on the specially made clothing Wu Tian had brought with him, a camouflage jacket and pants of a polyester-weave woven fabric coated with near-infrared absorbent dye. They blended in with the natural landscape, but the added dye masked them from modern night vision goggles. Something that didn't matter now but might when the sun set.

To help reduce their thermal signatures, silver-plated filaments had been inserted every centimeter into the fabric in weft and warp, but their clothing alone wasn't enough to keep them from being spotted. Once their brightly colored clothing had been replaced with the state-of-the-art camouflage, Wu Tian covered their entire hide site with camouflage netting to break up their outlines.

Hidden from view, Chen opened the duffel she had brought with her and handed a padded pouch to Wu Tian. He quickly unzipped it and assembled the broken-down submachine gun, then set it aside so he could focus on the most important tasks required for the operation. First, he removed the disassembled pieces from each dry sack and placed them deliberately around the hide site. While Chen went to work connecting them to make the weapon operational, he put together the satellite receiver required to download the software update once it had been completed.

"How long until it's ready?" he asked.

She looked up from the tablet she was working on. "It's ready now."

She glanced at the satellite receiver to see if any lights had illuminated. None had, but she knew that would soon change. Once the software update had been transmitted to the satellite in geosynchronous Earth orbit—over thirty-five thousand kilometers above them—it would immediately broadcast to their receiver and allow them to fine-tune the weapon's waveform. Only then could they commence the operation.

"Now we wait?" he asked.

"Now we wait," Chen replied.

She leaned back against the steep slope and closed her eyes, feeling the weight of her fatigue settle on top of her.

"Somebody's coming," a voice hissed in her ear.

Her eyes shot open, and she looked through the camouflage netting at the canyon wending up from Smuggler's Cove. Through the shimmering heat rising from the barren ground, she saw two heads bobbing in unison as the hikers ascended the steep slope. The one in the lead had shoulder-length dark hair wrapped in a red bandanna, and the other was blond, styled in pigtails.

"Two women," she whispered. "Let them pass."

Though her fatigue had dissipated, she knew the pair would pass their location soon and present no threat. Their position was well concealed and high above them, so there was little reason for the women to even look in their direction. But even if they did, it was unlikely the women would spot them.

Wu Tian prepared himself regardless. He lifted his H&K MP7 submachine gun and pointed the stubby suppressor through the netting at the hikers, tracing their winding movement through the canyon.

"I've got the one on the right," he said, sighting in on the blonde in pigtails.

"Steady," she cautioned, watching his short barrel drift slowly from right to left as he tracked his target. The women would never even know a trained commando had already calculated the lead, factoring in the swirling wind and drop of the heavy 4.6 x 30mm round. They were only a breath away from being killed and had no idea.

With relaxed curiosity, she watched Wu Tian following the hikers' movements and listened to the faint echo of their distant chattering when she heard a soft whir from over her left shoulder. Turning her head slowly, she saw a red light flicker on as the satellite transceiver began downloading the promised software patch.

Wu Tian ignored the sounds of the electronic equipment behind him, focused instead on keeping his weapon trained on the unsuspecting hikers less than one hundred yards down the slope. He shifted his body weight slightly, disturbing a small stone that tumbled a few feet before catching on the netting.

"Easy," she warned, holding her breath while watching the bobbing heads for any sign they had picked up the faint noise. But their chattering continued unabated, and their steady gait appeared unfazed. The wind lower in the canyon must have drowned out whatever sound the falling rock had caused.

"How much longer for the download?" Wu Tian asked.

She reached for the portable tablet computer and tapped on several icons before accessing the information she needed. "It's almost complete."

Wu Tian took his eyes off his target to glance over his shoulder at her, and the stone that had caught in the netting slipped underneath the loose material and tumbled down the hill, picking up speed at an alarming rate and bouncing off larger rocks with a clatter.

"Shit," he muttered, shifting targets to sight in on the brunette, whose head whipped in their direction.

"She heard that," Chen said, discarding the tablet for her MP7.

They held their breaths, listening to the fading echo of the falling rocks as they waited to see if the women would spook and bolt back down the canyon or just attribute the falling rocks as an expected part of nature.

Keep walking, she silently urged.

Then the blonde pointed directly at them and shielded her eyes against the sun, squinting through the glare to make out whatever had caught her attention.

"Take them," Chen ordered before uttering a quiet curse.

Wu Tian's MP7 submachine gun spat two rounds in quick succession, hitting the brunette high on her forehead, ripping the bandanna off as her head snapped back and showered the canyon in crimson. His second shot missed high. He pivoted slightly and fired two rounds at the blonde that missed completely. The last thing they saw was the frenzied whipping of blond pigtails as she looked at her fallen companion and ducked out of sight.

Chen rushed at Wu Tian and shoved him forward. "Get her!"

He ripped the camouflage netting up and tossed it over his head, exposing them to the deep blue sky above. Then, without another word, he hurled himself down the hill, sliding and leaping as he gave chase to the blonde.

"Don't let her get away!" Chen shouted.

29

Montgomery Field
San Diego, California

Colt dropped the parachute bag containing his flight gear on the ground near the double glass doors leading out onto the flight line. He had almost forgotten it inside the Corvette's trunk, but a flash of olive drab canvas through the splintered fiberglass reminded him that he had signed a sheet of paper taking responsibility for the almost half-million-dollar helmet. It seemed such a trivial thing, given the circumstances, but he was in enough hot water already.

"What's in there?" Punky asked, holding a rag against the gash she'd sustained on her forehead when it slammed into the unforgiving steering wheel.

Colt ignored the question and gave her a serious look. "I think it's time you told me what *the hell* is going on."

She glanced at the college co-eds working behind the desk, then back to Colt. "Can we go somewhere more private?"

He was getting tired of being jerked around but knew of no place more private than in the cockpit of his plane. He nodded at the receptionists and heard a *click* as the doors were unlocked. Retrieving the parachute bag once more, he turned and walked out onto the ramp with Punky hot on his heels.

"Where are we going?"

"Point Mugu," he said.

She pulled even with him and shook her head. "No, we're not. We need to go find my partner."

He stopped walking and turned to face her. The pain was still evident on her face, but she masked it behind a professional determination he recognized in almost every warrior he'd served alongside.

"Look," he said. "There's nothing we can do for him. You heard it same as me." She opened her mouth to argue, but he placed a gentle hand on her shoulder. "If you really want to do right by him, then help me figure out what is going on so we can stop more people from dying."

Her resolve seemed to harden as she considered his words. Finally, she said, "What do you think I've been doing? Rick was following a foreign intelligence operative code-named *TANDY*..." She trailed off, and her eyes glassed over.

"Is that who we heard on the phone?"

"I don't know," she said, struggling to fight back tears. "But who else could it be?"

Without realizing it, he reached up and felt for the thumb drive in his flight suit breast pocket. He wasn't sure how *KMART* and *TANDY* fit into what had happened to him the night before, but finding out what was wrong with the F-35 was his priority. He shook his head. "I'm sorry, but I need to go to Point Mugu."

He could tell she was losing her patience. She took a deep breath and looked around before speaking. "Okay, here's the deal. And this is classified."

He nodded.

"The NSA has been intercepting communications between our two subjects for several months. Last night, *KMART* sent a message to his handler stating the 'target aircraft survived' and that the 'operation failed.'"

"What operation?"

The words *aircraft carrier* flashed in his mind.

"We don't know," she replied, glancing away to watch a twin-engine

Cessna taxi to the runway. "But it gets worse. Last night, *KMART* told his handler that you had downloaded information that could compromise him—"

"What makes you think it's me?"

"This morning, he used your *name*."

He knew she had said the Chinese knew who he was, but it just didn't make sense. Sure, he was a TOPGUN instructor and helped develop tactics for the fleet, but... "Wait, are you saying those men were targeting me because of information they think I have?"

She pulled the rag away from her head and locked eyes with him. "What did you download, Colt?"

He opened his mouth to deny it, but a horrifying thought stopped him. If the Chinese were worried the information he had downloaded compromised their spy aboard the *Lincoln*, then that meant they were somehow responsible for the erratic behavior of his jet. "Nothing," he said, but even he knew it sounded unconvincing.

"I need to know," she pressed.

Despite all the training he'd received at SERE school in resisting interrogation, he found himself hopelessly unprepared to combat her fierce blue eyes. He likely would have failed the course in Survival, Evasion, Resistance and Escape if he had been questioned by a woman as determined as Punky. At last, he sighed. "I downloaded the squadron's maintenance data."

She cocked her head to the side. "Why?"

"I'm going to take it to a test pilot friend who's way smarter than I am. Maybe he can get it to engineers who can decipher what happened."

"Jug," she said, putting the pieces together.

He nodded. "You coming or not?"

They both heard the sirens at the same time and turned in the direction of the abandoned Corvette. Sooner or later, he knew the police would figure out who the car belonged to, and they'd spend the rest of their afternoon answering questions in an interrogation room instead of stopping whatever plot the Chinese had concocted. He knew she probably had broken protocol by leaving the scene, but he wasn't burdened by such bureaucracy.

"Let's go," she said.

Colt wasn't one to look a gift horse in the mouth, so he turned toward the dark gray experimental plane he had parked on the ramp a week earlier before flying an F-35 from Marine Corps Air Station Miramar out to the *Abraham Lincoln.*

"Is that your Carbon Cub?"

Colt stopped. "You know what that is?"

She gave him a wry smile. "Sure," she said. "I've got almost a hundred hours in one."

Colt took off from the shorter 3,400-foot runway, though the Carbon Cub needed only a fraction of that. The plane was designed for Short Takeoffs and Landings, or STOL, and when he wasn't flying fifth-generation fighters in the Fallon Range Training Complex, he was flying his pride and joy in the Nevada backcountry.

"Experimental Carbon Cub Four Four Three November Alpha, switch So Cal on nineteen six," the air traffic controller said.

"Nineteen six," he said, then reached up to dial in the new frequency.

After checking in, Colt steered the bush plane north of La Jolla, shooting the gap between Mount Soledad and the Mormon Temple, then leveled off at fifteen hundred feet. Crossing the shoreline, he banked north and passed underneath the Seawolf Corridor.

"Want to take the controls for a bit?"

"Sure," Punky said. "I've got the aircraft."

"You've got the aircraft." He relinquished controls to the NCIS agent in his back seat, then went heads-down in the cockpit to enter their planned route to Point Mugu into his navigation system.

His cell phone vibrated in his breast pocket, and he removed it and saw Jug's number on the screen. After connecting to his headset via Bluetooth, he answered the call. "Hey, Jug, I'm on my way."

"Colt?" There was a brief pause. "Where are you calling from?"

He looked through his window at the dark blue waters beneath them. "About a half mile off the coast."

"On a boat?"

He grinned. "In my plane. Flying up to Camarillo right now."

"When will you get here?"

Colt glanced at his navigation display and saw that they had a favorable tailwind and were cruising comfortably at just over one hundred miles per hour over the ground. "If we don't get slowed down going through Los Angeles, we should be there in an hour and a half."

"*We?*"

Colt turned and looked over his shoulder at Punky, who was effortlessly flying the plane while staring out over the water, lost in her own thoughts. She couldn't hear his conversation and probably didn't even know he was on the phone. "I've got an NCIS agent with me," he said. Then quickly added, "Long story."

"Roger that," Jug said. "Listen, you might be waiting awhile. I need to go flying to sanitize the range for a missile test tonight, so I'll be gone for a few hours."

The news made Colt slump in his seat. The car accident and shootout were still fresh in his mind, and he didn't want to think it had all been for nothing. "Okay," he said at last. "Give me a call when you get back."

"Will do."

After Jug ended the call, Colt selected the intercom system and spoke to his copilot. "Looks like we have a few hours to kill. Where do you want to go?"

"I don't...I don't know."

Colt turned and saw her staring back at him with a lost look in her eyes. "Can you figure out where Rick was when he called?" he asked.

The lost look disappeared.

Colt showed her how to connect her phone to her headset, and she scrolled through her contacts until she found the number for Rick's supervisor at the San Diego Field Office. She took a calming breath, then placed the call.

A deep baritone voice answered. "Special Agent Deacon."

"John, it's Special Agent King from NCIS—"

"Punky! What can I do for you?"

She squinted at the nickname. *Of course he told them.* Though she had always liked it, the nickname had new meaning now. Rick had used his final breath to let *TANDY* know Punky hunted her, and she wanted to look the bitch in the eyes when she realized Punky had found her. "Rick is conducting a solo vehicle surveillance, and I'm moving to join him. But I don't have the beacon ID code for the tracker on the subject's car."

"Ahhh," John said. "Let me see if I can find the requisition form."

"Thanks, John."

They were nearing Long Beach, and she could see the brewery where she and Rick had shared a few beers the night before. She could see his playful smile and his obnoxiously bright Hawaiian shirt, and she struggled to accept that her Uncle Rick was really gone.

"Punky?"

"Go ahead."

"Okay, the beacon ID code is Romeo Sierra Zero Three Zero Five."

"Got it," she said, tapping the code into the application on her phone that allowed her to home in on the tracker Rick had placed on *TANDY*'s vehicle. She watched the map zoom in on a location another one hundred and fifty miles up the coast.

"Have Rick call me—"

She hung up without replying and switched over to the intercom. "Santa Maria. Do we have the gas for that?"

Colt zoomed out on his map. "Sure. It'll take another hour to get there..."

"Good, it's settled."

Colt looked as if he were about to argue, but in the end, he gave a little shake of his head, took control of the plane, and banked left to put the Santa Monica Mountains on their nose. Punky turned and looked through the left window at Catalina Island rising up out of the water like a green sea monster.

I'm coming for you.

30

Smuggler's Cove
Santa Cruz Island, California

Cassidy opened her eyes and peered over the edge of the hammock at the waves crashing against the shore. It had been a long time since she'd felt this much peace, and she understood now why Jenny and Carrie liked to get out of the city and into nature. She hadn't wanted to come, but she was thankful they talked her into it.

She flopped back down into the hammock, letting it rock gently with the ocean breeze. She had strung her blue-and-gold ENO hammock between two trees, one a eucalyptus and the other she couldn't recognize. Maybe one of the other girls could.

Where are they, anyway?

She closed her eyes again, reveling in the absolute absence of stress. No cell phone service. No internet. No demanding boss ruining a perfectly good three-day weekend.

Cassidy took a deep breath of the fragrant air, then slid her body up into a reclined position and let her legs dangle over the sides. She looked at her watch and scrunched up her forehead when she saw the time.

They should be back by now.

After hiking almost four miles to Smuggler's Cove, Cassidy was spent and had wanted to sit in her hammock for a while and take a nap before they made the return trip to Scorpion Ranch to catch the ferry to the mainland. But Jenny and Carrie weren't done exploring and set off into the hills opposite the grove of olive trees they'd passed on their way in.

"We'll be back by two," Jenny had told her.

But it was already two thirty. The boat was scheduled to depart in two hours.

"Shit!"

Cassidy scrambled out of the hammock and slipped her feet back into her LOWA hiking shoes. Without bothering to lace them up, she jogged out from under the canopy of trees and craned her neck in both directions, looking up and down the beach for her friends.

"Jenny!" she yelled. "Carrie!"

Not seeing another soul, she turned and walked up the double-track dirt trail a short distance, looking up at the olive trees perched on the hillside.

"Jenny! Carrie!"

Her voice shook with a rising wave of anxiety.

I'm all alone.

She turned back to the shaded spot under the trees where only minutes before she had felt completely at peace. Only now, she felt a fear unlike anything she had ever known. She knew where she was, and she knew how to get back to Scorpion Ranch, but she didn't want to make the hike alone. She didn't want to leave her friends all alone.

"Jenny! Carrie!"

Cassidy choked back a sob as she quickly unclipped her hammock from the trees and packed it away in its built-in stuff sack. She tossed it and the straps into her backpack, slung it over her shoulder, then knelt to tie her shoes. Her fingers trembled as she worked the laces, but she finally managed. With one more hopeless look around the picnic area for clues that might lead to her friends, she took off running up the trail.

It was a steep climb out of the cove, and her legs burned after less than one hundred yards, but she dug deep into what her high school coach had called her "reservoir of desire" to push through it. By the time she had reached the top of the hill a mile later, her lungs were on fire, and she felt light-headed. But she pushed on.

Three miles to go, she thought.

She took a moment to sip from her hydration bladder, but she barely noticed the lukewarm water she swallowed. Her eyes were wide with fright, scanning the surrounding grass-covered hills and Montañon Ridge to her west but still not seeing another soul. She looked at her watch again, then spurred herself onward.

Two miles later, she spotted the cypress tree grove Jenny had insisted on visiting and felt an instant longing for her friend. "Where *are* you, Jenny?"

But she knew the grove meant she was close to her destination. The aching in her legs had faded away almost to numbness, but her lungs felt raw, and her breathing had a rasp to it that hadn't been there before.

Less than a mile.

She lowered her head and picked up her pace, refusing to look at her watch for fear that she would see she had failed. Jenny and Carrie had been the better hikers. They would have made it. She didn't want to let them down by missing the boat.

When she rounded the corner at the switchback, she looked down into Scorpion Anchorage and saw the catamaran pulling up to the pier. The beach was awash with other day-trippers clambering for the pier and their ride back to Ventura.

"No!" she shouted.

This part of the trail had a steep drop on her right into the valley below, but unlike when the three friends had hiked up earlier in the day, Cassidy abandoned all caution and sprinted down the hill. All that mattered was getting there before the boat left. Jenny and Carrie *had* to be there waiting for her.

When she reached the valley floor, Cassidy skittered around a dense clump of coastal pines and almost ran into a park ranger.

"Whoa," the blond woman said. "You're cutting it close, but you'll make it."

"My friends..." She was breathless and gasped for air as she gripped the ranger's shoulders and looked into her eyes. "My friends..."

The park ranger looked over Cassidy's shoulder as if to spot the danger she was fleeing from, then back down at her. "What about your friends? Are they okay?"

"They're..." She fought for control over her breathing and swallowed against the bile rising in her throat. "They're *missing!*"

If Tiffany was being honest, it wasn't the first time somebody had gone missing on the island. And it certainly wasn't the first time somebody had missed the boat back to the mainland either. But when the pale brunette practically bowled her over with panic, it took all her strength not to lash out at her for being irresponsible.

After calming the girl somewhat, she walked with her to the pier, where the catamaran was in the process of loading passengers for the return trip. Tiffany escorted the girl up the pier, casting questioning glances at other women about the girl's age who might have been the two potentially missing friends. Tiffany thought it likely the two girls had become disoriented and had decided on the smart course of action by returning to the pier.

But after a quick search of almost all sixty people already on board, she had to admit that maybe there was something to the girl's story. Just to be sure, she walked both the upper and lower decks a second time, then disembarked to the pier, where she scanned the beach and surrounding hills.

The brunette approached her. "What are we going to do?"

As the park ranger on duty, it was Tiffany's responsibility to find the missing persons. But she didn't need a frantic civilian rushing her search and rescue operation. She leveled her gaze on the girl. "*You* are going to get on the boat and go home. I have the information I need. I'll find them and get them back to the mainland."

"But..."

Tiffany guided her back onto the boat. "No buts," she said. "You three will be laughing about this over margaritas by Sunday."

The girl seemed to relax at that comment but still appeared a little hesitant as she returned to take her seat outside on the lower deck. Tiffany gave her a slight wave, then turned back for the ranch, where she could make her missing persons report and begin what was sure to be a long night looking for the women.

How hard is it to stick to the trails?

When she reached the ranger station, she walked inside and sat down in a cheap swivel chair in front of the duty desk. She knew the island like the back of her hand and would take the truck to search the roads most visitors used for hiking, but she wanted to notify Coast Guard Sector Los Angeles-Long Beach so they could begin mobilizing assets before it got too late. For as big as the island was, a helicopter with infrared search capability might make her job just a little bit easier.

"Why's it always happen on a Friday?"

31

USS *Mobile Bay* (CG-53)

Beth sat in her chair on the bridge and yawned, looking out across the bow of her ship as they crisscrossed the Point Mugu Sea Range. She had worried how her crew might respond to the excitement from the night before, but as she walked the deck plates earlier that morning, she was surprised to hear very little scuttlebutt on the topic. Nothing about the swirling orbs of light that had harassed them for half an hour. Nothing about the F-35C that had almost crashed into them.

"Afternoon, ma'am," Master Chief said in greeting as he approached.

"Master Chief."

"Beautiful day on the water," he said.

"Another fine Navy day." It sounded trite, but the water west of San Clemente Island was unusually calm and almost seemed to blend in with the horizon. If not for the faint outline of San Nicolas Island rising out of the water in front of them, it would have been hard to discern where the Pacific Ocean ended and the sky began.

He leaned forward and looked through the windows at the broad expanse of ocean surrounding them. "The surface picture is clear," he said in an offhanded manner.

She nodded. "It seems merchant vessels really *do* pay attention to the Notices to Mariner."

Master Chief knew she was telling a joke, but his face remained impassive. "We should be on station within the hour and can commence flight ops to clear the seascape around the...*target*."

She grinned.

"You don't like it, do you?" Beth saw it in his body language. He didn't like the idea of sinking what had once been a United States Navy ship any more than she did.

Ben turned and squared his body to her, then he narrowed his eyes. "No, ma'am. I served on the *Bonhomme Richard* back in the day. Have a lot of good memories of her, and I don't like the idea of sinking her just so the flyboys can test some new missile."

Like most sailors, Ben had his superstitions. She'd spent her entire adult life sailing the world's oceans and understood how the Master Chief felt. A Navy ship imprinted on her sailors' souls and became a part of their identities. She looked around the bridge, knowing that the *Mobile Bay* would hold a special place in her heart. Especially after this, her final voyage.

But as an officer, Beth knew that it was also for the greater good. Even after the reckless pilot had endangered her ship and crew the night before, she knew an aircraft carrier was powerless without the aircraft it carried. She didn't like the idea of sinking a former Navy ship either, but the "new missile" Master Chief referred to would enhance the Navy's lethality. And they needed it to face off against their future enemies.

"Happens all the time, Master Chief."

"Still don't like it, Skipper."

Beth leaned back in her chair and folded her hands in her lap. "Last summer, I was with the *Carl Vinson* Strike Group in the Hawaiian Island Operating Area when we sank the decommissioned guided-missile frigate *Ingraham*."

"I got no problem with sinking a frigate," he muttered.

She ignored the comment. "Jets from the carrier and the Third Marine Air Wing combined with Submarine Forces Pacific and the Army Multi-Domain Task Force to sink the ship."

The Master Chief didn't roll his eyes, but she could tell he wanted to. "But why does it have to be the *Bonhomme Richard*?"

She knew the answer to that because she had asked the same question when the admiral gave her their orders. The former *Bonhomme Richard* was a *Wasp*-class amphibious assault ship that had been home-ported in San Diego before a fire broke out on a lower vehicle-storage deck while undergoing routine maintenance. After four days of fighting the fire, the ship was scrapped.

"The version of the Joint Strike Missile they are testing has a larger warhead and is designed to penetrate an enemy carrier's defenses and sink it. They needed a vessel large enough to replicate the Russian *Kiev*-class and *Kuznetsov*-class carriers, the latter being the basis for Chinese aircraft carrier design. The former *Bonhomme Richard* is just under two hundred feet shorter than the former Soviet carrier, *Varyag*, that was sold to China and recommissioned as the *Liaoning*." She grinned, then added, "As my dad used to say, it's close enough for government work."

"What about that new Chinese carrier? What are they calling it?"

"The *Fujian*. Yeah, that thing's just as big as our *Nimitz*-class carriers."

"Will this Joint Strike Missile have any effect on that?"

Beth shrugged. She wasn't an expert in air-delivered ordnance by any means, but as Alpha Whiskey, she made the effort to read everything she could on anti-ship missiles. "I don't really know," she said. "But the Naval Strike Missile delivered the knockout punch on the *Ingraham*."

"How's that different than this?"

"Same missile, pretty much. Raytheon designed the Joint Strike Missile to fit inside the F-35's internal bay, providing an air-launched weapon capable of attacking both sea and land targets at ranges over one hundred nautical miles."

A commotion off her left shoulder caught her attention, and Beth looked away from Master Chief to the lieutenant standing Officer of the Deck. She saw him pick up a phone and speak into it before pulling up a chart on the Electronic Chart Display and Information System. When he saw Beth looking at him, he covered the handset and said, "Ma'am, the Coast Guard is sending the cutter *Blacktip* to Santa Cruz Island for a search and rescue operation."

"Will they be in our operating area?"

He held up a finger while he quickly plotted the cutter's location on the chart and compared it to the area where the missile test was to occur. She saw his body relax, then he looked up at her and shook his head. "No, ma'am."

"Very well. Ask the Coast Guard if they require any assistance. As long as it doesn't prevent us from completing our primary mission, I'm all for helping the puddle pirates out." She turned to the Master Chief. "Isn't the air det scheduled for a gun-ex before range clearance?"

Ben nodded, confirming that they had planned on allowing their helicopter detachment to practice shooting their .50-cal machine guns before clearing the target area. "Yes, ma'am."

"Let's go see our airdales and get them prepared to spin up."

Lieutenant Brian Little stood on the aft flight deck and watched his sailors pull the MH-60R Seahawk helicopter from its resting place in the *Mobile Bay's* hangar. What had been an offhanded suggestion by the ship's captain to prepare for a search and rescue operation had turned into a direct order from their detachment Officer-in-Charge. Whether the Coast Guard wanted the help or not, he would be flying his Romeo over the beach.

"Sir, we still loading the fifties?"

Brian looked at AWR1 Rose, the First Class Petty Officer who had been assigned to his bird for the mission, and grinned. "Maybe we can get a night shoot in," he said hopefully.

Rose disappeared back into the hangar to collect the gear they would need for the mission. Though they normally flew in support of anti-submarine operations for the strike group, their squadron trained for a wide range of missions. The Raptors of HSM-71, or Helicopter Maritime Strike Squadron Seven One, flew the most advanced helicopter in the fleet, and their aircrewmen were among the best trained in the Navy.

From supporting Naval Special Warfare and Combat Search and Rescue to conducting over-the-horizon anti-surface strikes, the Raptors were prepared for anything. And part of that was because guys like Brian saw the benefit in conducting live-fire training when opportunities presented themselves. This mission would be no different.

Sailors began crawling over the helicopter to prepare it for flight, and Brian turned back into the hangar to get dressed in his gear. As the HAC, or Helicopter Aircraft Commander, he was responsible for ensuring both his bird and his crew were ready for the mission. He spotted Lieutenant junior grade Dillon Bush, his H2P, or Helicopter Second Pilot, and walked up to him.

"I told Rose to go ahead and load the fifties anyway," Brian said. "If the SAR mission goes nowhere, we might as well get some training out of it."

Dillon ignored the comment. "So, they're actually going to send us after some missing hikers?"

"Isn't this what you signed up for?"

"Honestly, I thought I'd be doing something more exciting."

Brian slapped him on the shoulder. "Come on. Let's get suited up. I'm sure we can find some excitement before the night is over."

32

Santa Maria Valley, California

Almost an hour into their flight, Colt followed Punky's guidance and steered the Carbon Cub toward the vast and multi-hued green agricultural fields of the Santa Maria valley. Their flight up the coast had been quicker than he expected, and he thought there was still a chance they could make it back to Camarillo before Jug returned from his flight.

"What's that?" Punky asked, grounding him in the reality of what was at stake.

He looked at her over his shoulder and saw where she was pointing. On a rural highway just left of their nose, he spotted what looked like a car flipped onto its back with a large semitruck sitting idle on the shoulder nearby.

"Let's take a closer look," he said, pulling power and dipping the bush plane's nose to descend from fifteen hundred feet. They jostled through the up drafts and down drafts of the turbulent air sweeping across the crops, and he angled his approach to parallel the road, then reached up to add a notch of flaps.

He slowed to sixty-five knots, then added a second notch as he picked a freshly plowed field and aligned his nose with the orderly rows. Aside from the flashing red and blue lights of police cars surrounding the scene of the accident, the ground beneath them was deserted.

Colt slowed another ten knots, then added the final notch of flaps. He hadn't touched the throttle since setting the power to begin their descent, but his eyes never stopped scanning his intended landing area, and his mind never stopped processing the dozens of changing variables that went into an off-field landing. If he flew fourth- and fifth-generation fighters like they were an extension of his body, he flew the Carbon Cub like it *was* his body.

At forty-five knots, he pulled back slightly on the stick and rounded out the approach to slow further and positioned the bush plane for a three-point landing, setting both thirty-five-inch Alaska Bushwheel tires and tail Baby Bushwheel on the ground at the same time. The heavy-duty suspension absorbed most of the impact, but still the plane bucked when he applied brakes and raised the tailwheel off the ground to bleed off the rest of his speed. He came to a stop alongside the inverted car.

"Is that..." Punky's voice was faint.

Colt could hear her anguish. "What kind of car was Rick driving?" he asked.

She let out a little sob that confirmed his fear. "A silver BMW," she said.

The police officers on the scene appraised them with professional skepticism. Colt was sure they hadn't expected an experimental airplane to descend out of the sky and were probably wondering what the newcomers planned on doing. He answered that question by turning off the engine and opening his window.

When a uniformed sheriff's deputy saw him unstrapping, he walked over and raised a hand to stop him. "Whoa," he said. "You can't just land that here. This is a crime scene."

Colt heard him but didn't care. He climbed down from the front seat and approached the deputy. "What happened?"

"Who are you?" The deputy looked over his shoulder when Punky climbed out of the airplane behind him, then back to Colt. "Who's she?"

Colt had to admire Punky's grit. He knew Rick's phone call had shaken her and seeing the overturned car had only confirmed her fears, but she walked right past Colt and held her credentials up to the deputy. "Special Agent King with NCIS."

"This is our jurisdiction—"

"And *that's* my partner," she replied, pointing a finger at the wrecked BMW.

The deputy dropped his chin to his chest in a universal sign of respect, then quietly shook his head. "I'm sorry, ma'am. He was gone before we got here."

"Is he..."

Colt heard the tremor in her voice. "I don't think this is a good idea, Punky."

"I need to see," she said, her voice vibrating with fear and grief. But the look of determination on her face hadn't changed even after being presented with concrete evidence that Rick had fallen victim to foul play.

"Ma'am," the deputy said, holding out his hands to stop her. "You *really* don't want to see this."

Punky moved to step around him, but Colt reached out and gripped her shoulders, gently holding her in place. "Maybe you should listen to him."

The deputy appraised Colt again. "Who are you?"

"Just a friend," he replied.

At last, Punky stopped resisting Colt's attempt to keep her from crossing the road and seeing what was beyond the yellow crime scene tape. But he could tell she hadn't given up on avenging Rick's death. "What can you tell me?"

The deputy bit his lip, clearly uncomfortable with sharing information about an ongoing investigation, especially one that was so fresh. He looked at Punky and asked, "Were you investigating somebody at Cal Poly?"

She cocked her head to the side. "What makes you ask that?"

"We found a note that read, 'Cal Poly faculty, question mark.'"

Punky looked up at Colt, and he shrugged his shoulders in reply. He knew where Cal Poly was, and he could tell it meant something to her, but she wasn't willing to share that information with the deputy for some reason. She looked back at the deputy, then to the airplane. "Maybe we should leave."

Colt furrowed his brow, wondering why the sudden change of heart.

But he wasn't about to question her, at least not in front of the deputy. After everything she had been through, he knew she had her reasons. He tried putting himself in her shoes and tried feeling what she felt, but he couldn't imagine her loss. He knew she was committed to finding Rick's killer, and he was committed to helping her.

Without another word, Punky started walking back to the plane. Colt hurried to shake the deputy's hand and thank him for the information, then followed her back to the Carbon Cub. After several paces, he pulled even with her and asked, "Okay, what was that all about?"

"Rick told me he had followed *TANDY* to San Luis Obispo."

"And?"

"And if Rick thought somebody at Cal Poly was involved, then it's something we should look into."

"We're *not* flying to San Luis Obispo," he said. He was committed to helping her, but he had already entertained her curiosity enough by flying past Point Mugu to reach Santa Maria.

"We don't have to."

He puzzled over her answer for a moment, then looked back at the deputy. "Why didn't you tell him that?"

"Because this is personal."

Colt let her get situated in the back seat, then climbed back into his perch up front. She watched him run through the startup procedure from memory, setting the mixture to rich and opening the throttle half an inch. He looked to both sides, ensuring the prop arc was clear, then flipped on the master switch.

"You ready?" he asked.

"Let's do it," she replied.

"Clear prop!" Colt yelled through the open window.

He engaged the starter, and she watched the Borer prop turn over from the back seat as the engine coughed and caught with a belch of smoke. After turning on the avionics, he worked the stick between his legs in a box pattern to verify the control surfaces were free and functioning as they should.

Satisfied, he slowly advanced the throttle while dancing on the rudder pedals to steer the plane to an open stretch of dirt beyond the plowed rows. Then, without warning, he shoved the throttle to the stop and nosed forward on the stick to lift the tail off the ground. She felt the airspeed increasing, then watched as he reached up for the flap lever while pulling back on the stick at the same time to drop the tailwheel back onto the ground.

The immediate addition of lift from the flaps and increased angle of attack popped the Carbon Cub into the air. Despite her experience in the plane, she felt herself tense as he quickly lowered the nose and held their altitude barely ten feet in the air, accelerating to a comfortable climbing speed. She remained quiet until they had reached seventy miles per hour, when Colt eased back on the stick and let the airplane climb.

"I'm going to get some answers," she said over the intercom.

"From who?"

"It's better if you don't know." What she was going to be asking for wasn't exactly illegal, but it definitely toed the line. The less the Navy pilot knew, the less he could testify to if things didn't go according to plan. She connected her phone via Bluetooth to her headset, then placed a call to her contact at the NSA.

"Hello?"

"Margaret, it's me," Punky said. "I've got a favor to ask."

"Is it related to the case against *KMART*?"

"Yes. Rick..." She choked back a sob. No matter how hard she tried, she just couldn't bring herself to accept that he was gone. Really gone. Telling the analyst Rick was dead would have made it too real for her.

"Rick what?"

She took a deep breath and settled on a half-truth. "Rick was looking into a professor at Cal Poly who might be involved."

"Involved how?"

"I don't know," she said. "But I was hoping you could find out if there have been any irregular communications in or out of the Cal Poly campus in San Luis Obispo."

"This is highly irregular—"

Punky cut her off. "I wouldn't be asking if it wasn't important."

Margaret sighed. "What kind of communications?"

"I don't know that either."

"Well, what *do* you know?"

Punky wanted to snap at her, *I know Rick is dead!* But she composed herself and said, "I don't have much information to go on, but this is time sensitive."

"What does Rick say?"

Punky felt her throat tightening up again as she thought about Rick and what the Chinese spy had done to him. She was thankful the deputy stopped her before she saw something that would scar her for life, but the wound of his loss was still fresh. She cleared her throat to answer.

"Punky?"

Hearing the nickname brought her anguish roaring back, and she stifled a sob. Rick was the last person she truly cared about, and she would wear his nickname for her as a badge of honor. And a calling card she'd place at *TANDY*'s feet.

When she answered, her voice was little more than a whisper. "Can you do this for me?"

Margaret sighed again, then reluctantly answered, "Yes. Let me look into it, and I'll call you back."

"Thank you, Margaret. I owe you."

Punky ended the call and selected the intercom to speak with Colt. "I've got somebody looking into it."

"So, where to now?"

"Camarillo," she replied. "Let's go see Jug and find out what the hell is going on."

33

Santa Cruz Island, California

Tiffany tossed her backpack over the side into the pickup truck's bed, looking west toward the setting sun. It was always peaceful there, but without day-trippers scrambling to and fro over her island paradise, it seemed even more so. Still, she was thankful to have something to do, and she opened the driver's door and climbed inside, ignoring the aging truck's squeaking hinges.

Firing up the National Park Service truck, she backed it away from the building, then put it in drive and slowly inched down the hill toward Scorpion Ranch. She couldn't take the most direct route to Smuggler's Cove because the trail was too narrow, but she knew the island's roads intimately and knew the fastest way to get there in the truck.

Smiling and waving at several overnight campers who were walking toward their tents, Tiffany crossed the intersection onto Smuggler's Road and started ascending the hill in the growing darkness. She had wanted the Coast Guard to send a helicopter to aid in the search, because the island was just too big for one park ranger in a pickup truck, but instead they had sent a cutter from the Ventura Coast Guard station.

Cutters were useful for rescuing lost kayakers and divers with the bends, but she wasn't sure how they would help her find the missing hikers on land. Still, the added manpower off the coast might eliminate the possibility they had been caught in an undertow and pulled out to sea. That would allow her to focus her search on the island's interior.

Though the sun was still up, Tiffany knew it wouldn't be for long. The weather forecast was favorable with clear skies and evening temperatures expected to remain above sixty degrees, so she wasn't worried about the missing hikers being at risk due to exposure. But that didn't mean they weren't in danger.

"Ranger Reid, come in," squawked the handheld radio resting on the seat next to her.

She picked up the radio, pressed the push-to-talk button, and answered, "Go for Tiffany."

"Tiffany, this is Chief Romero on Cutter *Blacktip*."

Though the pickup truck had four-wheel drive and she felt confident on the island's roads, she still took care to guide it around the sharp corners as she crested the hill south of Scorpion Ranch. "Hey, Chief, I'm mobile and heading toward Smuggler's Cove. What's going on?"

"The Navy has a guided-missile cruiser in the area," he said. "They are offering to help with the search and rescue."

First a Coast Guard cutter, now a Navy cruiser?

"No offense, Chief, but what can a guided-missile cruiser do to help us find missing hikers on my island?"

"Well..." Chief Romero paused. "They have an MH-60R Seahawk helicopter with infrared sensors and dedicated search and rescue personnel."

"Oh!" she replied in surprise. "How soon can they be here?"

Tiffany had grown up in an Army family and knew little of Navy ships or their capabilities. She had always assumed they used their helicopters for ferrying personnel or finding submarines lurking under the waves. She knew they didn't have attack helicopters like the Apache her Uncle Don had flown, but she should have at least suspected they had some search and rescue capabilities.

"They will launch right around sunset," the chief replied. "Remain on this channel, and they will contact you once they get airborne."

"Good copy," she said.

The chief continued. "You can talk them onto your location and have them search the immediate area. They can direct you to any hot spots they find with their sensors."

The road Tiffany had been following cut back to the west and gave her an unobstructed view across the length of the island. She couldn't see Smuggler's Cove yet from where she was, but she was only minutes from descending to the isolated beach. "Thanks, Chief. What's your current position?"

"We are approaching Scorpion Anchorage now," he said. "Nothing here but a forty-foot sailboat at anchor. Looks like nobody is aboard."

Tiffany furrowed her brow. She had met every overnight visitor on the island, and she couldn't remember anybody coming ashore from a sailboat. But that was a problem for future Tiffany. Present Tiffany was focused on finding the missing hikers. "Copy. Go ahead and circle around to the south side of the island. I'm going to begin my search there."

She wanted to know if they would send a RHIB ashore with a few Coast Guardsmen to help with the search, but it was too much to ask. So, she kept her mouth shut.

"*Blacktip* out," the chief said, ending their communication.

Tiffany reached up and turned on the truck's headlights, casting a weak beam across the ground before her. Immediately, she saw pairs of glowing orbs hovering over the ground on either side of the road, and she grinned at the critters whose eyes reflected the light back at her. She continued driving onward, and the orbs disappeared as the animals scampered off into the darkness.

Her windows were down, and she enjoyed the cooling ocean air blowing into the stuffy truck's cab, but she was already looking forward to parking the truck and setting out on foot. With a Navy helicopter offering to help guide her search, she figured she would have the missing hikers in the truck and back at Scorpion Ranch within an hour. Two, tops.

USS *Mobile Bay* (CG-53)

Even in smooth seas, taking off from a naval vessel while underway was a challenge. As the HAC, Lieutenant Brian Little sat in the right seat and looked to the side at the faint green glow emanating from the thick glass windows of flight deck control, then at the yellow-shirted boatswain's mate serving as the Landing Signalman Enlisted, or LSE.

He waited until his engines stabilized, then set his external lights to dim flashing while making a circular gesture parallel to the flight deck with a red light in his hand. The LSE responded by rotating a single wand at chest level before the air officer turned on a yellow rotating beacon, authorizing him to engage rotors. Brian did so while completing his final checklist items.

"You guys ready?" he asked, looking to his left at Dillon, who gave him a thumbs-up.

"All set, boss," AWR1 Rose said over the intercom.

He set his lights to dim steady, then watched as the LSE gave the signal to break him down, directing two blue shirts to approach from either side of the MH-60R and remove the chocks and chains that kept them bound to the flight deck. Once removed, Brian saw a green rotating beacon flash on as the air officer gave the LSE permission to launch.

The yellow wands extended outward and moved in slow arcs above the LSE's head, and Brian responded by increasing torque and raising the collective to slowly lift his Seahawk into the air over the cruiser's flight deck. When he had pulled even with the top of the hangar, the LSE gave him a sweeping gesture, and he let the helicopter drift aft over the ship's wake.

She extended both wands out to the side, giving him the signal to hover, then swung her left arm in an arc over her head while keeping her right arm steady, pointed to the port side of the ship. He gave a little left pedal, keeping his eyes fixed on the LSE as he pivoted his nose to the left. At last, the LSE gestured for him to depart, and he turned to look through the forward windscreen while pushing forward on the cyclic to fly away from the ship.

"Red Crown, Raptor Two Four is airborne and proceeding north for tasking," Dillon said over the radio, letting the controllers in the *Mobile Bay*'s CIC know they were departing station.

"Raptor Two Four, copy. Push Cobalt for tasking."

"Raptor Two Four," Dillon replied.

Brian glanced down at his kneeboard card to check the frequency that had been assigned as "Cobalt." Like most things in the Navy, leadership tended to overcomplicate things for the sake of operational security, even when they were just off the coast of California. He watched Dillon change the radio frequency and verified he had entered it correctly, then returned his focus to the steering cue on his display pointing to the shadow rising out of the ocean in front of them.

"Cutter *Blacktip*, this is Raptor Two Four," Dillon said, hailing the Coast Guard vessel that had requested assistance for the search and rescue on Santa Cruz Island.

"Raptor Two Four, this is Chief Romero on *Blacktip*."

"We are ten mikes out, request SITREP."

Brian grinned, enjoying the younger pilot's use of military jargon and slang. Dillon was a good stick and would make a fine pilot, but he treated every mission as if he were flying over the beach in hostile territory. Reluctantly, Brian admitted he had once had the same youthful enthusiasm. But the Coast Guard chief understood the lingo and proceeded to give them a Situation Report in plain language.

"Copy. The National Park Service reported two missing hikers, both female in their late twenties. Their last known location was Smuggler's Cove on the south side at the east end of the island. Do you need the coordinates?"

Dillon referenced their chart before replying. "Negative. We have that location on board."

We have that location on board? Brian thought with a smile, wondering how much jargon Dillon could squeeze in.

"Copy that, Raptor Two Four. You'll want to contact Ranger Reid when you get on station, and she will provide further guidance."

"She's the ground force commander?"

Brian almost laughed.

"Um, she's the park ranger who is on the ground conducting the search," Chief Romero replied, deadpan.

"Raptor Two Four copies," Dillon said, then turned to Brian. "Sometimes I wonder if the Coast Guard is really even in the military."

"Just remember you said that when your boat runs out of gas and you're crying for them to come get you," Brian replied over the intercom.

"I'm with the LT on this one," AWRı Rose said from his station in the back. "They saved my bacon once when my boat's engine died with weather moving in. I used to give Coasties a hard time, but the shit conditions they do rescues in puts us to shame."

Dillon snapped his mouth shut and turned forward, looking through his night vision goggles at the rising terrain of Santa Cruz Island in front of them. Brian knew he saw the same thing and was probably focused on the glowing headlights of a lone vehicle near the shoreline on the east end.

"That must be *Ranger Reid*," Dillon said with a touch of sarcasm.

"Let's give her a call," Brian replied.

34

Santa Cruz Island, California

Tiffany slowed the truck at the bottom of the hill and looked through the dusty windshield at the black abyss of the Pacific Ocean. Putting the vehicle in park, she killed the ignition and listened to the waves lapping gently at the shore, the silence of the night deafening compared to the din of the city only fifty miles east. The silence was one of the reasons she became a park ranger in the first place.

Tiffany had grown up in California's Central Valley and spent much of her formative years in the national parks that were within driving distance. Sequoia, Kings Canyon, and the granddaddy of them all, Yosemite. When most of her friends were trolling the local mall for boys or a killer sale, she was hiking with her dog, Stella, high up in the Sierras. After graduating from Fresno State University with a degree in accounting and a brief, unsatisfying career chasing the almighty dollar, she quit her job and applied with the National Park Service.

Now here she was, sitting in a government vehicle, alone in the darkness on a mostly deserted island, and she couldn't have been happier. With a contented sigh, she opened the door and stepped out into the night, looking south across the water at the dim red and green navigation lights inching closer to her island.

"Ranger Reid," her handheld radio squawked. "This is Raptor Two Four."

She reached back into the truck and picked up the radio, bringing it to her mouth before keying the microphone. "Go ahead, Raptor Two Four."

"We're approaching your position from the south," the serious-sounding pilot said. "Please advise search grid, over."

"Well...the hikers' last known position was here at Smuggler's Cove. I was hoping you could search the surrounding hillsides for heat signatures and then pass the coordinates to me so I can investigate on foot." She paused for a beat, then added, "Over."

"Good copy, Ranger Reid," the pilot replied. "Will advise when on station. Out."

"It's just Tiffany," she said, then quickly added, "Over and out."

Raptor 24
Navy MH-60R

Brian piloted the MH-60R less than five hundred feet over the water, letting the rising moon illuminate the island's terrain through his night vision goggles. If he had been pointed west, the orange glow of the sun just below the horizon would have washed out his goggles and made them useless, but there was enough ambient light that he saw each undulation in the terrain as they neared Santa Cruz Island.

"Climbing up," he told his crew, pulling up on the collective to increase lift and climb higher into the air as they neared the shoreline. The truck's headlights had been turned off just before they made contact with the park ranger, but he knew precisely where Smuggler's Cove was located, even without the steering carat on his display.

"Pulling up the FLIR," AWR1 Rose said.

Brian glanced down at the display on his forward panel that showed the view from the helicopter's Forward-Looking Infrared. He watched as Rose manipulated the sensor and centered it on the National Park Service truck.

"Tallyho," Dillon said when the crosshairs settled on a lone figure standing alongside the truck. "Ranger Reid...er...Tiffany, this is Raptor Two Four. We are on station and have eyes on your pos. Over."

"Copy that, Raptor Two Four. Can you search a mile in either direction along the beach? Over."

"Affirm," Dillon said.

Brian responded by banking the Seahawk to the right, angling toward a spot on the beach east of Smuggler's Cove. He watched as Rose zoomed out on the FLIR, letting the sensor "snowplow" along the terrain as it moved along the beach at roughly the same speed as the helicopter.

"Few hot spots, but they look like animals to me," Rose said.

Brian glanced at the screen and nodded. "Yeah, I agree."

The sensor stopped snowplowing, and Petty Officer Rose guided it in arcing sweeps up the hillside, looking for a heat signature that resembled a human shape. After a few minutes of scanning the area, he keyed his intercom and said, "That's about it for a mile in this direction."

"Roger that." Brian banked the helicopter left, sweeping across the beach as he turned to search west of the cove.

"Tiffany, this is Raptor Two Four," Dillon said from the left seat. "No joy at the east end of the beach. Proceeding west to search the other end."

"Copy, Raptor."

Brian glanced down through his window as they passed over Smuggler's Cove, looking through his night vision goggles at the female park ranger. Her head was tilted up to the sky, and she waved as they flew past.

Santa Cruz Island, California

From their hide site on Montañon Ridge, Chen looked up from the tablet she had been working on when she heard the helicopter approaching. When Wu Tian had returned and informed her that he had eliminated both women and covered their corpses with brush, she knew they would eventually be discovered. She just hoped his hasty concealment of the bodies would keep them hidden long enough to allow them to complete their task.

"Are they here for us?"

She looked over at Wu Tian, who was staring at the dim silhouette of a military helicopter paralleling the shoreline near Smuggler's Cove. She shook her head. "They're probably searching for the women you killed."

"That's sooner than I would have expected," he said. "Any targets yet?"

She glanced at her watch, then back to the tablet. "It's still too early for the missile test, but there is one airborne above us now."

"How much longer until the patch has been installed?"

Chen slipped the VR goggles onto her head and picked up a controller in each hand. She rotated her head left and right, then up and down, orienting herself within the virtual reality environment. Holding out her hand, she swiped at a screen only she could see and saw the timer in the bottom right corner. "One more minute."

"Should we take this one?"

Chen shook her head. "Not yet."

"But if the helicopter finds us…"

"No," she said, her tone firm and commanding. "We wait."

While Chen immersed herself in the virtual reality framework she would use to hack into the Joint Strike Fighter, she knew Wu Tian was watching the approaching helicopter with unease. But they were hidden well. Their camouflage would keep them invisible from prying infrared sensors and night vision, and the netting disguised the assortment of nondescript black boxes and cables littering their hide site.

The weapon was unlike any she had ever used before. It was man-portable and contained a processor with immense computing power, but the real secret was in the interface she would manipulate once they initiated the hack. She was tempted to hack into the one above them, just to verify the professor had successfully modified the waveform, but she was worried it might tip her hand.

No, she reminded herself. *We wait.*

At last, she stopped swiping and tapping on the air in front of her and lifted the goggles from her head. "It is complete," she said with a tone of satisfaction.

Wu Tian looked back at her with emotionless eyes.

35

Devil 1
Navy F-35C
South of Santa Cruz Island, California

Lieutenant William "Jug" McFarland completed his last sweep of the airspace over the missile test range. Normally a P-3 Orion assigned to VX-30 at Point Mugu would have been tasked with performing the pre-mission sanitization, but the test squadron's only maritime patrol aircraft had been pulled to the Western Pacific for real-world tasking. Not that Jug minded. He was just happy for the excuse to squeeze in another sortie before the test.

The ocean beneath him was devoid of surface contacts, with the exception of the *Ticonderoga*-class guided-missile cruiser, *Mobile Bay*. He thought it fortunate the Pentagon had considered the test important enough to assign the *Mobile Bay* for area sanitization, and he looked down on the darkened ship as she steamed north toward Santa Cruz Island.

"*Mobile Bay*, this is Devil One."

"Go ahead, Devil One," the ship's controller said.

"My sweep of the airspace is complete. Your unit is the only surface contact in the test area. Confirm?"

"Copy that, Devil One," the man's voice replied. "We launched Raptor Two Four to aid the Coast Guard in a real-world search and rescue mission on Santa Cruz Island."

Jug activated his Distributed Aperture System and looked down at the darkened island, letting his jet's infrared sensors detect the MH-60R's hot exhaust. Within seconds, his jet's core processor had identified the helicopter and placed a digitally created box around it on his Helmet Mounted Display. The helicopter was flying low level over the island's southern coast.

He checked his fuel state and saw that he had enough gas for at least some loiter time over the island. *Well, why not?* he thought.

"*Mobile Bay*, is Raptor Two Four up Link Sixteen?"

"Affirm."

Jug pulled up his communication portal and selected the control page for his Link 16 datalink. Normally, the Joint Strike Fighter disguised itself from others within the network, but if he was going to be of any assistance in the search, he needed to reveal himself to the helicopter crew.

"Frequency?"

"Raptor Two Four is up Cobalt," the cruiser's controller replied.

"Devil One," Jug replied, then dialed in the new frequency. He banked left and set up a relaxed orbit over the island, letting the autopilot keep him in position as he manipulated his EOTS to put his infrared sensor on the ground beneath the helicopter. "Raptor Two Four, this is Devil One."

"Go ahead, Devil One," the new voice replied.

"Raptor Two Four, Devil One is a single F-35C overhead at angels twenty with one five minutes of playtime," Jug said. "How can I help?"

A few seconds of silence followed before the voice returned. "Uh, roger that, Devil One."

Jug knew the Seahawk crew was probably trying to figure out how best to integrate the fifth-generation fighter into their search. While he waited for instructions, he used his sensor to scan the eastern end of the island, designating hot spots as targets that he could transmit to the helicopter via datalink. Even if they told him to buzz off and go home, he wanted to at least give them something they could use.

"Devil One, this is Raptor Two Four," the helicopter pilot said. "We are searching along the beach on the south end of the island. Confirm you are visual."

"Devil One is visual Raptor Two Four."

"Copy, we would like you to scan the area north of our position. We are looking for any heat signatures that could be human so we can relay their location to the park ranger on the ground."

Jug knew the Seahawk crew had no way of knowing he was already using his EOTS to do just that. He had found half a dozen heat signatures near the helicopter's position that were potential hits, and he transmitted the target list to them over Link 16. "Roger, Raptor Two Four. Stand by for target package transmission."

"Uh, copy."

While he waited for the helicopter crew to confirm receipt of the target list, he continued scanning the east end of the island, noting a few surface contacts off the coast. They were both outside the missile test area, but one was close enough he wanted to get word to them to remain clear during the test later that evening. He zoomed in on the ship and saw what looked like a Coast Guard cutter steaming west toward the helicopter's position.

"Raptor Two Four, are you in comms with a Coast Guard vessel nearing your position from the east?"

"Affirm, that is Cutter *Blacktip*. They are up this frequency."

"Devil One, this is Chief Romero on the *Blacktip*," a new voice said.

"Hey, Chief, just wanted to make sure you were aware of the missile test later this evening and confirm you will remain clear."

"Affirm," the chief replied. "We will remain in the island's coastal waters and plan on returning to Ventura when we are complete with tasking."

"Thanks, Chief," Jug said.

"Devil One, Raptor Two Four received your target list."

Satisfied that he had given the SAR bubbas a place to start and that the airspace and seascape were sanitized for the test, Jug rolled out with Point Mugu on the nose. "Copy, Raptor Two Four. Devil One is departing station and RTB Point Mugu at this time. Happy hunting."

A few minutes later, Jug switched off the SAR coordination frequency and dialed in Mugu approach. Despite knowing Colt was flying up to Camarillo to see him, he wasn't in a hurry, and he pulled the throttle back and maintained his airspeed as he descended for the coastal naval air station.

He hadn't heard from Smitty in ages before his totally random phone call earlier that morning, and his first inclination had been to decline his college roommate's request for help. At least until after the missile test. But when he'd learned it was Colt Bancroft who needed the help, he relented. It had seemed odd that a TOPGUN instructor aboard the *Abraham Lincoln* had flown off that morning with technical data he needed help analyzing.

"Devil One, traffic at your ten o'clock for three zero miles. VFR at one thousand five hundred, maintain VFR at three thousand five hundred."

"Devil One, I've got him on radar," Jug replied, selecting the traffic on his AESA, or active electronically scanned array, radar. His jet calculated the closure at over two hundred and fifty knots, which meant that whatever he was gaining on was flying much, much slower. "What kind of aircraft is it?"

The controller paused for a moment, then said, "Experimental Carbon Cub."

Jug grinned. "Devil One."

He hadn't seen Colt since Hook a few years back. After being kicked out of Las Vegas—a feat most naval aviators were proud of—the Tailhook Association's annual convention had moved to Reno. It was part trade show and part reunion, but it was mostly just a big party. Colt had driven in from Fallon, where he was going through TOPGUN as a student, and Jug had flown in from Pax River after graduating Test Pilot School.

"Devil One, switch Mugu approach on twenty-eight, sixty-five."

"Twenty-eight, sixty-five," Jug replied. "See ya."

As he dialed in the new frequency, he slaved his IRST to the slow-moving traffic and zoomed in on a small taildragger flying east for the coast. His memory from Hook that year was fuzzy, but he recalled catching up with Colt in the TOPGUN admin for most of that first night. And, by catching up, he really meant getting drunker than a skunk while talking about their respective airplane purchases. Jug had been proud of the Mooney he'd bought from a fellow test pilot, but he had been more than a little jealous when Colt told him that he had just taken ownership of a Carbon Cub to do some backcountry flying in Nevada. There were few places more ideal for that kind of flying than the area around Fallon.

He stopped his descent at three thousand five hundred feet but inched closer to the taildragger. If it *was* Colt in the smaller plane, he was about to receive a personalized welcome message. Jug owed him at least that much for the hangover he'd suffered after Colt plied him with rum and Cokes— light on the Coke—at the Bug Roach mixer.

36

1,500 feet over the Pacific Ocean
South of Santa Barbara, California

As the sun dipped below the western horizon, Colt crossed the Santa Ynez Mountains and descended to fifteen hundred feet to remain clear of Santa Barbara's Class C airspace. He could have passed the airport to the north, but with fewer planes flying over the water, it was just easier. Maybe it had something to do with him being a carrier pilot, but he felt at home with nothing but the deep blue waters beneath them.

"What are you hoping Jug tells you?" Punky asked, breaking their silence.

Up until she came into his life and brought along a team of Chinese commandos intent on killing him, he had hoped that Jug would tell him it was nothing—just a fluke. But with all that had happened that morning, there was no way that was still a possibility. "I really don't know," he said.

"You want there to be a reason."

He shook his head. "I don't give two shits about the reason. I want some validation that I didn't just make up what happened to me. That I'm *not* crazy." He paused, then, "And I want to stop it from happening again."

When she didn't answer, he looked over his shoulder and saw her bright blue eyes reflecting the glow from his instrument panel back at him. "You're not crazy, Colt."

He wanted to say something trite, like *I know*. But the truth was, in the darkest recesses of his mind, part of him wondered if there was some truth to it. Maybe he *was* crazy. Maybe something *had* happened, but not the way he remembered it. But hearing her say those words, he believed her. "Thank you," he whispered.

"I'm serious, Colt. I've been investigating *KMART* for some time, and whatever happened to you was planned. You were in the wrong place at the wrong time, but you're the *right* person to stop something worse from happening."

They were halfway between Santa Barbara and Santa Cruz Island when Colt banked the Carbon Cub to the east and aimed just north of Point Mugu's rotating airport beacon. "What could be worse?" he asked. Again, the words *aircraft carrier* flashed like a neon sign in his mind.

"Won't matter if we can stop it," she said.

"Who did you..." He stopped when he heard somebody speaking to air traffic control through what sounded like an oxygen mask.

"Mugu approach, Devil One checking in VFR at one one thousand, RTB."

The air traffic controller's deep voice replied almost immediately. "Devil One, Mugu approach, radar contact, maintain VFR. Information Romeo is current, Mugu is landing two one. Say intentions."

Colt grinned as he listened to the exchange that would have sounded foreign to anybody but a pilot. He couldn't be certain, but he thought the "Devil" call sign belonged to the *Dust Devils* of test squadron VX-31 from China Lake. Jug's squadron. That he was returning to base, or RTB, from the Warning Areas off the coast meant there was a better than fifty-fifty chance the man he was flying to see was on the other end of the radio.

"Devil One's looking for the overhead."

Sure sounds like Jug.

Colt keyed the microphone switch and spoke quickly. "Jug, switch fingers."

Click. Click.

The double break in squelch was all the confirmation he needed that his friend was at the controls of Devil One. Still outside approach control's airspace, Colt switched off their frequency and dialed in 123.45 MHz. Known as "fingers" to almost every backcountry pilot, it was the unofficial air-to-air communication channel.

"Jug's up."

"Jug, it's Colt."

"Colt! You're not in Camarillo yet?"

"Had a little detour." Colt paused as a thought came to him. "Say, do you think you could coordinate permission for us to land at Point Mugu instead of going all the way to Camarillo?'

"Always looking for the easy way..."

Colt laughed, but he knew that if it was possible, Jug would make it happen. "Working smarter, not harder, brother," he said, then scanned the sky above him forward of his wing line, trying to spot the Joint Strike Fighter's blinking strobe lights against the canvas of stars. "Where are you, by the way?"

"Look over your left shoulder."

Colt turned his head and saw that Punky was also trying to spot the fifth-generation fighter in the growing darkness. Suddenly, a deafening thunderclap rocked the plane on their right side, and he spun his head around in time to see the orange-blue glow of a single Joint Strike Fighter in full afterburner, rocking its wings.

"You son of a...," Colt said.

"I'll talk to Mugu for you," Jug replied with obvious joy in his voice. "No promises."

"Thanks, Jug."

Click. Click.

Colt switched back to the Point Mugu approach control frequency, already feeling better about their prospects. With both Punky and Jug in his corner, the dark cloud looming over his head didn't seem so bleak and the threat to the JSF not quite as daunting.

"We're going to stop them," he told Punky over the intercom.

"Yes, we are," she replied. "And I'm going to kill her."

Colt wasn't sure she intended for him to hear that last part.

True to his word, Jug had coordinated with Point Mugu base operations and succeeded in securing authorization for him to land the experimental airplane at the base. Knowing Jug, he had probably told them an admiral was at the controls of the Carbon Cub, a suspicion made more likely by the excessive courtesy he was given as they set up to land on the shorter east-west runway. Once on the ground, they were *requested* to taxi clear to the north ramp.

Dammit, Jug! Colt thought with a smile. *What did you tell them?*

On the ramp, Colt saw two F-35C Joint Strike Fighters parked in front of one of the two hangars and a pilot suited up for flight waving lights in his hands to marshal the Carbon Cub into a parking spot. When Jug crossed his arms over his head, Colt came to a complete stop, then shut down the plane and jumped out. Jug walked around the front of the cowling with a huge grin on his face. "Isn't this a little slow for your liking?"

The two men embraced under the wing. "Can't always be supersonic with my hair on fire."

"Yeah, not with these pretty locks!" Jug reached up and tousled Colt's hair, then looked over his shoulder as Punky emerged from the Carbon Cub. His eyes grew wide, and even in the darkness, Colt noticed them scan up and down her body in a thinly veiled attempt at checking her out. "And who's this?"

Colt made the introductions, feeling more than a little jealous when their handshake lasted longer than what was socially acceptable. At last, Jug released his grip on her, then turned and led the pair across the ramp to the hangar.

"So, what's so important that you flew up from San Diego in that bug smasher?"

"Whoa! Easy how you talk about my plane," Colt said.

"Sorry, brother."

Colt knew he wasn't. "At least wait until we're out of earshot. You might hurt her feelings."

Jug shook his head and led them into the back corner of the hangar and a vacant room that had been temporarily converted into a paraloft. As he began stripping out of his flight gear to stow it neatly next to the only other set in the room, Colt leaned on a wooden bench pushed back against the cinder block wall and reached into his flight suit pocket for the thumb drive he had taken from the *Lincoln*. "I came to bring you this."

Jug paused what he was doing and looked at the memory stick perched between Colt's fingers. "What's that?"

Colt told him everything. From start to finish, he told the test pilot everything that had happened to his jet the night before. When he was done, Punky stepped forward and gave him a concise summary of her investigation into *KMART* and what had happened to them that morning.

"Holy shit," Jug said. "This sounds like a Mark Greaney novel."

"It's not fiction," Punky replied. "*KMART*'s Chinese handler killed my partner..."

"I'm sorry."

"...and we need to figure out what's going on before something worse happens."

Jug finished unzipping his anti-G suit and reached up to hang it on a peg bolted to the wall. "What could be worse than trying to ram an eighty-million-dollar jet into a guided-missile cruiser?"

"That's what we need to find out," Colt said. "Can you look at this data for me?"

Jug took the thumb drive from Colt, then shook his head. "I don't have the computing power here to analyze the data, but I might be able to get an engineer with VX-30 to look at it. Why don't I transfer it to my guy back at China Lake?"

"Thanks, Jug."

He leveled his gaze on Colt, his ever-present playful expression gone. "But if what you're telling me is true, then you probably don't have time for that."

"What choice do I have?"

Colt saw Punky reach into her pocket for her cell phone, then she excused herself and stepped out of the room to answer the call. He knew it had been a long shot that Jug would be able to give him the answers he desperately needed, but he still felt defeated they had come all this way for nothing.

"I'm sorry, brother. Wish there was more I could do."

He gave Jug a weak smile, changing the subject to keep from dwelling on his failure. "So, tell me about this test you're here for."

"We're calling it Project Rán, named for the Norse goddess of the sea. Raytheon teamed up with Kongsberg Defence and Aerospace to develop an air-launched version of the Naval Strike Missile that could be carried internally by the F-35."

"I've read up on that," Colt said. "Sounds promising."

He nodded. "The static tests have had positive results and the strikes against land targets have been successful, so now we're testing it against a ship."

"Which one?"

"That Devil Dog Uber that caught fire in San Diego a few years back."

"The *Bonhomme Richard*?" Colt whistled. "Pretty big boat."

"Yeah, well, the mucky-mucks in acquisitions at the Pentagon want to see if this weapon will be the next carrier killer."

...carrier killer...

Colt felt his heart thudding in his chest as he recalled *TANDY*'s words and swallowed against the dryness in his mouth. He cleared his throat. "When's the test?"

"Tonight."

Colt felt his face flush, but Punky burst through the door and interrupted his thoughts before he could speak them aloud. "Have either of you ever heard of the Amazon Elastic Compute Cloud?"

Both men turned to look at her, but neither answered.

"I just heard back from my contact with the NSA," she said. "It seems earlier today somebody at Cal Poly used the Amazon Elastic Compute Cloud, known as EC2, to modify an electronic waveform of unknown purpose that could be transmitted line-of-sight."

"You're speaking Greek," Colt said.

"It's a scalable cloud-computing service."

"Not helping me much."

Punky rolled her eyes, then looked at Jug. "When you want to run a complex computer program for one of your tests, what's the one thing you need?"

"Processing power. We have designated computers for tasks like that."

She nodded. "Think of this like a time-share cloud-based version. The more processing power you want, the more units you rent. You only pay for what you need."

Colt held up his hand to stop her. "Okay, I get it. It's a big computer. But what does that have to do with anything we've been worrying about?"

"If what happened to your jet was intentional, how would somebody go about gaining control?"

Jug leaned forward and answered for him. "Through a computer virus," he said. "A virus that could be transmitted wirelessly, maybe."

"What would that look like?" Punky asked, nodding her head as she saw the test pilot putting the pieces of the puzzle together.

"An electronic waveform transmitted line-of-sight," he said.

"Bingo."

Colt shook his head, still trying to make the leap the others had clearly already made. "Okay, so let's say this Cal Poly waveform is the one that was used to take control of my jet. I still don't see why we can't just send the FBI to the campus and raid the computer lab to prevent this new modified waveform from falling into the wrong hands."

"Because," Punky said, drawing out her answer. "The wrong hands already have it."

"What do you mean?"

Punky looked between the two pilots. "Whoever ordered the waveform modification already transmitted it using an X-band transceiver."

He stared at her with a blank look on his face.

"To a *Chinese* satellite in geosynchronous Earth orbit."

"Oh, shit," Colt said.

"It gets worse," she continued. "That satellite acted as a relay to re-broadcast the information."

"To where?"

"Somewhere in the Channel Islands."

37

Colt just stared at Punky and let the implication sink in, still trying to process the bombshell she had dropped on them. He had come to accept that what had happened to his jet the night before was no mere fluke but an act of overt sabotage. And it worried him to know that the Chinese weren't done meddling with the Joint Strike Fighter.

"So, what now?" Jug finally asked, breaking the trio's silence.

Punky turned and made eye contact with Colt. He knew she had her sights set on the woman who had killed Rick, and nothing was going to dissuade her from exacting vengeance on the Chinese operative. The only problem was that neither of them knew where she was, and even if they did, they couldn't ignore the bigger threat while seeking revenge. Colt broke her gaze and turned to Jug.

"What time is your test?"

Jug looked at this watch. "They should be loading the ordnance now."

"What's the load out?"

"Two AIM-120D AMRAAM and two Joint Strike Missiles," Jug replied.

Colt cocked his head to the side, wondering why they were loading two Advanced Medium Range Air-to-Air Missiles for what amounted to a SINK-EX. "AMRAAM? What for?"

Punky let out an exaggerated sigh, letting the two men know she lacked the patience for their technical banter. "Boys, maybe we could focus on the problem at hand."

Jug looked wounded, but he nodded in agreement. "You're right," he said. "You two should focus on stopping the Chinese threat. I need to get upstairs and finish my mission planning for this test."

"You can't really intend to go through with this test," Colt said.

"Why wouldn't I?"

"Oh, I don't know. Maybe because the waveform we suspect is the cause of my jet's erratic behavior last night was transmitted to an unknown location in the Channel Islands."

Jug huffed and walked out of the makeshift paraloft without waiting for Colt to finish his argument. Colt and Punky followed on his heels, walking quickly to keep pace with the test pilot.

"Hold up, Jug."

He wheeled on Colt. "Look, Smitty asked me to help you out. Hell, I would have helped even if he hadn't asked. But I've been preparing for this missile shoot for months. *Months*, Colt. Admirals at the Pentagon are interested in the results, and this will either make or break my career."

"I know. But Jug..."

He placed his palms flat on Colt's chest. "But nothing. Listen to me, brother, I think you and your lady friend..." He paused and looked over Colt's shoulder at Punky. "No offense. You two are on to something. I get that. But I still don't see why I should call my boss back in China Lake and tell him I couldn't get this done. Or call the three-star for acquisitions and tell him he's going to have to wait a little longer to pull the trigger on buying this weapon."

Colt understood what this test meant to his friend. They might have gone different routes in their careers, but he imagined the test track wasn't much different than the one he was on in the world of tactics. You advanced based on the merits of your contributions, and if you failed to provide something meaningful to your community, you were left sitting on the side of the road, wondering why the bus drove off without you.

"I hear you, brother," Colt said in a softer tone. "Maybe just postpone it? Delay it a day. Wait until we hear back from China Lake. Let us get some answers first."

Jug sighed, and Colt could tell he was at least questioning his decision to move forward. "I can't delay it, Colt. There is a *Ticonderoga*-class guided-missile cruiser off the coast right now providing range clearance. They launched one of their helos for a search and rescue mission, but—"

Punky interrupted him. "What search and rescue?"

"Apparently some hikers didn't show for their return trip to the mainland, so the National Park Service called in the Coast Guard to help with the search. The *Mobile Bay* was in the area, and—"

"Did you say the *Mobile Bay*?"

Jug squinted at Colt, wondering where this line of questioning was headed. "Yeah, she's on loan to us for the test. Why?"

"The *Mobile Bay* is the ship that was harassed by those orbs last night."

"You mean the one you almost crashed into?" Jug asked.

Colt nodded, unable to say more as the scene replayed again in his mind. He had successfully kept the worst of the memories at bay during the day, but with the sun now below the horizon, they had returned to haunt him. He could see the green-hued cruiser cutting through the water while dozens of orbs swarmed it, and he could feel the impotence when his jet rolled inverted and pulled down in an uncontrolled dive.

Punky's voice severed his nightmare. "Go back to the search and rescue for a minute," she said. "Where were these missing hikers?"

"Santa Cruz Island," Jug replied.

"That's one of the Channel Islands, right?" she asked.

When he nodded, she pulled her phone out of her pocket and placed a call. The two pilots could only hear her half of the conversation, but they watched transfixed as the NCIS agent took charge of the investigation and satisfied whatever had tickled her curiosity.

"Yeah, it's me...hey, this is a long shot, but can you pull some passenger manifests for me?" Punky turned her back on them as Colt and Jug traded confused looks. "Santa Cruz Island...oh, really?"

Jug leaned over and whispered conspiratorially to Colt, "What do you suppose is going through her mind?"

Colt shook his head. "I'm afraid to find out."

"Yes, I guess the Island Packers...what about flights?" Punky ripped a sheet of paper from the bulletin board mounted in the hall, then dug into her pocket for a pen. "Go ahead with that info...say that again? RLC?" She stopped writing and shot Colt a look. "Did you say Santa Maria?"

Colt grimaced when he saw the look on her face.

Punky ended the call. "She's on Santa Cruz Island."

"Who's on Santa Cruz Island?" Colt asked.

"*TANDY*," she said, with an edge to her voice. Her eyes glossed over, focused on a distant scene.

"That's a pretty big stretch."

Punky turned and looked through the open hangar doors at the Carbon Cub sitting idle on the ramp next to the larger Joint Strike Fighters. He could see her wheels turning but didn't know what was going through her mind. Fortunately, he didn't have to wait long.

"Not long after the police were called to the scene of an accident in the Santa Maria valley, a helicopter owned by RLC took off from Santa Maria airport and flew to Santa Cruz Island," she said, filling them in on what she had learned from her phone conversation.

"Who's RLC?" Colt asked.

She waved it away. "Totally legit. It's a Louisiana-based company that flies roughnecks to and from oil rigs off the coast. But this trip to Santa Cruz Island wasn't part of their normal routine."

"And you think *TANDY* was on that flight? That's pretty thin."

"What about the missing hikers?"

Jug added his two cents. "Hikers go missing all the time."

"On an island visited by a helicopter that departed an airport less than twenty miles from where my partner was shot dead?"

Neither pilot responded. Colt knew the evidence was circumstantial at best, but she was like a dog with a bone, and he knew she wasn't about to give up on this. At last, he spoke up. "So, what do you want to do?"

Punky didn't answer right away and instead turned to look at Jug. "If you were going to transmit a signal line-of-sight and get the greatest range, where would you do it?"

"At the top of a mountain," he replied.

"Any mountains on Santa Cruz Island?"

He shook his head. "There's some definite elevation on the island, but maybe only a couple thousand feet."

"Is there any way we can search for it? Some sort of electronic surveillance equipment?"

Again, Jug shook his head. "The F-35C has the AN/ASQ-239 electronic warfare suite. Once the engineers in China Lake have identified the waveform, we can use it to search for and jam the signal—"

"What's the other jet for?" Colt interrupted him, looking out at the jets on the ramp while feeling the familiar stirring in his gut of the sky calling his name. He had been ostracized from the *Abraham Lincoln* air wing, but his reputation was still mostly intact across the rest of the fleet. It might be enough.

Jug looked at the jets, then to Colt. "Uh-uh," he said. "I know what you're thinking."

"If you're hell-bent on going forward with this test, let me at least take the other bird and search for the signal. If we can pinpoint their location..."

"No way, Colt. Even if the other jet wasn't on tap to be a spare, are you forgetting that you'll be searching for an individual who is allegedly in possession of a weapon designed to defeat the JSF's defenses? *In a JSF?*" Colt opened his mouth to argue, but Jug cut him off. "Besides, you need to stay behind and wait to hear back from our engineers."

"What about your plane?" Punky asked Colt.

He wasn't sure whether he should laugh at that or not. The Carbon Cub was an amazing plane, but it wasn't designed to search for hostile forces and lacked the JSF's EW suite. Even if he did take her flying, there wasn't much he could do other than fly really low and scare *TANDY*. Finally, he answered her. "Nope."

"I'm serious," Punky said, unrelenting. "We can fly over to the island, find her, and then I can...arrest her."

There was a long enough pause that Colt knew she wasn't thinking about arresting her. But before he could answer, Jug jumped aboard Team Punky. "I can get you a pair of night vision goggles, but unless you know where to look, they won't help you much."

"You said there was a helicopter from the *Mobile Bay*?"

Almost as if Jug had forgotten Colt already ruled out the use of his airplane, he continued helping Punky formulate her strategy for flying the twenty-five miles across the Pacific Ocean to Santa Cruz Island to hunt down the Chinese intelligence operative who had murdered her partner. "When you get airborne, you can call Raptor Two Four on Cobalt."

"What's Cobalt?" Punky asked.

Jug read off the frequency, then realized it was in the ultrahigh frequency band. "Just come up Guard when you get to the island, and I'll have them reach you there."

Punky nodded, and Colt held up his hands. "Are you guys forgetting that it's *my* plane you're talking about taking?"

"Well, if you're staying here, what else is she going to fly?" Jug asked.

"No way." Colt shook his head, unable to believe what he was hearing. He had let other instructors on the staff fly his plane, but he was in the cockpit with them. The idea of letting a woman he had just met fly his pride and joy was ludicrous—especially given the head wound she had received during the assassination attempt earlier that morning.

"Colt."

He looked into her pale blue eyes and felt his resolving waning. Part of him knew he should trust her instincts the same way he trusted his own in a dogfight. But another part of him couldn't bear the thought of sitting on the sidelines while she went on the offensive. "No," he said, but with less conviction.

"Colt," she said again. "You know it's worth looking into."

He did, but that didn't make it easier for him to accept. "Fine," he said at last. "You can fly to the island, satisfy your curiosity, then come back."

Jug cleared his throat. "Let's get you those night vision goggles."

38

A little over an hour later, Jug watched Punky taxi away from the hangar in Colt's Carbon Cub. She handled the airplane like a pro, but he still understood why Colt was nervous just handing the keys over to her. He would have felt the same way if she had suggested taking his Mooney.

After her plane disappeared around the corner to takeoff on Runway 27, Jug returned to the makeshift paraloft and suited up for his flight. He had verified with the *Mobile Bay* that the airspace was still clear and that conditions remained ideal to execute the test. Despite Colt's best efforts at convincing him to postpone it, he felt a stir of excitement as he walked back through the empty hangar and onto the dark flight line to man up.

Walking up to his jet, Jug took a moment to appreciate the beautiful lines of the plane. Some considered the F-35C ugly in comparison to fighters of the previous generation, but he didn't agree. The composite skin had RAM, or Radar Absorbent Material, baked into the body panels, giving it a darker gray look compared to non-stealth carrier aircraft. But its sharp, crisp lines looked elegant from any angle. His jet's canopy was tilted forward in the open position, and a boarding ladder dropped down from an oddly shaped panel on the left side of the jet below the ejection seat.

Spotlights shone down on the aircraft, casting shadows across the ground as he walked closer and greeted his plane captain. Then, as he had done on every flight before, he completed an exterior preflight inspection, spending a few extra minutes inside the weapon bays with the ordies, inspecting his weapons for the mission. Underneath the nose and hidden behind a durable sapphire window was the EOTS, that combined Forward-Looking Infrared and Infrared Search and Track functionality. It was used for both air-to-surface and air-to-air targeting and would see action in both arenas during the test.

Following his walk-around, Jug climbed the ladder and stepped down into the Martin-Baker Mk16 ejection seat, spending a few minutes calming his nerves by methodically strapping himself into the seat and connecting his life-support systems to the jet. With each buckle that snapped together, he felt his stomach settle just a little bit more as everything going on around him faded away until he was left with total focus on the upcoming mission. It was the final step in combining man and machine and making them one.

Nothing would get in the way of that.

———————

As Punky climbed away from Runway 27, she reacquainted herself with the Carbon Cub's controls. The tower controller cleared her to depart to the west, and she turned left slightly and went feet wet just south of Port Hueneme.

Unlike the two naval aviators, Punky had never flown over the ocean at night. Her eyes strained to see anything that even remotely resembled a horizon, but she finally gave up and focused on the synthetic horizon displayed on the Garmin glass panel Colt had installed in the plane. Every private pilot had at least three hours of night time and ten takeoffs and landings in the dark, but even her own experience of double that was woefully inadequate to prepare her for the flight to Santa Cruz Island.

The calm voice of the air traffic controller broke through her growing fear. "Experimental Carbon Cub Four Four Three November Alpha, radar services terminated, change to advisory frequencies approved."

"Three November Alpha," she replied, then changed the radio's frequency to Guard.

The VHF Guard frequency, 121.5 MHz, was an international distress and emergency aviation frequency all civilian aircraft were expected to monitor. Though military aircraft monitored a like frequency in the UHF band, Jug understood that the Carbon Cub wasn't equipped to transmit or receive in UHF. Monitoring Guard was a smart call, as long as he could reach Raptor Two Four and have them contact her there.

"Raptor Two Four, this is Three November Alpha on Guard," she said.

Silence.

She tried reining in the growing dread that she had made a mistake by flying west into the night. After double-checking that she was pointed at Santa Cruz Island, she reached behind her for the night vision goggles bracket Jug had made for her, then slipped it on over her head. She cinched down the straps, then affixed the AN/AVS-9 night vision goggles to the bracket and powered them on.

After flipping the goggles down in front of her eyes, she made some last-minute adjustments to the fit and focus, then stared at the ominous dark green landmass rising out of the ocean in front of her.

"Three November Alpha, this is Raptor Two Four on Guard," a voice said.

She breathed a sigh of relief. "This is Three November Alpha, go ahead."

"I understand you are offering to assist with the search effort?"

"Negative," Punky replied. "I am with NCIS on a special mission and request your assistance."

The pause at the other end was long enough to let her know her pronouncement was news to them. If her suspicion proved accurate, their search and rescue mission should really be a search and recovery mission. But she wasn't about to tell them that.

After several minutes of Punky droning west toward the island in silence, the voice returned. "Go ahead with your request."

As much as she appreciated Colt letting her borrow his plane, it wasn't ideal for the interdiction mission she had in mind. She needed to put the Carbon Cub down someplace on the island and then convince the MH-60R crew to pick her up and help her search for a needle in the haystack.

Only this needle shot back.

"Request you meet me at airstrip located at..." She consulted the notes she had taken during her rudimentary target area study, then read back the coordinates for a grass strip located eight miles west of Smuggler's Cove. "Thirty-three decimal nine eight north, one nineteen decimal six eight west."

"Stand by, Three November Alpha."

As Punky neared the east coastline of Santa Cruz Island, she descended to three thousand feet and bisected the island at Scorpion Ranch. She glanced down and saw what looked like a sailboat anchored off the coast, but quickly looked back at the rising terrain, knowing that finding the grass strip at night would be a challenge. Fortunately, the night vision goggles made it easy for her to spot the orbiting MH-60R.

If only it were that easy to find *TANDY*.

The moon's dim glow illuminated the sharp ridges and valleys defining the island's terrain and cast long shadows across the ground. Punky steered the Carbon Cub north of the shoreline where the Seahawk orbited and looked down at the island through the forward windscreen and each side window.

"Three November Alpha, we are supporting an active search and rescue mission and are unable to grant your request," the helicopter pilot said, in what sounded like a rehearsed response.

She bit her tongue to keep from replying with a string of four-letter curse words, then casually keyed the microphone switch atop the stick. "Raptor Two Four, my mission takes precedence over your search and rescue."

A different voice answered her. "How do you figure?"

"Meet me at that location and I'll tell you," she said, breathing through her nose to control her temper.

"Tell me now, or you're on your own."

Punky eased back on the stick as she neared a ridge to the west of Smuggler's Cove. A blinking red light sat at the top, indicating an antenna or other man-made structure that posed a hazard to aviation. She was already above the height of the ridge, but she believed in the old aviation axiom: *Speed is life, altitude is life insurance.*

"It's classified..."

From the corner of her eye, Punky caught an irregular flash that seemed out of place lower on the ridge. She whipped her head to the left and focused through the goggles at the flashing light, just as it stopped.

"Say again," the helicopter pilot said.

But Punky didn't get the chance. Before she could respond, she heard the whip-snapping of bullets streaking through the air next to her airplane. She jerked the stick to the right, banking away from what she now recognized as muzzle flashes coming from the side of the ridge.

"I'm taking fire!" she yelled over the radio, not caring that every airplane monitoring the civilian Guard frequency had heard her panicked shout.

At Naval Air Station Point Mugu, Colt waited in a room on the hangar's second deck that Jug and his sailors had converted into a makeshift ready room. Jug had told his engineers in China Lake to rush the analysis, and Colt still hoped to have the results in time to provide Jug with jamming protection during his flight. But he hated waiting, and he passed the time by dialing in the civilian Guard frequency on a portable radio to listen in as Punky made her way across the water to Santa Cruz Island.

"Raptor Two Four, my mission takes precedence over your search and rescue."

Colt had to hand it to her. She was flying in the pitch black off the coast of Southern California, searching for the woman who had killed her partner, and still she refused to back down. Punky had balls, he decided. Bigger balls than most of the men he'd flown with.

He listened to the rest of the conversation with growing unease, recognizing the new voice on the radio as that of a more seasoned pilot not easily cowed by her assertiveness. But it sounded like she was slowly convincing them to at least meet her at the airstrip for a face-to-face. At least until the conversation took a chilling turn.

"I'm taking fire!"

Colt's heart leaped into his throat, recalling his own experiences in combat when the Hornet he had been piloting became the target for surface-to-air gunners. The enemy's Air Defense Artillery had largely been inaccurate, but it hadn't stopped him from believing he was in grave danger, danger he knew Punky was in at that very moment.

"I can't just sit here," he said to himself.

Spinning away from the radio, he raced from the ready room and down the hall to the stairwell at the end. Taking the steps two at a time, he raced for the ground floor and into another hall leading to the converted paraloft. In that moment, he was thankful he'd had the presence of mind to remove his own flight gear from the back of the Carbon Cub and stow it in the hangar.

Unzipping the parachute bag, Colt removed his flight equipment and quickly went about suiting up for flight. He didn't rush, but neither did he take his time, knowing that whatever engagement Punky had found herself in would likely be over before he managed to get airborne. Regardless, he wasn't about to sit on his hands in the safety of the ready room while listening to the radio as the woman who had saved his life was shot down over an island only twenty-five miles away.

After donning his gear, Colt left the paraloft in a rush and raced through the hangar to the darkened silhouette of a single F-35C Joint Strike Fighter at rest on the ramp. Jug wasn't likely to forgive him anytime soon for stealing his squadron's jet, but he'd get over it.

Hang on, Punky. I'm coming.

39

Santa Cruz Island, California

Chen stared in horror as Wu Tian swept the camouflage netting away and stood in the darkness, swinging the Heckler & Koch MP7 up to aim at the small plane flying directly at them. He flicked the selector to fire and let loose a short burst, adjusted his aim, then fired another.

"You *idiot!*" she shouted.

Wu Tian spun back to her with a menacing scowl on his face. "The helicopter might be coincidence, but an airplane flying directly for us?"

She looked away from him to the airplane as it banked north, trying to escape the barrage of gunfire. It was unlikely he hit the plane, but there was no question the pilot now knew somebody on the ground was armed and didn't care for an airplane flying over them. The plane's engine sounded strong, but it appeared to be descending for the butte north of Smuggler's Cove.

"You need to handle this," she hissed.

He looked down at the weapons kit at her feet and nodded to it. "Give me your spare magazines."

She hesitated, but in the end decided that her focus should be on using the weapon Mantis had entrusted to her. If she needed to use the silenced

MP7, things had gone terribly wrong. She leaned over and picked up three twenty-round magazines and handed them to the naval commando.

"Do not let the pilot escape," she said, then looked down as a notification appeared on her tablet. "And see that I am not disturbed. The target aircraft is within range."

He looked as if he wanted to say something in response, but he wisely kept his mouth shut. Stuffing the spare magazines into his pants' cargo pockets, he glanced over to the still descending plane, then began climbing the slope for the trail at the top of the ridge. Chen watched him disappear into the darkness, then surveyed the expansive Pacific Ocean, where she would meet her destiny.

With a deep breath, Chen slipped the VR goggles down over her eyes and stepped back into a digital world.

"Holy shit!" Punky shouted. She felt the impact through her seat frame and glanced over her shoulder at the four new holes that had appeared in the plane's fuselage just behind her.

"Say again, Three November Alpha?"

Punky gripped the stick and squeezed. "I'm taking fire!"

"From where?"

She had the throttle pushed forward to the stop and was straining the motor to its limits, but if she had any chance of surviving, she needed to get away from the muzzle flashes on the ridge. Scanning the ground ahead of her, Punky looked for a flat piece of land where she could put the plane down if one of the bullets had managed to find a critical component.

Thwap! Thwap! Thwap!

The sickening sound turned her stomach, and she slapped the stick over to her left leg to counter the almost immediate roll to the right.

"What the..."

Punky dropped her hand from the throttle to the stick as the airplane fought her, and she struggled to keep her wings level. The Carbon Cub tottered on its axis, wobbling like a drunk sailor as it yawed into the damaged wing. She added left rudder to keep the nose tracking straight and hazarded a glance through the side window.

"Oh, shit."

Through the green-tinted night vision, Punky saw a ragged strip of fabric fluttering on the outermost portion of her wing.

"Three November Alpha?" The helicopter pilot's concern was evident in his voice.

"I think he got me," she replied through gritted teeth. The hairs on the back of her neck stood on end as she fought to regain the composure she expected of herself in stressful situations. But regardless of her previous experiences, nothing could have prepared her for the multitude of emotions that descended on her as she limped away in an experimental airplane from an invisible gunman below.

"Say your intentions," the helicopter pilot said.

She had her hands full and fell back on her flight training, returning to the most basic of all aviation axioms: *aviate, navigate, communicate.* Before she could do anything else, she just needed to fly the damn plane.

"Three November Alpha?"

"I'm missing about two...maybe three feet of fabric from the top of my right wing. Aileron looks to be in good shape," she said, talking through the damage in a calm, almost detached manner.

"How's it flying?"

"Like a truck." After the impact's initial shock had worn off, Punky returned the Carbon Cub to a mostly stable attitude, but the damage she had sustained was making it difficult to keep her wings level. "It's pulling hard right."

"Copy. Can you make it to the airfield?"

She opened the window, letting it hinge upward against the wing, and craned her neck out into the slipstream to look back at the tail of the plane. Even at only sixty miles per hour, the wind blast took her breath away and almost knocked the night vision goggles free. Not seeing anything else that concerned her, she pulled her head back into the cockpit and scanned the ground in front of her for a suitable landing spot.

"Not with the way she's flying," she said.

She felt a shudder reverberate through the plane. When she pushed the stick forward, it got worse.

Fuck. Not good.

"Okay. What do you want to do?"

She leaned back into her seat and tried to ignore the sour feeling in her stomach. "I'm setting up for an off-field landing," she said.

It was a fancy way of saying she was going to crash.

Raptor 24
Navy MH-60R

Brian had no trouble spotting the experimental taildragger as it cruised above them heading west. He had even less trouble spotting the muzzle flashes from just below the ridgeline. He saw the gunfire, but his brain struggled to accept something like that could happen off the coast of California.

"Say again, Three November Alpha?" He banked right, tracking the airplane's movement to the north, then switched over to the intercom. "Rose, get on the fifty. Port side."

"I'm on it," Rose said.

The woman pilot's voice sounded shaken and almost incredulous. "I'm taking fire!"

"From where?" he asked, though he was almost certain he already had a bead on the point of origin. "Anything, Rose?"

The aircrewman shouted from the back to be heard over the wind noise. "Nothing yet!"

"Three November Alpha?"

"I think he got me."

He focused all his attention on the rising terrain in front of him, keeping the Seahawk close to the ground as he tracked closer to the stricken plane. It looked like the taildragger was making a turn back to the east, but he knew there were no runways on that end of the island.

Maybe she plans on bugging out back to the mainland, he thought.

"Say your intentions," he said.

He had always been taught to stay out of another pilot's cockpit in an emergency unless invited in, but he needed to know what she planned on doing if he was going to give her the appropriate support. When she remained silent, he knew she had her hands full.

"Three November Alpha?"

"I'm missing about two...maybe three feet of fabric from the top of my right wing. Aileron looks to be in good shape," she said.

"How's it flying?"

"Tallyho!" Rose shouted from the back. "One contact on the ridgeline moving north."

"Like a truck," the taildragger's pilot said. "It's pulling hard right."

"Copy. Can you make it to the airfield?" He switched over to the intercom. "Can you maintain a visual, Rose?"

"Negative. He's hard to make out, and I can only see his movement."

Brian had to make a tough decision, but that was why the skipper had entrusted him with the HAC qualification. He didn't have time to debate the merits of his choices. If he continued shadowing the stricken plane, Rose would lose sight of the gunman. But if he turned and gave Rose a chance to engage, he wouldn't be able to help the taildragger.

"Okay. What do you want to do?"

"I'm setting up for an off-field landing," she said.

Brian made his choice. "Okay, fellas, we're gonna help this lady pilot out. Rose, keep an eye on our six and let me know if you see any gunfire headed our way. Dillon, padlock that plane and make sure it looks like she's heading for a clear piece of land. Call out any obstructions you see."

"Aye aye, sir," Rose said.

"Copy that," Dillon replied. "She's running out of room."

"Three November Alpha, we are in trail on your right side and will meet you when you land."

She didn't reply, but Brian saw a pair of bright LED landing lights under the nose turn on. The taildragger was less than one hundred feet off the ground and looked to be on final approach.

40

Punky debated landing with the night vision goggles on, but she decided her lack of experience would offset any benefit she might gain from seeing more of the terrain. She knew her visual acuity would be better with traditional landing lights instead of on the goggles that hindered her depth perception, so she ripped them off her head and illuminated the ground in front of her with 175,000 candles.

"It's getting worse," she said.

"Copy, we're visual," the helicopter pilot replied. "That stab is shaking pretty bad."

Hold together, baby...

"What do you see?"

There was a delay, and she sensed a dark shadow hovering off to her right side and resisted the temptation to look at it. The helicopter pilot's voice was calm and reassuring. "It looks like you're missing some rigging that connects the horizontal stabilizer to the vertical stabilizer. The whole damn thing looks like it's trying to twist off."

"I'm giving it almost full left rudder," she said, as she fought to tame the bucking plane. "And the nose wants to run away on me."

"The area in front of you looks clear. Recommend you set her down there."

Yeah, no shit!

She depressed the push-to-talk to reply when the plane suddenly nosed over, and she felt her stomach leap into her throat.

"Watch your nose!"

She eased back on the stick and held her breath while she waited for the nose to respond.

One thousand feet per minute, she thought, reminding herself that she didn't have that much air beneath her. She glanced at the attitude indicator on the Garmin panel and saw the nose tracking slowly upward to the horizon.

"You've got it?"

"I've got it...I've got it," she said.

She strained against an increased pressure on the stick to keep her wings level, feeling beads of sweat forming on her brow. She had already fed in more rudder to keep her nose pointed straight, but the shaking tail only seemed to get worse. Without the night vision goggles, she could only see a narrow strip of ground in front of her illuminated by the twin LED landing lights, but she knew there was a pretty significant drop into the sea at the east end of the island. She couldn't mess around much longer.

"I'm putting her down."

"What do you need me to do?" the helicopter pilot asked.

"Nothing," she said, then pulled power and felt the nose yaw further left.

"Watch your nose!"

She eased off the rudder pedal, and the nose straightened out.

Her legs shook from the constant tension of fighting the controls. She wiggled her fingers and toes, a forced habit that reminded her to relax as she prepared for probably the most challenging landing of her life. But then the tail began shaking violently, and she struggled to control the bobbing and weaving plane and keep it tracking straight. With each weave to the left, she countered too far right and fought it going back to the left. When the nose dipped, she responded by lifting it too far, and she feared she might stall the wings and plummet to the earth.

"I'm losing it," she said.

"You're running out of room."

When the nose dropped again, she eased back on the stick and leveled off barely ten feet over the grassy butte as she waited for the violent shaking to subside. She kept her control inputs as smooth as possible, and when the shaking faded into only a mild tremor, she reached up to pull the lever and add one notch of flaps. She braced herself for the nose's natural tendency to drop while wondering what the added stress would do to the damaged airplane. But she held together.

She pulled power and held her speed constant until she had assured herself the plane wouldn't nose-dive for the ground. Then she cracked the power back even further.

Sixty-five knots, she thought, then added a second notch of flaps as her airspeed crept closer to the final approach speed.

Fifty-five knots.

"You need to put her down," the helicopter pilot said. "Now."

Forty-five knots. She reached up for the flap lever one last time and added a final notch, then established the proper attitude for a wheel landing.

She rounded out the bottom of the approach profile, and the tremor grew until the plane shook with surprising intensity. She waggled her stick from side to side, dumping air and lift from under the wings until the tundra tires settled onto the dirt. Not knowing how badly her tailwheel was damaged, she kept it off the ground and tracked in a straight line, using gentle rudder pedal inputs to avoid the biggest shrubs dotting her path.

"Stop!" the voice screamed at her.

As her airspeed continued to decay, she retracted her flaps and let the tailwheel fall as her landing lights illuminated what looked like the end of the earth racing toward her. She stood on the brake pedals and held her breath as the experimental plane struggled to stop before she ran out of ground.

When the Carbon Cub came to rest at last, she felt the tension trapped in her body evaporate in an instant.

Devil 1
Navy F-35C

Jug leaned his helmet against the head box as he plugged in the afterburner and watched his airspeed tick upward in his Helmet Mounted Display. He added back pressure to his side stick, and the Joint Strike Fighter climbed rapidly through the thin coastal air.

"Devil One climbing into the three block," he said over the datalink network, letting the test director back in China Lake know he was climbing to thirty thousand feet to begin the test.

"Copy," the emotionless voice replied.

It felt strange being the only aircraft in the large Pacific missile test complex, but at least he had a host of engineers, technicians, and other test pilots monitoring his flight from the command center back in China Lake. If he needed a second or third set of eyes and ears, he would have his pick.

He pulled the engine out of afterburner and climbed effortlessly at three hundred and fifty knots. With a subtle twitch of his hand, the plane responded to his command and banked to the right as he steered to follow the pre-programmed route on his display.

A little over a minute later, he flew over the first fix on his route. "Devil One, checkpoint Alpha," he said.

"Copy," the same emotionless voice answered.

He adjusted his heading to the southwest on a route that took him just north of San Nicolas Island, where the Navy had a myriad of radar emitters that would attempt to detect him while he engaged target drones orbiting in a simulated CAP.

His radar warning receiver chirped, and Jug noted the line of bearing from the emitter, figuring it was one of the Navy's longer-range systems. But so far, the ground-based system had not painted a return, and he was still piloting a phantom through the night sky. But he wasn't willing to risk Project Rán's success on chance, so he toggled over on the Panoramic Cockpit Display to the page for the AN/ASQ-239 electronic warfare suite.

The next-generation electronic warfare suite was always active and provided both offensive and defensive options to the pilot. But it was its all-aspect, broadband protection and suppression of enemy radars that Jug was most interested in. Even if a surveillance radar was able to paint a return against the radar-absorbent material baked into the skin of his jet, his EW system would jam it and create a blind spot for him to slip through. He grinned when he saw the system working as advertised.

"Devil One, buzzer on," he said, letting the observers in the command center know he was jamming along a radar's line of bearing.

"Copy, Devil One," the observer said. "Palmdale, how's the radar picture?"

The voice of their FAA representative broke in. "Picture clean."

"Devil One, continue to checkpoint Bravo."

"Roger," Jug said.

He scaled out on his moving map display to see more of the route that turned north after San Nicolas and paralleled the Air Defense Identification Zone at the far western edge of the test complex. He knew he would engage the target drones on that leg before reversing course to the south to launch his Joint Strike Missiles at the target ship.

Fighting off the temptation to relax and let his guard down, he pulled up his fuel system's display and compared his current fuel state with the plan. No matter how successful the test went, if he didn't have enough gas to make it back to base, that failure would overshadow everything else.

"Looking good," he said to himself. But any additional commentary was cut short when his display flickered. "What the..."

He half expected the oddity to be accompanied by a caution, warning of an impending electrical failure. But the flicker lasted less than a second and the display returned to normal, leaving him with only a slightly uneasy feeling that things weren't as kosher as they seemed. He had almost successfully brushed the incident under the rug of other more pressing matters when he remembered what Colt had told him earlier.

He switched off datalink comms to the frequency for the radio they had set up in the ready room back in Point Mugu. "Base, Devil One, is Lieutenant Bancroft around?"

"Wait one."

He knew Colt was focused on getting results back from China Lake, but he didn't think the TOPGUN instructor would be far from the radio where he could monitor the test. Even though he was certain he was letting his imagination get the better of him, he couldn't just dismiss the anomaly as a one-off gremlin that all newer fighters experienced.

"Devil One, he's not in the room at the moment."

He shrugged and decided to let it go in favor of focusing on the task at hand. He made a mental note to include the flickering displays in his report and reached up to the touchscreen display to select his weapons page. The screen flickered again, then shuffled through several pages on its own, causing his stomach to drop with a sudden onset of fear.

"What the hell is going on?"

"Jug, this is Colt."

Jug exhaled loudly, then keyed the button to transmit his reply. "Colt, something strange is going on."

"Abort the mission and return to base."

He recoiled as if slapped. "Say that again?"

"I said abort...abort the mission and return to base. Punky is taking fire over Santa Cruz Island, and I'm en route to provide air cover."

He didn't have a clue what was going on but didn't argue and pressed the button to disengage the autopilot, uncoupling the jet from the pre-programmed route. Then he added pressure to the side stick to turn his jet back to the east and the safety of Point Mugu. The test could wait.

But his wings remained level with his nose pointed at the dark mass of San Nicolas Island.

Oh, shit...

"Jug?"

The moisture in his mouth evaporated in an instant, and his tongue felt thick as he tried to speak. "Colt..." He paused. "I can't..."

"You have to!"

"You don't understand," he replied, awash with fear. "I can't control it."

41

USS *Mobile Bay* (CG-53)
South of Santa Cruz Island, California

Captain Bethany Lewis jerked upright with a start, her eyes wide with fright and staring into the darkness as she struggled to surface from her nightmare. The blue wool blanket was a little thinner than it had been when they issued it to her as a Plebe at the Naval Academy, but she tossed the "blue magnet" aside and swung her feet out onto the floor. Using the heels of her hands, she massaged away the fatigue from her eyes before glancing at the boxy battery-powered alarm clock on her desk.

21:57

She reached for the clock and, with practiced hands, turned off the alarm that was to go off in three more minutes. She had only intended for it to be a short power nap anyway. While she wasn't technically needed in CIC for either the missile test or the search and rescue mission, she wasn't about to put the burden on her crew while she sawed logs. Leadership bore responsibilities she was unwilling to pass on to others.

Beth still wore her blue coveralls but had kicked off her steel-toed boots before climbing into her rack. She bent over and slid her feet inside the worn leather footwear, then laced them up like she had done countless times before. It was pitch black, but she didn't need the benefit of light to navigate the scant furnishings of her stateroom, and she rose from her bed and walked through the door into the head, where she flipped on the fluorescent light above the sink.

She stared at her reflection for a long minute, studying the bags under her eyes and the creased worry lines on her forehead. It seemed like only yesterday when she had stared back at herself from a mirror in the fourth wing of Bancroft Hall, questioning her decision to leave her family and friends behind and travel across the country to pursue a career in the Navy. The lines hadn't been there then, but the worry had.

A distant knock on the door to the passageway broke her trance of reminiscence, and she glanced at her watch to see that the three minutes had elapsed.

Right on time, she thought.

She exited the head and made for the door on the far side of her office, opening it a crack. Master Chief Ben Ivy stood like a massive statue in the doorway, blotting out the red glow from the passageway beyond. "It's time, ma'am."

Beth nodded. "Let me brush my teeth. I'll be right out."

"Aye, ma'am."

She closed the door softly, wondering how long Master Chief had been standing outside her door, waiting for the minute hand to point due north so he could rouse his captain. Fortune smiled on her when the Navy ordered her to the *Mobile Bay* and gave her Ben Ivy as her Command Master Chief. He was one of the good ones.

She turned back to the head and quickly brushed the fuzz from her teeth, enjoying the way the peppermint toothpaste invigorated her and propelled her further from her sleep. Then she splashed water on her face to try to dampen the heavy bags that came with command at sea, before pulling the ship's ball cap down from the hook next to the sink and setting it onto her head.

Beth took a few moments to smooth back her hair, tucking loose strands up underneath the ball cap, then stepped back to study her reflection in the mirror. She knew Ben was waiting for her just beyond her stateroom door, but this last personal inspection had served her well since her very first day as a midshipman, and like all who called the sea their home, she was loath to break from tradition.

"You are the captain," she said to herself in the mirror.

She flipped off the fluorescent light and turned for the door.

Santa Cruz Island, California

Punky killed the engine and swung open the door, squinting against the maelstrom of wind and loose debris flung into the air by the helicopter's powerful rotors. After jumping out of the Carbon Cub, she reached back inside for the night vision goggles she had discarded before making her emergency landing, then turned to look at the edge of the cliff she had stopped less than a yard from.

That was close, she thought. *Too close.*

With the taste of bile in her mouth, she turned away from the cliff and shielded her eyes as she watched the military helicopter set down twenty yards from the Carbon Cub. She knew Colt wasn't going to be happy she left his plane damaged and stranded on an island in the middle of the Pacific Ocean, but she couldn't think about that now. The gunfire that had brought her down was enough confirmation she was on the right path.

She turned for the helicopter just as the side door slid open and a man in a green flight suit jumped to the ground and raced toward her. "Ma'am! I'm Petty Officer Rose, and I'm here to rescue you! Do you need any assistance?"

"I don't think so!" she shouted over the tumult of the rotor wash.

The aircrewman gripped her arm gently and guided her to the open rear door, bracing to help her climb inside. But she brushed him off, nauseous with anxiety from being shot down but determined to stop *TANDY* before she could do anything else.

The pilot in the right seat turned to look back at her. "Ma'am, are you okay?"

She nodded. "Thanks for your help."

"What the hell is going on? Why are you here?"

"We need to get in the air," she said. "Before somebody comes to finish off the job."

The pilot nodded at her, then turned back to the Seahawk's complex controls. "Rose, keep an eye out. Let's get her back to the *Mobile Bay*."

"No!" Punky shouted. "I can't leave." Her stomach dropped as the pilot raised the collective to lift the helicopter off the butte and quickly nosed over to accelerate in the air over the water on the east side of the island. He banked right and followed the coastline south as it bent back to the west.

"What the hell is going on?" he asked again.

The aircrewman in the back turned to look at her. She knew she needed their help to find *TANDY*, but she wasn't sure what to say that would convince them of that. So, she settled on the truth. "There is a hostile enemy force on the island."

The other pilot turned to look at her. "Say that again?"

"I have been investigating a sailor suspected of giving secrets to the Chinese, and we believe they used him to help develop a weapon that hacks into the Joint Strike Fighter."

"For what purpose?"

She thought that would be obvious, but it was really a question for Colt and Jug. Her only objective was to find *TANDY* before she could do it again. "I don't know. But I believe she is attempting—"

Rose did a double take out the window. "Contact, right!" he shouted.

Punky darted across the narrow cabin, scrambling to look over the aircrewman's shoulder, but she couldn't see anything but darkness. She slipped the NVG bracket on over her head, then affixed the goggles in place and powered them on. As the green image stabilized on the island's butte, she saw movement but couldn't make out anything else. It was only after seeing the unmistakable muzzle flashes of an automatic weapon firing up at them that she recognized a man's shape.

It's not her.

"Break left!" Rose shouted.

The first rounds plinked into the helicopter's skin as Punky felt the world tilt underneath her. She tumbled backward and fell hard on the deck as the aircrewman pulled himself hand-over-hand to the .50-caliber machine gun mounted in the door on the right side. She looked up and saw him jerk back on the charging handle, preparing to return fire.

"Talk to me, Rose," the pilot shouted, banking the helicopter back to the right while dropping low to the earth. "Is that our guy?"

"That's our guy!" he shouted.

It's not, Punky thought, then rose to her feet and inched closer to the door.

"Cleared hot!" the pilot shouted.

The aircrewman didn't hesitate, and the deafening blast of the heavy-caliber machine gun stunned her as she stared at the flaming tongue lapping at the man shooting up at them. The rounds impacted the earth and sent debris skyward as Rose delivered short, controlled bursts and inched his fire closer to the threat.

"Nose right!" Rose shouted.

The pilot responded by yawing right and shifting their position closer to the shooter as the heavy machine gun continued spitting fire down on the enemy gunner. She ignored the returning fire, barely noticing the dull hammering against the helicopter as she focused on Rose's rounds slicing through the air. She still couldn't see the target, but after what seemed like an impossibly long time, the tracers cut through a solid mass, and she again recognized the man's shadowed figure.

Why does he look so strange?

"Hit!" he shouted, ceasing fire and plunging them into relative silence. "Got him!"

That wasn't TANDY.

"Keep your eyes peeled," the pilot said. "There are probably more."

There are, Punky thought. *And I'm going to find her.*

USS *Mobile Bay* (CG-53)

Beth sat in her chair in the middle of the Combat Information Center and watched her sailors collect information from every source they had available to them. Aside from the AN/SPY-1 radar system, they had other onboard and off-board sensors they could use to build a complete picture of vessels and aircraft operating near them.

"Surface picture is electronically and visually clear, ma'am," Lieutenant Martin Schaeffer said.

Beth lifted the ceramic mug embossed with the ship's logo on one side and the command-at-sea badge on the other. She took a sip of the steaming coffee the TAO had brewed in anticipation of her arrival, thankful for the French-roasted organic Peru Cajamarca. It was a favorite among the officers in her wardroom, owing to the roast's unique name that linked it to the ship's heritage.

Damn the torpedoes, she thought, and took another sip of the Trident Coffee.

"Air picture too," he added. "Aside from Raptor Two Four."

"Very well."

Master Chief Ivy walked to the back of the room and sat down in the chair next to her. "Ma'am, you don't have to stay here for the duration of the test. I can come get you if anything comes up that needs your attention."

She turned and appraised him, thankful for the gesture. "I know you have things well under control," she said. "But I'd prefer to be here."

"Aye, ma'am," he said, then lifted the Styrofoam cup to his lips and sipped from the same blend.

Beth watched the steam rising from her cup and thought about the old saying that the Navy didn't float on water alone. She was sure the original quote had referred to the traditional ration of rum or grog for sailors at sea, but she couldn't help but think how much she had grown to rely on coffee to get her through her watch.

She hadn't even tasted coffee until reporting to the Naval Academy, and she even made it through her Plebe year without becoming hooked on it. But during her Youngster summer, a small flotilla of Yard Patrol craft sailed from the Annapolis seawall and through the Chesapeake Bay, making its way up the coast for port calls in New York City and Boston. The midshipmen on board manned the watch twenty-four hours a day, and she could still remember being roused from a deep sleep for her midnight shift and craving something to sustain her until sunrise.

Enter, coffee.

Beth had hated the taste. She hated the thick sludge the enlisted sailors on board the YP craft brewed for the midshipmen, and she hated how it scalded her tongue every time she tried taking a sip. But she needed the caffeine, so she learned to fill the Styrofoam cup half full and then top it off with water from the scuttlebutt. From that moment on, coffee became a religion to her, and she slowly learned how to enjoy finer roasts without having to water them down.

"Ma'am, it looks like the *Bonhomme Richard*—"

"Former *Bonhomme Richard*," she corrected.

Martin bobbed his head in acknowledgment of the gaffe. "Sorry, the former *Bonhomme Richard* is exactly where it's supposed to be. The sea picture around the target vessel is still clear and should remain that way for the duration of the test."

"Very well," she replied, then drained the rest of her coffee. "The Master Chief and I will be on the bridge to watch the fireworks. Please let me know as soon as you spot the test aircraft entering the airspace."

It was really a matter of "if" and not "when" they spotted the F-35C, but she ran a tight ship and expected her crew to deliver sometimes miraculous results. The newer versions of the AN/SPY-1 radar had increased capability against targets with smaller radar cross sections, like cruise missiles, but her ship was fitted with the first generation, albeit with several modifications that reduced weight and increased power output. It still performed well against steep-diving missiles and was more than capable against most air threats, but the Joint Strike Fighter was another animal altogether.

"Aye, ma'am," Martin replied with a slight grimace.

Beth stood and strode for the door, hanging her empty coffee mug on a hook above the coffeepot. She was one of the few on the ship who had her own mug in almost every space aboard the ship, and she relished the opportunity to practice her religion with the crew. Master Chief Ivy followed in her wake as she led him to the bridge.

"It's going to be hit or miss if they can spot the test aircraft," he said, hoping to temper her expectations.

"Oh, I know that," she replied over her shoulder. "But it never hurts to motivate the crew a little. Honestly, I'll be a little disappointed if we spot the stealth fighter, especially since he's supposed to be jamming against threat radars for the duration of the test."

"Do they know that?" he asked.

She stopped mid-stride and turned to look up into his placid face. As always, he challenged her when he thought she needed a subtle course-correction. It was a fine line between demanding excellence from her crew and safeguarding their morale. Beth had always believed that the crews with the highest morale were the ones who performed at the highest levels. But she appreciated Ben's counterpoint.

"Tell you what," she said. "Let's make a bet. Just between you and me."

He narrowed his eyes. "What's the wager?"

"I'll bet they can spot the inbound aircraft and alert me before he launches his missiles at the target ship. If they can't, I will personally praise the crew for their efforts to do so."

"And if they can?"

She grinned. "Then you can tell them you didn't think they could do it."

Ben opened his mouth to answer but stopped short when the radio clipped to her belt squawked with, "Captain to the bridge. Captain to the bridge."

42

Santa Cruz Island, California

Chen leaned back against the sloping terrain to ground herself in the reality surrounding her. The view through her virtual reality goggles was breathtaking, and it would be easy to get lost in the virtual environment. Feeling the warm dirt at her back, she pivoted and tilted her head in every direction while marveling at the interface the professor had constructed.

"This thing is incredible," she whispered to herself, though nobody was around to hear.

Initiating the hack had been surprisingly easy, but she wasn't ready to declare victory yet. After all, Xi Jian had achieved as much before the jet's electronic defenses repelled his attack. Manipulating the odd-looking controllers in her hands, she swiped at the air while searching for the display showing what ordnance had been loaded on the fighter. When she saw two radar-guided AIM-120D air-to-air missiles and two Joint Strike Missiles, she grinned.

"Just as Mantis expected," she said.

A notification suddenly appeared like a floating box in the lower left corner of her VR goggles' field of view. She turned her attention from the infrared video she was monitoring and focused on it briefly, noting that the target aircraft was nearing the next waypoint. She rotated her right hand as if manipulating the jet's side stick and grinned when the fighter turned in response. After rolling out, she pulled up the display and studied the pre-planned route.

"One hundred miles to the target," she said, reminding herself to remain on the route until the last possible moment. Eventually, she would break off and turn south for the real target, but she didn't want to risk tipping her hand too early. Even if it *was* a stealth aircraft, she wanted every advantage, and surprise was still the greatest one of all.

The box disappeared when she dismissed the notification, then she noted the distance until the next turn while continuing to swipe at the air in front of her. She drilled deeper into the Joint Strike Fighter's menus, becoming more familiar with the virtual reality interface's capabilities. As long as Wu Tian eliminated the threat and gave her the space to operate, she knew nothing would keep her from reaching her destiny.

Then she heard what sounded like a chainsaw, tearing the night's tranquility asunder.

Slowly lifting the goggles from her head, she turned toward the sound and waited for her eyes to adjust to the island's surrounding darkness. But in the distance, only a few miles away, machine gun fire streaked down at the ground from an orbiting helicopter and shredded the black veil of night.

"No..."

When the machine gun fell silent and the helicopter dipped low, she felt her hopes drop with it.

"No," she said again through gritted teeth, then pulled the goggles back down over her eyes.

Devil 1
Navy F-35C

Forty miles to the southwest, Jug was still trying to regain control of his aircraft while reining in the fear that threatened to overwhelm him. It wasn't the first time he'd experienced a system failure in an aircraft, or even the first time he'd thought there was nothing he could do to bring a jet back safely. In each prior instance, he'd suppressed his fear and approached the problem with methodical calmness. And each time, he'd returned home.

"Come on, Jug," he said to himself. "Think!"

He had stopped trying to use brute force to reclaim control of his jet and was mentally dissecting each system to figure out what was happening. Though his heart pounded in his chest, he leaned his helmet back against the headrest and observed the jet's behavior. Instead of feeling like a prisoner in the cockpit, he approached the situation like the test pilot he was.

Unlike what had happened to Colt the night before, his jet wasn't in a dive, and he had time to slow down and assess the situation. Watching the displays shifting and changing pages was disorienting, but he quickly recognized they weren't as random as he first thought but followed a logical pathway. At first, he noticed his moving map display pan out to show his entire route of flight, then saw the addition of a waypoint over the Pacific Ocean south of San Clemente Island. The map scaled back in to show his immediate route of flight, but his thoughts were already several hundred miles ahead of him.

What's south of San Clemente?

Over his nose, he saw a thin line where the broad tapestry of stars met with the vast nothingness of the dark ocean. He was slightly right of his planned route, but the EW suite was still actively repelling multiple surveillance radars searching for the darkened stealth fighter. Looking down at the moving map, he watched the icon representing his jet fly past the pre-programmed waypoint, then begin a turn north to parallel the planned route on what was to be the air-to-air engagement segment of the test.

"Command, Devil One is over checkpoint Bravo."

The reply was immediate. "Have you regained control, Devil One?"

"Negative," Jug replied, furrowing his brow in thought. "But I appear to be following the pre-planned route. It's definitely not flying as smooth as if it were on autopilot, but I'm paralleling the programmed track."

"Roger, Devil One. We still see you in the datalink. Palmdale, anything?"

The FAA representative responded, "Negative. Still clean."

Though the test plan called for a representative to monitor the radar picture and ensure separation of the test aircraft from civilian air traffic, the squadron was able to monitor his positioning through the same datalink that provided their communications. It was more granular than the Los Angeles ARTCC radar scope and allowed the test pilots and engineers in the command center to monitor the jet's systems.

"Command, what is...." Jug paused, questioning what he had seen on the moving map and wondering if he was allowing his imagination to run away from him.

"Say again."

The logical, analytical side of his brain knew there was no way the jet had spontaneously added a waypoint to his route of flight, but the fearful, human side of his brain knew what he saw. But was it enough to voice his concerns to the rest of the team back in China Lake? Or should he just keep his mouth shut and continue gathering information to figure out how to get out of this mess?

"Disregard," he said at last. He still had some time, and he needed to keep his focus on finding the target drones.

Not that he could do anything about it.

***

Devil 2
Navy F-35C

Colt fidgeted in his seat, second-guessing his decision to steal the second fighter. He knew there wasn't much he could do to help Punky from the air, but it was where he belonged. Now, after learning Jug's jet had been hijacked, he was torn between helping Punky and saving his friend. There was only so much he could do. From the moment the afterburner lit off and pushed him back into the Martin-Baker ejection seat, he knew he was on his own. No wingman. No airborne controller. No squadron rep. It was just Colt versus the world.

"Raptor Two Four, Devil Two," Colt said on Cobalt.

"Go ahead, Devil Two."

"What's the status on the emergency aircraft?"

There was a pause, and Colt held his breath. "We have the pilot on board now," the helicopter pilot said.

Colt exhaled and watched the airspeed ticking upward on his visor as the Joint Strike Fighter gained speed rolling down the darkened runway. When he felt the nose start to lift, he eased back on the stick and coaxed the stealth fighter into the air. Free from the Earth, he raised the landing gear and pointed his nose out to sea.

Punky's in good hands, he thought. He kept the afterburner lit to chase down the rogue fighter.

He had a hard time believing it had been only twenty-four hours since he had flown the same jet over the same waters. So much had taken place since then, he almost felt like a different person. He turned his head to look at the dark shape of Santa Cruz Island, and he felt his stomach knot up thinking about Punky down there fighting for her life. But nothing mattered more than catching up to the hijacked stealth fighter before something tragic happened. Not his fatigue, not his fear. Colt was a man on a mission, and he knew it was the most important mission of his life.

He looked at the moving map display on the large touchscreen in front of him, noticing the test aircraft's route of flight overlaid atop a sectional chart. He zoomed out and saw an icon representing Devil One barely fifty miles away, flying northwest along the planned route. Colt angled his jet right, setting a cutoff vector that would hopefully allow him to intercept the other F-35 at the western edge of the missile test complex.

He had never been particularly good at math. It was one of the reasons he became a pilot. But he was constantly amazed at the number of times he'd had to perform mental gymnastics to come up a number that nine times out of ten ended up being no better than a SWAG, a *scientific wild ass guess*.

Based on Devil One's speed and route of flight, Colt calculated it would take the hijacked jet just under six minutes to reach the next checkpoint and turn back south to engage the target ship. If he cut across the northern border near Santa Cruz Island, Colt would need to fly close to six hundred knots to complete the intercept before the other jet made the turn. At the altitude he was climbing to, the speed of sound was just over that, and thumping the island with a sonic boom wouldn't do him any favors.

It was a fine line. But like most things in Colt's life, he had become accustomed to toeing that line.

He keyed the microphone switch to transmit over the datalink network. "Jug, you up?"

"Yeah, I'm here."

He breathed a sigh of relief that the hack hadn't severed the communication channels. "How you doing, buddy?"

"How the hell do you think I'm doing?"

He figured the test pilot was still disoriented and confused by having his ability to fly the jet stripped from him. So, he kept his conversation casual, like they were just catching up over a few beers at the Country Luau in Kingsville. "I hear you, man. We'll figure this out."

"Where the hell are you?"

He had just passed over the eastern shore of Santa Cruz Island, but he wasn't ready to give up that bit of information just yet. He wasn't sure if the person who had hacked into the F-35 had the means of monitoring their datalink communications, but he wasn't willing to risk it. The only thing he had going for him was that nobody knew where he was.

"Never mind that," Colt said. "Let's focus on what your jet is doing."

There was a pause, and he could almost feel Jug's fear radiating across the night sky in that silence. "I don't know what's going on, Colt."

Colt watched his airspeed creep past six hundred knots, and he pulled the throttle back to come out of afterburner. If Punky was right and *TANDY* was on the island beneath him, the last thing he wanted to do was let her know he was there. He glanced down at the island again, then pulled up his EW page as an afterthought.

"I hear ya," Colt said, straining to keep his voice calm and soothing. "You just keep observing what's happening, and if you see anything that might give you an idea of the target, you just let me know."

"Target? What are you talking about?"

He probably should have kept his mouth shut. But Colt also believed in giving the man in the seat all the information he needed to make the best decisions, however limited those decisions might be. "Listen, Jug." Colt paused as he tried to find the right words. "The Chinese hacked into your jet for a reason. We don't know why, but there is definitely a target at the end of this road."

"Holy shit."

"So, if you see anything that—"

Jug interrupted him. "A waypoint was added to my route south of San Clemente."

A chill ran up Colt's spine. There were a lot of reasons why the hijacked jet might fly south of the Point Mugu Sea Range, but there was only one target Colt could think of that would be worth the effort. "Holy shit is right," he said without keying the microphone.

43

USS *Mobile Bay* (CG-53)

Beth blew onto the bridge, willing her eyes to adjust to the darkness as she made her way to the forward windows.

"Captain on the bridge," the boatswain said.

She half expected to see the same mysterious glowing orbs from the night before, but she breathed a sigh of relief at seeing only pitch black. Still half blind, Beth turned to the lieutenant who had summoned her. "What's going on?"

The Officer of the Deck walked up to give his report as Beth again surveyed the dark ocean outside. "The Anti-Submarine Tactical Air Controller reported Raptor Two Four taking fire over Santa Cruz Island."

Her head whipped up to look at him. "What?"

He ignored her incredulous expression and continued giving her the status update. "They observed a small plane being engaged with what appeared to be small arms."

"On Santa Cruz Island?" she asked, still not quite believing what she was hearing. She might have expected something like that off the coast of South America or Southeast Asia, but not less than one hundred miles from Los Angeles. She glanced at the ship's heading, then turned to look in the direction of the island.

"Yes, ma'am," he said, before continuing. "After the plane made an emergency landing, they recovered the pilot and were en route here when they came under fire themselves."

"Well, get them back here," she said.

"We tried—"

"Get them on the radio," she said. "Now."

"Aye aye, ma'am."

The Officer of the Deck turned back to hail the MH-60R crew when Master Chief stepped closer for a private discussion. "Ma'am, I recommend we divert them to Point Mugu and pass this off to Cutter *Blacktip*."

She looked into his dark brown eyes and considered his words before shaking her head. "Not until I know the helicopter crew is safe."

Having said his piece, Ben nodded his head in silence.

"Ma'am, I have Raptor Two Four," the OOD said, holding a radio handset that looked like a red 1950s telephone.

She took the handset from him and held the earpiece to the side of her head before pressing the push-to-talk. "Raptor Two Four, this is *Mobile Bay*, actual," she said.

"Yes, ma'am," the pilot said, his voice punctuated by the percussion of his rotor blades.

"Are you okay? Did you sustain any damage?"

"Negative. We're okay. We took accurate small arms fire, but all systems are green."

She exhaled slowly, thankful the crew seemed to have come away unscathed. "Understand you have a civilian on board?"

The pilot paused. "Sort of," he said. "She's a special agent with NCIS."

"NCIS?"

"Yes, ma'am. She said she tracked a hostile force to the island and that they are attempting to hack into the Joint Strike Fighter."

Beth stiffened. Images from the dive-bombing fighter the night before flashed into her mind, and she glanced down at the deck where she had huddled in fear as it raced overhead, narrowly missing her ship. If there was any truth to what the NCIS agent had told the crew of Raptor Two

Four, then maybe the previous night's events hadn't been the reckless flat-hatting of an overconfident jet jockey after all. It could have been a hostile act designed to take out her ship.

"Ma'am, are you there?"

"Wait one," she said, then thrust the handset back to the OOD. "Master Chief, a word?"

She stepped through the open hatch onto the bridge wing and waited for Ben to join her. He saw the worried look creased on her face and asked, "What's wrong?"

"The helicopter crew reported picking up an NCIS agent who is trying to stop an enemy force from hacking into the Joint Strike Fighter," she said, looking at the distant outline of Santa Cruz Island on the horizon.

"Hacking into..." His voice trailed off, and he looked up at the starscape above them.

Seeing the Master Chief looking into the sky inspired a sickening thought. "You don't think..."

"The Joint Strike Fighter," he said, then tilted his head down to her.

"The missile test!" she blurted, giving credence to her fears. She wheeled back onto the bridge and began shouting commands. "Lieutenant, call the crew to general quarters! Tell Raptor Two Four to remain on station and locate the hostile force, call Cutter *Blacktip* to mobilize a law enforcement response, then radio the *Abe* and warn them of a potential missile attack!"

The OOD looked stunned at her sudden and confusing change in demeanor. "Ma'am?"

"*Now*, Lieutenant!"

USS *Abraham Lincoln* (CVN-72)

Lance Corporal Adam Garett yawned and placed his tray on the empty table. He sat on the stool, looking at the mound of mashed potatoes and Salisbury steak soaked in gravy, suddenly missing the Gonzalez chow hall aboard Miramar. He picked up the steaming plastic mug and winced when he held it in front of his nose, inhaling the aroma of what they tried passing off as coffee.

He took a sip of the dirty bean water and almost spit it back into the cup, but he needed the caffeine before his shift. He swallowed a gulp of the burnt liquid while trying to suppress a burgeoning guilt at giving Chen what she'd asked for. Even after justifying his treasonous actions for months, he struggled now with the notion that the information he'd given her would most likely result in a man's death, an act that was tantamount to murder.

But you didn't do it, he reasoned.

It didn't matter that he didn't pull the trigger. If Lieutenant Bancroft befell some mysterious fate, he would always blame himself and live the rest of his life in shame. And it would kill his parents if they ever learned what he'd done. Honor and duty meant something to them.

"Anybody sitting here?" a voice asked over his shoulder.

Adam shook his head and gestured for the sailor to take a seat as he cut into his rubbery Salisbury steak. "Help yourself."

The sailor sat down across from Adam. "Pretty crazy about last night, huh?"

Adam popped a chunk of meat into his mouth after asking, "What about it?"

"You know, those strange lights over the *Mobile Bay*?"

He chewed several times and swallowed before answering. "Oh. That."

"Yeah, I heard some TOPGUN pilot almost crashed his jet into the ship." The sailor studied Adam closely, then added, "Say, wasn't that your squadron?"

Adam nodded and stabbed at another piece of meat, then dragged it through the sea of gravy, not really caring to recount the effects of his treason. But he still had to act interested. "Yeah. Pretty crazy. Wonder why he did that."

The sailor scooped a mound of mashed potatoes into his mouth and shrugged. "I dunno, man. Crazy."

This was why Adam didn't get along well with his fellow Marines or the ship's company sailors. They lived for scuttlebutt, even about the most inconsequential things, like some strange lights over a ship at sea. He had more important things to worry about. Unlike every sailor or Marine on the *Lincoln*, Adam didn't just have to do his job, but he also had to keep up regular communications with Chen and feed her enough information to stay in her good graces.

The sailor across from him swallowed the mouthful of potatoes and reached for the plastic cup full of soda. "Maybe those orbs will come back tonight and we—"

The sailor stopped mid-sentence when the *bong, bong, bong* of an alarm sounded over the 1MC followed by the rushed voice of a sailor with a Kentucky accent. "This is not a drill. This is not a drill. General quarters, general quarters. All hands, man your battle stations." The announcement was followed by a repeat of the alarm.

Adam dropped his fork and felt his blood run cold. "What the hell?"

The sailor took a long swallow of soda and set the cup down. "Gotta go!"

"What's going on?"

He shrugged. "Guess we'd better find out."

Adam pushed his tray of food away and stood up. His meal forgotten, he stepped back from the table and spun for the exit, his mind racing over what he knew he had to do. If he had been assigned a different military occupational specialty, his battle station might have been on the roof, preparing his squadron's jets to launch against an inbound enemy force. But instead, he was stuck reporting to Gunny in maintenance control, where he would sit out the action from behind an ODIN terminal.

The alarm sounded again, and the Kentuckian voice returned. "This is not a drill. This is not a drill. General quarters, general quarters. All hands, man your battle stations. The route of travel is forward and up to starboard, down and aft to port. Set material condition Zebra throughout the ship. Reason for general quarters is imminent missile attack. This is not a drill."

He bumped into a sailor running the wrong direction on the mess deck while puzzling over the call to quarters. *Imminent missile attack? This isn't good*, he thought.

"Hey! Watch where you're going!"

He ignored the shouting behind him and pushed through a growing throng of sailors on his way to the closest ladder. He didn't give a damn about the route of travel. He just needed to get to maintenance control as fast as he could and find out what was going on. His stomach turned, and he hoped with all his might his stupidity hadn't put the entire ship in jeopardy.

Or his life.

"Dammit!" he growled. "Move!"

44

Santa Cruz Island, California

Tiffany shone her penlight on the notepad, comparing the coordinates the Navy helicopter had given her with the ones displayed on her handheld GPS. The handwritten latitude and longitude only went out three decimal places, giving her a margin of plus or minus forty feet. With that degree of accuracy, her handheld unit could read the exact same thing and she still might miss whatever the pilot had spotted.

She swept her light across the ground around her, looking for anything that might indicate a human had been there. Boot prints. Litter. Anything that hadn't been made by the Almighty and worn down by the weather. But she only saw a bit of scat and a few paw prints hinting at the presence of an island fox. Slowly, she fanned her light outward, scanning in concentric rings around the center of the GPS coordinates.

"Tiffany, anything yet?" Chief Romero called over the radio.

"Negative, Chief. The first two locations were a bust. No evidence of human presence at either."

"You're at number three?"

She looked at the notepad again, confirming she had indeed trekked to the right spot. "Yeah, not much here either. I'm..."

She stopped when her flashlight illuminated a bush that looked...odd.

"You broke up," the *Blacktip* chief said.

"Hold on," Tiffany replied, carefully making her way up the steep slope to get a closer look at what had caught her attention. At a distance, she saw what looked like splintered light-colored sapwood, as if a thick branch had been ripped from a tree and tossed aside. She shone her light on the ground and placed her feet carefully, then lifted the beam back to the clump of irregular brush to make sure she was on the right track.

"Do you see something?" Chief Romero asked.

She stopped halfway to her destination and brought the radio to her mouth. "Give me a second."

Click. Click.

The chief had finally gotten the hint and remained quiet while she took her time traversing the uneven terrain. As she drew closer, she felt an uneasy feeling wash over her and squeeze her stomach in a viselike grip. Under her flashlight's weak beam, she saw a disheveled clump of blond hair tinged red, and she quickly turned her head and dry-heaved on the ground at her feet. She spat thick strings of sour saliva while trying to force the image from her mind and regain her composure. Slowly, she turned back to the gruesome scene and scanned the area around the bush.

Boot print. Drag marks. Loose leaves. Broken branches.

As her analytical side supplanted the emotional, she moved around the shrub while piecing together what might have happened. One thing was for certain, though. This woman...

Carrie. Her name was Carrie.

...had been moved there, and the branches had been placed on top of her body to hide it from view.

Somebody had murdered her.

"Chief," Tiffany whispered into the radio. "I found one of them."

His reply was equally somber. "Copy, Tiffany. Break. Raptor Two Four, can you proceed to location three and recover the body?"

Raptor 24
Navy MH-60R

Punky sat on a seat against the bulkhead at the rear of the helicopter, listening to the pilot coordinate recovery efforts with the Coast Guard personnel aboard the *Blacktip*. She had been right, but it gave her no joy that the missing hikers had fallen prey to the same woman who had murdered her Uncle Rick. Instead, it gave her even more motivation.

"We're moving overhead location three," the pilot said from the right seat. "Rose, stay on that fifty and keep your eyes peeled. We'll use the searchlight to look for the second body. It has to be nearby."

Punky looked over at the aircrewman as he prepared the swivel-mounted heavy-machine gun, thankful they had something more powerful than her SIG Sauer pistol if they came under fire again. But she thought they were focused on the wrong thing. "We need to put off searching for the other body until the threat's been neutralized," she said.

The pilot looked over his shoulder at her. "Ma'am, you heard our orders. We're to identify the threat, and we intend to do that. But if these hikers were killed by the same person you're looking for, then finding the second body might give us a place to start."

She bit her tongue and leaned forward to look through the open door opposite Rose. She still wore the night vision goggles on the bracket Jug had made for her and couldn't help scanning the island's terrain for a sign that might lead her to *TANDY*. She knew the Chinese operative was down there somewhere, and she didn't have the patience for a methodical search like the pilot was suggesting.

"Ranger Reid," the other pilot said over the radio. "We're coming overhead your position now."

"I see you," the park ranger replied.

"Copy, shine your light up at us, then close your eyes. We'll put a searchlight down on your position."

Punky craned her neck to look down at the ground beneath them, studying the green-hued terrain as if it were the surface of an alien planet. Suddenly, a bright light clicked on and blinded her, and she recoiled back into the darkened recess of the helicopter's interior.

"Raptor Two Four has visual," the left-seater said.

That makes one of us.

Punky ripped the goggles off her head and squeezed her eyes shut as she tried regaining some of the night vision the park ranger's flashlight had just ruined. Slowly, she opened her eyes and stared through the side door at the darkness beyond, waiting for her pupils to dilate. But the more she blinked, the more certain was her belief that she would never see the same again.

"Ready," the park ranger said.

As the pilot activated the powerful searchlight, Punky squinted her eyes and avoided looking down a second time, instead letting her eyes sweep across the blank horizon. The flashing red lights she had noticed earlier at the top of the ridgeline again caught her attention, and she pointed at them. "Hey, Rose, do you see those red lights over there?"

He turned and saw where she was pointing, then nodded. "Yeah, an antenna of some kind."

She knew the island was largely deserted with few permanent structures, but none of them were on Montañon Ridge. "Why would they put an antenna way out here?"

Rose shrugged. "Line of sight, I guess."

She rubbed her eyes and groaned, frustrated it had taken her so long to see what had been staring her in the face all along. Of course, *TANDY* would go to the highest place on the island to set up her weapon. If it was good enough for radio line-of-sight, then it would be good enough for her.

"I need you to get me on that ridge," she said.

The pilot in the right seat looked back at her. "We're a little busy at the moment."

"You don't understand," Punky said. "The person I'm looking for is on that ridge somewhere, and if I don't get there soon, something terrible is going to happen."

He traded glances with the other pilot, obviously hesitant to jump to the same conclusion. At last, he spoke. "We can't put you right on top of the ridge, but there's a finger on the west side that might work. Are you armed?"

She lifted her hoodie and reached back to feel the comforting grip of her service pistol. "I've got my handgun."

"You'll be on your own. Are you sure you want to do this?"

"I've *got* to do this," she said.

"Okay then," he said over the intercom before shifting back to the radio. "Ranger Reid, hang tight for a few minutes. We're going to drop our passenger on the other side of that ridge and will be right back."

"Oh," the park ranger said, sounding surprised. "Okay."

The searchlight went dark, and Punky opened her eyes wider as she stared across the sky at the distant ridgeline. She knew *TANDY* was down there somewhere, and she was going to make that bitch bleed for what she had done to Rick.

The MH-60R Seahawk nosed over and accelerated north across the island, demonstrating the crew's tactical proficiency. They were professionals who probably had experience inserting men like her father and Uncle Rick into dangerous places, and they certainly didn't need her giving them suggestions on how to make their approach as discreet as possible.

As they crossed feet wet over the northern shoreline, her stomach lurched when the pilot dropped the helicopter to just above the wave tops and banked left to return over land at an uncomfortably low altitude. She gripped the frame of her seat with her left hand in a white-knuckled grip, relaxing her right just enough to slip the night vision goggles back onto her head. When she saw the hills and sparse trees rising above the helicopter on both sides, she instantly regretted it.

"Thirty seconds," the pilot said.

Punky looked forward through the windscreen and saw the terrain rising in front of them, bracing herself to return to terra firma and resume her hunt.

I'm coming for you.

On the east side of the ridgeline below the antenna, Chen watched as the helicopter hovered dangerously close to her position and turned on a searchlight to scan the ground less than half a mile from her hide site. Had she been a jihadist on the side of a mountain in Afghanistan, she might have aimed a rocket-propelled grenade or shoulder-fired surface-to-air missile at the vulnerable machine. But she was off the coast of California. And she had something even better.

When the helicopter turned off its searchlight and raced north across the island, she exhaled slowly, half expecting it to vanish into the night for good. But despite its disappearance, she could still hear the sound of its rotors echoing off the surrounding terrain. It hadn't left for the mainland or whatever ship it had come from as she'd hoped, but was still searching.

But for who? The hikers? Me?

She glanced down the slope, as if Wu Tian might appear like a phantom in the night and offer his unsolicited counsel. But instead, all she saw was the weak beam of a flashlight searching the area where he had hidden one of the bodies. The sound of the helicopter grew louder, reverberating through the hard ground beneath her, and she set her jaw.

"Enough!" She pulled the VR goggles back down over her head and returned to the professor's digital world. In the framework he had developed, she had unfettered access to every sensor the Joint Strike Fighter possessed. From its AN/APG-81 active electronically scanned array radar to the AN/AAQ-37 Distributed Aperture System, comprising six electro-optical sensors that gave her three hundred and sixty degrees of spherical situational awareness, Chen had everything she needed at her fingertips.

"It's time for the hunter to become the hunted," she said.

She swiped at the air in front of her, manipulating the now familiar menus to pull up the two pages she needed most. The first was the air-to-air radar page, presenting her with information taken from the F-35C's AESA radar. She found the contact she was searching for and quickly designated it as a target. The second was the stores page, and she selected the AIM-120D air-to-air missile, linking it to the target she had just designated.

With a flick of her wrist, she armed the weapon, then paused. She took a deep breath and turned her head to take in the views surrounding the stealth jet. "Goodbye," she said.

Then she squeezed the trigger.

45

Devil 2
Navy F-35C

Colt watched the number in his helmet inch closer to Mach 1.0, but he kept the throttle back to prevent highlighting his location to whoever was on the island beneath him. Even though he was flying an advanced stealth fighter, a sonic boom would erase any of those benefits and jeopardize his mission.

He had "hooked" the icon representing Devil One, which meant that his jet's fusion cell was collating every available source of data on the other Joint Strike Fighter. Although his active electronically scanned array radar wasn't painting the target, the Infrared Search and Track function of his EOTS had locked onto the jet's exhaust and was providing him constant steering updates and guidance cues to ensure he completed his intercept.

"Hey, Colt," Jug said over the datalink communications network.

"Yeah, buddy?"

"Who do you think is flying this?"

As a TOPGUN instructor, Colt had access to the most sensitive intelligence reports as they related to threat nations. Only two had the technical know-how to make something as complex as this work, especially in the skies over the United States. But he knew Punky had narrowed that list to one.

"Has to be China," he said.

"Yeah, but who?"

"I have no idea."

"You have any idea why?"

That was the one thing that had stumped him. There was no question China benefitted from a weakened American military. And with over a dozen other countries having purchased the F-35, an exploitation of this magnitude would have far-reaching consequences. But why expose their capability to hack into the stealth fighter now? Why not keep that trick up their sleeve until it was needed? Unless it was to accomplish something that had an even greater impact.

"Good question," Colt said. "But I have a bad feeling I know what they plan on doing."

"What?"

"You said the Pentagon acquisitions people think the Joint Strike Missile could be a carrier killer, right?"

"Yeah."

Colt didn't respond, knowing Jug was already piecing it together.

"You don't think..."

"Yeah, Jug. I do think." Colt glanced down at his datalink display and saw the icon representing Jug's jet connected to another by a solid line, indicating that he had taken a radar lock on something. "Are you locking up an airborne target drone?"

"What?" His voice sounded confused, but he recovered quickly. "That can't be a drone."

"Why not?"

"It's all wrong," Jug replied with genuine surprise. "The BQM-177A is a subsonic target drone, but whatever I'm locked onto is way too slow. And it's the wrong altitude, too. This thing is barely above the ground, almost like it's a..."

Colt felt the hairs on the back of his neck stand on end. He placed his cursors over the icon representing whatever Jug's jet had locked onto and felt his blood run cold. "That's a helicopter, Jug!"

Devil 1
Navy F-35C

With a sick feeling in his stomach, Jug watched the solid line on his datalink page begin flashing as his radar sent command signals to the AIM-120D Advanced Medium Range Air-to-Air Missile tucked away in his weapon bay. But as long as the doors remained closed, the missile didn't pose a threat to the helicopter his jet had just locked up.

Then, the doors opened.

"Oh, shit."

"What?"

"My weapon bay doors just opened," Jug said, scrambling to think of any way he could keep the jet from doing what he thought it was about to do. But unlike the Hornet or Super Hornet, he couldn't simply jettison the weapons stored internally.

"You need to stop it," Colt said.

"Yeah, no shit!"

Jug reached down for the master arm switch and flipped it back and forth, hoping to disrupt the electrical signals being sent to his weapon system and prevent the missile from firing. Then he slammed against the side stick, trying in vain to move the jet's nose in any direction other than pointed at the targeted helicopter. He pulled the throttle to idle, then, in a fit of panic, pulled it beyond the idle stop and cut off fuel to the engine.

But the engine continued producing thrust, propelling him north toward Santa Cruz Island. His nose remained fixed on the helicopter's dim red and green position lights as it flew low along a ridgeline. And the X through the air-to-air missile on his stores page disappeared, letting him know the weapon was armed and ready to fire.

"Colt..."

Suddenly, he felt a subtle vibration in his seat as the missile fell free from his jet, and his breath caught in his mask. Less than a second later, the sky lit up with a bright flash underneath him as the missile's solid-fuel rocket motor ignited and sent the weapon accelerating forward to its top speed of three thousand miles per hour.

"Missile launch!" Colt screamed.

Jug stabbed at the EMCON button, trying to silence all electronic emissions from his jet, but his radar continued providing updated guidance to the missile. Not that it would have mattered, because within two seconds of leaving his weapon bay, the missile had transitioned to an active state and was using its own onboard radar to guide itself to the target. There was nothing else he could do but warn the helicopter crew and pray the missile failed to complete its intercept and shower the Seahawk with blast fragmentation.

"Raptor Two Four," Jug shouted over Cobalt. "Smoke in the air!"

Raptor 24
Navy MH-60R

Punky leaned forward at the edge of her seat as she felt the Seahawk nose up into a flare. The powerful rotor wash pushed dirt and lightweight debris away from the helicopter, then sent it skyward in a swirling vortex that temporarily blinded her. She rose off her seat and gripped the door's frame, perching her body at the edge in preparation to leap to the ground the moment the helicopter's wheels touched down.

"Raptor Two Four, smoke in the air!"

The panicked shout over the radio was met instantly by a surge in engine noise as the pilot reacted to the unseen threat. Punky acted on instinct alone and leaped through the door when she felt the helicopter's downward movement reverse direction. The rotor wash hit her like a tornado and tossed her about like a rag doll as she plummeted through the darkness for the barren earth beneath her. They had been higher than she guessed, and the fall took longer than expected, but when she hit, her momentum carried her onto her side in an awkward roll.

When she came to a stop, she looked up and saw the helicopter pivoting away from the ridgeline as it dropped closer to the ground and raced for the safety of a narrow valley. She scrabbled to her feet and swept her hand back for her pistol, drawing and presenting it up the hill in one smooth motion.

The sound of an object streaking through the air overhead distracted her, and she looked up in time to see a blur arcing away from the helicopter and across the stars in her night vision goggles' narrow field of view.

It missed, she thought.

Turning to look up the hill again, she spotted the flashing red lights of the antenna she had seen from the air, and she oriented herself on her mental map. Taking a hesitant step, she began slowly moving up the finger toward the ridgeline where she suspected *TANDY* would have positioned herself to hack into Jug's jet. And if the missile she had just seen was any indication, the hack had been successful. There was no time to waste.

With each step, Punky felt an increasing dread as she raced against an unseen clock. She didn't know what the woman's ultimate objective was, and she didn't really care. All that mattered was finding her and making her pay for what she had done to Uncle Rick. Her hesitant gait became a determined jog, and her legs screamed at the exertion of propelling herself up the hillside. But her eyes never strayed far from her pistol's glowing front sight post as she pivoted left and right, searching the darkness for the woman she had come to kill.

Early thirties. Five foot two or five foot three. One hundred and ten to one hundred and twenty pounds. Shoulder-length black hair. Narrow face with almond-shaped eyes.

46

Devil 2
Navy F-35C

Colt watched in horror as the missile streaked north from Jug's jet and arced through the sky for the Navy helicopter hovering over the island. His heart pounded as he thought about Punky. She had just survived being shot down in his Carbon Cub and was in danger of being shot down a second time. The helicopter just didn't stand a chance at evading the supersonic missile, and he looked away to avoid watching her die.

"It missed!" Jug shouted, sounding breathless with relief. "It missed."

Colt looked back toward the island and saw the missile's rocket motor burning bright as it flew harmlessly past the island and crashed into the ocean. He banked to the right, slowing his closure with Devil One as he drew within five miles of the hijacked jet. At that range, his datalink and IRST had provided cuing to the radar and allowed him to establish a radar lock, despite the other jet's electronic countermeasures attempting to jam him.

"Devil One, Base."

"Go ahead," he said, his voice shaking with tension.

"I think I've isolated the waveform," the China Lake engineer said. "I have a new profile that should allow you to jam the signal."

Colt felt optimistic for the first time since getting airborne. "Transmit it to Devil Two," he said.

"Copy that." There was a pause, then, "I'm uploading the new profile to your two thirty-nine now."

Colt tapped on the button to accept the linked profile. He remembered his days flying the Hornet when pilots had to use a cumbersome computer known as TAMPS, or Tactical Automated Mission Planning System, of which nothing was automated, to load profiles for their jet's electronic countermeasures. Even then, electronic warfare was in its infancy, and their jammers had limited capability against pulse-mode radar-guided threats. The ability to update the F-35's electronic countermeasures on the fly was a giant leap forward for the warfighter.

Of course, the enemy had used that capability to hijack the jet, so maybe it wasn't such a great idea after all.

"It's downloading now," Colt said. "Jug, do you still have a lock on the helicopter?"

"Negative," he replied. "Looks like it's using the terrain to mask its position."

Colt felt a surge of hope as he maneuvered his jet to rendezvous with Jug. The hijacked jet only had one air-to-air missile left, but more importantly, it was pointed in the wrong direction to employ its Joint Strike Missiles against the *Lincoln*. As long as the Seahawk continued to be a threat, *TANDY* would have no choice but to focus her efforts there, giving him the time he needed to figure out how to stop her.

"Copy. What's happening now?"

"Looks like they're using my IRST to try and regain a lock on the helicopter."

He had used his own Infrared Search and Track function of the jet's EOTS to cue his radar onto Jug's jet, so it made sense that the Chinese operative would manipulate the same system to target the Navy helicopter. But he didn't like it. He glanced down at his Panoramic Cockpit Display and saw Jug's jet banking into him. He pushed on the stick, dropping his altitude below the other jet, then banked left as he crossed under to the other side. "Where you going, Jug?"

There was a pause. "I'm turning through east."

Colt craned his neck to look up at the hijacked jet as it passed over his head and rolled out heading south.

"Hey, Colt?" Jug said.

"Yeah, buddy?"

"Where are you?"

Colt manipulated the side stick to adjust his angle of bank and stabilize his jet less than two miles from Devil One, on a forty-five-degree bearing line on his right side. The fact that Jug didn't know where he was meant that whoever was controlling his jet probably didn't know where he was either.

"Four o'clock for two miles," Colt replied.

Devil 1
Navy F-35C

Jug looked over his right shoulder and saw the faint outline of another F-35 rendezvousing on him. Colt was flying midnight and had every external light turned off, including the covert infrared lighting that should have been visible through his helmet's night vision. Even without that, the moon's illumination was enough that Jug could discern target aspect as the Joint Strike Fighter drew closer.

The helmet he wore was the one sensor he retained control over. By turning his head and seeing Colt approaching, it alerted every other sensor within the AN/AAQ-37 Distributed Aperture System and cued the six high-definition infrared cameras to the jet's presence. DAS had been designed to detect and track inbound missiles to aid in launch point detection and countermeasures, but it also provided aircraft detection and tracking and fed that information through the jet's core processor to provide situational awareness and air-to-air weapons cuing.

The moment DAS recognized another jet was on his wing, no matter how its presence was detected, it would track the contact using every available means and provide continuous guidance to the pilot. That was useful when the other aircraft was an enemy, but Jug thought nothing of it since he knew it was being flown by his friend.

"Visual," Jug said, letting Colt know he saw him.

Suddenly, his jet banked left, and he bounced his helmet off the canopy before being thrust down into his seat with the sudden onset of G-forces. His vision narrowed as he scrambled to perform the anti-G straining maneuver and keep blood in his head to prevent from blacking out.

Santa Cruz Island, California

"Holy shit!" Chen shouted, panning her head left and right while twitching both hands to manipulate the virtual reality controllers. The hijacked jet responded by breaking away from a second aircraft that her jet's Distributed Aperture System had detected less than two miles away. She didn't have any experience in aerial combat and reacted on instinct alone, hoping that would be enough.

Though she sat on solid ground and felt the comforting caress of the cool ocean breeze, her stomach knotted up and a thin sheen of perspiration coated her skin as she strained against the virtual G-forces. She felt the tension in her neck as she looked over her shoulder to maintain sight of the enemy fighter, struggling to believe he had found her.

Where did he come from?

She had worried something like this might happen but didn't think the Americans could have reacted fast enough to launch a counter-air mission. She thought she would at least have enough time to launch the two Joint Strike Missiles and complete the mission before the carrier launched its fighters to intercept her. That it had happened so early into the flight, before even turning south to begin her attack run, meant that the Americans were expecting her.

But how?

He couldn't have found me on radar, she thought hopefully, though it was impossible to ignore the reality. Besides, it didn't really matter anymore. For whatever reason, the Americans had been expecting her, and they sent another jet to stop her.

But she still had the advantage. She still had control over the jet and still had an air-to-air missile she could use to maintain her advantage. All she needed to do was shoot down the pursuing jet and continue with her mission.

"Let's see what you're made of," she whispered.

***

Devil 2
Navy F-35C

Colt watched Jug's jet break into him and had a moment of panic before his training kicked in. He banked to oppose the other jet's nose and kept his helmet against the head box as he strained against the growing G-forces to keep sight of the attacking Joint Strike Fighter as he maneuvered to the merge.

"What's going on, Jug?"

"Left-to-left...I think."

Colt pointed his nose to the right, and they passed each other with less than one hundred feet of separation. He checked across Jug's tail and watched the other jet giving up angles and pulling up into the vertical with cold lift vector placement.

That was a mistake, Colt thought.

He processed the myriad of tactical errors and capitalized on each by rolling inverted and pulling pure nose low to counter the other jet's nose high, but he kept the top of his helmet pointed right at his opponent. As his nose came up, he watched the other's come down, setting up for a classic low-to-high merge that gave Colt the distinct advantage. A good pilot would have tried flattening out the merge, but Colt knew his opponent wasn't that.

As they neared the second merge, this time in the vertical plane, Colt rolled his left vector ninety degrees and pulled back on the stick to early turn his opponent. His timing might have been off by a few tenths of a second, but he saw the other JSF reenter his field of view right where he expected. He added rudder and spiraled his jet down into Jug's control zone.

"Talk to me, Jug," Colt said.

"The pull's coming on..."

He watched Jug's nose slowly coming up to the horizon, but before it got there, the jet rolled onto its back in an ill-timed ditch maneuver. Colt shook his head, knowing that if it had been executed properly, it could have given him a closure problem to contend with.

"I think I just ditched..."

"Poorly," Colt replied.

A pilot with less experience might have overshot anyway and given up his offensive advantage, but there was nowhere Colt felt more comfortable than at the controls of a fighter. He quickly pulled his nose up to slow his closure and increase his vertical separation, waiting until he had passed over the top of the other F-35 before rolling inverted and pulling his nose down to follow.

The stick and rudder skills were easy, but this kind of fight wasn't something they had ever trained him for. He knew how to fight another jet and had trained against adversary pilots who were skilled in replicating all manner of threat aircraft, but he had never had to fight a pilot who wasn't in the jet. Or fight a jet without a pilot.

Except there is *a pilot, and he's your friend.*

Colt's nose was stuck in lag, behind the other jet, and he looked through the top of his canopy as the possessed JSF banked right to complicate him gaining a weapon's solution. Colt rolled left to preserve weapons separation and again avoided a costly overshoot that would put him on the defensive.

Acting on a honed instinct drilled into him over hundreds of hours of training, Colt put his jet into air-to-air mode and selected one of the two AIM-120D AMRAAM missiles. The last thing he wanted to do was shoot down his friend, but if the fight went from offensive to neutral, he would have no choice. There was no way he could risk losing this fight and allow the other jet to continue its mission and launch its Joint Strike Missiles at the unsuspecting aircraft carrier.

"I'm jamming you, Colt!" Jug said. Then, after realizing what that meant, added, "Wait...are you trying to shoot me?"

He glanced down at his radar display and saw indications that the other aircraft was indeed disrupting his attempt to maintain a lock. But his radar had its own built-in anti-jamming capabilities, and it was an even fight as to who would win—the most advanced radar in the fleet or the most advanced jammer.

"I don't want to!" he replied.

Hope it's the radar, he thought.

He banked right and descended in trail of the other JSF as it went into afterburner and extended, trying to race for the hapless carrier floating in the waters south of San Clemente. He shoved his own throttle forward, dumping fuel into the hot exhaust as his own afterburner shoved him back into the seat.

47

USS *Mobile Bay* (CG-53)

Beth stood tall at the center of the bridge, hiding her fear from the sailors around her as they performed the individual tasks required of them to keep the warship afloat. She marveled at how the Navy had taken kids from diverse backgrounds and trained each of them in specific skill sets, then placed them into positions of responsibility. She didn't know them all by name yet, but she knew they would all perform their jobs with flawless precision. "All ahead flank three," she ordered.

"All ahead flank three, aye, ma'am."

The lee helmsman at the central control station advanced the throttles slowly, tapping into all eighty-thousand-shaft horsepower available from the four gas turbines. Beth leaned forward onto the balls of her feet to counter the momentum of the ship surging forward under her, glowering behind her mask of indifference. In the days of her grandfather's Navy, the movement of the throttles was accomplished in the engine room after receiving a corresponding signal from the engine order telegraph, also known as a Chadburn. But in the modern Navy, the lee helmsman had a direct linkage to the engines. Even the advanced *Arleigh Burke*–class destroyers had reverted from touchscreen helm and throttle controls to more tactile mechanical connections. Sometimes, technology wasn't the asset ship designers thought it to be.

"Range to target," she said, staring through the windows at the darkness beyond the bow.

The sailor standing at the Mk-20 console fired a laser to update their distance from the former *Bonhomme Richard* as it bobbed in the water behind them, awaiting its fate in Davey Jones's Locker. "Eight point six nautical miles and opening, ma'am."

She felt his presence before smelling the coffee, and she turned to see Master Chief Ivy handing her a steaming ceramic mug. She accepted the coffee and brought it to her lips, savoring the subtle taste of chocolate, citrus, and brown sugar, as she looked up at the clock and noted the time. She knew it was running out but wasn't sure how many more grains of sand could fall.

"How much longer?" Ben asked, reading her thoughts.

"It will be close," she said.

"The crew are at their battle stations, material condition Zebra has been set, and all weapons are green," he said, giving her the confidence that if it came to a shooting war, the *Mobile Bay* was ready. She would have every available tool at her disposal.

"Very well."

He sipped from his own mug adorned with a fouled anchor and two inverted silver stars, then nodded in quiet contemplation. Much to the Master Chief's delight, the former warship turned floating target had been given a brief stay of execution, though Beth suspected he would have preferred seeing his former ship at the bottom of the ocean instead of the circumstances that saw them racing south to find the stealth fighter on their radar.

But now, finding the stealth fighter had taken on stakes far greater than a friendly wager she had made with the Master Chief.

"Captain, Combat," came the voice over Net 15.

She set the mug down and lifted the handset to her lips and pressed the button to reply. "This is the captain. Go ahead."

"New contact, Track Number One Eight Four Five, bearing zero zero five for eighty miles, altitude between ten and twenty thousand feet."

Lieutenant Schaeffer's voice echoed the fear she felt but still sounded hopeful.

Beth plotted the contact on her chart, then turned to Ben. "That's our target."

"How do we know it's him?"

"He's in the heart of the missile test complex," she said. "Other than Raptor Two Four, there have been no other aircraft in that airspace all day."

"We can't engage unless we're certain."

Even though his words echoed her own sentiment, she still resented the reminder. "Combat, how certain are we that this contact is our guy?"

"Fairly. The flight profile is too erratic for commercial traffic, and we are receiving jamming indications along that line of bearing. We only pick him up for a few seconds before losing him again, and it almost appears as if he's jumping around."

"Probably a result of the jamming," Beth said. "Designate Track Number One Eight Four Five as the primary target."

"Aye aye, ma'am," the TAO replied.

Beth set the handheld radio down and turned to Ben. "I don't like this. We need to find out what the hell is going on before that contact gets within range of—"

The TAO's voice interrupted her. "Captain, Combat!"

She felt a chill running down her spine at the panicked voice of the normally unflappable lieutenant. "Go ahead."

"We have two air contacts now, heading directly toward *Abe*!"

"Slow down, Martin," she said. "Give me details."

"Second contact designated Track Number Two Four One Eight is in close proximity to the first contact," Martin said.

"Designate Track Number Two Four One Eight as secondary target," Beth said, leaning forward in her chair as Ben reached over his head and turned on the speaker to listen in as their sailors in the Combat Information Center tried reaching the aircraft over both UHF and VHF Guard frequencies.

"...thirty-three decimal seven three degrees north, one nineteen decimal five one degrees west, you are approaching a US Navy warship and will be fired upon. Fly north immediately and identify yourself."

Beth furrowed her brow and held her breath as she waited for a response. Again, she reminded herself that they were off the coast of Southern California and not deployed downrange where the enemy probed the strike group's defenses in hopes of catching them with their guard down. She shouldn't have been in a position where she needed to employ her weapon system to defend the *Abraham Lincoln* from an air attack.

Beth brought the handset to her mouth again, "Combat, did you say the two contacts were in close proximity to each other?"

He replied immediately. "Yes, ma'am. Their track numbers appeared to swap contacts, but one broke away and headed directly for *Abe*. The track numbers are stable now."

She didn't like the sound of that, but she needed more information before she could act. As a cruiser skipper, she was intimately familiar with the errant shoot-down of Iran Air Flight 655 by the USS *Vincennes* in 1988. Though there were several technical factors that had contributed to misidentifying the Airbus 320 for an Iranian F-14 Tomcat, and all of those had been remedied through upgrades to the Aegis system, she couldn't discount the simplicity of the fog of war. No matter how much the technology or training had changed, it still came down to a human being making the decision.

You are the captain, she reminded herself.

Like the night before, she knew the burden fell on her to make the best possible decision to protect her crew and those aboard the *Abraham Lincoln* from a potential threat. She chewed on her lip as she listened to the speaker squawk with another attempted query of the unidentified aircraft streaking through the night sky toward the aircraft carrier.

"Unknown rider, unknown rider at thirty-three decimal seven three degrees north, one nineteen decimal five one degrees west, you are approaching a US Navy warship and will be fired upon. Turn north immediately and identify yourself."

She could hear the fear in the sailor's voice and knew she was running out of time. If an enemy force had hijacked the test aircraft loaded with air-to-surface missiles designed to sink large ships, they were an imminent threat to the carrier. But now there were two jets instead of the one she had expected. Was one friendly? Were both hostile? *I don't like it*, she concluded.

Beth pressed the button on the handset. "Maintain targeting track," she said. "But do *not* do anything else. I'm on my way there." She jumped off her chair. "TAO, contact *Abe* and tell them we are tracking two unidentified aircraft heading in their direction and will provide minute-by-minute updates."

"Aye, ma'am."

She spun away from her chair and left the ship in her executive officer's capable hands. As a ship driver, there was no place she would rather be than on the bridge. But as the captain, she knew she was needed in the Combat Information Center, where she would face the greatest challenge of her career.

As she raced through the door, she felt Master Chief's hulking presence trailing her. "Master Chief, have the Weapons Officer get in touch with China Lake and find out what *the fuck* is going on. If something doesn't happen soon, I'll be forced to engage."

Her stomach turned at the thought.

48

Santa Cruz Island, California

Punky crested the ridgeline in a combat crouch, counting her breaths as she inhaled slowly through her nose to calm her racing heart. She scanned in both directions along the trail, suddenly unsure which way she should turn to meet the threat. To her left, the trail descended toward the butte where she had crashed Colt's plane, but to her right, the terrain rose higher to a clearing with what looked like a small utility building supporting the radio antenna that had drawn her to that spot. She turned right.

She walked quickly in a smooth heel-toe motion, deftly placing her feet on the narrow trail as she ascended to the clearing with her pistol held low and ready. Even aided by the night vision goggles, she strained to see into the darkest shadows beyond the glowing tritium night sights while orienting herself to what she had seen from the helicopter. As best she could tell, the ground fell away into narrow valleys on either side, and the ridge continued south from the antenna, sloping gradually to the southern shore.

She could be anywhere.

She reached the structure at the top and darted for it, spinning to place her back against the smooth concrete wall as she scanned north in the direction she had come. Satisfied that she hadn't yet been spotted, she inched her way to the corner and paused, sticking her head out briefly to take a mental snapshot before quickly pulling it back behind cover. The assessment took less than a second, and she rolled out into the open with her pistol up in front of her.

On the opposite side of the building, she saw an array of solar panels angled up at the sky south of the island, and she sighted in on each one, scanning their shadows for a hidden threat. But the area in every direction appeared clear, and the ridge seemed deserted.

Where are you?

Punky stepped away from the building and crept between the solar panels, listening to the sound of darkness being carried up to her by the wind. Over the pounding of her heart, she heard the distant sound of the Navy helicopter's rotors echoing across the island, but she heard nothing that gave her a clue as to where Rick's murderer was hiding.

She dropped low to the ground and counted her breaths, alone with her ghosts.

Devil 2
Navy F-35C

South of Santa Cruz Island, Colt ignored his decreasing fuel quantity and watched his airspeed increase through Mach 1.0 as he gave chase to Jug's fleeing JSF. He didn't need to consult his moving map to know the other jet was flying closer to the *Abraham Lincoln* and that time was running out before it would be in a position to launch its Joint Strike Missiles at the carrier.

"What are you seeing, Jug?" Colt asked while tweaking his radar to maintain a radar lock. So far, his jet's jammer didn't seem to be having any effect on the hack, but at least the opening separation between the two aircraft had slowed, then stopped as Colt matched his speed.

"I don't like this," he replied with obvious tension dripping from each word.

"I know, buddy, but I'm working on it." He pulled up the display for the AN/ASQ-239 EW suite to verify he had loaded the program China Lake thought might have a chance at jamming the hack's waveform. "But you need to tell me if you go into air-to-surface mode, okay?"

"What aren't you telling me?"

Colt saw the faint blue flame in the distance disappear as the other jet came out of afterburner, and he resisted the temptation to pull back on his own throttle. Without even looking, he knew he wouldn't have enough gas to make it back to Point Mugu, but fortunately there were still plenty of suitable divert airfields along the Southern California coast.

Closest alligator to the canoe, Colt, he thought, reminding himself to prioritize and execute. He saw the icon for Devil One passing south of San Nicolas Island and decided it was time to share his fears with his friend. "I think whoever is controlling this is going after—"

"It just switched to air-to-surface mode, and the surface search radar is active," Jug said in a panicked voice.

Colt cursed at the advanced EW suite for not breaking the hack, knowing it left him with only one choice. "Listen to me, Jug," he said in an overly calm voice. "I'm going to need you to eject."

"*Eject?*"

"I think they're going after the *Abraham Lincoln*," he said. "I can't let that happen."

Jug was silent for a minute as he considered the new information. "Colt...I'm going supersonic."

He glanced at his own airspeed and blanched at the number, knowing exactly what Jug meant. During all their years of training in ejection seat aircraft, they'd heard horror stories about pilots who ejected while going too fast. The first pilot to survive a supersonic ejection was an Air Force test pilot in 1955, but his experience was one no pilot ever wanted for themselves.

His body had been subjected to a rapid deceleration upon ejection, instantaneously increasing his relative bodyweight eight thousand pounds. His internal organs pressed against the tissue holding them in place, the air pressure forced blood from his ears, and his eyes hemorrhaged as they very nearly burst from his skull. The force of the ejection ripped his helmet, gloves, boots, socks, and wristwatch off, and he was only saved by a lucky gust of wind that inflated his tattered parachute. He woke up five days later, badly bruised from head to toe, but alive.

Colt didn't blame Jug for not wanting to eject.

"I know, buddy. But I'm going to have to shoot you down."

He couldn't believe the words that came out of his mouth. His stomach turned at the thought of watching the AIM-120D AMRAAM streak through the night at the F-35C on his nose and blast his friend out of the sky.

"Colt."

"I don't want to, Jug—"

"No!" he shouted, interrupting Colt's plea. "The radar found a surface contact one hundred miles away, and the data is being fed to the Joint Strike Missiles."

"Shit. The carrier must have moved north in the working area. We don't have much time, Jug."

Whether or not his friend decided to eject, he was going to have to fire on him. He took a lock on the MADL track file, hoping that even if the other jet's defensive jamming prevented the missile's active seeker from guiding it to the target, the datalink would provide enough guidance to complete the intercept.

Complete the intercept, Colt thought. *That's a cold way of saying, 'Shoot down your friend.'*

"What about your jammer?" Jug implored.

"It's not doing anything."

"Give it time..."

"We don't *have* time, Jug!"

Colt flipped the master arm switch up to activate his weapons, then placed his finger on the trigger, prepared to fire the AIM-120D at his friend's jet, wishing the test birds had been loaded with the newer AIM-260 Joint Advanced Tactical Missile that had increased capabilities against jamming. But at a maximum intercept velocity of Mach 4, the Advanced Medium Range Air-to-Air Missile would detonate before the hijacked jet could defend itself.

"Colt?"

He said a silent prayer and squeezed the trigger.

49

Santa Cruz Island, California

"He's shooting at me!" Chen hissed in response to the high-pitched tone warning her of an enemy radar lock. She frantically swiped and slapped at the air in front of her, manipulating the Joint Strike Fighter's controls through the virtual interface to evade the very real missile.

Beads of sweat trickled down the sides of her face, and her heart raced with fear as if she were actually in the jet fifty miles out over the Pacific Ocean instead of on a small island. She slapped her left hand back, retarding the virtual throttle, while twisting her right hand to the left to break back into the missile. Craning to look over her left shoulder, she thumbed rapidly at the handheld controller, spitting out countermeasures to disrupt the radar lock.

"There you are," she said, staring at the digitally created symbol overlaid atop the missile plume being tracked by the hacked jet's Distributed Aperture System's infrared cameras.

She glanced forward for a brief instant, then back over her shoulder to regain sight of the missile. At the last possible moment, she yanked her right hand back toward her chest and pulled as many Gs as possible, hoping it was enough to cause the missile to overshoot.

"No!" she shouted, completely forgetting that she was sitting in the darkness on the side of a ridge and not in a jet being targeted by a supersonic missile. She panted as she waited for the screen to go dark, an undeniable clue that she had failed.

But after what seemed like an eternity, the jet returned to stable level flight, and she felt her body sag with relief. "It missed," she gasped. "It missed."

She knew it was only a temporary reprieve. The other jet wouldn't hesitate to take a second shot given the chance, and she needed to finish her mission before that happened. She turned forward and looked at the air-to-surface radar page she had pulled up, watching the target data transfer to the Joint Strike Missile.

"Just a little longer," she whispered.

***

Devil 1
Navy F-35C

Jug almost blacked out when the jet abruptly banked left and snapped back with a rapid onset of G-forces. His anti-G protection suit inflated, attempting to squeeze the blood pooling in his legs back up into his brain, but he was already behind the power curve and his vision narrowed to the size of a soda straw. But it was enough to see that the DAS had identified the missile and was directing the EW suite to jam its seeker while automatically dispensing chaff to further disrupt it.

He couldn't move his head to gain sight of the missile, but when the G-forces increased even further, he knew impact was imminent. He thought about reaching for the ejection handle, but his arms were pinned to the controls, and he couldn't lift them against the overwhelming force.

Suddenly, the Gs subsided, and his heart regained its foothold and pumped blood furiously into his brain. His vision returned, and he saw the missile streaking past his jet before disappearing into the darkness over the Pacific Ocean.

"Goddammit, Colt!"

"Get outta there, Jug!"

He shook his head to clear the fogginess of the uncontrolled missile avoidance maneuver, but he felt more disoriented than he had only moments before. On the one hand, he was thankful to still be alive. But, on the other, he knew Colt only had one more air-to-air missile to bring down the hijacked jet before whoever was controlling it could launch both Joint Strike Missiles at the unsuspecting aircraft carrier.

He glanced down at his display and saw his weapon bay doors opening. "Oh, shit."

Devil 2
Navy F-35C

Colt had closed the distance between the two aircraft to less than five miles, capitalizing on the loss of speed the hijacked jet had suffered while avoiding his missile attack. His heart hammered in his chest and a sour taste coated his mouth as he thought about how close he had been to killing his friend.

"Get outta there, Jug!"

He didn't want to bring down the other jet but couldn't see any other way around it. If he didn't stop Devil One soon, he would be in the launch window for his Joint Strike Missiles, and thousands of sailors and Marines aboard the Lincoln would suffer because of his failure. With a silent curse, he refocused his radar onto the F-35C and prepared to fire his second, and last, AIM-120D AMRAAM.

Colt wasn't much for appealing to the man upstairs when he needed something and thought it was disingenuous to only pray during his low points, but he was out of options. He closed his eyes briefly, said a clipped and hurried prayer, begging for divine intervention, then placed his finger on the trigger.

He opened his eyes and looked at the screen displaying a close-up view of Devil One from his IRST. His prayer had gone unanswered, and he saw the other jet's weapon bay doors opening. If he didn't shoot him down before the anti-ship missiles fell away, it would be too late.

"No, no, no..."

Suddenly, two light-colored shapes fell in tandem and dropped clear of the Joint Strike Fighter in his crosshairs.

"We're too late, Colt," Jug said.

God help us.

"Vampire."

50

Santa Cruz Island, California

Tiffany grew tired of waiting for the helicopter to return, and she clicked her flashlight on to survey the area around the woman's body. On the uphill side, in an area with sparse scrub brush, she saw a single boot print and froze. She had never been remarkably skilled at tracking, but she knew enough to estimate that it had been made that day. Most likely by the woman's murderer.

Carrie's murderer, she reminded herself.

Turning off her light, she knelt in the darkness and calmed her breathing while listening to the normal sounds of the island's fauna. She had never been terribly brave either, and she struggled with her decision to either wait for the helicopter to return or man up and find out for herself where the boot prints led.

She took one more deep breath, then turned on her flashlight and scanned up the slope for the next print while bringing her handheld radio to her mouth. "Chief, it's Tiffany," she said.

"Go ahead."

"I found a set of fresh prints leading away from location three—"

The *Blacktip* chief cut her off. "Do *not* follow that trail, Tiffany. We have officers coming."

She took another halting step, then paused. "But what if the other hiker is hurt?"

If Chief Romero responded, she didn't hear it. Her breath caught in her throat and a chill ran down her spine when she heard a woman's voice high above her and shrill with fear, screaming, "*No!*"

"I'm going," she said.

"What *was* that?"

Good, she thought. *At least now I know I wasn't making it up.*

She turned and cast her light onto the next boot print. Then the next. With each one, she felt a renewed confidence that she was doing the right thing, and the fear that had held her back faded away into the night. After several minutes climbing the hill, her flashlight's narrow beam reflected back at her from half a dozen tiny specks on the ground. She crept closer and knelt over one, examining the spots of light until she recognized what they were.

"Chief, I've got six or seven spent ammunition casings about twenty yards up from location three."

"Tiffany..."

She pressed the radio to her chest to muffle his reply when she heard the scrape of a boot heel against a rock only a few yards above her head. She kept the light at her feet but gradually brought it up in short, sweeping arcs to search for the source. Things always seemed much closer than they actually were at night, but she would have wagered anything she was less than ten yards from whatever had made the noise.

Tiffany heard the muffled chief's voice shouting against her chest, but she held down the push-to-talk to silence him and lifted the beam of light higher. She reached what looked like a narrow ledge protected by a boulder on one side and paused. Holding the light there, she scrunched up her face while trying to figure out what seemed off about that spot. Then she heard the scraping sound again, and the pieces fell into place in her mind.

She clicked off her light and dropped to the ground. Bringing the radio to her mouth, she keyed the microphone switch and whispered, "Chief, I see camouflage netting."

After calming herself, Punky rose from between the solar panels and moved across the trail toward the ridge's east slope. She closed her eyes and pictured where she had seen the very first muzzle flashes as she flew over the island in Colt's Carbon Cub. Looking over her shoulder at the antenna, she referenced the flashing red lights and figured they had come from less than halfway down the slope.

Her night vision goggles gave her an advantage, but she knew the enemy would have camouflaged their location. It would be difficult, but not impossible, so she took her time scanning the area she thought the most likely place to establish a hide site. Its size would depend on how many were in the party, but she imagined the footprint would be small.

"No!"

Punky dropped to the ground when she heard the woman's scream. It sounded close, but she couldn't see anything in the green-hued scenery that pointed at its origin. She ached with exhaustion and her limbs felt heavy, but the sudden shot of adrenaline fueled the athlete inside who wouldn't let her quit. Deep in her subconscious, she recalled back-to-back water polo matches and the overwhelming fatigue she had battled through to claim victory and knew this was no different. Ten years might have elapsed, but she was still the same girl who knew what it took to win.

It pays to be a winner, she thought.

There wasn't room for anything short of complete victory. In water polo. In school. In life. It was a lesson her father had imbued in her at a young age, and a lesson that propelled her up off the dirt and over the lip of the ridge. Bringing her pistol up in front of her, she carefully picked her way down the hillside, her head slowly panning left and right as she searched for her target.

After several minutes, she saw a beam of light arcing up from the bottom of the hill, and she froze. She lowered herself to the ground, suddenly wishing she had worn something other than a red hoodie. Even one of her black concert hoodies would have been more appropriate as she slinked through the night in search of her uncle's killer.

Keeping an eye on the light, she continued creeping down the slope and winced when her boot scraped against a rock. She froze as the flashlight's beam focused on a spot less than ten yards below her, then suddenly clicked off. Punky studied the ground that had been illuminated by the light, puzzling over the growing unease in the pit of her stomach. It looked like a narrow ledge, sheltered by a large boulder on one end, but the earth seemed to flutter in the breeze in an unnatural way.

What the hell is that?

She took another step, then froze. Through her night vision goggles, she saw several specks of light glowing from where the earth fluttered. She tilted her head up and looked at the same spot underneath her goggles, but she saw nothing. Tilting her head back down, the specks of light returned.

Then it dawned on her.

Camouflage netting.

Chen breathed a sigh of relief when the pair of Joint Strike Missiles fell away from the jet and began racing across the ocean toward the *Abraham Lincoln*. Whether or not the missiles succeeded in sinking the aircraft carrier, the damage would already be done. Within days, American news outlets would report on the emotionally distraught pilot who had attacked an American symbol of dominance and then martyred himself by ramming his jet into the badly damaged ship.

It was the perfect plan. It was a shame the one person who had made it all possible would die with his shipmates. And in doing so would usher forth her rise to prominence within the Ministry. Chen smiled as she thought about the accolades Shanghai would shower upon her when she returned home.

Only five more minutes, she thought, watching the timer countdown how much time remained until the anti-ship missiles reached their target. In five more minutes, she would have stirred the hornet's nest, but it would be too late. While the *Lincoln's* damage control sailors fought to extinguish fires and control flooding, the stealth fighter at her fingertips would slip through its air defenses and deliver the final blow. *Just five more minutes.*

Suddenly, a flash of light distracted her from the missiles' time of flight.

She craned her neck left and right, looking for whatever had caught her attention, but saw nothing through the jet's infrared cameras. She almost dismissed it—then the light disappeared, and she realized that it hadn't been shining on the jet but on her *actual* location.

She ripped the goggles off her head and stared through the camouflage netting into the night. She tilted her head to the side and listened for a clue that someone had discovered her hide site. Hearing nothing, she let go of one of her controllers, temporarily releasing the Joint Strike Fighter from her command, and reached for the silenced H&K MP7 submachine gun resting against a rock next to her.

A total victory would have been preferable, but even if only the anti-ship missiles reached the carrier, the American military would be weakened by the loss of public support and a key strategic asset. It was a victory Chen could live with.

She let go of the second controller and wrapped her fingers around the submachine gun's stubby forward vertical grip. She spun the barrel up the hill at the sound of a boot scraping against a rock above her head and stared through the camouflage netting at the shifting shadows while her heart pounded in her chest. She flicked the selector lever to fire and peered through the red dot optic, waiting for a target to present itself.

I need to get to the sailboat, she thought.

Wu Tian had stashed the dinghy on the beach at Scorpion Anchorage, what seemed like an impossibly far distance as phantoms closed in around her. But it was her only chance of escape. Backing off the ledge, she pulled the netting over her head and slowly descended from her hide site while keeping the MP7 pointed at where she'd heard the sound.

Suddenly, she was again awash with light, only it was coming from behind her.

"Freeze!" a woman yelled.

51

The sick feeling in Colt's stomach only grew worse when the solid fuel rocket boosters ignited and propelled both Joint Strike Missiles away from Jug's jet. He knew the boosters were only designed to get the cruise missiles up to speed before they descended to wave-top height and micro turbojets pushed them supersonic to the target.

Almost at the same time, his Distributed Aperture System designated both booster plumes as targets. He selected one—*eenie, meenie, miney, moe*—and fired his remaining AMRAAM. "Fox Three," he said, then watched his last air-to-air missile streak forward of his jet.

"Colt!"

"I'm not shooting at you."

Colt knew F-22 Raptor pilots trained to shoot down cruise missiles with the AIM-120, but he'd never tried. He gave it a less than fifty percent chance of working, especially from the rear quarter with the Joint Strike Missile already accelerating away from him, but it was worth a shot.

"Come on, baby."

He looked away from the retreating missiles to Jug's jet, just as its wings waggled from side to side and it started a shallow left turn to the east. Colt kept his nose pointed at the target and glanced down at his missile's flyout cue, watching it strain to reach the target. He knew it wouldn't be enough. The Joint Strike Missile had too big of a head start, and his AMRAAM would run out of energy before it caught up.

"I think..." Jug paused. "I think I have control."

"Say again?" Colt saw that his AMRAAM had gone into an active state, and he immediately banked left to follow Jug's jet toward the California shore.

"I've regained control of...oh, shit."

He felt his blood run cold, waiting to hear what could possibly make their situation any worse. "What?"

"Come up Guard."

Colt turned up the volume on the radio tuned to the International Air Distress frequency and caught the tail end of a stressed transmission: "... decimal seven three degrees north, one nineteen decimal five one degrees west, you are approaching a US Navy warship and will be fired upon. Turn north immediately and identify yourself."

He started to press the button to reply when he heard Jug's voice. "US Navy warship, this is US Navy aircraft call sign Devil One. I am in a turn to the north, do not fire on me."

Jug's jet banked left, and Colt turned to follow him, putting distance between them and the aircraft carrier. "Should we tell them about the missiles?"

"Shit. I don't know."

On the one hand, neither pilot wanted the carrier to be caught with its pants down with two anti-ship cruise missiles skimming the water's surface to sink it. But, on the other, if they admitted they had launched the missiles, Alpha Whiskey would likely declare them as hostile and target them with birds.

After several seconds, Colt finally spoke. "I think we have to."

"I don't know, man."

But Colt didn't give Jug the chance to argue. "US Navy warship, this is US Navy aircraft call sign Devil Two. You have two anti-ship cruise missiles targeting the carrier—"

The rest of his transmission was drowned out by the high-pitched tone of his radar warning receiver.

"They've locked us up!"

USS *Mobile Bay* (CG-53)

Beth hadn't even had time to sit in her chair in the middle of the Combat Information Center when the sailors operating the Aegis system identified two additional contacts. The chief continued manipulating the radar's controls while speaking quietly into his headset. "Two new contacts. Track Numbers Seven One Eight Seven and Six Five Eight Two, high supersonic and descending rapidly. Suspected cruise missiles."

Beth bolted forward across the darkened space and stared at the large screen showing the air picture around the *Mobile Bay*. "Status on the first two contacts," she said.

"Turning north," the sailor replied.

"Any response to our queries?"

Almost as if in answer to her request, she heard a pilot's voice come over the speaker. "US Navy warship, this is US Navy aircraft call sign Devil One. I am in a turn to the north, do not fire on me."

"What about the new contacts?" she asked.

"Passing ten thousand feet. Over one thousand miles per hour."

She glanced over to the Master Chief, who held a phone to his ear, waiting for word from the Weapons Officer who was trying to reach some-body at the Naval Air Weapons Station in China Lake. The aircraft had identified itself using the test aircraft's call sign, but the two new contacts were heading in the opposite direction of the former *Bonhomme Richard*.

You are the captain...

Shit!

She took a deep breath and spoke in a deliberately calm voice that carried across the room. "Kill Track Numbers Seven One Eight Seven and Six Five Eight Two. Monitor the first two contacts."

"Aye aye, ma'am," Martin said, then spun back to his console.

Based on the information she had available and the flight profiles of the two new contacts, she was relatively certain they were both cruise missiles. Whether they had targeted the carrier was irrelevant in her mind; she felt confident she could defend her decision to a board of inquiry if it ended up being the wrong choice.

"Missile one away," Martin said. "Missile two away."

She looked up at the display showing the symbols that represented two RIM-174 Standard Extended Range Active Missiles leaving the ship's vertical launcher to intercept the cruise missiles. She still felt good about her decision, but the other two contacts were another story altogether. She would make the same call if it came to that, but there was no way she was going to authorize launching one of her surface-to-air missiles at a *known* American aircraft unless she was one hundred percent certain their intentions were hostile.

In the brief silence that followed, she heard another voice come over the speaker. "US Navy warship, this is US Navy aircraft call sign Devil Two. You have two anti-ship cruise missiles targeting the carrier…"

She didn't wait for the rest of the transmission. "Target Track Numbers One Eight Four Five and Two Four One Eight!"

"Aye, ma'am!"

Again, she looked at Ben. "Master Chief! I need answers!"

Devil 2
Navy F-35C

Colt saw Jug engage his afterburner, and he matched him by advancing his throttle to the fire wall and nosing over to gain speed. Both pilots wanted to build as much separation as possible between them and the guided-missile cruiser targeting them. The radar warning receiver continued screeching at him, but the tone hadn't changed to indicate a missile had been fired yet.

"US Navy warship!" Colt shouted. "This is Devil Two. You are targeting a US Navy emergency aircraft squawking the appropriate code and complying with your instructions. Do *not* fire!"

"Devil Two, continue flowing north," the emotionless voice said.

Colt slammed his fist against the canopy in frustration, then looked down at his Panoramic Cockpit Display to assess his fuel state. If they continued flowing north, he would run out of gas before he could recover at Point Mugu, and he knew Jug's situation was even more dire. "Jug, what's your state?"

There was a pause. "Not good. I'm on fumes."

Looking at his moving map, he selected the closest base. "Can you make North Island?"

"I don't think so."

Jug took his jet out of afterburner, and Colt angled his jet to rendezvous on Jug's left side, closing to within a mile. He couldn't believe how close he had come to shooting the darkened Joint Strike Fighter out of the sky. And now he needed to somehow convince Alpha Whiskey they weren't a threat so he could get them to an airfield and land before fuel starvation caused them to flame out.

Dividing his time between flying formation and coming up with a solution, he looked down at the moving map display again and saw the narrow island representing the northern portion of the Southern California Offshore Range. The auxiliary landing field on the north end of San Clemente Island was their best bet.

"Let's circle back and descend for San Clemente," Colt suggested.

"They're not gonna like it."

Colt double-clicked the microphone switch to let Jug know he'd heard him, then did his best to assuage the cruiser crew's concerns. "US Navy warship, this is Devil Two. We are emergency aircraft descending to land at San Clemente Island. Do *not* fire on us. I say again, do *not* fire!"

The response was immediate. "Devil Two, if you turn south, you will be engaged. Continue flowing north."

Dammit!

Colt asked Jug, "What do you think, brother?"

"It wouldn't be the first time I've been shot at tonight."

Click. Click.

Colt fell back in trail and allowed Devil One to take the lead. Jug began a right-hand turn and descended for the airfield only thirty miles behind them. In most situations, he would have felt comfortable with where they were, but with the glowing FUEL LO caution staring him in the face from the Integrated Caution, Advisory and Warning System, he knew he was in an even more precarious position than his wingman.

"Buzzer on," Jug said.

Here we go.

52

Santa Cruz Island, California

When the flashlight turned on and illuminated a dark-haired woman dressed in camouflage, Punky reacted on instinct and shifted the pistol's front sight post to center mass. Out of habit, she shouted a command for the woman to freeze, but when she recognized the stubby submachine gun in her hand, she pressed back on the trigger.

But at the exact moment when she felt the trigger break, the flashlight shifted up the hill and blinded her in its brilliant beam. The gun recoiled in her hand, and she let the trigger reset but held off on firing a second round. Even without looking right at it, the white light had washed out her night vision goggles, and she lost sight of her target. She could only hear the soft scampering of feet retreating down the hill.

"Federal agent!" she yelled again, still blinded but hoping her command voice was enough to encourage the woman to stop.

Instead of surrendering, her target responded by letting loose a fusillade of submachine gun fire on full automatic, and Punky heard the sharp *cracks* of supersonic rounds impacting the hillside around her. She dove to her right, vaguely recalling that part of the slope being clear of jagged rocks, and hit the ground hard. The impact jarred the night vision goggles from the makeshift bracket, then she bounced, and her body plummeted down the hill.

But at least she managed to hold onto her pistol in the tumble.

After several seconds of falling, she finally came to a stop. Dizzy and disoriented, she rose on unsteady legs and scanned the darkness around her. Without the night vision goggles, she struggled to make sense of the scenery and couldn't tell up from down or north from south. Her ears rang from the gunfire, but she could just barely make out a few other distinct sounds. The bass drumbeat of a helicopter's rotor blades, ocean waves crashing ashore in Smuggler's Cove, and the faint crackle of twigs breaking under the weight of a boot.

She spun toward the sound with her eyes wide, searching for movement in the shadows. But all she saw was the inky black of night. Her heart hammered in her chest, and she felt her skin flush from her body's fear response, but she inhaled slowly through her nose to avoid giving in to the budding panic. Slowly, she lowered herself to the ground, letting her ears build a picture in her mind.

The helicopter's sound echoed from both over her shoulder and directly in front of her, and she looked up at the tapestry of stars that came to an abrupt end in a jagged line. She must have tumbled into the narrow valley on the east side of the ridgeline. The sound of the waves beating against the southern shore reached her right ear first, confirming that she was still facing east.

Snap.

It was quiet, barely loud enough to register over the other sounds, but she reacted to the snapping of twigs by turning slowly to her left. There, maybe ten feet away, was the dark silhouette of a woman moving toward her in a crouch. Punky raised the pistol and placed the front sight post on center mass, then began pressing back on the trigger.

But something didn't feel right.

A little voice in the back of her head told her to wait.

She relaxed her finger off the trigger just as she heard another twig breaking, this time up the slope to her left. The person in her sights also heard the sound and spun, offering Punky a faint profile that confirmed what she'd feared.

It's not her.

Suddenly, the darkness was split open by muzzle flashes twenty yards to her left. Punky shifted her aim and squeezed the trigger repeatedly while lunging for the dark shape just in front of her. She stopped firing as her feet left the ground and her shoulder caught the person in their ribs. Punky could tell she had hit a woman, but she continued driving through the tackle until they were both on the ground with automatic fire raking the air over their heads.

"Don't move," she growled.

The woman whimpered.

She rolled to her side and leveled her pistol on the now silent submachine gun, searching for her target in the valley's shadows. After several seconds, Punky looked down at the woman and asked, "Who are you?"

"Tiff...Tiffany," she said. "I'm the park ranger."

She must have been the one whose flashlight had taken away her element of surprise. Punky wanted to curse her incompetence but remembered they were all treading on new ground. To her knowledge, nobody had ever tracked a foreign agent to an island off the coast of Southern California. "Do you have a radio, Tiffany?"

The woman reached for a handheld radio clipped to her belt and handed it up to Punky. She took the radio and keyed the microphone, keeping her voice low as she continued scanning for a target. "Raptor Two Four, come in."

"Go ahead," the pilot's voice answered.

"This is Special Agent King," Punky said. "I'm here with Tiffany on the east side of the ridgeline."

"Stand by."

The sound of the helicopter grew louder and the echoes off the surrounding terrain overlapped as the Seahawk drew closer. She looked to her right and saw the shadowed outline of a helicopter approaching their position from the south.

"Raptor Two Four is visual two individuals," the pilot said.

She gave a little shake of her head. "There should be a third," she said. "We were taking fire from north-northwest at about twenty yards."

The pilot was silent for a moment. "Negative contact. We only see you and Tiffany on infrared."

What the hell?

Fifty yards north, Chen huddled next to a shrub while watching the approaching helicopter with some trepidation. She knew the helicopter likely had infrared search capability and its crew wore night vision goggles, but she hesitantly placed her trust in the clothing Wu Tian had brought for them to wear. The Ministry's scientists had touted that the specially made camouflage would make them invisible on infrared, and she gambled her life on their competence.

The helicopter descended closer to the ground, hovering over her pursuers for a few moments before lifting and spinning to the east to disappear over Montañon Ridge. She knew it would likely return to resume its search, so she used the brief opportunity and scurried north, away from the two individuals hunting her and down a narrow draw that might lead her into Smuggler's Canyon. From there, she knew she could reach the butte and escape north to the beach at Scorpion Anchorage.

At first, her movements were slow and methodical, but the deeper she went into the draw, the more she forsook noise discipline for an increase in speed. She had successfully escaped being caught in a pincer on the east slope, but with that treacherous part behind her, it quickly became more important to reach the beach than it was to stay and fight. The inflatable dinghy Wu Tian had stashed on the beach was her only lifeline to the sailboat at anchor off the coast.

And the sailboat was her only refuge.

As she made her way up onto the butte, she heard the helicopter several more times, crossing high overhead in a north-south zigzag pattern. Each time, she froze, listening to her ragged breathing and the blood pulsing in her brain, and she waited. Ten seconds. Twenty seconds. It was pure agony waiting for the helicopter to retreat out of sight so she could continue her movement north, but each time her confidence in the clothing increased. If they had spotted her, they would have engaged. That she was still alive counted for something.

By the time she reached Smuggler's Road, she had convinced herself she was invisible. She slung the H&K MP7 over her shoulder and ran like her life depended on it. The helicopter continued flying in a zigzag pattern behind her, and she allowed herself to revel in the taste of the salty ocean spray on her lips. She was close, and there was nothing the Americans could do to stop her.

53

USS *Mobile Bay* (CG-53)

"They're turning back!" the sailor monitoring the track files shouted.

Beth felt the knot in her stomach rising as her heart rate soared. She stared at the symbols representing the two air contacts she believed were Joint Strike Fighters. Though she had established firing solutions on both, she thought she had avoided making the tough decision. But the new cry put her firmly in the hot seat again.

"Altitude?" she asked.

"Descending through fifteen thousand feet rapidly," the sailor said.

Lieutenant Schaeffer added, "Could be trying to break our lock by hiding behind San Clemente."

She might have thought the exact same thing if they were operating off the coast of a hostile nation and were tracking a legitimate threat aircraft. But she was one hundred miles off the coast of California, and she knew they were tracking two Navy F-35C Joint Strike Fighters in a descending turn back to the south. They were both squawking the emergency beacon code of 7700 and had identified themselves to her.

But they had also fired on the *Lincoln*, and that tipped them toward hostile in her mind.

"They're jamming us!"

The shout carried across the cramped space and chilled her. Even getting a lock on the stealth fighters had been a challenge, but with the added electronic jamming against her radar, she knew time was running out. Beth turned to look at her Command Master Chief, who was with the Weapons Officer, still waiting to hear from somebody in China Lake. "Ben! I need answers!"

"They're descending through ten thousand feet," the sailor said over the din.

"Ma'am, you're going to have to make a call before we lose them," Lieutenant Schaeffer said.

Another sailor pumped his fist in the air. "Splash one! Track Number Seven One Eight Seven faded."

In the excitement of the two stealth fighters turning back toward the carrier, she had almost forgotten she had launched two surface-to-air missiles to intercept the cruise missiles racing for the *Lincoln*. She looked up and saw the first track file time out, leaving only the one labeled *TN6582* racing across the ocean at the carrier.

"What about the other?"

The sailor turned back to the console, and his shoulder sagged. "Miss."

"Do we still have a weapon solution?"

"We're out of range," the sailor replied.

Her blood turned cold. She was the strike group's Air Warfare Commander, Alpha Whiskey. It was her job to prevent something like this from happening, and she had failed. "Radio the *Abe*!" she shouted. "They have a missile inbound!"

"And the others?" Martin asked.

She had failed once and wouldn't fail again. She opened her mouth to give the one order she never thought she'd give when Ben Ivy slammed the phone down and shouted, "Stand down! Devils One and Two are bingo fuel and making emergency landings on San Clemente. They are *not* a threat."

She felt relief flood her, and as the icons representing the two Joint Strike Fighters faded from her screen, she was left staring at just one. For all the power the Navy had entrusted in her, there was nothing she could do to stop *TN6582* from reaching the *Abraham Lincoln*.

God help us.

Devil 2
Navy F-35C
San Clemente Island, California

Colt decided their saving grace had been their altitude when they decided to turn back for San Clemente. At less than thirty miles from the nine-thousand-foot-long airstrip on the north end of the island, they were able to keep their throttles pulled back to idle as they managed their altitude and airspeed in preparation for the emergency landing.

"Going dirty," Jug said, letting Colt know he was lowering his landing gear and flaps and preparing for his straight-in approach to the runway.

"Roger," Colt replied. He was two hundred feet above the other Joint Strike Fighter and had drifted half a mile aft, giving Jug room to maneuver and land his plane without distraction. But he would need to slow his speed to match the lead jet if he wanted to preserve that separation.

"One mile," Jug said.

Colt lowered his landing gear and flaps and felt the sudden deceleration of his jet as he slowed to his approach speed. The island runway was not illuminated, but the night vision and infrared images fed to his Helmet Mounted Display allowed him to establish a three-degree glide path to the approach end, where he saw Jug's jet touch down and roll out to the far end of the runway.

He felt his engine sputter with a sudden loss of thrust but kept his attention focused on the runway. There was nothing he could do to stretch the fuel he had remaining and knew the engine was likely running on what was left in the fuel lines. If it quit, he would have to punch out. But he was less than a mile from the runway and had a better than fifty-fifty chance of making it.

"*ENGINE...ENGINE...*"

He felt the engine spooling down and knew he had exhausted every drop of JP-5 jet fuel they had put into his aircraft. His rate of descent increased, and he glanced down at the ground, one thousand feet short of the runway where the earth ended at a steep cliff falling away to the ocean.

Come on, baby...

Colt kept his right hand on the stick, trying to stretch his glide to the concrete while shifting his left hand from the worthless throttle to the black-and-yellow-striped ring between his legs. His eyes were wide, absorbing his airspeed, altitude, and position over the ground as his exhausted brain performed a continuous assessment of whether or not he was going to make it.

Come on...

He sensed the coastline drift by underneath him, and he coaxed back on the stick to increase his angle of attack and arrest his descent. As his speed bled off, he knew the wings would eventually give up trying to create lift, and he would slam into the ground no matter what he did. He just hoped it happened over the runway and not the soft grass that would likely send him cartwheeling across the ground.

One hundred...fifty...thirty...

He counted down his altitude over the ground, still spring-loaded to pull the handle and eject from the fifth-generation fighter, when he felt his main landing gear touch down on the smooth concrete runway. He kept back pressure on the stick, keeping the nose off the ground as he used aerodynamic braking to slow his ground roll. When the nose fell to the earth, squarely on the runway centerline, he exhaled loudly in his mask.

"Thank you, Jesus," he said.

USS *Abraham Lincoln* (CVN-72)

Adam sat in the chair in front of his ODIN terminal, chewing on the inside of his lip. Gunny and Sarge bickered over his shoulder, but he hadn't heard a single thing either man said. He kept replaying the events of the last twenty-four hours over in his head, from the TOPGUN pilot who had almost crashed his jet into the strike group's cruiser to his communications with Chen.

When did it all go wrong?

She had made him feel important, worthy of her time and attention. She had given him her love and made him feel as if his job was the most important job in the world. His fellow Marines looked down on him for the job he performed, but Chen had seemed genuinely interested. She had wanted to know how it all worked and actually *listened* to him when he talked about his day.

Sure, he knew what he was doing when he started passing her information. He knew what she was and what that made him, but he was past caring. If the United States Marine Corps wouldn't value him, then maybe Chen could. He looked over his shoulder at Gunny as he spit a long stream of tobacco juice into his taped Gatorade bottle. All he wanted to do was escape to the aft Sea Sparrow launcher with his Nintendo Switch and check for messages.

Surely she's warned me.

He turned back to the computer in front of him, then abruptly stood.

Of course, Gunny took notice. "Where you think you're going, Garett?"

"I need to go—"

The bald senior staff noncommissioned officer interrupted him. "The head. I know."

He felt flustered but couldn't focus unless he checked for messages. "My stomach..."

"Just be quick about it," Gunny said, then turned back to berate Sergeant Narvaez for something he had said.

Adam darted for the door and a few minutes later had reached the watertight door he used to access the Sea Sparrow launcher. He rotated the long-armed handle and pushed it open, once again exposing only pitch black. He stepped out onto the catwalk, then closed and dogged the door behind him, standing with his back to the steel hull as he tried calming his racing heart and let his eyes adjust to the darkness.

Pushing through his fear, he made his way along the bulkhead to the railing aft of the Sea Sparrow launcher and stood on the platform just above the Phalanx Close-in Weapon System. With a furtive glance over his shoulder, he removed the Nintendo Switch and entered the faux-Konami code to access the Covert Communication Partition.

Unlike the night before, the flight deck was devoid of other sailors. With all hands at their battle stations to prepare for an imminent missile attack, he didn't worry about the device's glowing screen giving him away. He waited for it to connect to the satellites overhead, then tapped on "Receive" and held the device at arm's length to wait for the progress bar to fill. Once complete, he looked down at the words on the screen, fearing he already knew what they would say.

NO NEW MESSAGES.

He felt tears ring his tired eyes with the sting of betrayal. It had all been fake. He hadn't been important, hadn't been worthy of Chen's time or attention. She hadn't loved him or thought his job was the most important one in the world. She wasn't interested in him and had only used him to get what she wanted. She had abused his devotion to her, then tossed him out with the trash.

Adam reached back, then flung the Nintendo Switch as far as it would go into the inky darkness of the Pacific Ocean, watching it tumble end over end until it disappeared into the water. Suddenly, the R2-D2-looking Phalanx beneath him pivoted and tilted upward in a jerky motion.

"Missile inbound! Missile inbound! Brace for impact!"

Adam gripped the railing and watched the CIWS spin to the right. Then the night erupted with the sound of a dozen chainsaws as the Phalanx fired seventy-five armor-piercing tungsten penetrator rounds per second, sending a rope of fire arcing across the sky on the port side of the ship. He shrieked and covered his ears at the deafening roar but watched with morbid fascination as the 20mm Vulcan cannon engaged the supersonic cruise missile.

After five seconds of sustained firing, Adam saw a small explosion just above the water half a mile from the ship and tracked the ball of fire as it nosed over into the ocean with a quiet splash.

54

Santa Cruz Island, California

Punky stepped out from the shadows and looked down the beach at the woman hunched over the inflatable dinghy as she prepared to make her escape from the island. With shaking hands, she aimed her pistol at the woman and struggled to overcome the flood of conflicting emotions. On the one hand, only yards away was the woman who had killed her father's best friend and deserved to die the most painful of deaths. But, on the other, she was the only one who could lead her to *KMART*.

It was only her sense of honor and duty that kept her from pulling the trigger.

"Don't move," she growled.

The woman whipped her head around, startled by Punky's sudden appearance, and appraised her with narrow, surprised eyes. Punky side-stepped left, moving in a slow arc to put her back toward the water as she inched closer to her cornered prey. Even in the dim moonlight, she could see the woman's unique camouflage that she suspected had masked her from infrared and night vision—the same camouflage that had made the gunman appear strange to her before Rose cut him down, and the same camouflage that allowed her to escape from the ridge.

The woman shuffled her feet and pivoted to keep Punky in sight.

"I said, don't move!" She stepped into the cold surf, and her eyes flicked up to the Scorpion Ranch trail, where she had watched the woman make her approach. She heard the distant sound of a helicopter crisscrossing the island, pretending to search for the Chinese agent, and Punky lowered her eyes in time to see the woman's ears twitch as confusion etched her face.

Punky grinned and tilted her head. "Oh, you hear that too?"

The woman pursed her lips and glanced toward the submachine gun resting on the ground six feet away.

"Don't even think about it," Punky said, reminding her with the muzzle of her SIG Sauer pistol that she still had the upper hand.

The woman looked back up at her, and they locked eyes. Punky felt a chill run down her spine at the pure evil emanating from the woman's dark eyes. Her facial expression was passive, her body language submissive, but hidden behind those eyes was a hatred unlike anything she had ever seen before.

"Do you know who I am?" she asked.

The woman said nothing.

"On your knees," Punky said. "Hands behind your head."

The woman slowly lowered herself onto the sand and interlaced her fingers at the base of her skull. Punky shuffled closer, then reached down and grabbed a fistful of hair, jerking on it as she bent her forward to prevent her from standing up. She held her SIG close to her body, and her finger stroked the trigger, aching for an excuse to put several rounds into the Chinese woman's head.

Any excuse.

"You're going to die," the woman said in flawless English.

Her words dripped with venom, and again Punky felt the hatred and violence oozing from the slender woman. She was slight in size, but Punky felt a restrained strength, as if she were pushing against bamboo, and she kept her guard up against an attempt to overpower her.

"Shut up," Punky said, shoving the woman's head lower until it was almost between her knees.

Over the sound of her pounding heart, she heard a faint scraping noise over her head. Her eyes snapped up and her heart rate spiked as she released her hold on her prisoner's head and brought her weak hand up to the pistol. Assuming her comfortable two-handed grip, she aimed the glowing front sight post up at the darkness above them on the cliff.

"Don't move a muscle," she said to the woman at her feet, acutely aware that she was within striking distance if her prisoner wanted to lunge for her. Acting on instinct, she slid her feet backward in a shuffle-step motion that had been drilled into her in combative training, putting distance between her and the woman who had killed Rick.

Without warning, the woman dropped her hands from her head and grabbed a fistful of sand and flung it up into Punky's face. She reacted a beat too slow, clenching her eyes shut against the flurry of granules as she brought the pistol down and squeezed the trigger twice. But she knew the woman had moved and her shots had missed.

Pivoting left and right with her ears still ringing, she backed into the water and wiped at her face as she blinked her eyes several times to regain sight of her target.

But the woman was gone.

"Shit!"

Punky waded deeper into the water while sweeping her pistol across the beach, searching for the woman who had murdered Rick. Her foot hit a submerged rock, and she stepped over it, praying she hadn't made a fatal mistake by convincing the helicopter crew to drop her off at the beach and then return to Smuggler's Canyon. She remembered seeing the sailboat on her flight over and suspected that's where *TANDY* was headed, but now she regretted her decision to confront the woman on her own.

Where'd she go?

She felt a shift in the current around her ankles and glanced down just as a hand came out of the water on her right side and slid across her jawline, catching her neck in the crook of an unseen elbow. She recognized the beginning of a rear naked choke, and she shifted her body with a violent splash and twisted inward while stepping out to her right, catching the submerged rock again. They thrashed in the water as she brought the SIG Sauer up to fire into her attacker's mid-section, but the woman pulled her off-balance and dragged her backward under the water.

She could have panicked at being deprived of her life-sustaining oxygen supply, but her hours spent in the pool as a youngster playing water polo and on the mat as an adult, training in jiu-jitsu, had taught her the importance of one thing: never stop moving. She had already taken the first step in the escape, and as she felt the second hand clamp down on the back of her head, she bent forward and reached back for her attacker's leg.

It was thinner than she'd expected, almost feminine, but the strength of the arms clamped down on her neck and squeezing against her carotid arteries was anything but. She felt her heart thumping on the sides of her neck as her attacker cut off blood flow to her brain, but she knew drowning would be just as bad as blacking out from the choke.

Fortunately, Punky wasn't a stranger to the water.

Her father liked to say that she was born on the crest of a wave and rocked in the cradles of the deep. Instead of flailing to reach the surface, Punky kicked hard on top of her attacker and drove her down to the sandy bottom. The impact jarred loose the choke, and she felt blood rush to her head, but her lungs still screamed for air. She felt her attacker retreat in an attempt to return to the surface, but she wrapped her hand around the woman's neck and pulled her back down.

Like a saltwater crocodile, Punky wrapped her body around the other woman and rolled her along the bottom in the shallow surf. Disoriented and confused, the Chinese agent struggled to reach the surface, but Punky kept her pinned to the ocean floor. She fought against her instincts and an uncontrollable desire to fill her lungs with air, focused only on defeating the woman in her arms.

Finally, the woman fell still, but Punky still held her against the bottom until she could no longer control her body's instinct to breathe. She shoved off the sandy floor and leaped out of the water, gasping for air. The cool oxygen rejuvenated her, and she took several ragged breaths before reaching back under the surface for the still woman.

Dragging her to shore, Punky dumped the soaked body on the sand and collapsed with exhaustion on top of her.

"My name is Punky," she croaked.

After several minutes, she felt along the woman's neck for a pulse.

When she couldn't find one, she felt the tears she had kept at bay start to fill her eyes. All her ignored emotions flooded her in an instant, and she collapsed on the sandy beach and cried.

We did it, Uncle Rick.

55

San Clemente Island, California

After Colt's jet slowed on the runway, he had just enough speed to round the corner at the end and coast onto the taxiway before coming to a complete stop. He set the parking brake, safed up his ejection seat, and opened the canopy to breathe in the fresh, salty ocean air and enjoy the first moment in over twenty-four hours when somebody or something wasn't trying to kill him.

"Hey, flyboy," a voice called to him from the darkness. "You okay up there?"

He whipped his head to the right toward the barren ground just beyond the paved taxiway but saw nothing other than grass and low bushes between him and the black ocean crashing against the rocky shore. "Who's that?"

A light blinked on then off, and Colt homed in on the unmoving shadow that seemed to be its source.

"You need some help getting down?"

"I can manage," he called out, feeling silly for answering a phantom.

Colt removed his helmet and set it on the forward glare shield before lowering the boarding ladder and unstrapping from the ejection seat. With trembling arms, he pulled himself out of the seat and lifted a leg over the side, fishing for the top step with the toe of his boot.

"Damn, son. You just gonna park that there?"

He cursed under his breath while trying to ignore the unseen heckler and focused on descending from one peg to the next before finding solid ground. He stood at the bottom of the boarding ladder and began peeling off the flight gear, letting it fall to the ground in a heap at his feet.

"Seriously," the voice said, much closer this time. "You look nothing like any flyboy I've ever seen before."

Colt turned to the nose of the plane just as a bush rose from the ground and took a step toward him. He took an involuntary step backward before recognizing the faint outline of a man draped in a specially made camouflage ghillie suit. "What the hell?"

The man reached up with one hand and pulled the hood from his head, letting it flop down onto his back. Even in the darkness, he could tell the man had his face painted and had gone to considerable length to keep from being seen. He stepped up onto the taxiway and crossed the short distance to where Colt stood with his mouth agape. "Senior Chief Dave White," the man said, holding out his hand. "What the hell you doing on my island?"

The next morning, Colt opened his eyes and stared up at the ceiling of the storage shed. It took him a moment to remember where he was, and with the memory his heart started to race, pretty much eliminating any chance he had of falling back to sleep on the canvas cot underneath a well-used poncho liner.

He hadn't thought he was going to be able to sleep after the SEAL led him to where Jug had shut down his jet on the transient aircraft ramp and then set them both up with a place to crash while he called back to the beach to figure out what to do with them. The accommodations reminded him more of Boy Scout camp than anything else he had ever experienced in the Navy, but after what he'd been through, he was thankful for the respite.

After a brief awkwardness between the pilots, probably owing to the fact Colt had tried shooting Jug down, they settled into a mutually agreed-upon silence and tossed and turned on their cots until sleep finally claimed them. For Colt, it was a matter of minutes.

"You awake?"

He turned his head and saw Jug sitting on the edge of his cot. His poncho liner was folded neatly underneath his pillow, and it looked like the test pilot hadn't slept a wink.

"You sleep at all?" Colt asked.

Jug shook his head. "Not much. No way I could sleep after what just happened."

Colt pushed himself up onto his elbows and appraised the other pilot. "Look...Jug, I didn't..."

He waved the comment away. "I'm not talking about that. Hell, I would have done the same thing had I been in your shoes."

Colt swung his feet out from under the poncho liner and was surprised to see he was still wearing his black leather Red Wing flight boots. He must have been more overcome by exhaustion than he thought. He sat on the edge of the cot and faced his friend. "What's eating at you?"

"This thing isn't over," he said. "We still don't know how they managed it."

Colt shook his head. "Punky found the source of the waveform up at Cal Poly, and—"

"That's not what I mean."

Then Colt understood. Somebody in the Navy had fed the enemy the information they needed to make such a feat possible. And just because they had foiled the attempt to sink an American aircraft carrier with a hijacked Joint Strike Fighter didn't mean they were out of the woods. They still needed to find out who had turned on the Stars and Stripes and sold out their country.

Colt leaned forward and placed a hand on Jug's knee. "You and I did our part," he said. "We stopped the attack from happening. I know Punky is looking into who gave up the classified information, and I'm sure after last night there will be plenty of admirals willing to turn up the heat. But we did our job."

Jug nodded his head slowly, but his reply was cut off by the door opening and permitting a filtered ray of sunlight into the dark space. "You boys done playing grab ass in here?"

Colt recognized the Senior Chief from the night before, even though he had traded his ghillie suit for a pair of short khaki shorts and a dark blue T-shirt with the words "UDT/SEAL Instructor" written in gold on the chest.

"Thanks for the digs, Senior Chief," Colt said, slowly coming to his feet.

"The name's Dave, or Whitey if you prefer."

Colt held out his hand. "Colt, or Mother."

The SEAL gripped his hand with a smile. "Your name Goose or somethin'?"

He tried not to wince as Dave squeezed his hand with a little more pressure than he probably gave others and stared back at him with a wry smile. "Somethin' like that."

Dave nodded, then released his grip and looked down at Jug, who was still sitting on his cot. "Well, I just got off the phone with my boss back in Coronado. Seems there are some crazy rumors flying around about you two."

Colt and Jug exchanged looks but said nothing. Until they talked with their own bosses, they weren't sure how much of what had gone on the night before was going to be classified. And they knew there were going to be a lot of people looking into what went down and trying to find suitable scapegoats to shield them from any potential blowback.

"I have no idea what you're talking about, Dave," Colt said.

The SEAL pursed his lips and nodded. "Thought so. Anywho, somebody aboard the *Abraham Lincoln* wants to have a chat with you. There's an Osprey on its way here right now to take you back to the ship."

"Both of us?" Jug asked.

Dave shook his head. "Nope, just Mother here."

Colt knew CAG was the only one with enough juice to divert a Navy CMV-22B Osprey to San Clemente to pick up a single passenger and bring him out to the carrier. It was either to chew his ass some more or give him an "atta boy" for trying to stop the attack. Even for as good as he felt, Colt knew it could still go either way.

He looked down at Jug. "Let's get together when I get back to the beach."

"Drinks are on me," he said. "Even if you did try shooting me down."

Jug stood, and the two men embraced before Colt turned and followed the Senior Chief out into the morning light. He followed him down a worn trail to the parking apron a few hundred feet away, lost in his thoughts as he heard the faint beating of the tilt rotor's massive blades churning through the air on approach to the island.

When the Osprey came into view, its proprotors turned skyward like a helicopter, Dave turned to Colt and spoke with something akin to admiration. "If any of those rumors I heard were true, I have a feeling you're going to get a medal out of this."

Colt couldn't help himself, and he laughed. "And here I am thinking I'm being flown out to the ship to get my ass chewed!"

The SEAL slapped him on the back. "Either way, I think I may know of an opportunity you'd be perfect for."

The Osprey hover-taxied closer, and Colt turned to see it set down on the parking apron and roll toward them. He turned to look at Dave and saw a mischievous look in his eye. "Why do I get the feeling I'm being conned into something?"

The SEAL grinned broadly and nodded at the Osprey. "We'll be in touch, flyboy."

USS *Abraham Lincoln* (CVN-72)

A man named Chief Cooper led Colt from the back of the Osprey and across the flight deck. He wore a similar cranial, goggles, and life preserver unit to the ones he had been wearing when he departed the ship the morning before. He had barely been gone twenty-four hours, but already the flight deck seemed like a foreign place to him.

The VRM-30 chief walked across the flight deck with his head held high and guided him to a short set of stairs outboard of the carrier's superstructure. Colt knew exactly where he was. It was the same ladder he had taken down into the ship following his doomed flight, and the same one he had taken to the roof after CAG kicked him off the boat.

He stepped through the hatch having found some of the answers he had gone searching for and removed his cranial and goggles and handed them to Chief Cooper. "Thanks for the ride, Chief."

"No problem, sir. But you can hold onto those. We'll be taking off for North Island within the hour, and you're coming with us," he replied.

Yep, Colt thought. *Definitely getting my ass chewed.*

"Know where I'm supposed to go?"

Before the chief could answer, he heard Footloose's booming voice coming from the passageway behind him. "Lieutenant Bancroft!"

Colt spun and came to attention, feeling silly as he looked down at the ruddy-faced Navy captain in an olive drab flight suit striding toward him. The man's face gave nothing away, but Colt clearly remembered the dressing down he had received and braced himself for a continuation of that. Somehow, Colt suspected he had found out that he had stolen the JSF's maintenance data and probably blamed him for the attack on the ship the night before.

"I owe you an apology, young man," CAG said, reaching out to take Colt's stunned hand. "I don't have all the details yet...hell, I'm not even sure I'm cleared to have all the details...but I should have taken your warning more seriously."

Colt blinked away his surprise. "Thank you, sir."

"Everybody on this ship owes you an immense debt of gratitude, and I wanted to personally tell you that I fucked up. You tried warning me that something was wrong, and I blew you off. If there is anything you need from me in the future, don't hesitate to call on me."

"Thank you, sir," he said again, relaxing for the first time since Dave had told him an Osprey was coming to pluck him off San Clemente and take him to the carrier.

CAG released Colt's hand, slapped him on the shoulder, and with a grin said, "There's a certain cruiser CO who wants to know who she's putting a medal in for. Should I tell her it's the same one whose wings she wanted taken away?"

In spite of everything, Colt laughed.

CAG turned to Chief Cooper, who was standing quietly off to the side, and said, "You get this man back to North Island."

"Aye aye, sir," the chief replied.

"Bravo Zulu, Mother," CAG said. "Bravo *fucking* Zulu!"

56

San Jose, California

The woman known as Mantis sat in a chair on the front porch of her modest mid-century house in Willow Glen. It was a cool morning, and she enjoyed sipping on her tea as she watched the traffic passing in front of their house, young hipsters running the Silicon Valley rat race.

The door behind her opened, and her husband stepped out onto the porch, walking around her to sit in the chair at her side. She didn't acknowledge him, but he hadn't expected her to. She focused her attention on a bench in the park across the street in what had been a morning ritual every day for the last thirty years.

"Do you see it?" he asked.

She took another sip of her tea and nodded, replying with a muted, "Mmm."

He said nothing else, and she finished the cup in silence. She carried it back into the house and washed it along with the kettle she had used to prepare her morning oolong. She returned them to their places in the cupboard next to the stove, and the canister containing the tea leaves to the pantry.

Her husband remained in his chair, his eyes also fixed on the park bench, while he waited for his wife to return. When she did, he asked, "Shall we take a walk?"

The married couple walked from their front porch to the park across the busy street. The bench they had been watching was on the opposite side, hidden behind the thick bushes and trees lining the park's boundary, and only visible because she trimmed them down. If they could not see the bench from their front porch, it would complicate things.

They walked in silence along the sidewalk, circling the block to enter the park from the far side. The cement walkway angled in from the street, and they passed between steel bollards designed to prevent vehicles from accessing through the gate. It was cooler still in the park. The low clouds overhead clung to the valley and soaked everything in a thin layer of dew, and they dodged low-hanging fir branches bordering the path.

It was a short walk to the bench from there. They didn't hold hands or engage in idle conversation, surveying the park to look for something that wasn't there. School was in session for a few more weeks, although most families with young children had long since moved from Willow Glen. It had been years since they had heard the laughter of playing children in the open space, but still they looked.

When they reached the bench, they sat together near the middle. He Gang removed the newspaper he had tucked under his arm and opened it wide. It was a local paper, printed in Mandarin, but he wasn't interested in what it had to say and only pretended to read it as his eyes scanned across the top of the page.

"We're clear," he whispered.

Fu Zan reached under the bench and felt inside the cranny. She retrieved a small tube the size of a pack of gum and removed the lid to pull out a rolled scrap of paper. She handed it to her husband, replaced the lid, and returned the tube to the carved-out hollow in the bench's frame.

As he unrolled the slip, he turned the newspaper's page and looked for the correct key. His eyes danced between the scrap and the business section, completing a task that was all but second nature to him. As he did so, his wife swiped her hand along the edge of the bench near her right knee and wiped clean a thin chalk line that had not been there the day before.

"What does it say?" she asked.

Her husband rolled up the scrap of paper and slipped it into his pocket. When they returned to the house, he would set it on fire and watch it burn in an ashtray as he smoked a cigarette on their back porch. Then he would get into his car and go to work, doing his part to run the Silicon Valley rat race.

"It's about Chen," he replied.

Her heart jumped, but she made no outward reaction. She already knew the mission had failed and that Shanghai's darling had gone missing. "What about her?"

Her husband placed his hand on top of hers in a rare sign of public affection. Fu Zan turned and looked up at him with expectant eyes.

"They want you to assign a replacement for one of her assets," he said.

She furrowed her brow and asked, "Who?"

Her husband sighed, and he reached into his pocket for a cellophane-wrapped crumpled packet and the scrap of paper. He surprised her by drawing one of the unfiltered cigarettes and perching it between his lips with trembling fingers. Then he lifted a silver Zippo and sparked a flame, touched it to the tip, and took a long drag of the thick tobacco smoke while holding the scrap of paper over the flame. It flashed in an instant and incinerated to fluttering ash before he exhaled.

"Adam," he said.

Fear gripped her heart, and she struggled not to react to the news. When their adopted foster son had surprised them by enlisting in the US Marine Corps, she had purposely kept it a secret from their superiors in Shanghai, knowing they would demand she turn him into a Ministry asset.

"How?" Her voice was barely a whisper.

He didn't answer, but she hadn't risen to her level within the Ministry's operations directorate without the ability to piece together incomplete and unrelated morsels of information to create a cohesive picture. She knew she had failed to keep Adam's enlistment a secret and suspected Chen had recruited him to use as leverage over her. But how had she discovered Mantis's secret?

Racked with guilt, she reached across and placed her hand on top of his. "This is my fault," she whispered.

"No," he said. "It's mine."

Her husband turned to her with sad eyes and patted his hand on top of hers. Fu Zan turned and started to smile at him but stopped when she understood what he had meant. She had kept Adam a secret from the Ministry, but he had not. He lifted his hand, folded the newspaper and returned it to his breast pocket, and stood. She hesitated for only a moment, then joined him, and they walked back to their mid-century house in silence.

OUTLAW:
BATTLE BORN #2

A missing CIA officer.
A rogue terrorist faction.
A bioweapon more devastating than anything ever seen...
And that's just the beginning.

When a rogue military faction in China kidnaps a CIA case officer, global tensions ignite. Desperate to forestall the looming firestorm, the United States deploys an elite team of Navy SEALs to rescue the agent, protected by nothing but their training and a single pilot providing air cover from his FA-18E Super Hornet—normally, it wouldn't be enough.

But these aren't normal times...and this is no ordinary pilot.

Fresh off his latest mission, TOPGUN pilot Colt Bancroft is tasked with providing air support to the SEALs. But when Chinese jets engage him just as a bioweapon is simultaneously deployed against Colt's aircraft carrier, he realizes this is more than a simple kidnapping: it's a prelude to world war.

Now, aided by Emmy King—an intelligent and beautiful NCIS Agent with a score to settle—Colt will have to use everything he has to figure out who's behind the attacks. And more importantly, how to stop them before they strike again.

It's a race between national security and global catastrophe....and only a man used to flying supersonic has a chance in hell of winning.

ACKNOWLEDGMENTS

My dream of writing a novel has been a lifelong one, thanks to my parents, **John and Laurie Stewart**, who instilled in me a love for great stories and a thirst for adventure. To me, bookstores and libraries were portals to worlds of endless exploration, and I knew one day I would add my own books to their shelves. Thank you for always believing in me and encouraging me to chase my dreams, no matter how bold and unlikely.

But the bulk of the burden for the work that went into this has fallen on my family. I couldn't have written this without the enduring support of my wife **Sarah**, and my three amazingly talented children, **Tre, William**, and **Rebecca**. Your belief in my dream of becoming a published author gave me the strength I needed to push through in those moments when nagging doubt set in. I love you all dearly.

Life in a fighter squadron can be a bit harsh, especially when you expose your deepest desires to a ready room designed to humble you at every opportunity. The same cannot be said for the men and women of **Strike Fighter Squadron Two Zero Four**, who encouraged me at every step in my writing journey. In particular, I would like to thank **Billy Fraser, Layne Crowe, Luke Mixon**, and **Borya Celentano** for their enduring support. The spirit of the River Rattlers and Naval Aviation flows through this novel.

To my extended military family who offered their critical eye to scenes in their areas of expertise, I can't thank you enough. Any mistakes in this novel are mine alone, but where I nailed it, the credit is yours. To **Pat Corrigan, Derek Heinz, Casey Kyle, Rob Lightfoot, Charlie Mauzé**, and **Ben Romero**, thank you for ensuring I captured the heart and soul of our warrior culture.

One of the most amazing aspects of this journey has been forging new friendships with a group of extremely talented authors, who never fail to raise the bar or deliver on the promise that "a rising tide lifts all boats." **Ward Larsen**, your early support gave me the confidence I needed to believe this was possible. **Brian Andrews** and **Jeff Wilson**, you were among the first to reach out and welcome me into the fold, and I am truly blessed to consider you both friends.

To the heavy hitters in this business, I am eternally in your debt for taking a chance on a washed-up fighter pilot trying to become an author. **Mark Greaney**, I am so fortunate I was able to give you a glimpse into my former life, but I am even more thankful for your continued friendship. **Jack Carr**, thank you for your early words of advice that gave me the encouragement I needed to persevere and become a published author. **Brad Taylor**, thank you for showing me how to transition from a military career to one in publishing. Each of you will always be the standard I hold myself to.

To my "big brothers" in this business, thank you for never shying away from including me as part of your group. **Don Bentley, Simon Gervais, Chris Hauty, Josh Hood, David McCloskey, Taylor Moore,** and **Connor Sullivan**, I can never repay you for what you have done to keep me sane during this process. You are all extremely gifted writers, and I will forever be thankful for your mentorship. I hope I make you proud.

Steve Urszenyi, you were a lifesaver as I navigated the querying mine-fields, and you continued to offer sage counsel during the revision and submission process. You have a bright future ahead of you, my friend, and I look forward to watching your career take off. **Eric Bishop**, your journey to publication embodies the tenacious mindset required to succeed in this business, and I can't wait to see where it takes you. **Rip Rawlings**, your passion for this genre is only surpassed by your passion for doing the right thing, and your work in Ukraine speaks volumes about your character. I am proud to call you a friend. **James Brooks**, thank you for always lending an ear or offering words of encouragement when they're needed most. I can't wait to return the favor!

To my **International Thriller Writers** family, most importantly my critique group, thank you for providing your invaluable feedback on this and other projects. **Traci Abramson, Dave Elliott, Ann Feinstein, Brian Godden, Millie Hast, Don Saracen**, and **Steve Stratton**, I am humbled to be part of such a talented group of writers, and I can't wait to share our future projects with each other.

To **Mike Houtz, Chris Albanese**, and **Sean Cameron**, extremely talented writers in their own right and hosts of **The Crew Reviews** podcast, thank you for providing endless hours of entertainment and encouragement. To **David Temple**, you might be the new kid on the block, but your pedigree has made **The Thriller Zone** one of my favorite podcasts. Whether or not you know it, your shows gave me the motivation I needed to continue chasing my dream. Keep putting out content, and I'll keep tuning in!

To **Stuart Ashenbrenner, Ankit Dhirasaria, Kashif Hussain, Derek Luedtke, Chris Miller, Steve Netter, Todd Wilkins**, and the team behind **Best Thriller Books**, your reviews and coverage of the genre are among the very best, but your support of its authors is second-to-none. I have only met a few of you in person, but I am thankful to have had such staunch advocates of my work in my corner from the beginning.

To my amazingly talented super-agent, **John Talbot**, I am thankful for your patience and guidance as you helped hone this manuscript and find a home for it. To **Andrew Watts, Cate Streissguth, Randall Klein, Kate Schomaker**, and the unsung heroes behind Severn River Publishing, thank you for recognizing the potential and helping to mold this story into a finished product I am incredibly proud of. None of this would be possible without you.

Lastly, to you, my readers. I hope you enjoyed reading this as much as I enjoyed writing it. Thank you for taking a chance on a debut author and giving up your most precious commodity to spend time with Colt and Punky. I hope you found new friends between these pages and look forward to seeing them again. I know I look forward to delivering them to you.

I'm out.
Farley

ABOUT THE AUTHOR

Jack Stewart grew up in Seattle, Washington and graduated from the U.S. Naval Academy before serving twenty-three years as a fighter pilot. During that time, he flew combat missions from three different aircraft carriers and deployed to Afghanistan as a member of an Air Force Tactical Air Control Party. His last deployment was with a joint special operations counter-terrorism task force in Africa.

Jack is a graduate of the U.S. Navy Fighter Weapons School (TOPGUN) and holds a Master of Science in Global Leadership from the University of San Diego. He is an airline pilot and has appeared as a military and commercial aviation expert on international cable news. He lives in Dallas, Texas with his wife and three children.

Sign up for Jack Stewarts's reader list at
severnriverbooks.com